AROUND THE
WAY GIRLS 5

AROUND THE WAY GIRLS 5

TYSHA,
ERIC GRAY,
MARK ANTHONY

www.urbanbooks.net

Urban Books
1199 Straight Path
West Babylon, NY 11704

ISBN 13: 978-1-60162-055-2
ISBN 10: 1-60162-055-1

First Printing June 2008
Printed in the United States of America

10 9 8 7 6 5 4 3 2 1

Submit Wholesale Orders to:
Kensington Publishing Corp.
C/O Penguin Group (USA) Inc.
Attention: Order Processing
405 Murray Hill Parkway
East Rutherford, NJ 07073-2316
Phone: 1-800-526-0275
Fax: 1-800-227-9604

Ashley "Da Street Diva" Acknowledgments

Hey everybody! This is only a short story so I'm going to follow the script and keep my acknowledgments short and sweet. I want to thank . . .

*God for allowing me to learn from the negative in my life and overcome my past by turning it into something positive and life-changing. These stories are truly a reflection of me and I am so grateful to have been blessed with the talent to share myself with the world through my pen.

*Carl Weber for continuing to believe in my craft and for expanding my knowledge of the literary industry. You are giving me an opportunity to learn the business and become a prominent figure in this game.

*JaQuavis Coleman for all that you do. May we continue to do big business together and get this money like only we can.

*All of my loved ones, family and friends alike for your continued support. I love you!

*Denard, Natalie, and the entire Urban Books Family for all of your hard work and support.

*Keisha Ervin, for reaching out and showing me so much love. I don't deal with people that ain't like me and you are truly one of a kind, girl. Real bitches keep real friends, lol. Love ya.

*Sharonda from Augusta, Georgia. I believe that you truly are my #1 fan. Your email truly touched me and it is because of you that I am positive that these books need to be read by young people. I was just you a few years ago, so I am honored that you look up to me in the way that you do.

*Last, but definitely not least, to the readers and book clubs that have supported JaQuavis and me thus far. Your opinions are the ones that matter the most. We do this for you and I hope that you all enjoy my first solo venture. Don't worry, Ashley JaQuavis ain't going nowhere. JaQuavis and I will always write together, we're just expanding so that you can get to know us individually as well. Anyway, I hope y'all enjoy! I guess it wasn't short, but it was most definitely sweet. Make sure you hit me up at www.ashleyjaquavis.com with your reviews.

Ash

Acknowledgments

I want to thank any and everyone who had a hand in my literary success and it's very much appreciated. I want to thank God first and foremost for giving me the talent to paint pictures with words. I also want to thank Ashley Snell for being my biggest critique and best friend, you know how we do. Thank you to my brother, my nigga Denard Breland for being a stand-up dude. Thank you to Carl Weber for mentoring and helping me become a better businessman and writer. A big thanks goes to Natalie Weber for helping me in this journey and making everything run smoothly, I truly appreciate your time and patience. I want to THANK YOU, MARIA, for being the best editor ever and making sure my work is on point. Last, but not least, I want to thank the readers for continued support. You guys make all of this possible.

One,
JaQuavis Coleman

www.ashleyjaquavis.com

Acknowledgments

First and foremost I'd like to thank God for giving me this gift of visual writing. I want to thank Urban Books for giving me a voice and a chance to bring "Class to Hood Literature". I want to thank my agent and friend Tracy Brown for being my #1 fan and always being honest with me about my work. I want to thank my girl Carmen Bautista for believing in me so much that she introduced me to Tracy, who, in my opinion, is just the bomb! I want to thank the "hood" for being my inspiration behind so many things that I write. I want to thank "the struggle" for pushing me to want more and do better. I believe in Expression through Experience, which allows my work to come off as real because I write about what I know. I want to personally thank my friends and family that constantly push me and give me their blessings. I want to thank my mother for the tough love, if I had it easy I'd probably be lazy. My oldest brother Courtney for always being a fan and believer and my twin and other brother Taff (Black) for just being my sidekick....(we ride we ride we riiiiide LOL) my only sister Tana (mah-kee-dah-dah) (we K-ci and Jo-jo for life) and the rest of the breakfast club (Knisha, Wendy, Kherra and Pilot) for keeping me laughing on emails all day. (Gotchya Bit**es!LOL) My girl Evette Maisonet for being the angel on my shoulder, Tamara Jolly for listening to everything I write and recite, Dale Robinson for being my little sis and friend, Lorraine Stanislaus for pushing me out of New York, Eneida and Sybil (London Fischer) for being the realest co-workers a girl could have, Hughette Jasper and Felicia Jasper (40 Granite) I love you both so much. You held me down when I couldn't hold myself and I will always love you

both for being a mother and grandmother to me and my daughter even when you didn't have to, and last but not least I want to thank my ladybug, my daughter Nia. You are my hero and I'm doing it all for you, lil mama. Thank you everyone for your support in advance. To everyone else that I did not mention, blame it on the mind, not the heart.

Ayana Ellis

Keepin' It in the Family

By Tysha

Acknowledgments

This story would not have been born without the seed planted by my agent, editor and friend—Joylynn M. Jossel. I thank you and am blessed to have you in my life. I thank my husband, Vincent, and our children, Je'Vohn, Reese, Isaiah and India, for never disturbing me when they see the 'Writer at Work—Do Not Disturb' sign hanging on my door. Thank you all for always supporting me and giving me the time and encouragement I need to write. To my publicist, Earth: keep it moving girl, I got you.

To my family and friends, thank you all for the support, love, financial donations and assistance with promoting my work. My prayer is that God continues to bless you all.

To my fans, I appreciate and thank you for supporting me. Please feel free to email me your comments, suggestions and questions any time. My goal is to continue with my creative writing so that you may have a happy reading experience. Smooches!!!

Tysha@NovelsByTysha.com
www.NovelsByTysha.com

July 30, 1997—Family Court Hearing

Dallas Collins sat on the right side of the Franklin County family courtroom listening to the social worker address the judge on behalf of the three daughters he'd abandoned over ten years before. He kept looking down at his watch, hoping the hearing would come to a close and let him go on about his day.

"Per her living will, Ms. Isis Fernando wished for her three minor daughters, Diamond, Essence, and Chanel to be permanently placed in the care of their godmother, a Ms. Deborah Holmes," the social worker, Susan Bardwell, stated matter-of-factly. "However, the Franklin County children social services has uncovered some troubling issues in doing so."

"I'm listening, Ms. Bardwell, please continue on," instructed Judge Lawless.

"Yes, Your Honor, we have investigated Miss Holmes and we find that it would not be in the children's best interest to be permanently placed with her. We have found that Ms. Holmes has three children of her own; all under the age of twelve and one child suffers from chronic asthma. It appears that Ms. Holmes loves the girls and has their best interest at heart but she is financially incapable of taking on additional mouths to feed. She and her children receive aid from the government,

live in subsidized housing, and Ms. Holmes collects Social Security disability for the disabled child. It is our opinion that even
with the child support from Mr. Collins, Ms. Holmes would not
be capable of properly caring for the three girls," explained
Ms. Bardwell. "Therefore, it is our opinion that the three girls
be placed in the permanent custody of their father, Mr. Dallas
Keith Collins of Columbus, Ohio."

Dallas looked the middle-aged white woman up and down
and smirked. *There is no way I'm gonna be shackled by
some kids. I don't give a shit what the circumstances are*,
thought Dallas.

The judge read from the file provided by Ms. Susan Bardwell, before speaking directly to Paul Simmons, Dallas's
lawyer.

"Mr. Simmons, how does your client feel about taking custody of his three daughters?"

"Your Honor, Mr. Collins has no interest in taking custody
of the children in question. It is his intent to relinquish all
parental rights and allow the children to be placed in foster
care or perhaps even permanent adoption by Ms. Deborah
Holmes."

"I don't understand this decision, Mr. Simmons. Why
would a father willingly and knowingly cut all ties with his
children and put them up for adoption?" asked Judge Lawless with a tone of disgust in her voice.

"Your Honor, Mr. Collins has not been in the children's
lives since the youngest child was born. He is, in essence, a
stranger to them and Mr. Collins can find no need to intro-
duce himself to the three girls now," explained Mr. Simmons.
He could tell the judge was agitated by his client and he felt
the same way, but his only objective was to follow orders and
get paid.

"Per our own investigation, it appears that Ms. Holmes,
who is seated to the left of Your Honor, has kept the three
girls in her home for the last thirty days. If it pleases the

court, Mr. Collins suggests the children be kept together and placed in the custody of Ms. Holmes," Mr. Simmons continued.

"While it puzzles me why your client would turn his back on the very children he helped to create, I think it may be in the children's best interest to be placed in a home where they are wanted," said Judge Lawless. "Ms. Bardwell, have you considered the option of placing the girls in foster homes until they can be legally adopted?"

"Your Honor, it is very unlikely that adoption would be an option, due to their ages. The other obstacle will be keeping the girls together. They may have to be separated or placed into a group home if Mr. Collins will not own up to his parental responsibility. Seeing that our office feels Ms. Holmes is unfit to properly care for the girls, we are hard-pressed to find a foster family willing to take all three of the girls at one time."

"That's not true, Your Honor!" shouted Deborah. "The girls have been with me since the day their mother died and they need me. Please, Judge, I'm begging you to let me raise the girls. I promised my best friend on her deathbed that I would watch over her girls," cried Deborah.

"Ms. Holmes, please grab a hold of yourself. As emotional as this is, we must and will have order in my courtroom," stated Judge Lawless. "Well, Mr. Simmons, it seems we have a dilemma. The children's godmother is financially unable to care for three additional mouths, and your client is the only blood relative alive. Mr. Collins will take custody of his children. Whether he has been a part of their lives or not, he will care for them."

"Come on, Judge, I don't have time for any kids, especially not girls. What am I going to do with three little mixed-breed girls? I mean, I can't give them a good home. They will be better off with—"

Dallas was interrupted by the doors to the courtroom

being pushed open. He turned and laid eyes on the daughters he'd left years before without a second thought. There stood the most beautiful sight Dallas had ever seen: thirteen-year-old Diamond Ebony, twelve-year-old Essence Ta'Neal, and eleven-year-old Chanel Micah.

"Well, Mr. Collins, if you're that adamant about not taking them, you leave me with no other choice. The girls are to be placed in—"

"Excuse me, Your Honor; it seems that I may have made a grave mistake. I would love to take custody of my girls. Please, disregard my previous statement. I was wrong to say the girls should be placed elsewhere."

Everyone in the room stared at Dallas with confused looks on their faces. Deborah saw a look in Dallas's eyes that she had seen before and it let her know that he was up to no good.

"Well, Mr. Collins, while your decision is welcoming, in that the girls shall remain together as their mother had wished, the court must ask, why the sudden change of heart?"

"Today is the first time I've seen my daughters in ten years," stated Dallas, while never taking his eyes off the girls, "and I must confess that in doing so, I realize how much of their lives I've already missed out on. After seeing them, there is no way I can turn my back on them again, especially since they have suffered such a devastating loss. It would be cruel for me to hand them over to the system, force them to be separated from each other and for me to go on pretending as if they don't exist. They will reside with me," said Dallas, smiling like a mischievous cartoon character.

"If it pleases the court, my client will assume full responsibility for his three minor daughters and take custody of them today," announced Mr. Simmons.

"Mrs. Bardwell, how does your office feel about this?" quizzed Judge Lawless with some reservation in her voice.

"We suggest the girls be placed with their father and rec-

ommend Mr. Collins agrees to a trial period of six months, where our office will make periodic visits to the home. It is also suggested that Mr. Collins place the girls in counseling for at least one year to help them grieve for their mother. Lastly, Ms. Holmes is to have regular, unsupervised visitation. The girls should be able to maintain their relationship with Ms. Holmes and her children."

Deborah lowered as the social worker, the judge, and Dallas's lawyer mapped out the future of girls who were complete strangers to them and asked God to send down his guardian angels to keep watch over Diamond, Essence, and Chanel. Something inside told her they would need all of the protection they could get. When she raised her head and looked over at Dallas, a chill went up her spine as tears ran down her face.

Unable to take his eyes off of the three young women he helped create, Dallas thought to himself, *This just may be the best thing to ever happen to me.*

Chapter One

They Call Me Miss Bitch

"Ah, hell to the no! Muthafucka, let me tell you something!" snapped Essence. Her honey-bronzed flawless skin shimmered in the moonlight seeping between the vertical blinds. Essence shifted all her weight to her left leg, placed her left hand on her hip and ran her slim fingers through her light brown mane. She had just given the man standing in front of her the best night of his damn life and he had shit fucked-up if he thought her pretty ass didn't come with a high price tag stamped on it.

"My titties are laced in bronze, my pussy is lined with gold and my ass is muthafuckin' platinum. You can search the world and you'll never find a bitch better than me. That fact alone makes my time priceless."

Bill Bowman turned pale-faced and lock-jawed, not sure of how to handle the situation. When he called the escort service to schedule the date, he requested the best girl available. He explained that the woman had to be classy, proper, and beautiful. Bill was adamant about the woman's ability to know the difference between a salad fork and a dinner fork. She had to be familiar with the difference between a Merlot and a Zinfandel wine. Most importantly, she had to be up on world affairs and speak the King's English.

After placing his order, Maria Petrilo quoted him an estimated price and provided him with an address and instructions on picking up his date.

Upon arriving at the Easton area Hilton Hotel located in the heart of Columbus, Ohio, Bill was speechless when he laid eyes on his date for the evening. Twenty-two-year-old Essence Ta'Neal Fernando-Collins introduced herself with a ladylike handshake and a pretend peck on each of Bill's cheeks. Her hair was in a perfect double French roll, accentuated with diamond crest hoop earrings and a matching choker. The sequined black evening gown hung to her firm body as if Ann Taylor had designed it just for her.

Luscious, voluptuous, and *tempting* were the words running through Bill's mind all evening. As they sat at the mayor's table for the annual Urban League fund-raiser, Bill found it difficult to peel his eyes off of Essence. He wondered if she wore a black satin thong underneath her black evening gown or if she was confident enough not to wear any panties at all.

"What the fuck is ya problem?" barked Essence, snapping Bill back to reality. "Are you listening to me?" Essence was not known for being a patient person.

The phrase *a woman in the streets but a freak in the bedroom* originated with her, if you let Essence tell it. As she delivered the worse tongue-lashing she could muster, her size six feet began throbbing in the five-inch stilettos she sported.

"Look, I got other things to do than stand here arguing about *my* money. Just give me what the fuck you owe me and I'll be on my beautiful way," fumed Essence as she extended her open hand out to receive her fee.

"I don't have any more cash on me," lied Bill. "Like I told you, Maria quoted me a fee of three thousand dollars for the evening, not the ten thousand dollars you're asking for." His voice cracked and beads of sweat formed on his forehead.

"See, you got me fucked-up. That little petty-ass three thousand dollars was for me to escort you to a formal dinner, after-hours drinks and a half hour of you busting a nut in my one-of-a-kind pussy."

"Yes, Miss Essence, I know that much, and most impor tantly, that was all we did. I don't understand where the additional fees are coming from," stuttered a nervous Bill.

"Okay, pour me another shot of brandy to help me calm the fuck down because you're about to make me show my Columbus, Ohio short-north ass," Essence said with her eyes closed as she searched for her center to help regain her composure. This was the second date in a row that Maria had tried to shortchange her by quoting the wrong price. Essence made a mental note to check Maria first thing in the morning.

Bill walked so fast over to the minibar that he left a puff of smoke behind him. Essence smirked behind Bill's back as the clink of the small liquor bottle hit the drinking glass and echoed throughout the overpriced hotel suite.

Essence sat on the flowered couch and kicked her stilettos off. Bill handed Essence her drink before taking a seat on the love seat facing her. As Bill watched Essence gulp down the brown liquor, he wondered what happened to the classy, refined woman he'd met just hours before. He didn't know how much more his nerves could take. The desire for one of his little white pills was sudden but not unexpected.

"You must look at me and think, *Dis whore don't know shit,* 'cause you playing me like I'm stupid." Essence paused to make Bill feel like the walls were closing in on him. She stood up and walked closer to him. She wanted him to feel the heat rising from inside of her. "Daddy ain't raise no dummy and don't either one of us take no mess. I didn't just start selling pussy yesterday. Shit, I'm a veteran at taming perverts like you."

Failing to think before allowing the words to escape his

mouth, Bill replied, "Miss Essence, you are a whore, and this is not a negotiable business transaction." Although he was trying to sound threatening, his words came out gentle and compassionate.

Essence jumped up from her seat and screamed, "Oh, hell to the no! You got me fucked-up for real. That is all this is, muthafucka—a damn business transaction."

"How do you come to that conclusion?"

"I offer a service which you've received. That service has concluded and your bill is now due," snapped Essence.

"Like I said before, the receptionist told me the evening would be three thousand dollars, not the ten you are asking for."

"Why don't I break it down for you? After dinner and drinks with those stiff shirts, we went dancing with even more stuck-up muthafuckas who think the world twirls only for them. Then you bring me here and ask for me to allow you to handcuff me and use my perfectly toned body like a garden tool." Essence frowned at the thought of Bill's definition of a fantasy sexual escapade. "Being that you upgraded your package deal, you owe me another seven thousand dollars, plus tip." Essence snapped her fingers and rolled her eyes.

Bill stood before Essence looking dumbfounded. *I'll be damned if some high-priced whore is going to strong-arm me,* thought Bill as he tried to map out in his head a route of exit.

As if on cue, there was a hard, aggressive knock on the door. Essence glanced over at Bill, who was now visibly shaking, and instructed him to open the door. He slowly did as he was told.

When he opened the door the sight before him almost caused Bill to lose control of his bowels.

"Do we have a problem here?" asked the deepest voice Bill had ever heard.

"I'm so sorry if we disturbed you, but everything is fine in

here. My lady friend and I were just having a misunderstanding," explained Bill. He attempted a smile, but his fear would not allow it. Bill tried to shut the door but the man's foot was in the way.

"I know you and your lady friend are having a misunderstanding, that's why I'm here, to help you come to an understanding," mocked Houston Collins in a voice as deep as the ocean. While Houston was the younger brother of Dallas, he stood taller, weighed more and was quick to anger, so he was assigned to protect the girls while out on dates. He had been watching Essence all evening, and though she never saw him, she knew that Houston was never far away.

Bill quickly looked away from the six-foot, two-hundred-something-pound muscular man standing before him and turned his attention to Essence. "I don't understand," said Bill.

"Bill, that's Houston. He is never far away from me on date nights," explained Essence. "Come on in, Houston, because like Daddy would say, 'Houston, we have a problem.'"

Houston closed the door behind him and nudged Bill out of his way before walking over to where Essence sat. He scanned the room before checking over Essence to make sure there were not physical signs of trouble.

"So, what's the problem?" inquired Houston.

"Well, it seems like Mr. Bill doesn't want to pay me in full," explained Essence.

"No, no, no," said Bill with a quivering voice. "I only have three thousand in cash on me, but I can mail you a cashier's check in the morning if you'd like."

Essence shook her head before replying, "We don't take checks, but I do accept credit cards." She reached inside of her bag to retrieve a manual credit card machine to make an imprint of Bill's platinum credit card.

With a pale face and shaking hands, Bill fought against himself to get his wallet out of his suit jacket.

"Well, Houston, it seems that once again, you have fixed the problem." Essence laughed after completing the business transaction.

Bill almost jumped out of his skin as Houston led Essence to the door and laughed the way a cartoon villain does. To Bill, no freaky sex in the world was worth physical danger. He was happy to see his high-priced ho and her bodyguard leave. As Bill watched Houston close the door, he knew that despite all of the drama, he had to admit, Essence was one of a kind and he would be calling on Miss Essence to service him again in the near future.

Chapter Two

A Place All My Own

DJ Easy Rock was spinning his best mixes, and when Chanel heard the sounds of the Shop Boyz number-one hit "Party Like a Rockstar" blaring from the huge speakers, she headed straight for the dance floor.

"Oh, girl that is my jam," screamed Chanel over the music. She and her friend, Shalonda, began moving their bodies to the tunes as all eyes became fixed on them.

"Party like a rock star, party like a rock star," Chanel and Shalonda sang in unison.

The crowd at Club Ice in downtown Columbus was just as Chanel liked for it to be: not too crowded and void of ghetto fabulous queens envious of her style. Chanel Micah Fernando-Collins wore a cute little Baby Phat jean skirt with just enough material to show off her shapely twenty-one-year-old legs. The matching crop shirt offered a peek at her flat stomach and showed off her plump thirty-six C-cups just the way she liked it. The six-inch-heel stilettos with the straps accentuated her toned calf muscles.

After dancing to a few more songs, Chanel wished she would have worn shoes easier to take off. She knew that bending over to remove them from her aching feet would allow everyone in the club to see what God had given her, so

she decided to dance through the pain. As soon as the song ended, Chanel and Shalonda made their way back to their favorite VIP section of the club.

"Girl, the club is hot tonight," hollered Shalonda.

"Yeah, you got that right. This is the place to be," screamed Chanel. "We are going to close this bitch down."

Chanel and Shalonda toasted and sipped down their green apple martinis like true ladies should. For as long as she could remember, Chanel had been instructed on the proper way to conduct herself when in public and even more so when in the presence of a man.

The girls began their "hoes in training lifestyles" regimen one week after being placed in their father's care. To begin with, Dallas hired a personal trainer to teach the girls how to tone their bodies and strength train without bulking up to look like female bodybuilders. He then brought in a petite, proper speaking teacher to train the girls on etiquette. Twice a week, they studied which fork to use during dinners, the King's English, how to walk in heels even when their feet hurt, and how to be submissive.

Dallas drilled different things into the girls every day and all day. He told them that because of their mixed heritage, Hispanic and African American, they were blessed to be some of the most beautiful beings walking the earth. In Dallas's opinion, Diamond, Essence, and Chanel inherited their mother's greatest attributes: honey complexion, long, dark, wavy hair, and beautiful almond-shaped light brown eyes. All three girls' hips spread perfectly during puberty as well as their C-cup breasts. Dallas often told them that their full, heart-shaped lips and petite frames came from his side of the family. The girls could only take Dallas's word for it because the only other Collins relative they knew was Houston. And if the rest of the Collins family was anything like their father and uncle, they were better off not knowing them.

Dallas never allowed the girls to roller-skate or play outside for fear they might fall and scrape their knees. He told them that beauty was hard work that came at a price and that, one day, it would pay them well.

The weekends were usually Chanel's busiest days, due to all of her repeat clients requesting an hour or so of her time. Chanel had begged and pleaded with Dallas to allow her one weekend off a month. She explained that if he were to approve her request, she'd be more apt to pleasing her clients. As a result, Chanel was given the third weekend of every month off. Chanel put her free time to use by clubbing it with her best friend, Shalonda Harris, and spending quality time with her boyfriend, Maurice.

"Do the ladies run dis muthafucka?" sang DJ Easy Rock.

"Heeellll yaaaaaaa!" answered all the ladies in the club.

The sounds of Lloyd's, "Get It Shawty," kept the club jumpin' and Chanel decided it was time to kick off her stilettos and dance the night away. As she swayed her hips back over to the dance floor, she could hear the faint whispers of two women hating on her.

"Would you look at that bitch? Thinking she's God's gift to men," said a woman with cinnamon skin and hair to match. "That's one of them Collins girls. I think she's the baby."

Though the music was too loud for Chanel to hear exactly what the two women were saying about her, it was obvious that she was the topic of their conversation. Chanel put more of a switch in her hips and slowly swept her slim fingers through her flat-ironed mid–back-length hair. After looking over her shoulders at the two women dressed in knockoff Apple Bottoms outfits, Chanel winked her right eye at them and smiled. *I love this shit. If they hate me, they want to be me,* she thought as she danced her way to the bar.

"What's up with those two bitches? Do you know them?" inquired Shalonda.

"The usual; bitches hate—but fuck 'em. I ain't letting two fat-ass, broke chicks from the projects block my fun. Not tonight," Chanel shouted over the music.

"I hear you, girl," said Shalonda, smiling, as she and Chanel raised their drinks to toast to their having fun. After taking a swig of her Hennessy on the rocks, Shalonda felt that all-familiar urge creeping up on her. "Girl, are you straight? I need to go powder my nose."

"Yeah, girl, I'm cool. Trust me when I say them two poor-ass bitches don't want a piece of my ass. Not tonight, girl, not tonight," said Chanel, smiling.

"Cool. I will be back in less than five minutes," said Shalonda. "Don't move from this spot or we'll never catch up with each other because the crowd is getting thick."

"You're right about that. If it keeps up, I'm raising up out of here," Chanel yelled into her best friend's ear.

Chanel watched Shalonda make her way to the restrooms before returning her attention to her drink. She caught a glimpse of herself in the mirrors lined along the wall and smiled to herself. *Mommy sho' nuff broke the mold when she made my perfect ass*, thought Chanel.

"Hey, excuse you," said Chanel to the woman who had just bumped into her. She stood with her hand on her hip as she looked the woman up and down like she was an alien from outer space. She noticed that it was one of the two women that had been eyeing her.

"Nah, bitch, excuse you!" countered the woman.

"Oh fat-ass, I got cha bitch right here," threatened Chanel, waving her middle finger in the woman's face.

"You ain't special," screamed the woman. "Ya little yellow ass walking around here like you own the fuckin' place. Bitch, you ain't shit!"

Chanel could not understand why the woman was fucking with her, nor did she give a damn. She did not know the

woman from a hole in the wall, yet here she was acting as if she had just caught Chanel giving head to her husband.

Deciding not to bow down and join the woman in her self-hatred pity party, Chanel turned her back on her and took another sip of her drink. Just as the hot liquid slid down the back of her throat, Chanel felt a shove and the drink flew out of her hand. *No, this bitch did not just put her ashy hands on me*, thought Chanel as she spun around to put an end to the impending altercation.

Chanel refused to argue anymore and caught the woman on the chin with a strong right hook. The blow sent the woman backward, knocking over two couples seated behind her. Onlookers scattered, attempting to get out of the way before any more fists were thrown.

"Ah bitch, I'm gon' fuck you up now," threatened the woman. "I don't know who in the hell you think you are but I—"

Chanel hit the woman again as she to struggled to stay on her feet.

Coming out of the ladies' room, Shalonda saw the commotion over by the bar and rushed to see if Chanel was somehow involved. It was not uncommon for a woman to get jealous because she caught her man flirting with Chanel or Shalonda. Shalonda figured that might be the case. She got to the bar just in time to see Chanel throw a mean right hook followed quickly by a left jab. Her opponent grossly under-estimated Chanel's physical strength as she went flying into a small table occupied by unsuspecting patrons. As any true friend would do, Shalonda joined in on the melee and got in a few punches and kicks of her own. The woman's attempts to block the blows were futile and she regretted instigating the altercation. She breathed a sigh of relief when the bouncers put an end to the fight.

The club's hired security guards grabbed Chanel and

Shalonda and led them out the back door. Once outside, the two women burst out laughing so hard that their sides hurt and tears ran down their faces. Almost ten minutes later, Chanel and Shalonda regained control of their senses and decided to call it a night instead of driving up north to another club like they had initially planned on doing. The friends walked around to the front of the establishment to wait for the valet to bring both of their cars around.

"Girl, what in the fuck was that about?" inquired Shalonda.

"I have no idea what that bitch's problem was. Girl, she had the nerve to push my ass and left me no choice but to get at her," explained Chanel. "Shit, these women out here always hate on me. I know I'm fine, but damn, sometimes that petty jealousy gets on my damn nerves. Most of the time, I let that shit slide, but tonight I was forced to beat a bitch to the ground. When someone puts their hands on me, I do not hasten to give them a knockdown, knockout fight. You feel me?"

"I feel you on that, girl. That's why we get along so well, 'cause we both real with it," said Shalonda.

The valets finally arrived with Chanel's pearl colored, 2008 Mercedes-Benz convertible and Shalonda's 2007 silver gray Lexus coupe. The friends gave each other a hug and promised to meet up in a few days for lunch. Chanel got behind the wheel of her car and thought, *She my girl and all but Shalonda probably want to be me too.*

Chapter Three

Diamond in the Rough

Twenty-three-year-old Diamond Ebony Fernando-Collins's—also known as the eldest Collins sister—favorite pastime was being pampered by the staff of Charles Penzone Day Spa. Every Monday, early afternoon, Diamond treated herself to the You Deserve This spa package. It consisted of an hour-long full body massage, a one-hour facial, catered lunch, a forty-five-minute pedicure, and a half-hour manicure. Diamond's weekly massage appointments were always with Sabrina Riaz. After experiencing her massage techniques for the first time, Diamond was hooked. The Dominican-born twenty-five-year-old arrived in the States as a teenager with her parents and four siblings. Her bronze skin always glistened and her hair always smelled of tea tree and rose petals.

Sabrina worked as a masseuse in order to pay for nursing school. When she first began at the spa, Sabrina was having a hard time building clientele, and Diamond felt sorry for her. Next to Diamond's mother and sisters, Sabrina was one of the prettiest women she had ever laid eyes on. Though it went against the day spa's regulations and procedures for employees to fraternize with customers for fear of giveaways or discounted prices, Diamond and Sabrina held a conversation during their initial session and realized that they had

much in common. From that day on, Diamond was Sabrina's 11:00 appointment every Monday.

Like any pampered woman, Diamond spent the rest of her off days shopping in Ann Taylor's and Macy's department stores. She was so much of a fixture that the sales representative called Diamond to inform her of new arrivals and unadvertised sales where employees and their families received special coupons and discounts.

After hours of shopping, Diamond's routine led her northeast to her second favorite place to spend time alone with herself. Old Bag of Nails Restaurant was a great place to enjoy a meal without disruption. Diamond treasured her alone time. It was during those times that she daydreamed about her life before her mother died and wrote her dreams in one of her many journals.

"Hello, Miss Diamond, I've been expecting you," welcomed the restaurant's greeter. "We have your patio table ready. Please follow me."

"Thank you," said Diamond as she followed behind. "I'm going to mix it up a bit, so will you have my drink brought to me now instead of after my meal, the way I usually have it?"

"Sure thing, one cosmopolitian coming right up. Will you be having the fisherman's platter today?"

"Yes, I will," said Diamond, smiling. "Wait, no, I won't. Let me try the baked salmon, dirty mashed potatoes, and Caesar salad."

Staying in routine had recently become very old to her so she decided to switch things up. While waiting for her drink, she scanned the patio and watched as fellow patrons ate, drank, and conversed with one another.

"Here we are, Miss Diamond," announced the waiter, Mike, "a perfect cosmo for a perfect lady." He carefully sat the drink in front of Diamond as she smiled up at him.

Diamond really liked Mike's free spirit and his obvious comfort within his own skin. She had never met a black man so comfortable with his sexuality, but Mike wore it in bright neon colors visible from the moon.

"Thank you, Mike. How are you today?"

"Honey, I'm as fine as I want to be and as cool as a Fudgsicle," joked Mike. "Miss Diamond, I must return to work, but I'll join you during my break. Duty calls." Before turning on his heels to walk away, Mike complimented Diamond on the new gold hoop earrings she sported and the glow of her skin.

Diamond was described as a diamond in the rough by her late mother, Isis Fernando. When she was a little girl, her mother would call her into the house from playing with her sisters and neighborhood friends by yelling, "Where is my Diamond? She must be in the rough because I can't find her." Diamond would give her left arm now to hear her mother's soothing voice just one more time.

It had been a little over ten years since she and her sisters heard their mother's beautiful voice sing out their names. At times, like when she was laying on a massage table with calming sounds filling the room, Diamond could hear her mother call out her name. That voice allowed Diamond to remember times of yesteryear clear as day.

Diamond sat looking out onto the empty sidewalks of State Street and felt eyes on her. She looked up from her now open journal to find a nice-looking man with an almond complexion and deep brown eyes glaring at her. Diamond smiled at the stranger and returned her attention to her journal. Standing at five feet nine with a tiny waist, plump breasts, and shapely hips, Diamond was used to drawing attention from men and women alike. Her shyness prevented her from introducing herself to strangers, and as far as she was concerned, it was best that way. Diamond was young in age but old in life experience. She had learned early not to

trust a soul who had not earned it. So, with the exception of her two sisters, Essence and Chanel, and their godmother, Deborah, she trusted no one. Not even their father.

"Here is your meal, madam," Mike said.

"Thank you, love. As always, you're right on time. You can probably hear my stomach growling," giggled Diamond.

"My pleasure, Miss Diamond. Will your friend be joining you today? It is the first week of the month?"

Sabrina would usually join Diamond for lunch on the first Monday of the month, but her growing list of repeat clientele wouldn't allow it as much anymore, so Diamond would be forced to enjoy her meal alone.

"You know what, Mike?" said Diamond, smiling. "You know me so well. My friend should be joining me today, but unfortunately, she was asked to work, so she will not be coming."

Mike asked Diamond if she needed anything before going off to tend to his other customers. Diamond caught the man at the bar looking her way again, and for a split second, they made eye contact. He stood up from his stool and, with drink in hand, walked over to Diamond's table.

"Excuse me, ma'am. I didn't mean to stare at you, but I think we've met before," the stranger said.

"No, I think you are mistaken," answered Diamond without looking up from her plate. She hoped the man would get the hint and walk away. Unfortunately for her, the man had other plans.

"I am sure we know each other, but I just can remember your name," lied the man. He knew exactly where he'd met Diamond and was determined to jog her memory.

"Sir, I apologize, but we have never met before," said Diamond, smiling, hoping that would be enough for the man to go back to his bar stool.

"Your name is Diamond, isn't it?"

"Yes, it is, but I've never seen you before."

"Oh, you knew me when you collected my money from me," the man spat loudly.

Diamond's tan complexion began to turn red from embarrassment with the mention of collection of money. Her memory wasn't quite jogging, but it was starting to do a little speed walking. All Diamond could think of was swallowing one of her anxiety pills with the aid of her now watered-down cosmopolitan and going home. It was times like that she wished one of her sisters would run to her rescue.

The smell of cheap beer coming from the man's direction turned Diamond's stomach. "Sir, please understand, but I am sorry, we do not know each other," Diamond said in a whisper. She put her fork down and gathered her belongings to leave.

The man grabbed her wrist when she tried to stand up and refused to let her get away. "Sit down, bitch. You ain't goin' nowhere," slurred the man as he jerked her arm.

"Please don't do this," Diamond pleaded as she fought back tears. "I have to be leaving now and you're hurting me."

"I'm hurting you? Ain't that some shit! Bitch, you don't know what hurt means."

"I do not know what you're talking about. Please let go of my arm," begged Diamond.

"Keep ya sorry ass in that chair, bitch, or I will show you what hurt feels like," threatened the man.

Diamond did as she was told and returned to her seat. She began to scan the restaurant in search of someone to come to her assistance. At that moment, Mike sauntered over to a table next to hers and asked to take their orders. Diamond tried as she might to get his attention without causing a scene.

"Yeah, hours after we met you took more than just my three thousand dollars. You took my happy home life from me and now I'm left with nothing," he vented through clenched teeth.

Diamond had prayed she never saw Sean Tillery again. He was a client who hired her to accompany him to some Christmas party he had been invited to during the holiday season. The evening started off fine; they danced, mingled, and ate one of the best dinners Diamond had ever experienced. When the party ended, Sean took Diamond to his hotel room. Diamond excused herself and went into the bathroom to freshen up and undress. She wore a matching lace bra and panty set under her evening gown and wanted to get their hour of sexual escapades over with as quickly as possible.

She returned to the bedroom to find Sean draped in leather chaps, cowboy boots, and a mask, holding a whip and keychains. Under no circumstances did Diamond do dominatrix-type shit, and she damn sure wasn't going to do it that night.

When she refused to be dominated, Sean became enraged and smacked the shit out of her. Diamond was able to grab her purse and run into the bathroom and alert her bodyguard, via cell phone, to the situation.

Houston arrived within seconds and beat Sean into the ground. After Diamond collected her things, including her fee for the evening, she and Houston left Sean Tillery on the carpeted floor, bleeding from every opening the good Lord had given him. Now here he was, in Diamond's face, ready to get revenge.

"Yeah, ho, you know who the fuck I am now, don't you?" Sean tightened his grip on Diamond's wrist that he refused to let go of and continued his ranting. "I said, don't you, bitch!"

"Please, Mr. Tillery, we can talk this out quietly. You don't have to do this to me," pleaded Diamond.

"Don't do this!" yelled Sean, drawing attention to their table. "Bitch, you got me fucked-up. Where is your bodyguard now? Who's going to save you today?"

Sean was now close enough to her to stick his tongue in her mouth, and she could smell the beer on his breath. Dia-

mond scanned the patio for Mike but failed to find him, causing her heart to beat faster with each passing second.

Again, Diamond tried to stand to leave, and again Sean grabbed her wrist and pulled her back down. Diamond began shaking and silently praying for someone to stop what was happening to her. The tears flowed down her cheeks as Sean continued his verbal assault.

"Do you know what you did to me? I ended up in the hospital for three days where they gave me a blood transfusion from all of the blood I lost before the maid found me the next morning. I got stitches in places you could never imagine and I will never regain sight in my left eye. I paid you all of that money, and all I got out of it was a straight-up beat-down."

"Excuse me, Miss Diamond, is everything okay?" interrupted Mike.

"No, it isn't, Mike. Please help me," cried Diamond.

"Man, get the fuck away from here before I hurt ya punk ass!" demanded Sean.

"Look, I have no idea what the problem is, but the lady wants to be left alone and you should leave," said Mike.

"Listen to me, punk, this don't have nothin' to do with you, so mind ya fuckin' business!" Sean stood up and released his grip on Diamond's wrist.

Without warning, Mike threw a power punch that connected to the left side of Sean's face, knocking him unconscious. Mike stood over a lifeless Sean to make sure he was still breathing before turning his attention to Diamond.

"Women beaters will never step to a man." Mike smacked his lips and snapped his fingers in a twirling motion. "I may be a punk, but I'm a proud one who has no problem putting a beat-down on dumb asses like him. Diamond, sweetheart, are you okay?" Mike gave Diamond a quick hug and walked her to her car.

The restaurant manager was trying to calm everyone down but not before calling the police.

"Thank you so much, Mike. I have to get out of here before the police arrive," explained Diamond. "I just don't have the energy to answer their questions right now."

"You don't want to press charges on him for what he did to you?"

"No, I don't. My schedule won't allow me to be running back and forth to a court hearing, only to have him let go with a suspended sentence. Anyway, I don't think he will be bothering me anymore."

Diamond tried to calm her nerves before she lost it right there in the parking lot. She would give anything to have one of her sisters by her side. For as far back as Diamond could remember, she and her sisters had always had each other's backs. If one of them had a problem with a bully at the playground, that bully had a problem with all three of them. As little girls they would be playing dress up in their mother's small closet and pretending to be successful business owners, mothers, nurses or whatever; they all shared the same profession and the same dream: to grow up and be together forever, or like they used to say, three the hard way.

"Well, let me drive you home or at least call you a cab," Mike said softly, rubbing Diamond's back in an effort to relax her. "You are in no condition to drive right now."

"I'll be fine, but I appreciate your concern for me. You are a lifesaver. I have no idea what he would have done if you hadn't stepped in when you did."

Diamond got in her car, pulled out of the parking lot, and drove down State Street to Westerville Road en route to the place she called home. She drove less than a mile away from the restaurant when she had to pull off the road and gather herself before driving any further. Unable to control her shaking, Diamond picked up her cell phone and called her sister,

Essence. Diamond was sure Essence would come to her rescue.

"Hi, Essence, it's me." Diamond began crying into the phone receiver as soon as Essence picked up. "I need your help. Please come get me."

"Just tell me where you're at," Essence said with both concern and urgency as she raced around her bedroom in search of her shoes and purse. After finding out where her big sister was, Essence ran down the stairs as fast as she could. "I'm on my way, baby. I'm on my way."

Essence then chirped their bodyguard on her Nextel. "Houston, we have a problem."

Chapter Four
Head of the Family

Dallas sat behind his massive desk watching the back of his receptionist's head as she sucked on his stiff dick. Performing oral sex on him was something the nineteen-year-old did with pleasure, but for Dallas, it was on-the-job training. Maria Rose Petrilo was oblivious to the real reason she was hired to schedule meetings, run errands, and make a good pot of coffee. Dallas was grooming her to become one of the highest paid escorts in the greater Columbus, Ohio metropolitan area. Just a few more hours of sucking her boss's dick and learning a few more sexual positions, and Maria would be like prime rib in a lion's den to high-rolling clientele willing to pay for what Dallas got for free.

"You coming along real good, girl," hummed Dallas, "but slurp more like you're tasting a candy apple at the state fair."

Maria did as she was told and took more of Dallas inside her mouth. She was able to handle his length better than the last time she got on her knees to please her boss. The first time Dallas wanted her to taste his manhood, Maria almost died from shock and embarrassment, because she had never been with a man before.

Dallas stroked her back and promised her they would never do anything that made her feel uncomfortable. After

she calmed down, Dallas undressed the nervous girl and broke her cherry the way Bruce Lee use to break cinder blocks with his bare hand.

Dallas intended on adding his first snow bunny to his stable of beautiful female specimens and he knew from experience that he was going to have to take things slow with Maria. He would run the risk of scaring her off to the point of running for the hills if he pushed her too soon, too fast. He knew it would be easy to make her fall in love with him, and after she sang those four little words all pimps love to hear, he would manipulate her as only he could. By his estimates, Maria would be purring, "I love you, Daddy" in a few more weeks and would be ready to serve her first trick shortly thereafter.

"Just swallow hard, baby. It will slide down the back of your throat with ease," instructed Dallas after he came. He was proud of his latest project and could not wait to share her with those unsuspecting, lonely, misguided men who were so insecure with themselves that they had to pay for the pussy.

As always, Maria rose up from her knees and walked into the private bathroom connected to Dallas's office. After gurgling with some mouthwash and fixing herself up, Maria returned to her post as receptionist.

Just outside of Dallas's office doors, Houston patiently waited with the man scheduled for the last meeting of the day. After Maria had returned to her desk, Houston led the man into the room to find Dallas seated in his leather lounge chair, sipping on cognac and smoking a Cuban cigar.

"Sit ya punk ass down in that corner chair, bitch," belittled Houston.

Knowing his odds of walking out of the meeting alive were against him, the man did as he was told without one attempt at defending his manhood

"Well, we all know why you're here, Mr. Tillery. It is Tillery, isn't it?" teased Dallas.

"Yes, yes, it is," responded Sean as his voice quivered.

"Good, but do you mind if I call you by your first name?" teased Dallas. "I mean, we don't have to make this meeting a formal one."

"You may address me as Sean if you like," he agreed.

"Well, Sean, most men who have a problem with one of my girls still know not to disrespect them. For some reason, you thought that calling out Diamond in a public setting was an option for you," stated Dallas matter-of-factly.

"I can explain if—" Sean started.

"Shut the fuck up! Did I tell you it was your time to talk?"

"No, sir, I'm sorry," apologized Sean. He sat in the chair as still as possible with his head down and both his hands tucked between his legs. As he sat visibly shaking, Sean wished he could turn back the hands of time and undo the scene with Diamond. *If I knew things would get out of hand like this, I'd of ignored that ho,* thought Sean.

"You got that shit right; you's a sorry ass!" barked Houston.

"Now, as I was saying before ya punk ass interrupted me." Dallas then paused to clear his throat and prolong Sean's torture. "The first time you took advantage of the services we offer here at Match Set Companions, you signed a contract that completely and clearly outlined our service. By signing the questionnaire form, you confirmed that all answers and information provided to be true and concise. The whole point of having a contract is to avoid uncomfortable situations like the one you caused yesterday." Dallas took a sip of his drink and flicked his cigar into his favorite ashtray engraved with the initials *D.C.* "I know there was a problem during the end of your night with Diamond, but that was your fault, not ours. Each girl under our employment has a certain level of experience, a variety of talents and other specialties. Now, had you been honest on the questionnaire, we would have coupled you with one of the girls who would have gladly played

your freaky little sex game. Based on the limited information you provided, we matched you with a date without having been properly informed on your wants."

After Dallas laid out the reason Sean was summoned to the meeting, Houston stepped in to explain the rest. Not only was Houston always taking care of the girls, he was always around to do whatever his brother needed him to do.

Growing up on the dangerous streets of the short north area of Columbus was a sign of poverty to most people, but to Dallas Keith Collins, it was a big schoolyard. Dallas had the ability to take in everything around him. He watched the drug dealers flaunt their material trophies acquired by spreading poison to the very people they lived among. Seeing women willing to sell their bodies for a twenty-dollar piece of crack, a can of baby formula or the overdue rent amazed Dallas the most. Dallas was the oldest of five children born to parents who could never seem to escape the lonely world of poverty. It fell upon him to watch out for his family while their father slaved for a dollar every day as a garbage collector. His father's job paid well and offered health insurance, but when he gambled and drank it up before making it home to pay the monthly bills, he may as well have been unemployed.

As he grew older, Dallas began to resent his mother for never leaving their father. His father's addictions finally came to a head one cold winter's night when Dallas was fourteen. His father had come home drunk and began beating his wife, for no apparent reason at all. That night both Dallas and Houston, the only male children at home at the time, came to the aid of their mother. After they overpowered their father, Dallas and Houston beat him within an inch of his life and drug him outside to lay with the dog. The next morning when the family woke, their father was nowhere to be found and never returned home.

Each of the children rallied to do what they could to make

life easier for their mother. By the time he was sixteen, Dallas had dropped out of school and made hustling a full-time job. His younger siblings did their share around the house, graduated high school and worked hard in college to make a better life for themselves while Dallas proudly flipped the bill. The only thing he asked in return was for his only sister to take good care of their mother and to move her away from Columbus.

His brother, Austin, was offered a position with a prestigious law firm out in Phoenix, Arizona after graduating Ohio State University and he took their mother with him. After getting himself situated, Austin sent for his brothers, Tyler, Houston, and the baby of the family, Autumn, to come live with him in Phoenix. Houston did not fare well in Arizona and began running with a gang and disrespecting their mother. When Dallas received word of Houston's arrest, he decided it best for his baby brother to return to Ohio. By then, Dallas had a girlfriend, Isis Fernando, with whom he lived and was expecting their first child.

Houston tried to stay out of the way of his big brother and his new family. He would do housework, help with the baby, and never missed a day of school for fear of disappointing Dallas. Houston always looked up to his eldest brother, who had been more of a father figure to him than their own father was.

Dallas was proud to have Houston around and began teaching him the grind of the streets. It was during one lesson, while out on the grind, that Houston proved to be in a foreign land when it came to the world of hustling. Unbeknownst to Dallas, the Columbus police department had set up a sting and busted him for selling to an undercover narcotics officer. Dallas kept little weight in his pockets and knew he would probably spend one night in jail at the most. What he hadn't counted on was Houston leading the cops to

their stash of three ounces of crack cocaine and two pounds of weed. It took the defense lawyer, Paul Simmons, who Isis found in the yellow pages, a week to get the felony charges reduced to misdemeanor counts of possession. Due to the evil look in Houston's eyes and his size, none of the other inmates dared to mess with him, but Dallas was not so lucky.

Dallas found himself locked up with people he had crossed on the street by shorting them with weight and jail was the perfect place for retaliation. The piercing pain in his midsection woke Dallas to find three shadows beating and kicking him in his ribs. Before Dallas could attempt to make a move, his mouth was stuffed with a dingy sock that had never been in contact with bleach, soap or water. All of the twists, turns, and swarming Dallas did was in vain because his enemies were far too strong and determined to not let their prey get away.

The next morning, guards found a bruised and battered Dallas laying face down on the cold concrete, fighting to breathe. He had suffered three broken ribs, two slipped vertebrae, and a huge loss of his manhood. After each man had his turn raping Dallas, his attackers sodomized him with some type of foreign object to further break his soul.

Because his needs were more than the county infirmity could offer, Dallas was transferred to Grant Hospital for medical care. For months after his release from the hospital, Dallas tried everything he could to feel like a complete man again. He vowed to never be caught slipping again and began blaming Houston for what happened to him.

It was during that time that Dallas realized that Houston was weak and would be swallowed up by the streets without the proper guidance. The experience changed Dallas in many ways, the biggest being his definition of a man. Only a weak man worked his fingers to the bone, gave his last penny to a woman, and sacrificed his existence to his seeds. To him, a real man led, ruled, used, and abused those around

him. It was then that Dallas decided that if he could not turn his brother into his protégé, he would hand the reins over to his firstborn son.

"You see, Sean, we pride ourselves on pleasing our consumers, but we also take great care of our employees. That is why I was there to protect Diamond that night you scared the shit out of her." Houston spoke with a devilish smile.

Sean was afraid to open his mouth and felt as though he might piss on himself. He looked from Houston to Dallas, then from Dallas to Houston, searching for a sign that it was okay for him to speak. After a few tense minutes, no sign was given, so no words were spoken by Sean. He had no idea exactly where this meeting was going to take him, but he prayed they would have mercy on him and send him on his way . . . all limbs intact.

"As if that was not enough, you broke our number one rule. Here, take this contract and read the first line out loud," instructed Dallas.

Sean reached out with trembling hands and grabbed the contract being extended to him by Dallas. He cleared his throat and tried to speak, but he couldn't find his voice. Inhaling a few long breaths helped Sean calm his nerves and he began to read. "Under no circumstances will any Match Set Companions customers or employees acknowledge each other in a public setting unless said persons are on a scheduled, prepaid date."

"Exactly, Sean, exactly. That rule is to protect your privacy and that of our employees. For some reason unbeknownst to us, you chose to throw Diamond out on Front Street like she wasn't shit. Man, what the fuck was on your mind?" quizzed Dallas.

Sean just stared at Dallas, unsure if he should answer him.

"What the fuck is wrong with you, I said!" Dallas slammed his fist on his desk, not too keen on being ignored.

"I'm so, so, sorry," he gulped. Now, more than clear on the signal that it was okay to speak, Sean stuttered, "See, the night of our date, I was charged a fee much higher than what was quoted to me, and that took my credit card over the limit without my knowledge. My wife tried to charge our children's summer clothes on that card and it was declined. That sent her on a tirade because she's the one who handles paying our household bills. When she saw the ten-thousand-dollar charge on the monthly bill, she did some snooping. After finding other signs of my infidelity, she put me out of the house and hasn't allowed me to see our four children since. She won't forgive me and has filed for a legal separation and wants me to get checked for HIV and any other sexually transmitted disease. My entire life has been ruined all because of some high-priced ho that I didn't even sleep with. When I saw Diamond all dressed and relaxed as if she didn't have a care in the world, something inside of me just snapped."

Sean was now crying like a baby, and Dallas and Houston stared at him blankly. The broken man felt low and wished for death.

"Oh, I must have been left out of the loop somewhere along the line," said Dallas.

"Yeah, me too," chimed Houston.

"I don't understand what you mean," said Sean.

"Well, I listened to you closely, and nowhere in your story did you mention Diamond having a gun to your head." Dallas's tone suggested a hint of sincerity.

"What do you mean? Diamond never brandished a gun during our evening together," answered Sean.

"My point exactly, dumb ass." Dallas jumped to his feet. "Didn't nobody put a gun to ya fuckin' head and force you to take advantage of our services. You cheatin' on ya wife is your problem, not Diamond's."

Dallas was offended by the lack of responsibility Sean was

willing to take for the state of his marriage. Weak men like Sean insulted men everywhere, as far as Dallas was concerned.

"Look, punk ass, I brought you here today to ensure you'd never disrespect Diamond ever again. I was prepared to have you taken out of here in a black bag, but now I'm thinking better of it. You have me thinking that death would be too easy for you. So, I'm gonna let you live," teased Dallas.

"Oh, thank God," Sean sighed under his breath. "I will never do anything to disrespect you, Diamond or your company ever again," promised Sean as he fell to his knees in front of Dallas.

Dallas turned toward the French doors leading to his indoor pool and let out a chilling laugh.

"Don't thank him just yet," chimed Houston, "because you ain't made it out the door yet."

"Houston, take care of this problem," instructed Dallas.

"Done," replied Houston.

"What? What are you going to do to me?" cried Sean.

"I'm going to make sure you never walk up on Diamond or any other woman again. You will leave here with your life, but I'm not sure how much of a life it will be," retorted Houston.

"Oh, dear God, no!"

Chapter Five

Order, Routine, and Profit

Five years ago, the escort service coupled with Dallas's drug sales moved the dysfunctional family from the northeast side of the city to the most expensive suburb surrounding the city of Columbus. His drug sales led to one of the biggest cartels in the state.

While Diamond, Essence, and Chanel brought in the most money, Shalonda and three other girls also worked for the escort service, but they had the privilege of living in a four-bedroom house in the Gahanna area of the city. The mansion on the golf course held two wings, one inhabited by Dallas and Houston, leaving the other for the girls. There were two state-of-the-art home gyms, both indoor and outdoor pools, seven bedrooms, eight bathrooms, one gourmet kitchen, and a home office custom designed for Dallas.

Until the girls were old enough to question where their money was going, Dallas pocketed every dime in order to buy the nine-thousand-square-foot mansion they lived in, along with their cars, designer clothes, two maids, one personal assistant, and anything else Dallas's heart desired. Dallas kept the girls on a tight leash in order to keep the cash flow coming in.

The three sisters were up and engrossed in their morning routine by daybreak. Diamond was the first to rise and get her

hour-long morning workout done. After eating her regular break-fast consisting of brown sugar and cinnamon–flavored oat-meal, fresh fruits, and pulp-free orange juice, Diamond found a comfortable spot in the sitting room the girls shared and opened her journal to document the beginning of another day. By the time Essence and Chanel joined her, *The Young and the Restless* was on. The shows' characters, Neil and Dru, were kissing as their children looked on with smiles on their faces.

"Diamond, why are you watching this show?" Essence in-terrupted Diamond's concentration. "Shit, our life is a fuckin' soap opera and some reality television for ya ass. I can see it now: *Match Set Companions* would be the name of the show. Cameras would follow us around and document how professional escorts con men out of their hard-earned money. Or, we could base the show on a man so much in love with money, he pimps out his own daughters to the highest bid-ders." Essence plopped down on the burgundy suede sofa before Chanel could hog the spot for herself.

Knowing it would lead to a drawn-out debate, Diamond chose not to respond to Essence's snide comment. Diamond continued to focus on her journal entry to finish getting her thoughts documented.

"Can I ask you something, Essence?" Diamond finally asked.

"Only if you want an answer," Essence replied.

"Do you think we could be the focus of a reality show? I mean, would anyone on the outside looking in believe the way we live?" Diamond's words brought a measure of disbe-lief with them.

To Essence, it sounded as if Diamond herself didn't be-lieve the lives they led. "Diamond, what is going on with you? Where is that question coming from?" inquired Essence with confusion. "Lately you seem to be spaced-out."

"She's probably had that dream again," interjected Chanel, who was sitting there removing the polish from her toenails.

"Well, what about you, Chanel, do you believe in happily ever after?" asked Diamond.

"Not for high-priced hoes like us," laughed Chanel. "What did you ask that question for?"

"You're right, I did have *that* dream again," confessed Diamond.

"What did she say this time?" inquired Essence.

"She told me that it is time for us to break loose and start traveling down the right road," Diamond replied almost in a whisper.

The three sisters sat silent for a few minutes, allowing the words to sink in. For months now, each one of them had been experiencing their mother visiting them in their dreams. In each dream, at first, she wouldn't say anything. She would just be combing their hair, fixing them breakfast or watching a movie with them, but before the dream ended, she would always speak. With each visit, they awoke with a measure of weight on their hearts. When she was alive, Isis Fernando was never one to bite her tongue. She was forthright and honest with everything and everyone. True to form, she was the same way when she visited them in their dreams.

"What would you have us do if we tried to walk away from this life? The only thing we have been taught to do is sell pussy. So unless we up and move to Nevada, we are ass the fuck out," spat Essence to her older sister. She hated when Diamond talked about running away from themselves. No matter where they went, they had to take *them* along.

Being the middle child, Essence Ta'Neal often felt over-looked when they were children. She had to fight for attention all of the time. After their mother died from ovarian cancer, Essence's role in the family took a dynamic turn. Diamond Ebony was the oldest and knew their mother the

best. The loss sent Diamond into a depression that continued to go untreated. The once active and happy child grew into a quiet and withdrawn woman. Diamond was a mirror image of their beautiful, happy, spirited parental guide. When their mother died, Diamond felt a piece of her heart died with her.

When the courts first put them with their father, the baby of the family, Chanel Micah, found the transition into their current home frightening. As a motherless child, she clung to Essence as if they were Siamese twins. Essence became a mother to both of her sisters and she protected them as best she could. When the man who fathered them was forced by the courts to take custody of them, Essence's parental status went into full gear, but she was no match for their father's reign of terror.

Dallas sat at the table with his lawyer during the custody hearing adamant about relinquishing his parental rights, until he laid eyes on his seeds for the first time in ten years.

They were as beautiful as their mother had been. To Dallas, it was evident that men would fall at their feet for a chance to get close enough to smell them. The very moment he laid eyes on them, was the moment he decided to profit from them.

Diamond, Essence, and Chanel were three high-priced hoes in high demand, and their own daddy was their pimp.

"Haven't you been depositing money into our rainy-day fund? We should have enough to start a life all our own. The three of us are of age now, and they can't stop us," said Diamond with sadness in her voice.

"Of course I have been putting money to the side, and you know that, but none of us knows what a *real life* is. This is the only life we've known since Mommy died. What else can we do?"

"We could open our own business, maybe a boutique featuring our own line of designer clothes," offered Chanel with

excitement. "Maybe one day we will each find a man to love us and take care of us like Mommy wanted."

"Shit, both of y'all are dreaming. What man do you know could love a woman who sold her pussy to every dick willing to pay for it? Besides, bitches like us sell so much ass that when it comes to the dick, we end up feeling one of three ways about it."

"How is that?" asked Diamond.

"We end up loving it, hating it or just fuckin' tolerating it," Essence said while smacking her lips, twisting her neck and rolling her eyes.

"Tolerate what?" asked a confused Chanel, who was half listening to her sister's sarcasm.

"The dick, bitch, tolerate da dick," Essence spat.

"Whatever," retorted Diamond in disgust of her sister's pessimism. She closed her journal and headed down the long hallway and retreated into her personally designed bedroom. It was the one place in the massive nine-thousand-square-foot home she felt safe, secure, and alone with her mother.

Essence and Chanel remained in the sitting room on the upper floor of the mini-mansion they helped finance by selling their souls to the devil himself. The two sat in silence for a few minutes to see if Diamond would return. When it became evident that she would not, Chanel broke the silence.

"Should we go see about her?" asked Chanel with concern.

"Naw, she probably just needs some time to herself. She'll come back when she's ready," said Essence matter-of-factly.

Chanel felt at ease with her big sister's take on the matter. She always put her trust into Essence, no matter what the situation.

"If you say so," Chanel said. "Since we waiting on her, pass me that bronze fingernail polish and that bottle of

Belvedere. I need to calm my nerves before our weekly staff meeting because who knows how this one will end."

"Seven o'clock on the muthafuckin' dot! Every week, Wednesday evenings, seven o'clock on da muthafuckin' dot. What da fuck I got to do to get you on the same time frame as me and all of the other people living in the Eastern Time zone?"

It was half-past dinnertime, and Essence had just sat down and joined the others for their weekly staff meeting. Dallas was so mad, he had steam coming out of his ears, but Essence didn't give a fuck. She felt that Dallas had way too many rules and stipulations in the house, and no matter how he felt about it, Essence was gonna do her damn thang.

"Shit, I'm here now," said Essence as she placed her napkin across her lap. "I mean, damn, I'm sure that nothing at this meeting is that fuckin' pressing any damn way."

Despite the years of training, discipline, and abuse, Essence remained true to form. She spoke her mind and allowed whatever was on her mind to roll off of it. Essence didn't give a damn whose feelings she hurt, or who she pissed off. Besides her sisters, ain't nobody ever gave a fuck about her feelings.

Dallas would argue with Essence all day, every day if need be. Like father, like daughter, the two never got along because they were both stubborn, bullheaded, and strong. Dallas appreciated her boldness and lack of fear. He realized that she was the chosen one. The one who could take over the business after his reign.

It was dinner meetings like this that Dallas regretted never allowing his other hoes to attend. *Maybe some fresh meat thrown into the mix could shut Essence the fuck down for me,* thought Dallas. Even as the thought ran through his mind, Dallas had to be honest with himself about his reasoning for not having Shalonda and the other girls involved. If

they witnessed the strength and fearlessness in Essence, they might get the courage to walk away from him, believing him to be weak.

"Girl, can the fuckin' attitude before I fine ya ass. Shit, I got other things to do tonight and you done fucked-up my entire schedule," said an irritated Dallas.

"Dallas, if what you got to do is that pressin' why in the hell wouldn't you start this so-called staff meeting without me? Seriously, why wouldn't you?"

Dallas, Houston, and Diamond and all looked at Essence like she had just grown a second head right before their eyes. Chanel snickered and shook her head at her sister's antics but failed to understand why everyone besides her was surprised. Essence always had a smart mouth loaded with a slick tongue. Essence just didn't give a fuck what she said and who she said it to. Diamond and Chanel would not dare speak to Dallas the way Essence had, but for different reasons.

Diamond's personality did a total 360 after their mother's death, and ten years later, the fence she built around her seemed to have grown even higher. There was a door into Diamond's world, but only her sisters knew where the key was hidden.

Chanel was born optimistic and always saw the glass half full and the sun bright as all hell. No matter what the situation, Chanel would smile, make light of the situation and move on like she didn't have a care in the world. Things in Chanel's world worked for her because she never stressed on things she could not change.

Essence was dead smack in the middle of the two. Though she tried to live her life looking on the positive side of everything, she was guarded and investigated anything in her path. Essence demanded people to earn her trust; she never gave it up for free. Getting on her bad side was so not a good thing to do, because if that one chance was blown, Essence

would never give them another one. The worst sin in Essence's eyes was to fuck with her sisters. She would gladly run through hell with a panty and bra set drenched in gasoline, if it meant protecting her sisters.

"You done ranting and raving about nothing?" Dallas asked Essence sarcastically.

"Whatever, Dallas. I mean, it's your show, ain't it?" spat Essence.

"From what I hear, the three of you had various problems last week. Diamond, I heard one of your former dates from a month ago was a fuckin' pervert and into things that are not your specialty. That client has been dealt with, and I apologize for what you had to go through. That situation could have been prevented if the right question had been asked at scheduling. I will see to it that from now on, Maria will be asking more in-depth questions when scheduling and assigning dates."

"I don't know why, because the clients don't always answer honestly when they call for a date," said Essence.

"Like I just said, you will be asking more in-depth questions. I will inform Maria that I want to see a new questionnaire by noon tomorrow right after we finish dinner.

"Now, back to Diamond. Again, the situation that arose at the restaurant has been handled, and his punk ass will never walk up on you again," promised Dallas.

"What situation at the restaurant?" asked Chanel with concern.

"It's not important, and like Dallas just said, it has been handled," replied Diamond, not wanting to be embarrassed all over again.

"Fuck that, I want to know what happened to you," said Chanel, pouting.

"One of her clients blamed her for his misery and made a scene at her favorite restaurant. He tried to get physical, but

one of the waiters took good care of Diamond until I took over," explained Houston. "While I'm thinking about it, Diamond, we rewarded your friendly waiter handsomely for his having your back."

Chanel was satisfied with the explanation enough to leave it alone for now, but later that night, she planned on getting the full story from Diamond herself.

"Now to you, Essence, please tell me when you will fuckin' learn to follow the rules?" Dallas asked, but was not looking for an answer.

"It got handled, didn't it? Shit, that punk-ass lonely-hearted rich businessman paid for my services, didn't he?" Essence rolled her eyes toward the three-tier chandelier placed directly above the eight-chair formal dining room table.

"Yeah, it got handled, but the situation could have been more contained if you would have just followed protocol and signaled for me," complained Houston.

"He is right, Essence, and you know it," interjected Dallas. "Just let Houston guard and protect you as the rules state. If a client doesn't want to pay for the services he has received, continue to let Houston know immediately, not after you've tried to explain it yourself more than once," instructed Dallas.

"Naw, that trick paying me wasn't the issue; he was quoted three thousand dollars by Maria, but the package he received was a ten-thousand-dollar one. Maria has been making a lot of mistakes lately, and I'm sick of her unqualified ass," Essence said, looking directly at Maria.

"That's true, Dallas. She has been fuckin' up," added Chanel. "Last week she had me waiting in the wrong hotel to be picked up by a longtime client who pays me well. We can't have that," Chanel said with an attitude.

"How can y'all just talk about her like she's not sitting across from us?" Diamond asked in disgust.

Dallas was well aware of her weak qualifications for the re-

ceptionist and scheduling position. The only reason he'd kept her around was because he planned to put her to the money-making position of one of his hoes. He was enjoying training her during their lunch-hour sexual escapades.

"I'll double-check the schedule for the next week or so and help Maria earn her position with the company," explained Dallas.

"Okay, ladies, it's that time of year again, and it's time for your physicals," Dallas informed them. "You each have an appointment with Dr. Blackman this week. The individual appointment times will be penciled in on your appointment log for the week. I will quickly recount the rules for you ladies if I have to. Since none of you have been having unprotected sex, including when giving and receiving oral sex, I'm certain each of you will have a clean bill of health. Besides an alcoholic drink every now and then, no illegal drugs will be revealed and all of you have remained at your target weight. Having that state-of-the-art home gym built in the wing of the house you all occupy better be paying off," threatened Dallas, though it seemed no one was listening to him.

Dallas was a hustler in every sense of the word and never missed a chance to benefit from things that fell into his lap. Diamond, Essence, and Chanel had turned out to be his best hustle ever. Their African American and Hispanic heritage molded them into three of the most beautiful beings he had ever laid eyes on.

When Isis first became pregnant, Dallas was ecstatic at the thought of having a son. When the doctor announced, "It's a girl," Dallas was disappointed, but loved his daughter. Isis knew Dallas felt let down that their firstborn child wasn't a boy, and to make him happy, she got pregnant immediately after her six-week checkup. When the baby was born one month after Diamond Ebony turned one, Isis, once again, saw the look of disappointment in the eyes of the first man she'd ever loved.

It was after Essence Ta'Neal made her loud entrance into the world that the couple's relationship changed. Dallas became distant and began disrespecting Isis like she was some bum on the street begging for a dollar. The day Isis brought their second baby girl home from the hospital, Dallas gave her an ultimatum.

"You will give me a son or I am out the door. Shit, what in the fuck is wrong with you that ya ass can't give me a son?" fumed a drunk Dallas.

Isis was beside herself and couldn't believe her ears. It was bad enough that Dallas didn't pick her and the baby up from the hospital, but now he was making demands on her that she had no control over.

"Dallas, why are you mad at me? It's not my fault our baby is a girl. I don't know about you, but if I remember my high school health class correctly, it's the man who determines the sex of the baby," argued Isis.

When Dallas hauled off and hit her, Isis was in a state of shock. In the five years they'd been together, Dallas had never touched her in anger. Hitting her was bad enough, but the fact that he'd done it while Essence was in her arms was unforgivable. Isis calmly walked into the baby's room and gently placed Essence in her crib. She peeked into the bathroom, where her best friend Deborah was watching Diamond play in her tiny tub, and closed the door. Isis returned to the front room to find Dallas gulping down a beer and flicking through the sports channels. Isis stared at Dallas for a moment and rubbed her hand on the side of her face that still stung from the strike he'd surprised her with.

Isis slowly removed a sword from its case that Dallas had proudly hung on the wall and snuck up behind him.

"Listen to me closely, papi," instructed Isis through clenched teeth. "I have been beat on and abused my entire life growing up in foster care. There was one piece of shit of a man who robbed me of my virginity before I even understood what my

womanhood was worth." The blade was so sharp, it pierced Dallas's skin with little force being applied, causing blood to trickle down his white wife beater he always wore as a shirt. "You may think I'm weak-minded, worthless or beneath you, and that very well may be the case. But let me tell you one thing, papi, today was the first and the last time you ever lay hands on me in anger. Should it happen again, I will fuckin' kill you."

Isis pulled the sword from Dallas's neck, wiped it clean on her shirt, returned it to its proper place and went to see about her babies.

Dallas was in shock and could not move. He was stunned by Isis threatening his life, but she left no doubt that she would indeed kill him for disrespecting her the way he had.

For three weeks following that incident, Dallas helped out with the babies, brought dinner home so Isis would not have to cook, and rubbed her feet at night without being asked to. During this period, Isis agreed to try for a son and have one more baby. Two months after Diamond turned two, and one month after Ebony turned one, Isis gave birth to Chanel Micah.

The day Isis was released from the hospital, Dallas was a no-show. Isis called Deborah, who was caring for the girls at her place, to pick her and the baby up. They were both shocked by what they found waiting for them when Isis arrived at home.

At first glance, the apartment looked as if it had been burglarized, but after taking a closer look, Isis discovered that the only things missing were Dallas's. In three years, Isis bore Dallas three babies, all girls. After her last failed try at having a son, Dallas kept his word and left Isis to raise *her* daughters on her own.

The day Isis gave birth to her third daughter was the last day she ever saw or heard from Dallas. She did the best she

could in her situation and showered her girls with love, protection, and a sense of belonging.

It devastated Isis when the oncologist told her the ovarian cancer was so advanced that it had already spread to her stomach. Besides her daughters and her best friend, Isis had no one. Even if she'd wanted to, contacting Dallas was not an option at all. He had turned his back on them once, and she would be damned to hell if she allowed him to do it again. Isis and Deborah talked endlessly about the care and upbringing of her girls after she passed on. Deborah promised her best friend that her three daughters would stay together and that she would love them unconditionally.

Isis penned her wishes on paper and slipped into darkness at ease, believing her daughters would be placed with Deborah. The social workers, lawyers, and judge felt differently. It was law that the children be placed with a blood relative if one existed. Social services tracked Dallas down, using the girls' birth certificates and old hospital information. Dallas wanted nothing to do with taking custody of the daughters he never wanted in the first place. Both his lawyer and the social worker begged Dallas to take responsibility, to make the process easier, but he wouldn't have it. Dallas chose to sign away his parental rights and let the system swallow the eleven- , twelve- , and thirteen-year-olds whole.

Chapter Six

Not the Girl Next Door

The night after their weekly staff meeting, Chanel decided to spend as much time as possible with Maurice. Spending alone time together was extremely difficult for the couple due to their busy schedules. Maurice dedicated his time to his life's work, running a successful upscale restaurant, and it was beginning to pay off. He had recently hired two managers, one for the restaurant and the other for his catering service. At only twenty-six, Maurice was truly a successful businessman. When he was young, his hardworking single father taught him that working for himself, at a job he loved, would afford him the freedom to earn a living by doing what he loved.

Maurice and Chanel had been dating for five months and they had both fallen in love. As Maurice stood over his kitchen counter chopping vegetable for his eggplant manicotti and spaghetti sauce, his thoughts remained on Chanel. Her beautiful light brown eyes drew Maurice to her on Chanel's first visit to Ruby Jae's Joint. Maurice stopped by the best table in the restaurant to inquire about the taste of their meal and was instantly hypnotized by Chanel's flawless skin and her perfect smile. Maurice stopped himself from staring, introduced himself, and offered Chanel his business card. Chanel

returned to the restaurant the following evening, and so began the best relationship either of them had known.

"Sunshine, I'm here," shouted Chanel in search of Maurice in his huge loft apartment above his restaurant.

"I'm in the kitchen, baby girl," responded Maurice as he wiped his hands on a towel. "I've been looking forward to seeing you all day." Maurice greeted Chanel with a hug and passionate kiss.

Chanel returned the affection with the same level of emotion she had received it. Just as the two released each other, the ding of the oven timer forced Maurice to release Chanel from his arms.

"It smells good in here as usual," complimented Chanel with a smile. "What's for dinner?"

"One of your favorite dishes, eggplant manicotti."

"Good, I am so hungry. I'll set the table while you finish up. You have the wine on chill already, don't you?"

"Yes, grab it out of the fridge and place it inside the bucket next to the table. Baby girl, make sure to open the window sheers so we get the full view of the city lights," instructed Maurice.

Chanel did as she was asked and felt her heart smile, sending a warm chill up her spine. She stared out the window and hugged herself. The only form of love Chanel ever experienced was from her sisters. Meeting Maurice allowed Chanel to receive the type of love from a man she'd only seen on television or read about in novels. Whenever she was away from Maurice, Chanel counted the hours and sometimes days until they would see each other again. While they were together, Chanel wished the time would stand still and she could form a cocoon around them.

The two sat down at the smoked-glass dining room table, bowed their heads and blessed the gourmet meal before them. Chanel hadn't eaten much during the day in anticipation of her dinner plans with Maurice. As she now prepared to

partake of the dish, a feeling of nausea washed over her out of the blue. She took a few deep breaths, trying to calm her stomach and fight off the sick feeling.

"What's wrong, baby? Did I use too much garlic for you this time?"

"No, everything tastes wonderful as always. I don't know what has been wrong with me lately, but my appetite has been all over the place," apologized Chanel.

"Would you like some ginger ale to calm your stomach?" Maurice rose from his seat before Chanel could accept his offer.

Chanel sipped on the Canada Dry cranberry ginger ale Maurice prepared for her and took a few deep breaths, trying to rid herself of the nausea. Trying as hard as she could, Chanel could not get past the smell of the meal in front of her.

Maurice watched Chanel with worry. "Here, come with me over to the couch. Maybe lying down will help you feel better."

Chanel allowed Maurice to lead her over to his cream-colored, microfiber oversized couch and laid her head on his lap. Maurice wrapped Chanel's favorite blanket around her and pushed play on the remote to his state-of-the-art entertainment center, starting their favorite movie, *Lackawanna Blues*.

By the end of the movie, Chanel was feeling much better, but remained in the same position. She felt comfortable and safe with Maurice and didn't want the moment to end. Maurice stroked Chanel's mid–shoulder-length hair, allowing her to relax. She lifted herself up and wrapped Maurice's left arm around her.

"How are you feeling now?" he inquired.

"Like I want to become one with you," whispered Chanel seductively. Chanel gave Maurice a soft, warm kiss and sucked on his bottom lip the way he liked. Maurice returned the kiss

and pulled Chanel on top of him in a straddled position. For a moment, Chanel pulled away to look into Maurice's eyes. She never thought it possible, but Chanel could see the love Maurice had for her.

"I love you," proclaimed Maurice.

"I love you back," said Chanel, smiling.

Maurice wrapped Chanel's smooth, bare legs around his waist and stood up. He enjoyed the soft, sensual kisses Chanel planted on his neck and earlobes as he gently laid her on top of his California king-sized bed. Chanel rested on her back, watching Maurice undress as the moisture between her legs beckoned him to enter her.

Maurice bent down on his knees and pulled Chanel closer to the edge of the bed. He slowly removed the pink satin G-string and placed each of her legs on his shoulders.

The warmth of his tongue on her thighs caused Chanel to gasp. If she had her way, Chanel would forgo the foreplay and immediately allow her lover to enter her, causing them to become one.

The moans escaping Chanel's perfect mouth was turning Maurice on, willing him to kiss and suck on her clit with as much gentle force he could muster without hurting her.

After Chanel experienced her third orgasm, Maurice began kissing her navel before moving up to her plump C-cup breasts.

Chanel could not take it anymore. As her womanly juices slowly formed a puddle under her hips, Chanel moved her body and pushed Maurice on his back. She immediately straddled her lover and watched his thick manhood disappear inside of her.

Maurice gripped Chanel's hips and helped her move up and down on his dick as if it were a roller-coaster ride.

Moving fast, slow, and then fast again, Chanel placed her right ring finger in his mouth and used her left hand to play with her clit.

When Maurice was about to cum, Chanel suddenly stopped her joy ride, and the lovers flipped into the doggy-style position. The two moaned, groaned, and begged for more and more. Maurice stood up straight and laid Chanel on her back. With her hips on the edge of the bed, Chanel lifted her legs on Maurice's shoulders and enjoyed the butterfly position.

An hour later, the couple had enjoyed the pleasure of the arch, frog leap, and the sleeping beauty positions as they lay spooning each other, spent.

"You are wonderful," sighed Chanel.

"You don't love me, you just love my doggy style," teased Maurice.

Chanel could only laugh at her lover as they wished the moment would never end. The time was quickly approaching for Chanel to say the words Maurice hated to hear. In an effort to prolong the evening, Chanel asked Maurice to shower with her. He gladly accepted the invitation and followed Chanel into his chocolate and lime green master bath. The smell of sex filled the air as the lovers stepped into the double shower and began another round of love making. The hot water turning simultaneously cool and then cold, brought an end to the intimate shower and the evening.

Maurice reached for the lotion and caught a reflection of Chanel in the mirror. The look of satisfaction and love on her face was now replaced with sadness and regret.

"What are you doing?" whispered Maurice, though his heart already knew the answer.

"I'm so sorry, Maurice, but I have to go now," said Chanel.

"Why do you always do this?"

"Please understand, Maurice, that I have to go. I would love to stay the night with you and wake up with your arms around me, but I can't," explained Chanel with sadness.

"If that's the case, why don't you?" Maurice asked with great disappointment behind his words.

"I don't know how else to explain this to you, but I still live

at home and I have a curfew to keep and rules to live by. You know this, and I'm tired of having this same argument."

"Chanel, there are many twenty-one-year-olds who live at home and don't have a fraction of the rules you live by," replied Maurice. "You are a grown woman and you can't spend the night with your man?"

"I have no control of the rules our father makes for us. My sisters don't like it either, but we have no choice," Chanel desperately tried to explain.

When they first began dating, Maurice was patient and understanding with Chanel not being able to spend the night with him. As their relationship grew closer and he found himself falling in love with her, that patience was running thin. Maurice tried to control both his disappointment and anger as he carefully chose his words.

"Maybe it's not that you *can't* spend the night with me; it's that you don't want to. I mean, Chanel, tell me the truth," demanded Maurice.

"I have always told you the truth, Maurice. Please know that. You don't know my father, but I do. If I broke this rule, I would have to pay for it dearly," whined Chanel.

"What is he going to do? Put you out? I've told you we can live here together. If you don't want to move in with me here because this is my space, I will sell my loft and we can find a home together. A nice home that will belong to the both of us. Chanel, I love you more than you know, and I will do whatever it takes to make you happy and keep you safe," Maurice said in a more sensitive voice. He walked closer to Chanel and looked deep into her light brown eyes for a hint of truth. What he found was a deep sadness he never knew existed.

Chanel dropped her eyes to focus on anything but the hurt staring back at her. At that moment, the thing Chanel wanted most was to tell the man she loved the hard, abusive reality that was her life, but her heart just wouldn't let her. Although

she knew he loved her, Chanel doubted that any relationship could survive her reality.

"I know you will, Maurice, but I have to ask you to be patient with me just a little while longer. Things will change between us soon, very soon," promised Chanel. She did not know how, but Chanel was determined to make it happen.

Since the loss of her mother, Chanel and her sisters were taught that life was about rules, guidelines, and money. After meeting Maurice, those teachings felt misguided and wrong. Chanel loved the way he made her feel and yearned to be with him in a faraway place where no one knew her or how she made a living. The day she was made to go live with the father she had never known, Chanel's life was flipped upside down. Selling her body was not easy. It was filled with long, demanding training sessions that still continued to be critiqued. But like their father had told them, beauty was hard work, but it would pay off.

At first Chanel never understood what he meant by that, until the day their lessons with Houston began.

One day, Houston approached Diamond and told her to follow him. She did as she was told and asked no questions when her uncle closed the bedroom door and locked it behind him. He saw the look of fear on the thirteen-year-old Diamond's face and tried to put her mind at ease.

Houston had begun sexually abusing neighborhood girls when he reached puberty. It was by sheer luck that none of them ever told about the abuse. When they were growing up, Dallas had caught Houston fondling a little girl he was supposed to be babysitting. It was because of this that Dallas knew his brother would have no problem having sexual relations with his own nieces.

"We are going to do some things you may not like, but in life, all of us are forced to do things we don't like. Do you un-

derstand?" Houston asked the question more as a statement and Diamond did not respond.

Shortly after her thirteenth birthday, Essence took the same walk behind their uncle that her sister had. Chanel watched and noticed how Diamond and Essence seemed to change after being behind the closed door with Houston. Chanel noticed her sisters' eyes turn sad and seemed to be crying out for help.

Essence had always been the quiet one and always trying to make peace whenever the sisters disagreed and argued. After her first session with Houston, Essence's personality took a dramatic change, and she became defiant, angry, and out-spoken. Her refusal to do as Dallas and Houston told her often resulted in her being whipped with leather belts or locked in her room for days at a time. The two men were always careful to physically beat her while she was fully clothed to avoid leaving any marks or scars on her body.

Chanel had no idea what took place when alone with Houston, she just knew that she did not want to find out.

Just one week after she turned thirteen, Houston came for a frightened Chanel. Once locked in the room with him, Chanel quickly discovered the reason behind it all.

"I want you to undress," said Houston.

"Why do I have to undress in front of you?" Chanel asked, tears forming in her eyes.

"Like I told your sisters, sometimes in life we have to do things we don't like. Now, start by taking of your shirt," instructed Houston.

"No!" screamed Chanel as she ran toward the locked door.

"Come here," barked Houston as he snatched Chanel by her arm. "You will do what the fuck I tell you, and you will like it. Now, don't make me tell you again—Take off your clothes."

"I don't want to. Where is Dallas? Does he know about this?" cried Chanel. "I want my sisters."

Smack!

Chanel was stunned by being hit across her face. She immediately covered her cheek, trying to stop the stinging. Her crying made Houston treat her harshly.

"Take off your fucking clothes, starting with your top. Then move down to your skirt and stand before me," said Houston through clenched teeth.

Chanel did as she was told, with the tears steadily rolling down her face. When she was down to her undergarments, Chanel was forced to her knees and received instruction on performing oral sex on her uncle. Chanel was ashamed and wanted to die that night. She was forced to relive that scene multiple times before her uncle raped her for the first time. All three girls were threatened with harm and the thought of being separated from each other. Dallas began telling them that all girls their age did those same things; it was just something people didn't talk about.

For a little under a year, the girls were molested by their uncle, beaten by their father, and had their self-worth stripped from them. Though they didn't understand it at the time, everything they had gone through was in preparation of being sold to the highest bidders. The price they paid for room and board was their sexual being. When Houston would report back to Dallas about the girls being defiant, the psychological abuse would begin.

"Look, I fail to see the reason behind the three of y'all acting all ungrateful and shit," Dallas fumed. "It ain't like you hungry, got worn-out shoes on ya feet or some fucked-up shit like that."

"Why do we have to do all that nasty stuff? You know this ain't right," cried Diamond.

"He don't care anything about us. For all we know, he getting a check for us being here and we buying our own food and clothes any damn way," spat Essence.

"One day you gon' learn how to watch that foul-ass mouth of yours."

"It ain't no worse than yours."

"I'm gonna let that slide, Essence, 'cause I know it's been a hard day, but don't get comfortable with speaking to me like that. Shit, if I'd let you go to some foster home, some man, someplace would rape you any fuckin' way, so you may as well get paid for the shit," Dallas reasoned. Each time Dallas berated his daughters, thoughts of his own rape surfaced. While in his own twisted way he loved his daughters, he resented that he never had a son to build into the strong man he wished he had been the night he was unable to fight off his offenders.

Chanel had never lied to Maurice about anything besides how she made a living. As far as he knew, Chanel worked for a local graphic design firm as a corporate secretary.

"Maurice, do you know why I call you Sunshine?" asked Chanel as she held onto Maurice as tight as she could.

"Yes, baby girl, I do. You've told me it's because of the bright light I've brought into your life," replied Maurice.

"No matter what happens with us, I want you to know how happy I am when I'm with you and how much I love you," confessed Chanel.

"If that's the case, why don't you let me take care of you? Why can't we wake up together?"

"Maurice, I would love to do just that, but unfortunately, I am forced to abide by my father's rules." Chanel felt the tears escape from her eyes and roll down her cheeks. "Because of that, I have to say good night."

"I don't know how understanding you expect me to be. I love you, but I don't know how much longer I can wait for you to truly be with me," said Maurice from his heart.

"Maurice, at times, we all have to do some things we just

don't like to do. I'm just asking you to be patient with me a little while longer as I straighten out things at home with my father," requested Chanel.

Not wanting to continue the argument, Chanel wrapped her arms around her man before leaving him to sleep alone, again.

Maurice watched Chanel gather her things and walk out the door. Standing on the outside of the door, Chanel prayed that she had not lost the only man who ever loved her. It was at that moment she vowed to make dramatic changes and take control of her life. The first step in doing so was to get her sisters to do the same. Chanel walked outside into the humid air, looked up to the sky and said, "Mommy, please help us break away from Dallas, please."

Chapter Seven

My Life or Yours

It had been two weeks since Chanel and Maurice had spent any quality time together, and she was in a panic that Maurice might leave her. Chanel paced back and forth in front of the Cheesecake Factory contemplating her situation. No matter how many scenarios came to mind, the outcome remained the same. *Where are they*, thought Chanel as she looked around for her sisters whom she had called twenty minutes ago. It was Monday, their only off day, and as usual, Diamond and Essence were off doing their own thing. When Chanel called her sisters in a panic, they both dropped what they were doing and rushed to the restaurant to be with their sister.

After what felt like twelve hours later, Chanel spotted Diamond and Essence sprinting past Barnes & Noble to join her in the patio area of the restaurant. They were both filled with panic and fear when they saw the traces of tears on Chanel's face.

"What is wrong? Did somebody hurt you? Just tell me who hurt you and I promise you that muthafucka with never harm you again. Shit, this is some bullshit," Essence said in one breath.

"Essence, would you calm down? How is Chanel going to tell us what's wrong, with you ranting and raving like that?" Diamond asked.

"I'm just saying . . . Shit, I will fuck a muthafucka up for messing with mine," vented Essence with a nervous air. She was trying to be strong, but the thought of Chanel being in pain and her not being able to protect her scared the hell out of Essence.

"Okay, Chanel, we are both here now, so tell us what is wrong," soothed Diamond.

Chanel looked back and forth between her big sisters as she tried to find her voice. She knew that they loved her and would support any decision she might make, but she struggled to find the right words. "I'm pregnant," whispered Chanel.

"Ah, hell to da muthafuckin' no," responded Essence.

"Essence, keep your voice down; people are looking at us," said Diamond, embarrassed by the unwanted attention. "Chanel, are you positive about this?"

"Yes, I'm positive. For the last few weeks, I've had morning sickness and cravings for unbaked cake batter. When I couldn't keep any food down, I initially thought I had the flu or a summer cold, but when my period didn't come, I bought a home pregnancy test," confessed Chanel.

"Those home pregnancy test aren't always right, I don't care what nobody says. You need to go to someone's clinic for a real test or at least get a doctor's opinion or something," voiced Essence.

"I did go to the clinic, and I'm two months pregnant," Chanel explained. She put her head down in shame and allowed the tears to fall on her lap. The last thing Chanel wanted to do was let down her sisters. Besides Maurice, Diamond and Essence were the only two people on the earth that Chanel loved and trusted. She had always

looked up to her sisters and Chanel tried her best to be just like them.

"Chanel, what are you going to do?" asked Diamond.

"What do you mean by what is she going to do? She's going to abort it," snapped Essence.

"I don't know what I'm going to do yet. I haven't had time to process all of this; and anyway, Dallas is going to kill me when he finds out," cried Chanel.

"Don't cry, baby girl. You know that whatever your decision is we will be by your side," comforted Diamond.

"Chanel, how did this happen? You know the number one rule is to always use protection."

"When I'm working I follow the rules, especially that one. Essence, do you really think I'm that stupid and irresponsible that I would slip up and get pregnant by a trick?" Chanel was fighting the urge to run out of the restaurant like a spoiled child, but Essence wasn't making it easy for her.

Chanel was fifteen when Dallas started selling her out to the highest bidder, and not once in the last six years did she not protect herself. While Dallas hired teachers to instruct them how to be a lady, it was teachers at school, BET advertisements, and pamphlets that taught Diamond, Essence, and Chanel facts about sexually transmitted diseases. Dallas only threw condoms at them and never explained why.

"For the first time since Mommy died, I have been able to experience love from someone other than the two of you," Chanel told her sisters. "Maurice treats me good, and I feel special when I'm with him. Maurice loves me and he cares about the things that make me happy. Is it so wrong to enjoy a relationship with a man who cares about me without having to pay for my time?"

"No, it isn't wrong to love a man. At least that's what Dr. Phil

said in an *O* magazine article. Shit, the only thing I get from men has a price tag stapled to it," admitted Essence.

The sisters sat in silence for a minute, each one of them contemplating the idea of loving a man who loved them back. Diamond and Essence had never come close to experiencing love from a man. In all honesty, they would have no idea how to live a life without being paid for their time. The idea of living in a two-story house surrounded by a white picket fence was just that, an idea movie producers and romance writers imagined in their heads and put down on a piece of paper to entertain their fans.

"Do y'all remember Mommy promising us that one day she would move us out of that roach-infested two-bedroom apartment on Livingston Avenue? The way we would sit on Mommy's bed doing our toenails and listening to her sing them old songs on the radio?" reminisced Diamond.

"Yeah, she said one day we would live in a four-bedroom house out in Reynoldsburg or Pickerington," remembered Essence. "She said her bedroom would have its own bathroom, and we would share one big enough to be another bedroom. On Sunday mornings, we would lay in bed with her and watch that real estate show that lets you see the inside of houses for sale. Mommy would say, 'After you girls graduate college, get married and have me some grandbabies, they'll come visit their 'Dea every weekend, and I'll redecorate y'all's bedrooms for them. By that time, I'll be working as a phlebotomist at Mt. Carmel East Hospital or one of those urgent care clinics making good money.' She was a dreamer," added Essence.

"I miss her so much," Diamond said with a sigh. "It's been ten years since we lost her, but some days it feels like it just happened."

The sisters sat silent for a moment as each of them daydreamed about how their lives might have turned out if their

mother was still alive. Not a day went by that they didn't think about their mother. Sometimes when Chanel prayed, she would ask God to give their mother a message for her.

"Okay, enough of this. If we don't stop crying, people will start thinking we're crazy," stated Essence. "We have to decide what to do about Chanel."

"What do you mean by 'what to do with Chanel'?" Chanel rolled her eyes at her sister. "I love Maurice, and there is no way I could abort the child inside of me," she confessed.

"So, you love Maurice and want to be with him, that's all good; but how will he react once he finds out how you make your money? I'm not trying to hurt your feelings, but we have to look at the pros and cons of you having this baby," Essence said.

"I know, Essence, you're right. What if Dallas puts me out and Maurice turns his back on me and the baby? We've never talked about a future together, and I have no idea how he will feel about this pregnancy," cried Chanel.

"Can we just focus on one problem at a time? I mean, damn, every problem can't be ironed out over a slice of cheesecake. As far as I'm concerned, we are in this together," chimed Diamond.

"Diamond is right," countered Essence. "We will be by your side no matter what the situation. We will hold your hand when you break the news to Dallas."

"What do you think he's going to do? What if he puts me out of the house?" asked Chanel.

"Fuck that shit!" Essence proclaimed. "Let his ass try to put you out. If one goes, we all muthafuckin' go. Shit, we pull in money for him and we are his bread and butter. His punk ass is too scared to get in too deep selling them drugs, which means he needs us. Anyway, between the three of us, we have a nice stash put up for a rainy day. Even if it rained nonstop, we straight."

"Three the hard way?" asked Diamond as she extended her hand to the middle of the table.

"Three the hard way," replied Essence and Chanel, while simultaneously placing their hands on top of their sister's.

The three then proclaimed again, "Three the hard way."

Chapter Eight

Insubordinate Ho!

As soon as the sisters made it home, Essence was on the intercom barking instructions to Maria. Diamond and Chanel sat back listening to her make threats and promises to beat the shit out of her, and they knew Essence meant every word.

Maria was lucky Essence didn't feel like walking to the wing of the house that held Dallas's office. "No, I said we need to speak with him today, bitch. Don't make me march my pretty ass to the other side of the house just to smack ya dumb ass."

"No matter what you say to me, Essence, it doesn't change the fact that Dallas has a full schedule today," explained Maria. She felt no need to let Essence know that her sucking Dallas off under his desk again was part of his schedule.

"You know what? I don't even know why I'm fucking with ya simple ass. I don't need you to get us in to see Dallas." *Click.*

"Why did you do that?" asked Diamond.

"Like I said, Maria ain't worth my time. I'll have Houston get us in to speak with Dallas."

Essence picked up her Nextel from the foot of the bed and

chirped Houston. The conversation was quick, direct, and to the point. As promised, ten minutes later, Houston informed the girls that their meeting time with Dallas would be later that evening. After tossing her cell back onto the bed, Essence patted herself on the back and smirked.

Diamond looked at her sister and wondered how she could go from a refined, prissy socialite to a straight-up around the way girl in the blink of an eye.

Essence sat back on the plush soft leather couch that occupied the seating area in her bedroom and kicked off her shoes. She lifted her head long enough to take a swig of her Long Island iced tea and noticed Chanel had disappeared.

"Where is Chanel?" she asked Diamond.

"She wasn't feeling well, so I told her to go lay down," explained Diamond. "She went into her bedroom to relax and call Maurice."

"Good, because I want to know how you feel about this situation. Do you think Chanel is making the best decision?" Essence asked with a serious look on her face.

"I don't know if it's the best decision or not, but I will tell you one thing," Diamond said, pausing. "Raising a child in this house around Dallas and Houston would be the biggest mistake in the world."

Essence shook her head in agreement with Diamond and took another sip of her drink to relax her nerves.

Houston had done what was asked of him and got the girls in to meet with Dallas. Diamond, Essence, and Chanel held hands as they entered the massive room Dallas called an office, and sat down on the couch across from where Dallas sat. For what felt like forever, the sisters sat in silence with a blank stare on their faces.

Dallas wondered what was so pressing that Houston had to be involved. "Come on, ladies, don't just sit there looking at me. Time is fuckin' money, and right now, the three of you ain't making me no money," said Dallas, grinning.

The sisters all took a deep breath and squeezed each other's hand, giving Chanel the strength she needed to make her announcement.

"I'm pregnant," blurted Chanel.

"No, no, the fuck you ain't," countered Dallas.

"What da fuck you mean you pregnant? Don't you know the number one rule around here? Condoms! Use fucking condoms!" said Houston.

"I know the rules, Houston, and I always use protection with my dates," Chanel tried to explain.

"How the fuck did this happen? I know you didn't miss your appointment for a fresh IUD because I paid the bill in full," said Dallas, who was now pacing the room. He kept his eyes on the floor as he tried to figure things out in his head. He knew the girls had a better chance against pregnancy by using the Depo-Provera shot, but Dallas couldn't chance the added weight that came along with it.

The girls were each one year, two years, and three days old when he had left them for dead, not giving a fuck if they had food to eat or a place to lay their heads. When Dallas saw his daughters in that courtroom, he failed to see three children who had just lost their mother. Dallas saw three beautiful beings he could transform into dollar signs. Chanel being the youngest was the easiest to train. She did as she was told and when she was told. Now standing before Dallas announcing she was pregnant was completely out of character for her. Dallas thought Essence would be the one running back and forth to the damn clinic.

The room was quiet enough to hear a mouse taking a piss in the corner on a cotton ball, as everyone waited for Dallas to say or do something. Diamond watched him as he paced back and forth and saw how dark his eyes were for the first time. It was if he had no soul, thought Diamond. She wondered what her mother ever saw in a man like him. Isis Fernando was a beautiful woman, and not just on the outside.

Her spirit filled a room whenever she walked in. She was dependable, kindhearted, free-loving, and giving. Diamond could not find one aspect of the man who helped father her that her mother could have found appealing. Dallas possessed a cold, vengeful, and defiant spirit that kept a dark cloud around him and those in his presence.

"Houston, pour me a fuckin' drink, now!" demanded Dallas.

Houston made his way over to the bar and did as he was told. He wanted to ask some questions of Chanel, but thought better of it. No matter what the situation, he knew that Dallas would grab control over it in due time. "Here, man, drink this." Houston offered Dallas a shot of whiskey.

"Let me get this shit straight," began Dallas. "You had your scheduled birth control shot on time, and you use rubbers with each and every sexual encounter, right?"

"Well, yeah, sort of," confessed Chanel. The volume in which Dallas was speaking to her caused her to be nervous, and she tightened her grip on her sisters' hands. "When I'm working, I am always careful and use protection. Dallas, there is someone in my life that's very important and special to me. And, in all honesty, I missed my ob-gyn appointment."

The room grew silent again as everyone waited for Dallas to respond. Just when it looked as if he would break his silence, Maria knocked on the door and came in without being invited.

"Dallas, sorry to interrupt but it's dinnertime and you shouldn't miss this meeting," said Maria.

"Bitch, if you don't getcha stupid ass the fuck up out of here—" shouted Dallas.

Maria turned on her heels and slammed the door behind her.

"What in da fuck do you mean, you missed your appointment? What the fuck you mean, you got somebody special? What the fuck is special? 'Cause the nigga spends a little

money on you and tells you how beautiful you are? Shit, you get paid to hear that shit almost every other day," fussed Dallas. "I don't need to be dealing with this bullshit right now!"

"No, Dallas, it's not that simple. He means a lot to me, and he has no idea what I do to make money," cried Chanel.

"How the fuck you gon' explain that to this special man?" Dallas asked sarcastically.

"I don't know," cried Chanel and placed her face into her hands. "I just don't know."

"Shit, this is some bullshit for ya ass, I know that damn much. Here I am taking care of the three of y'all for the past ten years and now you tryin' to get me with another kid? Shit, Houston, we have a muthafuckin' problem."

"Fuck, Dallas, you ain't got to be so fuckin' cold to her," screamed Diamond.

Everyone in the room looked at Diamond with shocked expressions on their faces. Her outburst took everyone by surprise, but it got their attention.

"So what, you had to take care of us? Ain't that what you should have been doing when our mother was alive? We ate portions of food, wore used clothes and shared one blanket in the winter, but that ain't mean shit to you. If you had taken care of your responsibilities, our mother would still be alive. She would have had the money and health insurance to treat her cancer instead of suffering and dying on us." It was now Diamond pacing the floor and wringing her hands.

"I don't know what the fuck done came over you, but I know one fucking thing," Dallas stood toe to toe with Diamond. "You better watch how you fuckin' talk to me."

"You know what, Dallas? We aren't as stupid and naive as you think. Do you really think we don't know the reason you took custody of us? Because you could have given us up to Miss Deborah. At least then we would have had a fuckin' chance," fumed Diamond.

"I took y'all in because I had no other choice," responded

Dallas with venom, "and I'm not going to tell you again to watch ya damn mouth."

"You took us in because you saw dollar signs. Not one day in our lives have you been a father to us. You ain't been nothin' but our pimp and now you wanna be mad because your daughter is pregnant? Fuck you, Dallas!" screamed Diamond.

Smack!

Diamond stared at Dallas like he was the devil himself. Houston rushed over to father and daughter to help Diamond get away from Dallas, but his efforts were in vain. Diamond stood as still as a statue and refused to back down.

Dallas took three steps backward, never taking his eyes off Diamond.

Chanel and Essence watched on with wide eyes and dropped jaws. Essence jumped up from her seat and rushed to stand in front of her sister. She would die before letting anyone harm her sister.

"What now, Dallas? As children you used us, abused us emotionally and sold our souls." Essence stared deep into eyes that reflected a blackened heart. "And pimped us out. Now you gonna start beating on us as grown women too?"

"What in the hell has come over the three of you? Chanel thinks she's found love and gotten herself pregnant." Dallas pointed an accusatory finger in her direction. "Diamond is standing in my face being as disrespectful as Essence has. I know this is a stressful time, but the three of you better grab control of yourselves before all hell breaks loose in here."

Houston braced himself for another physical encounter as Essence balled her fingers into tight fists. Chanel remained seated, rocking herself back and forth, her hands over her ears and crying.

Diamond had had enough of being used and abused by her own father, and at that moment, she decided she would

take no more. "Dallas, we are done with you. My sisters and I quit, and you can rot in hell for all we care."

"Diamond, it's about time you grew some balls. You have been a punk since the day I got you. I wondered how long it would take you to find that strength you've always possessed. You are the one most like your mother. She was quiet, strong, and determined, just the way you are," responded Dallas, while walking behind his desk to put flame to a cigar. He had always known that this day would come, but he thought the confrontation would begin with Essence.

Dallas sat down and took a long look at his daughters before speaking. "The three of you have no skills and no idea how the workforce operates. The life I've given you is the same life you will continue to live until the day your looks and age betray you. There will be no more talk of anyone quitting," Dallas calmly said.

Diamond and Essence sat next to Chanel, who could not stop crying and shaking. They barely heard a word Dallas said thereafter, nor did they give a damn. Diamond rubbed her baby sister's back, while Essence wiped her face and assisted her with drinking a small glass of water.

Houston stepped away from the girls to fix himself a drink at the bar. He wished the events of the day could be erased and forgotten. Knowing full well Dallas would never forgive the girls for being insubordinate and defiant sent a chill over Houston.

Dallas stared over at his daughters. He noticed just how much they all resembled their mother in one way or another. Diamond had inherited her mother's hazel eyes and smooth pecan complexion, enhanced by the daily toning exercises and trips to the day spa. Essence got Isis's courage, perfect posture, pretentious character, and heart-shaped lips. Just like her, Essence strutted when she walked and appeared to glide when she danced. Chanel's wavy hair with natural

brown tones and her perfectly grown eyebrows made her light brown eyes light up and sparkle when she laughed. For the first time ever, Dallas looked at his daughters as human beings instead of a windfall of money.

He smirked to himself as he watched his beautiful, appealing, and—in his opinion—dependent daughters. An idea came to mind he felt would end the entire situation, allowing everyone to get their way.

"Diamond, Essence, and Chanel, I owe the three of you an apology," said Dallas.

The sisters offered their father their undivided attention.

"Why is that, Dallas? Because you don't allow your children to address you as Daddy? Because instead of being our father when we needed you, it was more cost-effective to be our pimp? Go ahead, Dallas, tell us why you owe us an apology," Essence said as sarcastically as she could muster while continuing to tend to Chanel.

"Chanel can have her baby. I will not force her to have an abortion or give the child away," promised Dallas, ignoring the truth Essence had just thrown at him.

"Why? Why are you making this so easy for her now?" Diamond demanded through clenched teeth.

"I had a moment to reflect, and it hit me," teased Dallas.

"What hit you?" asked Chanel through her tears.

"You probably already know this from all of the bullshit talk your mother did about me when you girls were younger, but—"

"Dallas, watch yaself about our mother. We'll have you know that she never talked negatively about you, nor did she allow anyone else to. Our opinion of you was formed based on your actions," interrupted Diamond.

"What do you mean, formed based on my actions? In the courtroom was the first time I'd laid eyes on you since Chanel was one day old," said a clueless Dallas.

"Exactly," said Diamond, Essence, and Chanel simultaneously.

Embarrassed by his failure to get the point, Dallas continued to speak. "Like I was saying, I wanted a son. Your mother tried three times to give me that son and she failed," explained Dallas.

Houston stood by the bar, knowing exactly where the conversation was about to go, shaking his head in disapproval of his brother's words as he continued on.

"Shit, Dallas, you the one that failed. Don't you know it's the man's sperm that determined the sex of the baby? Don't you know shit?" Essence asked in disgust.

"I am not putting up with or standing for any more disrespect," warned Dallas. "Again, like I was saying. I always wanted a son to carry on my legacy."

"What does that have to do with my baby?" asked Chanel.

"Since I don't have a son to carry on the Collins name, it will have to fall upon my grandson," said Dallas matter-of-factly.

"I would die before allowing my baby to live the life you forced us to live," cried Chanel.

Dallas appeared to be daydreaming and oblivious to his surroundings. After a few still minutes, he picked up where he'd left off.

"Yeah, a grandson will carry on my legacy." Dallas smiled for a second. He walked past Houston to the bar for another shot of whiskey, this time with ice and a Coke chaser.

The sisters watched his every move as their hate for him grew stronger and stronger with each passing minute.

Dallas walked over to the bay window overlooking the golf course and felt on top of the world. He turned around to dismiss the girls from their exhausting meeting.

Just then, a thought came to Chanel's mind. She turned around and faced her father. "What if it's a girl?"

"Huh?" replied Dallas, his mind off in pimp fantasy land somewhere.

"What if the baby I'm carrying isn't a boy?" repeated Chanel.

"On the off chance the baby you're carrying is a girl, she can start training to work in the family business. I mean, hell, how old were you Chanel, ten?"

Chapter Nine
Daddy's Little Girls

It had been one month since the meeting with Dallas and Houston, and the sisters' bond was tighter than ever. Chanel had gone to her initial ob-gyn appointment with her big sisters holding her hand the entire way. Diamond made certain Chanel ate breakfast every morning, even if it was only a bowl of fresh fruit. Dr. Johnson suggested Chanel keep some saltine crackers and Canada Dry ginger ale next to her bed. She also suggested that Chanel nibble on the crackers and sip on the soda pop before her feet touched the floor in the mornings. Chanel found it did help alleviate the morning sickness and was grateful for the suggestion.

Dallas demanded that Chanel worked until she began showing. After that, she could help do the scheduling and other menial task, that Maria took care of.

"Essence, I don't know who the fuck you think you are, but I suggest you watch just how in hell you talk to me," demanded Dallas.

"What the fuck ever, Dallas. If you haven't noticed by now, I ain't afraid of your ass," spat Essence with her hands on her hips. "Just so you know, you done made that shit up about Chanel continuing to work. She is now officially in retirement."

As Essence talked, rolled her neck, and refused to back down, Dallas remembered the night their mother caught him slipping and put his prized sword to his neck. Dallas would never admit it, but he was afraid of Essence and he knew she would kill him and go out dancing afterward.

When his demands weren't taken seriously, Dallas threatened to cut off their money supply. Again, Essence told Dallas he had pulled that shit out of his ass. She explained to him that, since he wanted to be a punk ass, he would be penalized and Diamond was officially on paid leave and would be taking care of Chanel during her pregnancy. Essence proved not to be fucked with and concluded the failed business talks by announcing that she was the only one who would be making any fucking money and, from that point on, would control the purse strings. As far as Essence and Diamond were concerned, Dallas could go fuck his damn self.

"Shit, I hope that muthafucka gets hit by a Mack truck and lives through that shit," Essence said with venom.

"Well, damn, Essence, why don't you tell us how you really feel?" giggled Chanel, who was enjoying a foot rub from Diamond.

It was Monday afternoon, and instead of the sisters going their separate ways, they stayed together and enjoyed each other's company. While lounging in their sitting room watching the classic movie *Lady Sings the Blues,* and snacking on a fresh fruit salad, the girls tried to brainstorm, to come up with ways to get back at Dallas. Voicing his desire to train his own granddaughter to please any man willing to pay for her time was the straw that broke the camel's back. They weren't sure how they would do it, but they were damn sure going to try.

"How close do you think this movie accurately portrayed Billie Holiday's life?" quizzed Chanel.

"Who knows? I mean, someone close to her would have had to write her story. Unless she documented her life, the

movie was probably pieced together from her loved one's memories. From what we just watched, Billie Holiday went through a lot of shit in a short period of time," answered Diamond. "On another subject, why don't we make some margaritas, Essence? Chanel is the one who's pregnant and can't drink, but a sister like me wants a frosty alcoholic beverage. Are you with me?"

"Hell yeah!" shouted Essence with glee.

"What about my foot rub?" whined Chanel.

"Girl, please, you ain't even in your second trimester and you always complaining about cha back or ya feet. I'm going to make you an appointment for a spa package at my favorite spot," said Diamond.

Essence and Diamond made their way into the gourmet kitchen designed with granite and stainless steel appliances. Until recently, they weren't allowed in the common areas of the house. It was another one of Dallas's rules the girls decided to break without fear of being disciplined.

Diamond placed the blender on top of the counter while Essence retrieved the margarita mix from the refrigerator when an idea hit Diamond in the face.

"Wait!" shouted Diamond, startling Essence.

"What is it?" asked Essence with her hand over her heart.

"Documented, that's it, that's it," said Diamond, smiling.

"What da fuck are you talking about, girl? You scared the living daylights out of me."

"I know how we can get Dallas. It's been in our faces all of this time. We can bring him down, Essence, we can bring him down!" Diamond shouted as she raced up the stairs.

Essence returned from the kitchen with two margaritas, a bottled water, and popcorn on a serving tray, to find an unexpected guest sitting with her sisters.

"What in the hell is this bitch doin' here, and why the fuck is my sister crying?" demanded Essence.

"Calm down, Essence," said Diamond as she jumped up

from her seat next to Chanel. "First, Chanel called Maurice, and they had a small disagreement about them spending time together. Since she made a decision to keep the baby, Chanel feels bad about lying to him."

"And?"

"And she is here because she wants to ask some questions about Dallas," concluded Diamond.

Essence set down the tray she'd been holding and returned to her seat next to Diamond. Though she was skeptical about Maria, she decided to feel her out before telling her to hit the fuckin' road.

"What do you want, Maria?" said Essence, frowning.

"Well, to be honest, I have a confession to make," said Maria with her head down and her voice low. "That day you all had a meeting with Dallas and he cussed me out for interrupting . . ." trailed Maria.

"Come on, bitch, spit it out," demanded Essence.

"Essence, calm down and give the girl a chance. Damn," said Chanel.

"After he embarrassed me, I stood outside of the door and I overheard most of the conversation."

The sisters looked at Maria with blank expressions on their faces. None of them were worried about Maria running her mouth about the business, because they knew she wasn't brave enough to cross Dallas.

"First of all, I'd just like to say I owe you all an apology, especially you, Essence."

"Why? An apology for what?" inquired Diamond.

"Until that day, I thought one of you had a relationship with Dallas and I viewed all of you as competition."

Diamond, Essence, and Chanel continued to look at Maria with blank expressions. The thought of being *involved* with Dallas would be funny, if the entire situation wasn't so sad.

"Anyway, I had no idea that Dallas is your father. I have never heard him addressed as anything but Dallas."

"That's because he wants it that way. What father do you know would be pimping out his daughters?" asked Essence with a bad taste in her mouth.

"That brings me to the other reason I'm here." Maria paused before continuing. "I really thought this was a reputable business. I mean, what other type of business would you expect to find at a local job fair? I thought the prices were high, but what do I know? I should have known something was wrong when Essence kept blaming me for quoting customers that wrong price. I was only following orders from Dallas."

"We know how it is to be working for an asshole; we've been doing it for ten years. Knowing Dallas, he was probably setting you up to dock your pay for being inadequate," said Chanel.

"I am so sorry for the way I've acted toward each of you, and now that I know what is really going on, everything makes sense," said Maria.

"What does that mean?" asked Essence.

"Well, I'm ashamed to say it, but Dallas and I have been involved."

"That's no surprise to us; he was probably trying to groom you for a promotion into his stable. The other girls you schedule dates for live about ten or fifteen minutes from here. They don't make as much money as we do and they don't have the dishonor of sharing a bloodline, so they get to live under a separate roof. Lucky bitches," laughed Essence.

"I feel humiliated and stupid to fall for his lies. I thought he cared about me, and all this time he was just playing with my heart," cried Maria.

"Fuck Dallas! He ain't worth shedding one tear," spat Essence.

The four women sat quiet for a few minutes, each with the same thought running through their heads. Maria continued to cry silently as Chanel sat running her hands over her stom-

ach. Essence grabbed her now watery drink and gulped it down. Diamond sat looking back and forth between her sisters, with thoughts of a better way of life.

"We have got to do something," said Chanel.

"I agree, but what can we do? Dallas won't let us just walk away from him without harsh penalties," added Diamond. "What we are gonna have to do is lay this muthafucka down."

"We will lay both Dallas and Houston down. I know exactly how to do it but, Maria, we are going to need your help," said Essence.

"Just tell me what you need me to do," said Maria.

For the next two hours, they threw ideas at each other, drank more frosty alcoholic beverages, and shed a few tears.

As the girls sat with Maria trying to map out a plan to make Dallas and Houston pay for all the years of emotional, psychological, physical, and sexual abuse, time floated away like ice cream on a humid day. They went back and forth with each other, a few times getting into heated arguments, about the best way to retaliate against their abusers.

After exhausting every idea, thought, and ounce of energy, Diamond, Essence, Chanel, and Maria sat quietly as the local evening news played on the muted television.

"Hey, look, y'all, look!" screeched Diamond excitedly.

"Oh my God!" screamed Essence. "Turn up the volume. Is that her, Diamond? Is that really her?"

The sisters scooted up to the edge of their seats as they watched the reporter recount an investigative report she had been researching for months. Unable to believe their eyes, Diamond and Chanel cried tears of joy at the sight of their godmother reporting the nightly news.

"Oh, do y'all know her? She is the investigative reporter for this news channel. She goes into a lot of issues important to the African American community," explained Maria.

Diamond, Essence, and Chanel all turned their heads and gave Maria a look that warned her to watch her mouth.

"Well, that's what she says at the end of her reports. Her name is Deborah Holmes. Isn't she a beautiful woman?" Maria tried to lighten the mood in the room before the sisters turned on her.

The group listened intently to the story and sat quietly after it wrapped up.

"Our answer has just been sent down to us from above," said Diamond.

The next morning, the girls traveled back to their old neighborhood in hopes that they could locate Deborah. They had plans to go to the television station if none of the neighbors knew how to get in contact with her. As luck would have it, Deborah was right where they left her.

Chapter Ten

Blast From Da Past!

After ten long years, Deborah's prayers had been answered. When she answered her front door to find the daughters of her deceased best friend standing before her, she thought her eyes were playing tricks on her.

"Oh my Heavenly Father," cried Deborah.

Diamond, Essence, and Chanel smiled as Deborah thanked God and hugged them as tight as she could.

"Girls, I have been trying to communicate with you all for the past ten years only to be turned away each time," cried Deborah. "I have done my best to keep in touch with the three of you, but Dallas blocked me at every turn. My phone calls went unanswered, my letters were returned to me, and the door was slammed in my face so many times that I lost count. But I never—I mean never—gave up trying to see y'all."

"We are so happy to finally see you," cried Diamond, a smile on her face.

"Oh, how I've prayed for this day to come," confessed Deborah with a steady stream of tears pouring down her face.

It wasn't hard for Diamond to track Deborah down. She remained in the same duplex family home in hopes that one day her three goddaughters would reach out to her. She kept the same address, but everything in her life was much im-

proved since back when the courts refused to grant her custody of the girls. Deborah had returned to school and earned a degree in communications from Ohio Dominican University. She began working for the local CBS station as a reporter. Her own children were grown and living on their own.

One of the first things Dallas did when he took custody of the girls was sever all ties with anyone who had the girls' best interest at heart. After the first field visit from children services, Dallas turned on the charm, fucked Susan Bardwell from behind, proved the myth about black men to be true, and paid her a hefty fee to never return. There was no way Dallas could allow them to keep in touch with Deborah without her finding out how they were being raised. The last thing he needed was the courts finding out he was pimping his daughters out for money.

Deborah invited the girls inside the apartment, where they used to play while their mother would visit. Silence surrounded them like an old blanket as old memories flooded back. Diamond smiled and closed her eyes, trying to hear her mother's voice calling out for her, "Diamond in the rough."

Essence peeked inside the small kitchen where their mother and Miss Deborah once played cards and laughed about old times.

Chanel thought she heard the faint cries of a woman, not realizing she was remembering her mother sobbing at night but never knew why. Chanel would crawl into bed with her mother and sleep in her eyes. The comfort of the unconditional love from her girls always dried up Isis's tears.

The initial reconciliation was awkward for them all, but the warm reception the girls received from Deborah let them know they had made the right decision by reaching out to her for help.

Having made her guests comfortable with cold drinks and light snacks, Deborah laughed with the girls with stories of their beloved mother. The afternoon seemed to fly by, and

the missed years between them seemed to have never happened.

After hours of reminiscing, Deborah realized she had done all of the talking. She looked into her goddaughters' eyes and saw emptiness, sorrow, and pain. Deborah knew their eyes were trying to tell her something, and whatever it was, she was certain Dallas was the cause of it all.

"So, girls, tell me what I've done to deserve this much welcomed visit today? What can I do to help you?" asked Deborah with an uneasy smile, afraid of what the answer would be.

Diamond and Essence smiled at the question, while Chanel diverted her eyes to a picture on the wall of their mother. She remained focused on the portrait while her sisters described the lifestyle they had been forced to live the last ten years.

Deborah listened intently as the girls spoke. A multitude of feelings washed over Deborah as Essence recalled the sexual molestation they suffered at the hands of their own uncle.

Tears were shed when Diamond explained how Dallas kept them under his thumb and isolated from any normalcy outside of his four walls.

Joy filled the room when Chanel explained her relationship with Maurice and the baby she now carried.

Once Deborah was brought up to date on everything, Essence jumped right to the reason for their visit.

"Miss Deborah, we think that your position as news reporter can help us escape the hell we've been living the past ten years," began Essence. "We have decided to get away from Dallas, but not until he pays for the things he's done to us over the years, and that is why we're here. We need your help escaping from him."

"What do you need me to do?" asked Deborah.

Chapter Eleven

Payback Is A Mutha

Dallas was beside himself and livid with his ungrateful daughters. He had lost control of them so fast that he had not seen it coming. After Chanel announced her pregnancy, Dallas relented and gave her permission to have the child, but he'd be damned if he was going to be forced to raise another ungrateful bitch. *Shit, fuck this mess. If Isis had taken care of herself, she would be the one dealing with an unwanted pregnancy. She was a pro at that,* thought Dallas.

As he paced the room talking to himself, he could not shake the feeling that he was being watched. For the last few weeks, Dallas had a wired feeling that someone was out to get him. He and Houston worried that their drug connection might be an undercover cop, so they put a halt to dealing with him.

Dallas's pockets felt empty, and he hated the feeling of being broke. He was pushed into a corner and was now forced to throw Maria out on the stroll. She wasn't as pretty and alluring as Diamond, Essence, and Chanel, but she was the next best thing.

While his drug dealings kept on rolling with great profits, Dallas never realized how much money his escort service

was bringing in until it ceased to be profitable. The girls were right about who actually controlled the purse strings. Essence had him by the balls and had no plans on releasing her grip.

"Yeah, come on in," Dallas instructed his visitor.

"You wanted to see me?" said Maria. She had found the note on her desk Dallas had left when she returned from lunch and thought he was finally ready to resume their afternoon escapades.

"Come on in and let me holler at you for a minute," instructed Dallas.

Maria made herself comfortable on the sofa and waited for Dallas to join her. When he didn't make his way over to her, Maria thought she'd done something wrong.

"Have I done something to offend you, Dallas?"

"No. Why would you ask me that?"

"You have been avoiding me lately, and there hasn't been much work for me either. Are you letting me go?"

"Absolutely not," said Dallas. He knew he would have to slide into the reason for her visit with caution, or he would run the risk of losing her too. "I want to promote you. I think you have earned a new position."

Maria was beside herself. Just as Essence had predicted, Dallas was reeling her in for the kill. Maria's laughter came out as a squeal, and her cheeks turned as red as roses. She hugged Dallas and accepted the long kiss he met her with.

"Oh, I'm so happy, I can't believe it. Tell me what I will be doing," gushed Maria, insincerely.

"Well, you will never have to schedule another appointment or run another errand for anyone other than yourself." Dallas smiled at Maria and began rubbing her back as he spoke. "The new position will expose you to the finer things in life and the amount of money you earn is up to you."

"I don't understand what you mean. Is it some type of commission-based position?"

"You could say that. Diamond, Essence, and Chanel have forced my hand, and I had to let them go. So you would be taking over as much of their job descriptions as you can—that is, if you can handle it." Dallas spoke with caution. He knew that coming on too strong would run the innocent young girl off. "In addition to a high salary and company credit card, you have the option of moving into one of the lavish bedrooms on the other end of the house and driving one of the sports cars outside."

"Wow, this all sounds too good to be true. You have my attention, but you still haven't told me what this new position is," said Maria, smiling.

"All you would have to do is date businessmen who need a companion for an evening. As you know from doing the interviews of potential clients, the evenings spent with them pay as little as three thousand dollars and as much as ten thousand dollars for just a few hours of your time," explained Dallas.

"What? Are you asking me to sleep with strange men? Is that what the other girls were doing for you?" Maria asked in a panic. She sounded offended and a little frightened by what she was hearing.

"Calm down, Maria, calm down. I would never ask you to do anything you didn't want to do. All I'm asking is for you to accompany these high-ranking businessmen to various events, pay them a little attention, and make them look good."

"Is that all? You know I have never been with another man in that way. Dallas, you were my first, and I don't think I could have sex with a strange man, especially not for money."

"All I'm asking of you is your time. You would be paid handsomely for it, but how you end those dates is up to you. If you are just trying to earn some pocket change, say good night at the door and walk away. On the other hand, if you

want to make some real money, use your new sexual skills before calling it a night." Dallas spoke seductively and kissed Maria before she could ask another question.

Maria placed her hands on Dallas's chest as he tried to push her down onto the couch. She was able to stop him before he ran his hand up her skirt.

"So, let me understand what you want me to do. I can go out on dates, rub elbows with the rich and famous, and collect a nice fee at the end of the night," reviewed Maria.

"Yes, baby, exactly. See, that's what I like about you; you know how to listen to a man," cooed Dallas.

"If I chose to, I can make a higher fee just by sleeping with my dates?" asked Maria for clarity.

Dallas continued to kiss on Maria's neck and shoulders in such a seductive way that she had a hard time fighting his advances.

"Yes, you got it right, baby. Just because you sleep with your dates don't mean you're making love to them. It just means you have an ambitious soul," whispered Dallas.

The sudden boom startled Dallas and sent him diving for cover.

"Freeze!" commanded a deep voice.

"Dallas Keith Collins, you are under arrest! Don't move!"

In one single wave, the room was filled with federal agents and local police.

"Ma'am, are you all right?" one of the feds asked.

Maria jumped to her feet and straightened out her clothes before responding. "Yes, I'm fine, but it took y'all long enough. I mean, damn," complained Maria. "Please tell me you have all we need to lock this piece of shit up for a very long time."

"Thanks to you, yes, we do," answered the commander.

"What the fuck is all of this?" demanded Dallas.

"This, dear *Daddy*, is muthafuckin' payback," teased Essence.

Dallas looked up to see Diamond, Essence, Chanel, and Deborah standing by the door. As he continued to search the room, he spotted Houston handcuffed in a corner. Dallas wondered where Houston had been for the last couple of hours and now he knew.

"Fuck all of y'all! Ain't nothin' you can do to me. Can't none of y'all prove shit. Fuck each and every one of y'all," ranted Dallas as he was being led away in handcuffs. Outside of the lavish golf course estate were numerous onlookers, news reporters, cameras, vans, and nosy neighbors. This only added fuel to the fire exploding inside of Dallas as he continued his tirade.

Two months later, during the preliminary hearing, Diamond, Essence, and Chanel took the witness stand to give testimony about the sexual molestation, prostitution, and drug deals of their father and uncle. They all gave testimony about being forced to perform sexual acts on their uncle and described the emotional and physical abuse they suffered at the hands of their father.

The courtroom was hushed while the girls recounted life under their father's roof. When Dallas and Houston's lawyer tried to question the validity of the girls' testimony by citing the state's lack of proof, the prosecution brought out the various journals Diamond had kept over the years. She had documented every single day, crime, and neglectful act she and her sisters suffered in her journals that she kept in a safe. The names of clients, the dates, times, and money she collected was also listed for the court's viewing. The pages painted a broad, sad picture of the most brutal child abuse to ever be documented in the State of Ohio.

Diamond seemed to gain strength as she told her story. Her soul seemed to be mending as she bravely sat in the witness seat.

After Chanel recounted her years of abuse at the hands of

her father and uncle, the state showed their final ace card: Maria Petrilo.

The feds had built an indestructible case against Dallas and Houston, thanks to a very disgruntled customer, Sean Tillery. After Dallas and Houston put Sean in a wheelchair for the rest of his life, he reported the crime to the local police. After looking into the complaint, the case was handed over to the feds, who had more resources to take the operation down to its knees.

Before the bust, Maria was able to obtain financial records, dates of drug deals that were disguised as lunch and dinner meetings, and other tax evasion infractions.

The federal case against Dallas and Houston was so strong that Houston decided it would be in his best interest to turn state's evidence in exchange for a guilty plea and a sentence of twenty years. Dallas was left standing alone as a broken man.

The story was so sensational, it was reported around the world. The sisters received an outpouring of support from children advocates, child abuse protestors, and various ministries from across the country. Initially, because the crimes against them began when they were minors, the sisters' faces were hidden for news cameras and in newspaper articles. After the community rallied around them, the sisters decided to allow their faces to be shown. They hoped their story would give hope to abused children everywhere.

On the day of sentencing, Diamond, Essence, and Chanel sat behind the prosecution table wearing buttons with a picture of their mother and matching Ann Taylor pantsuits.

"Mr. Collins, would you please rise?" asked the court's bailiff.

"In my thirty years on the bench, I have never witnessed this degree of abuse to a child by their own parent. The system and you as their father truly and undeniably let these three young women down," explained the judge. "Mr. Dallas

Keith Collins, having been found guilty of three counts of child abuse, multiple counts of rape on a minor, multiple counts of physical child abuse, tax evasion, kidnapping, attempted rape . . ."

It took the judge thirty minutes to read off each charge before sentencing Dallas to life plus four hundred years in a federal prison.

After the sentencing, Diamond, Essence, and Chanel walked out of the courtroom hand in hand. When asked by a reporter how they found the courage to finally escape from their father's hell on earth, the sisters answered in unison, "Three the hard way."

Chapter Twelve

And Life Goes On

"Do you, Maurice Derick Paine, take Chanel Micah Fernando-Collins to be your wife?" asked the minister. "Yes, I do," replied Maurice.

"Do you, Chanel Micah Fernando-Collins, take Maurice Derick Paine to be your husband in—"

"Ahhhh! Yes, I do!" screamed Chanel between contractions.

"I now pronounce you husband and wife," said the minister, "but if I were you, Mr. Paine, I would not try kissing the bride right now."

Maurice, Diamond, Essence, Deborah, and Shalonda laughed at the minister, but Chanel found nothing funny as she pushed and pushed and pushed.

Maurice had seen the breaking news reports on all of the local and national news channels and felt terrible for the three women who were forced to sell their bodies by the man who was supposed to protect them from the world. Since initially their faces were being withheld from the cameras, He had no idea that the woman he loved and believed he'd lost was one of the victims in the story. It wasn't until one reporter stood outside of the New Albany home and the camera caught a picture of Chanel's car in the driveway that Maurice

began putting the pieces together. Chanel had cut off all communication with him, for fear that he would reject her and their baby once he found out how she made her money.

When Maurice met Chanel outside of the courthouse the day of sentencing, they embraced each other and promised to never let go. Maurice asked Chanel to marry him after getting permission from Diamond and Essence. Chanel was determined to get married before the baby arrived, and that's exactly what they did. Her water broke in the middle of the ceremony, and the minister followed them to the hospital to complete the vows. A seven-pound, eleven-ounce baby girl made her entrance into the world on Saturday, April 27, 2008 at six o'clock in the evening. The happy couple named her Isis Diamond Essence Fernando-Paine.

The money Diamond, Essence, and Chanel had stashed away for a rainy day added up to more than enough money to take care of them for a long, long time. Diamond and Essence purchased a nice-sized condo in walking distance from the house Maurice was having built for Chanel and their baby. They were scheduled to finalize a book and movie deal as soon as Chanel was out of the hospital.

Deborah was ecstatic to have the girls back in her life, and she doted on baby Isis just like any proud grandmother would. Diamond and Essence took the legal steps needed to drop the Collins from their names. They wanted to rid themselves of everything associated with Dallas. He had stolen ten years of their lives, but they would be damned if they allowed his dark cloud to hover over them once they found the courage to fight back. Diamond, Essence, and Chanel; three the hard way, forever.

Pound-cake

By Eric Gray

Coney Island, Brooklyn . . .

June 21—the first day of summer for so many in the grungy, brutal projects called Gravesend. It was the first ninety-degree day of the month, and residents in the community tried to fight the sweltering heat by getting wet in the fire hydrants, maybe downing a cold glass of ice-cold water or cold lemonade, or just trying to keep still and relax, trying not to exert themselves too much in the heat.

Dusk was hours away, and Brooklyn felt like the sun was personally giving the borough a bear hug, as the hot afternoon made T-shirts and tank tops stick to peoples' backs with sweat, and utility bills soared from the massive use of air-conditioners blasting through the many project apartments.

No one paid much attention to the silver 750i BMW that came to a stop at a red light on Neptune Avenue. Mary J. Blige's "We Ride" blared from the car, as Sweety and Carissa nodded to the track. Dressed in their finest outfits—short Fendi skirt, tight-fitted Seven jeans, and stilettos, with their hair done up in the city, both women looked like video vixens.

"He calls me every night, begging for some pussy,"

Carissa said to Sweety. She had her manicured hand gripped around the steering wheel, and quickly glanced at her image in the rearview mirror and loved what she saw.

"You still fuckin' him, Carissa. I thought you only wanted to fuck him, only to get back at that bitch Veronica," Sweety said.

"Yeah, and the dick is good . . . but fuck that bitch. Her man got a taste of it, and now he lovin' it. Nigga be buying me shit, eating my pussy out. And now he wanna take me to Barbados for the summer," she boasted.

"Girl, you better break a piece off for me after you done with him," Sweety joked.

"I can't help it, Sweety, if I'm a fly bitch, and these niggas wanna trick on me instead of their girlfriends," she said with poise.

Carissa and Sweety were known for their wild, gold-digging ways. It was no secret that both ladies were about that money, and would fuck a bitch's man just to get theirs in life. Carissa paid for nothing. The 750i she pushed; she had a nigga from Manhattan paying her car note. The ice she sported—paid for by an old banker in New Jersey who she would bless with hand jobs on occasions. And the well-furnished apartment with the sixty-inch screen she had in the projects, she fucked a young hustler nigga with some paper, and had the nigga open like the freeway at four in the morning, that the following week he dropped an easy five grand at Best Buy and Furniture World for her.

For years, the two got over with using men, and upsetting the girlfriends and wives who would receive outlandish bills in the mail, from the limitless shopping sprees their counterpart would spend on Carissa and Sweety, and someday, karma would finally catch up to them.

"Damn, this light be taking fuckin' forever," Carissa cursed. She sighed and was ready to just run the red light and take her chances.

It would be a risk that she would soon wish she did take, running the red light. As both ladies sat and discussed the niggas that they had tricking on them, they didn't notice the group of young girls suddenly approaching their car.

"Get out da fuckin' car, bitch!" Pound-cake screamed, snatching the unlocked door open and viciously grabbing Carissa by her DKNY top and striking her with several blows.

Carissa screamed as she was being pulled out of the car. She tried to grip onto the steering wheel tightly, trying to resist being dragged out the car. But Pound-cake was relentless and beat on Carissa like she was some dog.

Sweety tried to come to her aid, but the passenger door abruptly swung open and two more malicious females began attacking Sweety, aggressively yanking her out of the car by her long weave and making her kiss the pavement.

With the car still in drive, and the driver no longer behind the wheel for control, the BMW began rolling into the intersection of Neptune and Bayview on its own, and an oncoming car slammed into the Beamer, crashing that shit.

But the accident was the least of Carissa's problems. Two girls tore into her like lions, as they beat her in the head with fists and combs. Pound-cake pulled at Carissa's tight DKNY shirt until it almost ripped in half. Sweety tried to run, but was knocked down by the other two girls of the group, and they beat her until she became unconscious.

"Yeah, bitch! You wanna be fuckin' my cousin's man like that, huh. That's right, bitch, get yours, bitch!" Sabrina yelled, with Carissa's weave wrapped around her fist strongly. She yanked and flung Carissa around like some rag doll, and had that bitch taking in punches from every which way from her and Pound-cake.

A crowd began to gather around the fight that was taking place in the middle of the street. The sweltering heat no long bothered the people as they were being entertained like it was fight night in Las Vegas.

"Fuck dat bitch up!" one of the homegirls shouted, hyping the situation.

Pound-cake was ruthless against Carissa. She hated bitches like Carissa and knew about that bitch's reputation around the way. She shredded Carissa's top like it was paper-thin, and left her exposed to the public as her nipples saw the light of day.

Pound-cake had a fierce knuckle game, and her reputation carried through the streets like the wind. She was ready for a fight any day, her hair styled in a tightly knit ponytail, and sporting no loose jewelry for a bitch to snatch out during a fight. She rocked a pair of baggy sweatpants and a large T-shirt, with some white Uptowns. She had angelic features on the outside, but within, she was like a female Mike Tyson, ruthless and known for beating bitches down with her crew. It wasn't a shock for the residents of Gravesend housing to see Pound-cake, Sabrina, Lady Rah, and Joy beat down bitches and, on occasions, niggas too in the hood—they got down like that.

Carissa looked a fuckin' mess, shirtless and with her business exposed, half her weave was gripped in Pound-cake's fist, with her car smashed up across the street.

"Yo, yo, cops are coming. Y'all better book," a young teenage boy warned the four.

"C'mon, Pound-cake, we out," Sabrina yelled, taking off running into the projects.

Five-oh quickly erupted onto the chaotic scene, and a female officer jumped out of the passenger side of the squad car and started to run after the girls. She had her sights on the young Pound-cake and swiftly gave chase.

But Pound-cake was no easy chase; she was slim, petite, thick in the right place, and fast like a racehorse. She ran track her first two years of high school, and had plenty of gold medals and trophies to show for it.

With Sabrina and the rest far ahead of her, Pound-cake was at risk of being caught. She sprinted through the pro-

jects like she was running on air. The female cop was not too far behind. Pound-cake dipped and turned through the court-yards and playgrounds like a ball in a pinball machine. She scaled a short fence and sprinted toward West Thirty-third Street and ran into the tall high-rises.

The lady officer was weighted down with too much gear, and was two times Pound-cake's age and knew she didn't have a chance in hell catching up to her. She huffed and uttered out, "Damn, that little bitch is fast."

When the cop finally crossed Thirty-third street and was about to continue pursuit into the high-rises, another squad car hastily drove up to her, and two black males got out, ready to jump into the mix of the action.

"They ran into the high-rises," the female cop shouted out in one breath.

One cop ran into the buildings with the lady cop, while the second officer jumped back into the car, backed up with tremendous speed, spun the car around, and sped off around the corner for a better chance at apprehension. But it was too late—by then, Pound-cake and her crew were on the ninth floor of one of the high-rises 'bout ready to take safety in a friend's apartment.

Once all four ladies were safe from arrest, they all laughed and took comfort on one of the tattered sofas that decorated the place.

"Damn, what y'all bitches do?" Minnie asked, knowing that her friends were always fighting, stealing, or fucking.

"Yo, we just beat that bitch Carissa down and crashed her car," Sabrina said to Minnie with a sadistic smile on her face.

"Y'all serious?"

"Hells yeah, that bitch think she's ill. I can't stand that gold-diggin' bitch. She fucked my cousin's man and gonna talk shit about it like it's all good. That's why that bitch ain't got a car now," Sabrina said smugly.

"Y'all crazy," Minnie spoke.

"Minnie, you ain't got shit to drink in here? A bitch is thirsty and shit," Lady Rah said.

"I got some sodas."

"You ain't got no E and J, Hennessy, Coronas or sumthin'?" Joy asked.

"Y'all better go to the store for dat," Minnie said.

Minnie was the youngest, sixteen, and both her parents were constant users of the pipe. She was practically raising herself. She was the only child, barely in school, and was two months pregnant with her first child. She loved being around Sabrina and Pound-cake; they were like the older sisters she never had. She would travel to the end of the world for them.

Minnie was five feet two, cute as a button with her honey brown skin and her hair in two long pigtails, but she could be so naive at times. Sabrina tried to warn her about Winter. She hated how Winter took advantage of Minnie because she was so young and in a vulnerable situation with life and her parents.

Winter was twenty-six, and didn't care about Minnie's age when he fucked her raw countless of times, gave her an STD twice, and now impregnated her. He hardly took care of her.

He was very disrespectful to Minnie, and Sabrina and Pound-cake hated him with a passion. When she was only fifteen, Winter had Minnie give him blow jobs on the park benches late nights while his boys watched and hoped for next. And, sometimes, if he was bored with her, he would let his boys fuck her—for a small price, of course.

But the worst was, he was very abusive to Minnie, and would sometimes beat on her until she could no longer stand. Sabrina and Pound-cake got into so many altercations with Winter that it was common to see the trio ready to go for blows in the ghetto. To the two ladies, Minnie was like their younger sister that they had to protect, but with Winter around, and having Minnie believe that she was in love with him, and her being brainwashed, believing that her boo Win-

ter could do no wrong, the girls hated how Winter had control over their young friend.

"Minnie, go to the store for us and get some drinks," Lady Rah suggested.

"Nah, Minnie, you stay here. Lady Rah, is you crazy sending Minnie to the store in this heat when you know she's pregnant?" Sabrina barked.

"Well, you know I can't go. Cops probably all over the place looking for us," Lady Rah said.

"And that's why we're gonna chill out here for a few hours until the drama calms down," Sabrina said. She was like the surrogate leader of the pack—witty, beautiful, smart, and down for her crew.

Men and women were easily intimidated by her beauty, while at the same time they feared her reputation of cutting bitches with razors, with having Pound-cake by her side.

Sabrina sat on the sofa and pulled out a White Owl and began dissecting it with a small razor she carried on her. She cut off the tip of the cigar and emptied the guts into the wastebasket, while her friends waited and watched. She then removed the cancer paper from between two layers and wet the edges with her tongue so the layers didn't come apart. When it came to rolling up an *L*, Sabrina was the best and fastest at it. She was a true weedhead, and didn't give a fuck who knew.

"Joy, give me that," Sabrina said, ready to plug up the blunt with that good shit.

Joy passed Sabrina a phat dime bag of haze, and Sabrina emptied the bag of weed on a magazine nearby and began inspecting the product for any unwanted seeds. She sifted through the haze like she was a pharmacist, and when everything was good to her eyes, she began to fill up the *L* with the product. And as easy as she took everything apart, within a short moment, it was back together again, ready for their enjoyment.

"Yo, I need a light," Sabrina said, the *L* dangling from her lips.

"Here." Joy tossed her a lighter, and Sabrina quickly put flames to the paper and took two lengthy pulls, inhaling every bit of that haze and then passed it over to Pound-cake, who sat next to her on the arm of the sofa.

Pound-cake took two long pulls and passed the burning haze over to Joy, and then it went to Lady Rah. Lady Rah took her two pulls, and was about to pass it over to Minnie.

Minnie reached for the blunt, 'bout ready to get her smoke on, when she heard Sabrina shout out, "Nah, you pregnant."

"So," Minnie said.

"So . . . you ain't about to make my godchild slow or retarded because you wanna get high," Sabrina said.

"Yo, weed is from the earth, and so are we, Sabrina. Why you trippin'? Let her smoke," Lady Rah said forcefully, trying to help Minnie out.

"Lady Rah, mind your business. She's only sixteen and pregnant. She don't need to be smoking," Sabrina snapped.

"Yo, you be actin' like you her moms and shit," Lady Rah returned, sucking her teeth and becoming frustrated with Sabrina acting like she was the queen bitch.

Minnie looked at Sabrina, begging to take a pull. But Sabrina didn't back down. As long as she was around, she was going to make sure that Minnie took care of her unborn child. Minnie caught an attitude and stormed off downstairs into her bedroom.

"Yo, that's fucked-up, Sabrina. You know she's stressed, and we chillin' up in her people's spot," Joy said.

"And she don't need to get high . . . her baby don't need to be comin' out fucked-up like y'all two," Sabrina said with authority.

Joy and Lady Rah both gave Sabrina the bird with their middle fingers and smirked at her.

The *L* was passed back to Sabrina and continued to rotate

throughout the room. The girls continued to pass the hours by listening to the radio, smoking, talking about dick, and raiding the fridge in the kitchen for whatever what was left, which was only some cold Domino's pizza, expired milk, left-over pasta that Minnie cooked, and a two-liter bottle of Pepsi. The pizza and the pasta was the first to go, and then they downed the Pepsi.

When dusk finally settled, the ladies assumed that it was safe to go back out. It was ten at night, and Lady Rah and Joy had boyfriends that they were dying to see, their pussy tingled for some dick, and after the beat-down they done gave Sweety, Lady Rah wanted to cozy up against some dick and call it a night.

Lady Rah stood up, with her long cornrows reaching down to her back and her white coochie-cutting shorts revealing too much skin. She was sexy, in a thug kind of way.

"Yo, anyone of y'all bitches got a fuckin' cigarette?" Lady Rah asked, dying for a smoke.

"Bitch, you better take that shit to da store," Joy answered.

"Y'all bitches ain't never got shit, always wanna be bumming a loosy off of me," Lady-Rah said jokingly.

"Bitch, you da one askin' for a fuckin' cigarette," Sabrina replied back with a smirk.

" 'Cuz y'all done smoked all of mines. Y'all like some bird bitches, fo' real," Lady Rah said.

Joy laughed and replied with, "Yeah, you need some dick, bitch. She gettin' all grumpy and shit."

"Bitch, you about to go and fuck your nigga tonight too, so I don't know what da fuck you talkin' about," Lady Rah returned.

"Yo, both of y'all need to shut da fuck up, fo' real. Don't anybody give a fuck about y'all weak-ass niggas," Sabrina chided.

Lady Rah sucked her teeth and came back with, "I don't

know what da fuck you talkin' about, Sabrina, but my nigga definitely ain't weak. What you need to do is stop all that carpet munching you be doin' and get a broomstick pushed up in you."

Joy and Pound-cake laughed. It was no secret that Sabrina was a dyke. She played the part, but definitely didn't look the part. She was a cutie. Most of the time she had her hair wrapped up under a multicolored scarf, and her body was sick with more curves than the letters *S* and *B* put together. Dudes and bitches always tried to holla, but Sabrina had herself a little shortie out in Queens that she loved to go see.

And there were rumors that her and Pound-cake got down like that, because they was so tight and were always around each other. But Pound-cake was no carpet muncher; it may have played in her head a few times, but she never acted out on it. Unlike her friends, Pound-cake wasn't fuckin' niggas like that. Niggas were always willing to give it, but she wasn't so willing to take.

After the jokes, sarcasm, smoking, and having the munchies, Lady Rah and Joy decided to leave to meet up with their fellows. And Sabrina was right behind them.

"Pound-cake, you coming?" Sabrina asked.

"Nah, I'm gonna chill here with Minnie for a minute," Pound-cake told them.

"Ayyite, you be safe, bitch," Sabrina said, and walked out into the hallway.

Minnie's crib was one of the few places Pound-cake could find peace at. She loved going to the window, drawing back the roller blinds and peering outside, staring over the neighborhood and gazing at the water, the beach, and the Verrazano Bridge from a distance. She would sit on the armrest of the couch and lose herself by gazing into the night.

"They all left?" Minnie asked, coming up the short flight of steps from her bedroom.

Pound-cake nodded.

"What you lookin' at?" Minnie asked.

"What do I always look at when I come over here?" Pound-cake said.

Minnie smiled. "You love lookin' at that bridge."

"Where do you think they all go?" Pound-cake asked in a rhetorical manner. "I mean, so many cars coming and going from the city. It must be nice just to go somewhere far."

With her eyes fixated on the illuminated bridge and staring at hundreds of headlights and taillights crossing the bridge and traveling back and forth on the Belt Parkway, she thought about so many places that were across the bridge. Pound-cake had never been outside of Brooklyn. Pound-cake was Coney Island, Brooklyn.

"You stayin' da night, Pound-cake?" Minnie asked.

"You scared to be by yourself?" Pound-cake asked without turning to look at her. Her eyes were still glued out that window.

Minnie nodded. She looked so innocent, so pure in her SpongeBob SquarePants pajama pants and small white top, with her stomach about to show soon. She knew both her parents wouldn't be home anytime soon—they were always out, always getting high, and always scheming to get by on the system, from shoplifting to check fraud, to public assistance, they knew how to get over on the system. And if push came to shove, Minnie's father would revert back to old-fashioned stickups around the way. He did ten years upstate for armed robbery, and would risk doing another bid just to satisfy his crack addiction.

"I hate sleeping in this place when I'm alone. I be hearing noises and shit," Minnie stated.

Pound-cake smiled. She went over to Minnie, who was seated on the couch, clutching a pillow between her legs, as she sat Indian-style.

"I thought you were a big girl," Pound-cake joked.

"I am a big girl," she cracked back, smiling.

"You scared of the dark?" Pound-cake said, turning off the lights to the apartment.

"Pound-cake, stop," Minnie hollered.

"Boo!" Pound-cake playfully shouted.

"I'm gonna hurt you," Minnie said, laughing.

Pound-cake turned on the lights and saw Minnie coming at her swinging the pillow. She mischievously hit Pound-cake against the head with the pillow, and Pound-cake laughed. Minnie ran, and Pound-cake threw the pillow back at Minnie, hitting her in the back. Both ladies laughed. It felt good to act like kids for once, without any drama.

As the night went on, Minnie sat on the floor, in between Pound-cake's legs, with her back against the bottom of the couch, as Pound-cake braided her hair.

"Pound-cake, how come you don't have a boyfriend?" Minnie asked.

" 'Cuz I don't need one."

"But everybody else is fuckin' somebody. I mean, even Sabrina is gettin' hers. Even though she be doin' the licky split . . . she still be gettin' hers," Minnie said.

"Licky split?" Pound-cake questioned with a smile.

"Yeah, I don't know about you, but I can't eat another bitch's pussy. I need me some dick plugging me up, ya know," Minnie said.

"Minnie, you is too much, with your fast ass, that's why you pregnant now."

"I can't help it if I love dick. But, Pound-cake, what you think I should name my baby if it's a girl?"

"I don't know."

"I wanna name her Ferrari or Porsche, or how about Mercedes? I think that's a cute name for a girl, 'cuz I know my baby is goin' to be so fly and so ill."

Pound-cake chuckled. "And what about if it's a boy?"

"I like Kareem, Raheem, and Hasheem. I think them are some cute names for a boy, 'cuz my lil' nigga is gonna be so

fly and a cutie. When he grow up, he gonna be havin' these bitches goin' crazy for him, watch, Pound-cake. I know me and Winter are goin' to be makin' some cute-ass babies," Minnie proclaimed excitedly.

Pound-cake frowned when she mentioned that bitch-ass nigga. But she kept her cool and let Minnie have her moment fantasizing about her baby's name.

"Pound-cake, I'm gonna give you a makeover one day, 'cuz you is too cute and too ill to be wearing them sweat-pants, pullovers, and sneakers every day. Girl, you know how many niggas be wanting to holla at you. But you got these niggas out here intimidated. You ain't gonna never get no dick if niggas is too scared to talk. Shit, niggas be asking me, 'Yo, Minnie, what's up wit' your girl? Why she be actin' like that? I know she be holdin' sumthin' under them clothes.' And I be like, 'Yo, just go do you, she ain't gonna bite'. Shit, if you want, you can borrow some of my clothes. I know I'm about to not fit in them anymore, with me gaining this weight."

"Minnie, you is too much," Pound-cake replied, working on her fourth braid.

Minnie definitely had a wardrobe of gear that was top-notch, and some so skimpy that it would even make Lil' Kim skeptical to wear. Minnie got her clothing from either boost-ing with her clique, who called themselves the flavor crew, or from Winter, who liked to see his bitch fly and sexy when she was around him. Minnie loved sporting tight, short denim skirts, tight jeans, revealing halter tops, stilettos, and every-thing else that showed off her body and was high-quality shit. At sixteen, Minnie was young and short, but had the body of a woman, with thick meaty thighs, and a figure that tempted so many to fuck, despite her age.

When Pound-cake began workin' on the last braid in Min-nie's hair, Minnie became sleepy and began nodding off. Min-nie was a talker, dressed like a slut most of the time, had

parents that didn't give a fuck about her, and niggas around the way done ran up in her a few times, making much talk about her being a ho, but to Pound-cake, she was still her friend. Minnie was still innocent in her eyes. Minnie could be naive, but she was about to become a young mother, like so many in the world today. At sixteen, Minnie was growing up before her time. At sixteen, Minnie thought she knew it all, and to her, the world was just this one big party that never ended. And at sixteen is when she would find out that she was HIV positive.

Done with the last braid, Pound-cake helped Minnie off to bed. Like a surrogate mother, who was not too much older than Minnie, Pound-cake tucked Minnie in and kissed her good night. She then went into the living room, gazed out into the night of Coney Island one last time, and then passed out on the couch.

The next morning, Pound-cake woke to the morning sun glaring intensely in her face from leaving the blinds open all night, and hearing the door opening to the apartment. She had covered herself with a thin sheet and used a pillow from Minnie's room to support her head. She slept like a baby, and hated waking up to seeing Minnie's father walking in after getting high and doing whatever he did all night.

Pound-cake got up, yawned and stretched and peeped Joseph standing in the kitchen staring at her.

"What?" Pound-cake asked with attitude.

"Where da fuck is Minnie?" Joseph asked in his gruff voice, holding a torn plastic bag in his hand.

His appearance was rough and not so easy on the eyes. He had an unkempt Afro, and his stained, tattered jeans, dirty wife-beater, and worn-out boots had seen better days.

"She's in her room, 'sleep. Let her be, Joseph," Pound-cake said.

"Well, go wake dat lil' bitch up and tell her to cook sumthin'. I'm fuckin' hungry," Joseph spat.

"Let her be, Joseph. She's pregnant and don't need any shit from you," Pound-cake barked. She stood up and was ready to get in Joseph's face to prove that she was serious.

Joseph knew not to get into it with Pound-cake, and even though he had a fierce reputation back in the days, that was twenty-years ago and his gangsta had faded since the days he started getting high. And now the new generation was taking over, and he needed to remove himself from off the tracks to keep from being run over by the oncoming trains.

Pound-cake glared at Joseph, ready to pop off if necessary.

Joseph glared back, but he was jelly on the inside and his hard gaze meant nothing to Pound-cake. He sucked his teeth and uttered, "Y'all bitches think y'all are so bad." He then walked back out the door, letting the two be in peace.

Pound-cake felt at ease, hoping that the morning and the day would be peaceful. Pound-cake took a seat on the couch and sighed. She looked at the time on the wall, and saw that it was only ten in the morning. Her stomach began to growl, indicating that she was hungry like a pig. She had ten bucks in her pocket and thought about going down to the deli or bodega to get an egg, bacon, and cheese sandwich on a roll, along with a grape Snapple. It was cheap, and would probably hold her hunger till later in the day.

She got up, walked over to the window and peered outside. From nine floors up, Coney Island seemed so quiet, so peaceful, so out of town for her, but being down in the belly of the beast, Coney Island was a place of hardship for many—murders, drug use and abuse and gangs, hustlers, pimps, and thugs that saturated the projects and streets. But among the negative, you also had the community outreach programs, the meals on wheels for the elderly, the PAL for

the kids in the parks and schools, detox programs for the users of many drugs that flooded the streets, and parents that were still there for their children, raising them to become decent human beings in society and refusing to relinquish their children to the streets.

Unfortunately for Pound-cake, Minnie, and the rest of the crew, they didn't have parents who cared and wanted to be there for them. Since they were young, all these girls knew were each other, the streets, and the everyday shit that went down in Brooklyn.

"You want sumthin' to eat?" Minnie asked, walking into the living room, still in her bedtime attire.

Pound-cake turned and said to her, "I didn't even hear you get up."

"I been up. I heard my father in here talking shit, so I decided to stay in my room until he was gone."

"You okay?" Pound-cake asked.

Minnie nodded. "I'll make us some scrambled eggs and toast. It's all we got left to eat in here," Minnie said, as she looked in the fridge.

"That's cool."

Pound-cake stayed with Minnie until noon and then headed back to her crib across the way in Gravesend. It was the second day of summer for everyone, and already the drama was happening. It was about to be one crazy-ass summer.

Pound-cake strutted to her building on Bayview Avenue. She lived in the second building down from Neptune Avenue, and from her apartment window, she had a good view of Kaiser Park.

When she reached the front of her building, she saw a handful of dudes lingering outside, gambling. They already had their hands clutched around a few forty-ounce malt liquor bottles, and it wasn't even mid-afternoon yet.

Everyone noticed Pound-cake coming their way, and out of respect, they cleared the way for her to enter the lobby.

"Pound-cake, what's good, luv," one of the thugs greeted, with a bottle in his hand, having his shirt off, exposing the six-pack he got from being in prison, and a do-rag on his head.

"Hey, Bones," Pound-cake greeted.

"I heard you and your crew popped off on Carissa yesterday. Damn, y'all bitches is wild. Just watch your back, five-oh still lookin' and shit," Bones informed, smiling about the incident.

Pound-cake smiled and said, "Thanks."

She walked into the lobby and knew that everyone's eyes were still on her, staring at her ass and shit. But what Pound-cake had on, loose-fitted sweats and a T-shirt, they could only use their imagination.

"Yo, I wanna fuck dat bitch so fuckin' bad," Bones proclaimed, squeezing his dick through his jeans, thinking about that pussy.

"Nigga, ain't she a dyke or sumthin'," Bones's man, Sick, said.

"Pound-cake, I don't know, but I know she be about her fuckin' business. Bitch is bad though, and cute," Bones stated.

Pound-cake was a quick discussion, and then the dice game and heavy alcohol consumption continued.

Pound-cake got on the elevator and pressed for the third floor. She became disgusted when she noticed that someone had used the elevator to be their personal bathroom again and pissed in the corner. It reeked, and she tried to hold her breath until she got off.

Pound-cake walked into her apartment, and the thought of her mother turning tricks in the back bedroom turned her stomach. The apartment was hardly furnished, with a ragged brown couch and an end table next to it that was chipped

and moldy. The filthy brown carpet on the floor was ringed by cigarette burns, and an old television with a broken antenna and a nonworking remote sat on a milk crate for support. Pound-cake's apartment was the epitome of being poor and filthy in the ghetto. Her mother didn't cook or clean, all she did was fuck, get high, and fuck again to get high.

The kitchen was bare with cracked tiled floors and peeling paint, with dishes so dirty that they began to smell, and her fridge was far worse than Minnie's, only displaying expired milk, a half-empty bottle of vodka, and some rotten cheese that began to change color.

Pound-cake walked down the narrow hallway toward her room and heard the moans and screams of her mother getting fucked in the bedroom across from hers. She sighed and slammed the door to her bedroom very hard, indicating to her mother that she was sick of this shit.

Pound-cake's bedroom wasn't much of an improvement from the rest of the apartment. Her small mattress rested on a chipped particleboard frame. The blanket was stained, and her bedspread torn and her room was lit by a single bulb in the ceiling fixture. Posters of her favorite rappers and singers like 50 Cent, Mary J. Blige, T.I, and Chris Brown lined her soiled walls. It may have looked like hell for many, but for Pound-cake it had been home to her for nineteen years.

Mary Jacobs, Pound-cake's mother, gripped the frayed headboard with a tight grip, as Duck slammed his eight-inch dick deep into her from the back. Sweat poured from Duck's brow as he thrust into Mary, trying to get his nut on. Duck's boy, June, watched the action as he stood next to the bed, butt naked with only some white tube socks on, jerking his dick and waiting for his turn with the ho.

Both men were having their sweet way with Mary Jacobs, as they did things to her that many would see as very disre-

spectful. They tore her asshole open with their size and thickness, they came down her throat, chewed on her nipples, causing the woman to cry out in pain, but she tolerated it, just so she could afford to get high. They fucked her simultaneously, with one penetrating her asshole, and the other deep in her pussy, and left marks and bruises on her neck.

Duck and June were two sadistic perverts who liked to cause women much pain as they sexed them down. The louder a woman cried out from their abuse, the more turned on they both got. But many ladies didn't fuck with the duo; only the ones desperate for the cash fell prey to Duck and June's brutal and sadistic world of kinky and deadly way of sex and foreplay.

June fastened a belt around Mary's thin neck and had her gasping for air, as he pulled the belt strap tightly, pounding his erection deep into her ass and slapping her ass red. When it seemed that she was about to pass out, he would quickly let loose of the strap, and start the routine all over again. He did this until he came. He pulled out and shot his huge load all over her back and then rubbed it in like lotion. When both men were satisfied, leaving Mary looking worn, beaten, and black and blue, they started to get dressed.

Mary remained sprawled out on the bed, unaware that her daughter was home. She massaged her neck where the belt almost burned into her skin from the constant pulling and tugging.

Duck fastened his jeans and stared down at Mary. She was a fiend, but her body was still good, and she still had some look to her. To him, pussy was still pussy, no matter where it came from, and it didn't bother Duck that Mary was a dope fiend. He loved what she allowed them to do for some quick cash.

Mary propped herself up on the headboard, scratching at her neck and asked, "Where's my money?"

Duck smiled. He went into his pocket, pulled out a fifty-dollar bill, crumbled it in his hand, and tossed it at Mary, hitting her on the forehead with it.

"There you go, bitch. Go get your fuckin' high," he cursed.

Mary cared nothing about the disrespect to her. As long as she had money in her hands for her drugs, she cared less about what they said or did to her. She knew she would get paid, because she was one of the few women in the hood that would allow the two to go to the extreme with her.

Duck and June were fully dressed and left out of the apartment laughing and plotting for their next bitch to get at, and tried coming up with more sick ways to get off with a woman.

With the men out of her room, Mary wasted no time getting dressed. Her bedroom smelled heavily of sweat and sex, with mice droppings not too far from the bed. But the only thing on Mary's mind was getting a fix. She threw on some old shapeless sweatpants, an oversized T-shirt, and slippers, and strutted out her apartment and traveled down to the next floor. She quickly knocked on the second-floor apartment, and soon a burly-looking man in a wife-beater, with large arms, a gut, and wearing a blue Yankees fitted cap answered the door.

"Big Jerry, I need a fix," Mary told him.

Jerry stared down at the small woman from his six-three frame and let out a smirk. "You got cash this time, bitch, 'cuz you know Big Jerry don't give out freebies."

Mary quickly reached into her sweatpants pockets and pulled out her fifty-dollar bill. "I need it, Big Jerry. I'm crashing, baby," she cried out.

Big Jerry took the money and nodded. "Wait here," he said.

He closed his door, leaving Mary waiting impatiently. Soon the apartment door came open again, and Big Jerry passed Mary a good-sized pack for her money. She snatched her works and left like there was a chase.

Big Jerry smiled and went about his business inside the apartment. He cared less about the exposed drug transaction he did in the hallway. He intimidated his fellow neighbors and knew how to handle any snitches.

Mary rushed back into her apartment and made a beeline for her bedroom, without her daughter being once on her mind. She removed her works from a top drawer, which was a syringe, a few bottle caps, cotton balls, and a lighter.

She carefully put some heroin inside of the bottle cap and added a little water. She then took the lighter and heated the bottle cap over a small fire to liquefy the substance. When it was ready, she took a cotton ball and drew the poisonous fluid from the bottle cap with a syringe to filter out anything other than the liquefied heroin.

A good high excited her and she was good at shooting up. Mary stood up and removed her sweatpants, exposing the bushy tangled mass of dark hairs on her mound. She positioned herself on the bed with her back against the headboard and spread her legs. She anxiously ran her fingers up and down her thighs until she could feel the vein she was searching for. And when she found the perfect spot, without any hesitation, she forced the needle down into her groin and shot up. For her, a high was better than sex, better than some dick. It made her get off, and she loved every fuckin' minute of it. She soon began to do the dope-fiend nod, and closed her eyes, trying to savor her high.

Pound-cake was curious about her mother and came from out her bedroom and slowly pushed her mother's bedroom door in. And she soon saw her mother nodding out, a syringe dangling from her inner thigh, and blood on the sheets. It was an appalling sight, but for Pound-cake, she had seen the display one time too many. She sighed, looked at her mother with disgust and went back to her bedroom, where she knew it was another place for her to be at peace for a moment. She closed and locked her door, then pulled out her pen and jour-

nal from under her mattress and began writing. For Pound-cake, life in the projects was no movie, no fantasy, just realism for her every day she woke up.

Queens, N.Y

Sabrina emerged from the subway station on Sutphin and Hillside Avenue, dressed like she was about to hit the club up. She paraded down Sutphin Boulevard clad in a butterfly geometric ruffled halter minidress with the spiral hemline and some stilettos, her long legs gleaming like a diamond off the sun. She had just gotten off the crowded F train, which was about an hour ride from Coney Island and couldn't wait to see and spend time with her boo, Shanice.

Sabrina was a display of beauty, with her long hair curving in the wind, and her cleavage exposed for all to see. But she was a pit bull in a skirt, a Brooklyn girl who roamed through the streets of Queens like she had a chip on her shoulder. Besides her girlfriend, Sabrina thought all Queens girls were stuck-up bitches and fake-ass hoes who couldn't fuck wit' a real bitch like her.

Sabrina got down to Archer and Sutphin, and was making cars slow down just to get a better sight of her, and some dudes took the initiative trying to holla at her, not knowing that she liked the same thing as men—pussy.

But Sabrina paid them no mind, and hailed a gypsy cab and quickly got in. She sighed, sat back in the backseat and told the African driver, who was black like tar, "Take me to Merrick and Linden."

The driver nodded, glanced at the raving hood beauty from his rearview mirror and said, "It's a fifteen-dollar fare."

"I don't give a fuck about the cost, just drive, nigga," she barked.

He nodded, knowing to mind his business and drove off. Sabrina rode quietly in the back for a short moment and then said to the driver, "Yo, where is y'all nearest liquor store out here?"

The driver shrugged, indicating that he had no idea. "I don't drink."

"You don't drink. What kind of nigga are you? Yo, I swear, I hate comin' da fuck out here. Y'all niggas is weak out here," she chided.

"You still wan' go to Merrick?" the driver asked.

"Yeah, muthafucka, didn't I say that in the first place? Yo, I just need to go to a fuckin' liquor store first."

Sabrina peered hard out the window, scanning for a place to get her shit. She couldn't go over to Shanice's place empty-handed. She had a dime bag on her, and needed some brown juice and a Dutch for her to roll up. It was a long train ride, and the cabbie was making her upset.

They finally found a liquor store further down Sutphin Boulevard. Sabrina quickly got out, bought her a bottle of Grey Goose and a bottle of E & J, and then she went next door to the bodega and copped two Philly blunts. She jumped back in the cab, after having him wait for ten extra minutes and said, "Now, nigga, take me to Linden and Merrick, and hurry da fuck up. I ain't got all day."

The cabbie sucked his teeth and drove off with an attitude. He couldn't wait to let the bitch out of his cab and be gone.

When they got to her destination, Sabrina handed him a ten and a five, but the cabdriver wasn't satisfied. He turned to look at Sabrina who was about to get out of his cab and said, "No, it's twenty."

"Twenty? Nigga, you told me fifteen," she replied.

"You had me drive around, so it's an extra five dollars," he proclaimed.

"Nigga, fuck you. You better go 'head wit' that shit," she

barked and jumped out of his cab with the goods clutched in her hand.

The cabdriver jumped out from the driver's side and shouted, "You owe me five dollars . . . gas is expensive."

"Nigga, you better get da fuck away from me. Don't get fucked-up out here, Kunta Kinte," she yelled.

"I want my five dollars," he demanded. "Why you gotta be a cheap bitch?"

Sabrina had a low tolerance for stupidity and niggas screaming at her. A small crowd noticed the confrontation and stared on.

"Nigga, what da fuck you call me?"

"Why you a cheap bitch?" he angrily retorted.

Without any thought, Sabrina picked up an empty glass bottle from off the curb and threw it at him. He moved out the way, and the bottle smashed against his car.

"Nigga, don't get fucked-up for five fuckin' dollars!" Sabrina yelled.

"I'm call police."

"Call police, bitch, I don't give a fuck." Sabrina picked up another bottle nearby and threw it at the car, and it smashed against the hood.

"Yo, shortie, you need to chill," a young teenager said, witnessing the act and smiling about it.

"Fuck that!" she shouted.

The driver got scared, jumped back in the car, and before he could pull off, he pointed to Sabrina and shouted, "You get yours!"

"Fuck you!" Sabrina threw up her middle finger at the car, watching it speed off.

"I swear, niggas out here are whack," she shouted. She then walked off down the block with the bag still in her grip.

Shanice lived a block away from Merrick Boulevard. Sabrina got there in a five-minute walk, fuming about the cabbie

and coming out to Queens in such heat. She couldn't wait to
roll up an *L,* get her drink on, and rub against her boo, and
get busy.

Sabrina came to a stop in front of a colonial home, with three
bedrooms, two and a half bathrooms, and a finished basement apartment that was in mint condition. Her girlfriend lived
in the basement apartment. She cut through the paved walk-
way, and didn't notice the upstairs tenant eyeing her like she
was a piece of meat.

"Damn," the middle-aged man uttered, feeling his dick getting hard as he watched Sabrina walk toward the back.

Sabrina came down a short flight of concrete steps and
knocked on the wood screen door. A short moment later, her
boo answered the door, wrapped in a white towel and her
hair draped up in a towel. It was obvious that Shanice just
came out the shower.

"Damn, boo, you're early," Shanice said, opening up the
screen door for Sabrina.

"You need to come out to Brooklyn, fo' real. Feel like I'm
on the other side of the fuckin' world, comin' out here to
Queens to see you," Sabrina stated.

"I thought you would be used to it by now," Shanice said,
walking up to Sabrina, giving her a hug and a passionate
kiss.

"You know I hate it out here. I almost had to fuck a cabdriver up just now," Sabrina informed.

"Why?"

"Nigga tried to jerk me on the fare, wanted me to pay an
extra five dollars because I had him take me to da liquor
store. Muthafucka, that's your fuckin' job. That bitch-ass
nigga got scared and drove off because I started throwing
bottles at his ride," Sabrina said, smiling.

"You're too much, baby. What I tell you about that temper?" Shanice said.

"I had to hold it down."

Shanice chuckled, and then took a good look at Sabrina in her outfit. "Um, damn, baby, you lookin' good in that dress. You know I'm jealous, right."

"You like, bitch?"

"Of course," Shanice said, stepping up to Sabrina and placing her arms around her. "Damn, you feel so soft."

"Ditto," Sabrina replied, moving her hands up Shanice's towel and getting a quick feel on.

Shanice's legs quivered a bit, loving how her boo touched her, rough, but gentle in many ways.

"You're beautiful, baby," Sabrina praised.

Sabrina cupped Shanice's succulent ass and squeezed like she was a nigga handling that booty.

Shanice loved Sabrina's roughneck touch and ways, but loved even looking into a prettier face more. To her, she got the best of both worlds, a dyke with the persona, but not the appearance. Sabrina could look good in a skirt and some heels, or dressed down in some jeans, Timberlands, and her hair wrapped in a scarf. But today, Shanice was happy that her girlfriend came dressed to kill, looking like a lady, but still having that raw ghetto attitude.

Shanice wrapped her arms around her boo's neck and shoved her tongue down her mouth, with Sabrina's hand still gripping her ass tightly.

Shanice was a beauty queen, five feet seven, with meaty thighs, a Coke bottle waistline, and tits like balloons. She had a thick caramel complexion with light brown eyes, and sported a ginger short-cropped hairstyle that brought the beauty out in her face more.

The two first met almost a year ago, on Eastern Parkway in Brooklyn, at the West Indian Day parade. The streets were filled with hordes of people crowding the dozens of island floats that moved unhurried through the jamming crowd of

thousands—with calypso, reggae, and soca blaring up and down the congested parkway that looked like a pack of Skittles exploded on the streets with the radical and extreme costumes, outfits, and headpieces the majority wore.

Sabrina was with Pound-cake and her crew, enjoying the music, the times, and getting high off two *L*'s that they had blazing, as they moved and danced behind the Barbados float, with the blue and yellow flags, with the black pitchfork in between the colors swinging consistently from dozens of hands that danced to the ear-piercing tunes of Rupee's "Tempted to Touch."

"This is my shit right here," Sabrina shouted, as she swayed her hips along with the crowd.

Both girls, Pound-cake and Sabrina, sported almost the same outfits, white tight coochie-cutting shorts, white Uptowns with no socks, and tight wife-beaters, their tits protruding, along with a blue and white Yankees fitted. They both looked sweaty and sexy, having nearby fellows tempted to get a dance and, if they were lucky, fuck one of two ladies before the night ended.

But Sabrina and Pound-cake were out to have a good time and do them, and ignored the many niggas that tried to give them rhythm. All four ladies danced up on each other and got tipsy off of beer and wine coolers, with a blunt being passed around from hand to hand.

But between Nostrand and New York Avenues, Shanice caught Sabrina's attention, as she watched Shanice wind and gyrate her backside like a true island girl and loved what she saw. Sabrina stepped away from her group and daringly approached Shanice. She gently placed her arms around Shanice and grinded her pelvis into Shanice's backside. Shanice turned around, thinking it was some nigga that she was about to push off her, but when she noticed Sabrina, she smiled and continued on with her movements.

They both danced and flirted with each other from Nos-

trand down to Washington Avenue. Many eyes watched the duo, envying them, some trying to step in between the show, but were quickly pushed away, indicating that they didn't want any company. Shanice in her tight cut-off denim shorts, sandals, and body-hugging Trinidadian T-shirt, sporting a Trinidadian bandanna, was definite eye candy for the day.

From that day on, they exchanged numbers, found out that they both liked pussy, and adored each other's company.

Sabrina pulled out her bag of goodies and took a seat on the plush tan leather couch, 'bout ready to roll an *L* for the evening. She watched Shanice walk from in and out of the kitchen, trying to tidy up the place. She was still in her bath towel, and was somewhat meticulous when it came to her home.

Shanice's place was well furnished. She had two tan plush leather couches, a small dining table with a fifteen-millimeter-thick transparent glass top and a tempered glass base—which Sabrina chose to roll her *L* on—and there was a sprawling rich brown carpet put down, a thirty-two-inch Sony wide-screen for everyone's entertainment and a ceiling fan above.

Sabrina dissected the Dutch quickly, laced it with some good 'ol haze and swiftly rolled it back together with her tongue and saliva, like a spider spinning her web.

"Yo, baby, take a break from that cleaning and come chill wit' your boo and enjoy this *L* with me," Sabrina said, tapping the seat next to her. "I ain't come out this way from BK to watch you act like Mr. Clean in a fuckin' towel."

Shanice walked out of the kitchen holding a can of air freshener in her hand. "You had to roll that up on my dining table?"

"It's only glass."

Shanice shrugged, and couldn't resist not getting high. She had a long day at work, and was happy Sabrina was

there to help her relax. Shanice had Sabrina beat in age by five years. She was twenty-four, and had her associate degree from Queens Borough Community College and did data entry at a hospital in the city. She was making good money, and looked to get her bachelor's degree soon.

Shanice walked over to where Sabrina was seated, plopped down next to her, and then threw her legs across Sabrina's lap, while Sabrina began burning up the haze and took two nice long pulls. She then passed the *L* to Shanice, who had her back rested against the armrest of the couch, with her feet still up on Sabrina's lap. She took the *L*, took three long pulls, and felt the haze working through her system, making her body relax, and forgot about her troubles at work. The smoke lingered above her head, and she passed it back to Sabrina.

The two got weeded out lovely, and then Sabrina opened the bottle of Grey Goose and took it to the head like an alcoholic. She downed a good mouthful and then passed it to Shanice.

"Damn, no glass, no mixture," Shanice said.

"Just drink it, baby . . . it does the body good," Sabrina stated.

Shanice smiled and took the bottle from Sabrina and downed it. The two continued to get high, tipsy, and soon the foreplay followed.

Sabrina stared at Shanice with lust burning in her eyes. She began massaging her feet gently and then asked, "What you workin' wit' under that towel?"

Shanice chuckled and returned with, "You already know what I'm workin' wit' . . . it ain't like you never saw it before . . . unless you wanna see it again."

"You fresh out the shower too. You know it's on."

"You know it," Shanice added.

Sabrina began kissing Shanice's feet slowly but surely, making her way up to her ankles and soon her shins. She then looked up at Shanice again, and reached for the towel

and began undoing the knot that held the white cloth against Shanice's skin. She unwrapped the towel, and let it fall against Shanice's sides, displaying Shanice's womanly curves in the buff, with her caramel mound shaved smooth like ice, and her dark Hershey nipples rigid from Sabrina's touch.

Shanice propped herself up more against the armrest, spreading her legs for her boo and quivered when she felt Sabrina's hands run up her thighs. Within time, she felt Sabrina's tongue swimming around in her, her juices mixing in with saliva from her lover's action. The haze had her in a frenzy, she was horny and arched her back from off the couch for better aerial support, as Sabrina sucked, chewed, and ate her pussy out with some tender, loving care.

"Aaaaaahhhhhhhhhh," Shanice cried out, feeling her body reaching an orgasm. She clutched Sabrina's shoulders, holding on for the ride. Her lover was like a beast down there. Her pants came in bursts, her heartbeat raced like there was danger.

Sabrina ate and fingered her lover simultaneously, causing Shanice's legs to clamp down on her when she came like hell.

Soon, both women were butt naked and sweaty on the cool, tan leather couch. Sabrina was faced on one end of the couch and Shanice opposite, with their legs clamped around each other like two scissors pressed together in a vertical and horizontal position, rubbing pussies and about to cause a bushfire.

Sabrina's legs trembled, as she gripped the couch and felt a orgasm coming. "Oh shit!" she shrieked, feeling Shanice cum against her. And soon she did the same.

After the intense episode between the two, Sabrina began rolling up another *L* butt naked. Shanice looked spent and remained sprawled out on the couch, waiting for her boo to finish rolling.

"Baby, I gotta go after this," Sabrina informed.

"What? Go? Why?" Shanice asked, clearly disappointed.

Sabrina spliced the *L* together with her tongue before an-

swering Shanice. She made sure everything was tight and then said, "I gotta meet up wit' Pound-cake tonight."

"Are you serious?" Shanice said, rising up from her slouching position and staring at Sabrina. "You fuckin' her too, Sabrina?"

"What? Nah, that's my girl from way back. I ride wit' that bitch, Shanice. Don't get shit twisted," Sabrina let known.

"Well, you be spending more time with Pound-cake than you do with me. I mean, I'm your wifey, right? So why you gotta be running back off to C.I to go check her for?" Shanice asked, anger in her voice.

"Shanice, you trippin', baby. Maybe if you moved out to Brooklyn and stop being out in corny-ass Queens, and be around some real bitches, then you wouldn't be actin' all insecure and shit. It takes a bitch like a day to come out here for some pussy," Sabrina proclaimed.

Shanice sucked her teeth and couldn't help but to be jealous of Pound-cake. She knew that her and Sabrina been best friends since they were six, but that bitch was cutting into her time with Sabrina. It was hard enough that she worked all day and rarely got to play, but now that she had time to play, Sabrina was off to the ghetto to do God knows what.

"You mad?" Sabrina asked.

Shanice sucked her teeth, lay back down, and turned her head.

Sabrina chuckled, took a pull from the burning haze and said, "You be ayyite."

"Whatever."

Shanice thought, *Fuck it*. It is what it is, and at least she got hers for the night. But she hated to hear the name Pound-cake come from Sabrina's lips. It angered her.

Shanice took the burning *L*, took a few pulls, and tried to let her anger for Sabrina's ways subside.

*   *   *

"The doctor says I need to take some tests," Minnie said, staring out the F train window as it roared down the elevated tracks above Brooklyn, soon coming to the last stop in Coney Island.

"What kind of tests?" Pound-cake asked in a concerned tone.

"I don't know. This is my second time seeing the doctor. I don't know what I'm doin,' Pound-cake. I just got put on Medicaid, and now I need to get this WIC to help me feed this baby. I don't know why we gotta go back to that fuckin' office. I was 'bout ready to slap the shit outta that black bitch for lookin' at me all stink," Minnie proclaimed.

Pound-cake smiled. They had just gotten back from the WIC office in downtown Brooklyn, and it was almost an all-day thang for the two ladies—from dealing with the crowds, the long waits, the shuffling around from office to office, and dealing with some workers who looked at them judgmental. Pound-cake and Minnie just wanted to go home, relax, and probably get their smoke on.

Minnie didn't want to go down to the office alone, so she asked Pound-cake to tag along for company and support, and Pound-cake did without any hesitation. It was a cold world, and Pound-cake knew that Minnie needed some support to get through her pregnancy comfortably.

"Winter was supposed to drive me, but I haven't spoken to him in two days." Just the thought of Winter not being there for her and her pregnancy put Minnie in a somber mood as she peered out at Brooklyn from above. She heard rumors around the way that she was not the only girl pregnant by Winter. There was talk in the buildings that Monique, who lived two floors underneath Minnie's, was having Winter's baby too, and she was three months pregnant.

"You think he loves me, Pound-cake?" Minnie blurted out.

"Who . . . Winter? Fuck that faggot, Minnie. You don't need

him to help take care of this baby," Pound-cake said. "You got me, Sabrina, and the crew. We family, baby girl."

Minnie looked at her with a look of uncertainty, and admitted, "I'm scared, Pound-cake. I don't know what I'm doing. I'm scared." Minnie started to cry, not caring who was watching or listening.

Pound-cake took a deep breath, pulled Minnie to her, and embraced her in her arms, having her head rest against her shoulders for support, and then Pound-cake propped her feet up against adjacent seats and held her friend until the F train came to its last stop.

It was a little after five when the two finally made it home and around the way. It was a balmy day, and everyone was outside catching a cool breeze and trying to make plans for the night.

Pound-cake and Minnie caught up with Sabrina, Lady Rah, Joy, and a few others chilling on a park bench, smoking and drinking, with a radio blaring some Mary J. Blige.

"Where y'all bitches comin' from?" Sabrina shouted out, sitting on the top of the bench with an L in her hand and flanked by her crew.

"Downtown Brooklyn. Went wit' Minnie to apply for WIC," Pound-cake informed, taking the burning haze from Sabrina and taking a few pulls.

"How's my godchild doin'?" Sabrina asked, rubbing Minnie's stomach gently.

"He or she is behaving themselves," Minnie stated with a smile, forgetting about the troubles that she worried about on the train ride.

"Next time, y'all need to let me come wit' y'all. I know how them assholes be actin' down at da WIC office. You gotta get in their fuckin' faces for respect," Sabrina stated.

"I know, girl. I was ready to smack them bitches today," Minnie replied.

"Bitch, you should have. Let 'em know how we get down," Sabrina said. "Anyway, Pound-cake, what you doin' tonight?"

"Nuthin'. Why? What's the four-one-one?"

"We 'bout to hit the club up tonight in Bed-Stuy. Whatcha-macallit is performing tonight . . . Ox. You know he's about to get put on, right," Sabrina said, sounding so excited.

"Oh word," Pound-cake uttered out.

"We all rollin' through deep, to show dat nigga some sup-port . . . let niggas know how C I gets down."

"I'm there, bitch," Pound-cake said.

Ox was Sabrina's cousin's man. La-La, who was Sabrina's cousin, was doing a six-month bid on Rikers Island for a pos-session charge. La-La was a ride-or-die bitch that was holding shit down on the streets before her incarceration. Her and Ox been together since high school, and been through it all, from fights with each other, to having each other's back in rough situations, the drugs, the gangs, the police, the war-rants, even the loss of their child when La-La had a miscar-riage—they had stories to tell. They were like the real ghetto Whitney and Bobby.

Sabrina loved her older cousin like a sister and was furious with Ox when she found out that he was fucking that bitch Carissa. Everyone knew how Carissa got down, and she knew Carissa was only fuckin' with Ox because he was com-ing up in the rap game. Ox was twenty-three and a ghetto superstar. His rhymes were tight and so was his abs, and even though his baby La-La was locked down, he still showed his love for her by having her name tattooed across his chest, covering his heart.

But tonight, even though Sabrina was still upset with Ox for doing what he did while La-La was locked down, she still was going to show up at his show and support him. But she knew once La-La came home, which would be in November,

it would be war with the two. And Sabrina had her cousin's back till the end of time.

"Yo, I need some muthafuckin' smokes," Lady Rah said, rising off the bench and looking like a hoochie in her extremely short denim skirt, which almost had her ass cheeks showing, and a skimpy top that highlighted her big tits.

"Take your ass to the store then," Joy shouted.

"Someone come wit' me," Lady Rah said.

Joy sucked her teeth. "Why you always want someone to come wit' you?"

" 'Cuz I ain't tryin' to pay for shit. Besides, Mr. Bean is in there, and you know he don't like a bitch," she said.

Mr. Bean was the nickname that the girls gave the owner of the bodega. To them, he looked exactly like Rowan Atkinson from the hit show *Mr. Bean*. He was tall and lanky and had the same goofy look of Mr. Bean.

Lady Rah, Joy, and Sabrina were known for always stealing out of his store. When Mr. Bean was there, it was always hard to do, because he would watch them like a hawk, and when they got bold and stole shit, he would curse at them and even chase them out of his store, threatening them not to come back.

But it was a different story when Mr. Bean's eighteen-year-old-son, Abdul, was behind the counter. Abdul was a sweetheart to the ladies, and the ladies had a strategy that would always work with him. One of the girls would distract Abdul's attention by flirting with him at the counter, while the others wandered through the store and would take whatever they needed and casually walk out. It was a flawless system for the ladies.

"Fuck it, we all go. I'm thirsty anyway," Sabrina said, stepping off the bench.

Lady Rah, Joy, Pound-cake, and another young hood chick

named Shannon followed Sabrina to the store, while Minnie stayed behind in the park with a friend named Bubbles.

Sabrina got to the entrance and smiled when she saw Abdul working the counter. She turned and told her crew, and they all knew it was on,

"Who's gonna be the decoy this time?" Sabrina asked.

"Fuck it, I'll do it," Lady Rah said. "Y'all just make sure to snatch me up a Pepsi and some diapers for my son."

Lady Rah walked into the bodega with a smile on her face and strutted her way up to the counter, where Abdul had his eyes on the old dusty tube that was mounted over the potato chips, watching a Mets game.

"Hey, Abdul," Lady Rah called out.

Abdul turned with a huge smile plastered across his face.

"What you watching?" Lady Rah asked, looking up to see and then said, "You like baseball?"

"Of course," Abdul said.

"You need to teach me how to play baseball," Lady Rah said. She leaned over against the counter, with her short skirt rising from behind, and gently grabbed Abdul's hand, massaging his fingertips.

Abdul smiled and didn't even notice Sabrina, Pound-cake, Shannon, and Joy walking into the store.

All three girls immediately went toward the back of the store and began their boosting. Sabrina grabbed a few sodas from the freezer and stuffed them into a small handbag, while Pound-cake and Joy went for the snacks.

"I didn't know you like baseball," Abdul said, looking at Lady Rah and loving the way she touched him.

"I like any sport that can get a nigga sweaty and lookin' good in a uniform," Lady Rah said, as she now massaged Abdul's wrist.

Abdul took a deep breath and felt a sudden bulge in his jeans. He was unaware of the thievery going on in the store, as his mind was distracted by pussy.

"So, Abdul, what kind of girls do you like?" Lady Rah asked.

Abdul smiled and eyed Lady Rah in her lustful attire and thought about so many nasty things.

"You like what you see?" Lady Rah asked.

"I love what I see," he replied.

Lady Rah took a step back and allowed for Abdul to get a full view of what she had on. Her tight mini-denim skirt was riding up her thighs, exposing parts that shouldn't be seen in public.

Abdul licked his lips and wished he wasn't working at the moment.

Meanwhile, Pound-cake discreetly opened up a pack of Pampers with the razor she carried and took out a handful of diapers for Lady Rah's son and stuffed them under her shirt, while Joy and Sabrina were about ready to make their exit, concealing a handful of goodies.

Lady Rah stepped up to Abdul again and said, "You ever been with a sista, Abdul?"

"Yeah, a few times. There's nothing like the sistas," Abdul said.

"You ever thought about getting wit' me?" Lady Rah asked.

Abdul shrugged.

"You like what you see?"

"Yeah, of course."

Lady Rah glanced up at the huge dome security mirror near the counter and peeped Sabrina and Joy 'bout ready to make their exit. She smiled and then took Abdul's hand again and said, "C'mere, let me show you sumthin'."

She gently pressed Abdul's hand against her breast and allowed for him to squeeze and molest her in public.

He didn't hesitate, squeezing Lady Rah's breast through her shirt, and hearing her moan with his touch.

"You like 'em?" Lady Rah asked.

"You crazy," he said.

"So, you wanna link up tonight and I can show you a lot more in person?" she said.

"I get off at seven."

"Ayyite," Lady Rah said, removing his hand from her goodies and stepping back. "Oh, can I get a loosy, baby?"

Abdul pulled out a pack of Newports and passed Lady Rah three single cigarettes and then said, "Just take them, they're on me."

Lady Rah smiled, took her cigarettes and said, "See you soon, cutie." She walked out of the bodega feeling, *Mission accomplished.*

She saw her crew standing at the corner and shouted, "I hope one of y'all bitches got my son some Pampers."

Pound-cake pulled out a stack of Pampers from under her shirt and tossed her a few. The girls laughed and crossed the street on their way back to the park benches to chill and enjoy the snacks and drinks they done snatched up for free.

"Winter, get off her!" the ladies heard Bubbles yelled as they were near the park entrance.

Sabrina, Pound-cake, and the rest looked and noticed Winter pulling on Minnie like some dog. Minnie was crying, trying to resist, but Winter slapped the shit out of her, shouting, "Get in da fuckin' truck, Minnie!"

Without a second thought in their heads, Sabrina and the rest ran over to help out Minnie and was 'bout ready to fuck Winter up. Pound-cake charged at him with her fists balled tightly and prepared to come to blows. Minnie was scared, and Bubbles was terrified of Winter, but she tried to help her friend by pulling on Minnie's arm, trying to free her friend from Winter's grip.

But Winter was furious with Minnie; he had his boy, Moe, by his side, watching his back. Moe glanced over and saw a crew coming at them. He tapped Winter, saying, "Yo, yo, we got company."

Winter turned and looked, and his eyes lit up, knowing that

Pound-cake and Sabrina wasn't running over to come and reason with him—they was coming for war. Moe was ready for anything, knowing Sabrina's and Pound-cake's reputation. He was ready to wild out on a bitch, if necessary.

Winter still had his stronghold grip on Minnie, and in one quick reaction, he reached for his .45 with his free hand, pulling out the weapon and had it aimed at all four ladies charging at him. "Yo, y'all bitches better back da fuck down!" he shouted.

"Oh, so that's how you want it, you pussy muthafucka? You gotta pull out on us, you bitch-ass nigga!" Sabrina cursed and shouted.

"Shut da fuck up, Sabrina. This shit don't concern you," Winter shouted.

"I'm gonna fuck you up, Winter!" Sabrina retorted.

Winter continued to pull on Minnie, his other arm outstretched with the weapon. He glared at everyone, hating how Minnie's friends were always in their business. Minnie was his to deal with, and he wanted no bitch filling her head with nonsense about his constant cheating, or her needing to leave him alone. He was ready to wild out and shoot everyone around, before he lost control over Minnie.

Winter was six feet two, well built, with long cornrows that ran down to his back. He was a hustler and a pimp, and was always draped in the nicest clothing from Sean John to Versace. He was a product of the ghetto, in and out of jail continually. He had eight kids spread all over from Brooklyn to New Jersey. He sold drugs, pimped hoes, and smoked crack from time to time. He wasn't pussy, but when it came to beefing with Sabrina and Pound-cake, he knew that they were two bitches who could get down, and he knew not to underestimate them, because they got wild and crazy just like him.

"Winter, you know she's pregnant, why you fuckin' pulling and beating on her like that?" Pound-cake yelled, stepping to Winter with fire in her eyes.

"Yo, back da fuck up, Pound-cake. I ain't playin' wit' you, bitch!"

"Nigga, without that gun in your hand, you ain't shit, nigga!" Sabrina yelled out.

Pound-cake picked up an empty bottle from off the concrete, and was ready to bash Winter over the head with it. She continued to move closer, testing him, daring him to be stupid and pull the trigger.

Winter continued to drag Minnie toward his truck, a polished black Escalade sitting on twenty-four-inch chromed rims. Moe had his back, watching the fury in the ladies' eyes as he back stepped toward the truck.

"Pussy . . . pussy . . . pussy . . . pussy," Sabrina taunted, as her and her crew followed Winter and Moe to the truck. "You pussy, nigga. I'm gonna catch you without that gun, pussy, and we gonna fuck you up!"

"Yeah, ayyite . . . whatever, bitch, step da fuck off," Winter said. "I ain't playin' games wit' y'all bitch, anymore."

Pound-cake had nothing else to say. She was ready for action, the bottle clutched tightly in her hand, but she knew not to leap forward because Winter had the advantage for the moment. She watched Minnie being dragged away like some child.

Minnie stared at Pound-cake with pleading eyes, because Minnie knew that once Winter had her in his truck, his attack on her would be relentless. But with the gun in his hand, Pound-cake and Sabrina were at a handicap against him.

With Moe having his back, Winter pushed Minnie into the backseat of the truck and shut the door. Then him and Moe quickly jumped into the front seats and hastily drove off, leaving Sabrina, Pound-cake, and everyone else fuming and ready to war with Winter.

"I'm gonna kill that nigga!" Sabrina screamed. "He wanna pull out a gun on me and don't buss . . . pussy-ass nigga!"

The whole crew was fuming with rage, knowing that if you

pull a gun, then you better use it. Sabrina wanted to see Winter bodied. She asked Joy for her cell phone and called up Pain, a thoroughbred thugged-out nigga, who had Brooklyn blocks on lock.

Pain answered, saying, "Yo, who dis be?"

"Pain, where you at?" Sabrina shouted through the phone.

"Who da fuck is dis?" Pain asked, not getting too excited.

"It's Sabrina, yo. That nigga Winter need to go. He just pulled out a gat on me and my girls and disrespected us, yo. Fo' real, I'm ready to body dat nigga," Sabrina informed.

Pain chuckled, knowing how wild and crazy Sabrina could get. But that was his bitch from back in da day, and he knew he needed to swing through and see what went down.

"Yo, Sabrina, I'll be out that way in a half, just be cool," Pain said.

"Ayyite, you know where we be," Sabrina said. She hung up and passed Joy back her phone and then said, "Yo, it's on. Winter gone get his."

Joy, Lady Rah, and the rest nodded, knowing that if Pain was coming through, it was about to pop off. Pain was ol'-skool nigga who ran with Chills and Corey-D back in his heyday, when niggas was getting money like that back in the nineties and the body count was causing the city some problems.

But Pain knew that there were too many young niggas running around trying to be gangsters and trying to get money, and today, niggas didn't have a foundation, structure, or an organization that knew how to wash money, or that knew how to handle things without it turning into Dodge City and making the block hot for police activity.

Pain was thirty-five, and he kept tabs on the block, and he knew Sabrina from her being kin to Corey-D, who was notorious with murders and getting money back in the days, until he was killed in '99. And he remembered when Sabrina used to be in diapers. He practically watched her grow up.

* * *

"Bitch, what I told you, huh . . . don't fuck wit' me!" Winter screamed, as he slammed Minnie's head against the glass window in the truck, almost shattering it.

He had climbed into the backseat with Minnie and began assaulting her while Moe drove down Neptune Avenue. He beat her like she was a nigga, and had Minnie balled into the fetal position in the backseat, pressed against the door, crying hysterically, her eye bruised.

"I told you, don't fuckin' be around them bitches. All they gonna do is get you into trouble, bitch! You don't fuckin' listen, you stupid bitch!" Winter screamed, grabbing Minnie by her neck and applying force to her windpipe.

Minnie began to gasp and clutched Winter's wrist, begging for her life.

With his fist balled tightly, Winter swung again, and struck Minnie violently in the face, causing her nose to bleed, with tears of hurt and pain following and her bottom lip quivering with fear. She was no match for Winter's size and brute force that he bestowed down on her.

"Keep fuckin' wit' them bitches if you want, and I'll fuckin' kill you and that fuckin' baby in you," he warned. "Ayyite, you fuckin' bitch!"

Minnie nodded meekly, tears staining to her face, and her nose and lip bleeding blood. But seeing her in a submissive posture didn't ease Winter's relentless onslaught. Winter's eyes were cold against her, and he was sick of looking at her. He thought about the shit that Pound-cake and Sabrina were putting in his girl's head, trying to turn Minnie against him, and thinking about them two bitches angered him to the point where he definitely took it out on Minnie at the moment.

He grabbed Minnie by her shirt, slamming her against the car door with brute force, raising his fist in the air, and pounded on her with no remorse. He didn't even think about

her being sixteen and being pregnant. Winter wanted Minnie to fear him, and he was succeeding with his goal.

Minnie's painful cries were muted from the streets of Brooklyn, with her encased in the sleek Escalade as it moved through Brooklyn.

Moe just drove, remaining nonchalant, as his boy beat on one of his girls in the backseat. To Moe, it didn't concern him; he had no love for the hoes, just the love for the pussy. As far as he was concerned, Minnie deserved it.

Pain pulled up to Sabrina and her girls, who were lingering outside of Pound-cake's building, in a gleaming black 335i BMW convertible. He was with his right-hand man, Coupe, who was like one of Brooklyn's deadliest dozen.

Pain stepped out the BMW, followed by Coupe. Pain had a deadpan look about him as he approached Sabrina, clad in a white T, denim jeans, and beige Timberlands. Coupe puffed on a Black and Mild, as he stood behind Pain like the loyal soldier he was.

Sabrina walked up to Pain, attitude written across her face. "Yo, dat nigga needs to get murdered," Sabrina shouted. "I'm gonna fuck dat nigga up when I see him, Pain."

"Yo, Sabrina, calm your tone, and tell me what happened," Pain said to her coolly.

"He gonna pull out a gun on me and my girls and don't buss his. He is pussy, Pain," Sabrina shouted, her arms flailing around.

"What you beefin' with Winter about?"

"Nah, he gonna snatch up Minnie like she some dog, and then pull out on me, and diss me," she explained.

Pain chuckled and returned with, "So this is over his bitch? "Yeah . . . but . . ."

"Minnie's his bitch, right? I know that's your girl, but that his bitch, first off, and that's his problem, not yours," Pain instructed.

"But she's only sixteen, Pain," Sabrina said.

"And if she's old enough to get fucked and have his baby, then you need to let her be, and let Winter handle his."

"But he gonna point a gun in my face, and I'm suppose to let it be," Sabrina said.

"I'll talk to him, Sabrina. But let it be. Winter's my problem and he runs the block for me. I don't need any problems with y'all too. So we cool about this, right?" Pain said, looking at Sabrina with certainty.

Sabrina knew that whatever Pain said was final. She looked up at him and reluctantly said, "Yeah, we cool."

"Ayyite, that's good to hear," Pain said. He then reached into his pocket and pulled out a small wad of hundreds and peeled off five C-notes and pressed them into her hand. "Ox is performing tonight, right? So you and your girls go out and have a good time on me."

Sabrina took the money; she wasn't a fool. She nodded and watched Pain and Coupe get back into the 335i and drive off, with her and her girls standing at the curb watching.

"What he say?" Joy asked.

"Nuthin', just let it be, and get ready for the club tonight," Sabrina said.

"That's it?" Joy asked, watching Sabrina walk toward the building lobby.

Pound-cake just stood there thinking about her girl Minnie and hated thinking what abuse that asshole Winter was putting her through. She wanted to be there for Minnie and felt helpless that she couldn't—and she hated feeling helpless. She knew truly in her heart that Winter would get his soon, either by her hands or someone else.

"Be cool, baby girl, you'll get help soon," Pound-cake said to no one in particular. She then followed behind Sabrina into the building lobby to get their smoke on.

* * *

The Lab on Fulton Street was jumping with a crowd of hundreds out front, and the streets lined up and down the block with high-end cars and the latest trends being sported for all to see and admire. The ladies pranced around on Fulton Street in their tight skirts and pants, stilettos, with their hair done up, manicures showing, and so much skin showing that it looked like an African village.

The fellows were dressed in baggy denim jeans, Timbs, designer shirts, and sporting ice and platinum like they were the next up-and-coming rap star. Everyone was out to come see Ox and his peoples perform. Ox was becoming a ghetto celeb, with his strong stage presence and serious street credibility. The ladies loved him, and the niggas and thugs respected him and his crew.

Sabrina and her crew rolled up to the club around one in the morning, stepping out of a cab dressed like some hoochies, wearing short denim skirts, tight coochie cutting shorts, stilettos, and skimpy tops that exposed much cleavage and tattoos.

Pound-cake looked like a lady for once, as she walked behind Sabrina and the rest, in a pair of tight denim capris, a hot pink tie halter top, and balancing herself in a pair of four-inch sandals, her hair reaching down to her shoulders. She looked good, and by the heads that turned when she passed the fellows, they agreed.

Sabrina smiled when she noticed Shanice waiting for her in front of the club. Pound-cake and the rest didn't look so happy. They didn't like Shanice. They felt that she was not one of them. She was from Queens, and thought that she was some stuck-up prissy bitch who was messing with Sabrina's head. The crew gave Shanice a smug look, like, *Whatever, bitch*, and ignored her as they made their way inside.

Shanice cared nothing for the bitches that hated on her, she was only there for her boo, Sabrina. And Shanice knew

she looked better than anyone of them hoes, as she walked arm in arm with Sabrina into the club, wearing the hell out of a black outrageous deep-plunge mini-dress and strutting in some five-inch wedge heels.

Ox had put Sabrina and her girls on the list and had them set up in VIP. So the ladies walked into the Lab looking like all stars, as they made their way through the dense crowd with some T.I. blaring throughout the club, the revelers getting tipsy and hyped. They were ready to see Ox get onstage to do his thang.

The night was still young, and the music was on point and diverse, with reggae, hip-hop, and rap playing. The ladies walked into the VIP section and greeted Ox's entourage of thugs, groupies, and wannabes. Bottles of Moët and Cristal were being popped opened, and Sabrina could smell the welcoming of that haze and piff being passed around the room.

Ox was nowhere to be found, but that didn't stop Sabrina and her crew from getting their smoke on and mingling with the crowd, drinking Cristal and Moët, and partying like a rock star. Everyone showed everyone some love.

Pound-cake took a seat on one of the lounge chairs, and pressed the haze to her lips and took a long pull, nodding her head to a Biggie track. She tried to black out the ugly thoughts of Minnie being hauled off by Winter. She took two long pulls and then passed the weed over to Joy, who already had some of that dark brown liquor in her hand.

"What's your name, beautiful?" one of Ox's people asked as he took a seat next to Pound-cake and admired her outfit and her beauty.

Pound-cake looked at him and knew he wasn't her type. He was too chunky, not cute, and had a lazy eye that bothered her. He was dressed nice, with jewelry, but Pound-cake just came to the club to show Ox some support and be around her girls. She didn't come to look for some dick.

"Not interested," she said frankly.

"I'm sayin' though, ma . . . I be seeing you around the way, always dressed in sweats and shit. You look nice, though, like a lady, fo' real. I'm sayin', let me get you a drink," he said.

"I'm good, nigga," Pound-cake said.

"Your name Pound-cake, right?" he asked, like he wasn't hearing what she first said to him. He was slouched down, with his elbows pressed against his knees, and trying hard to mack to her.

"I know you ain't got a man, because I don't be seeing you fuckin' wit' niggas around the way," he continued. "But, yo, they call me Meatball."

Pound-cake laughed, knowing that the name truly did fit him, *With his portly self*, she thought.

"You laughing at my name or me, shortie?" Meatball asked, looking a bit offended.

Pound-cake rolled her eyes and wished Meatball would step off.

But Meatball wasn't the type to give up on something he liked or, in better terms, some bitch he wanted to fuck.

"Yo, luv . . . I got paper for days, I can buy you anything, or pay for it if I want," Meatball stated, flashing hundred-dollar bills in front of her.

"Ohmygod, nigga, what da fuck! You thirsty like dat for some pussy!" Pound-cake cursed, jumping up and walking away.

Meatball stood up and glared at Pound-cake's backside, watching her strut off over to her friends. He was thirsty for Pound-cake. He loved her style and always knew she had a wicked body under them sweats, baggy jeans, and T-shirts, and tonight she was definitely showing it off, having niggas go, *Got damn!*

Pound-cake took a few sips of Joy's dark liquor and then turned to see Ox walk in, his crew of hounds closely behind him. It was all eyes on Ox and his peoples as they walked in looking like rap stars already selling platinum.

Ox had on a black tank top with the diamond and platinum chain draped around his neck, his designer braids were
freshly done, his baggy Sean John jeans sagging off his ass,
a fraction of his boxers showing, his Timberlands fresh off
the shelf. He was black like Wesley Snipes, and his chiseled
features along with his groomed dark beard made him eye
candy for the ladies around.

Ox flexed his toned biceps as he clutched onto a bottle of
Cristal, diamonds twinkling in his ears. He was a gangster
first and a rapper afterward. His rough demeanor and rowdy
entourage almost made him unapproachable, because they
intimidated so many. But his street credibility was selling him
some records, and he was definitely making a name for himself. Some say he was becoming the next 50 Cent.

Pound-cake watched as the groupies and wanna bes piled
over to Ox and his crew, trying to make themselves noticed.
But Pound-cake knew the nigga since the days of going to
P.S. 188, and she knew better than to act like some fuckin'
groupie for a nigga that was like an older brother to her.

But one of the men in Ox's entourage definitely did catch
her attention. She stared over at Ordeal and thought about
the last time she saw him. It had been months since they
linked up. She'd fucked him plenty of times. Pound-cake
kept her sex life discreet and kept her goodies mostly under
lock and key. She didn't crave for sex like her girls, but when
she wanted it, she knew the right nigga to call, and that was
Ordeal.

She stared over at Ordeal standing behind Ox, clad in a
throwback Miami Heats jersey, tattoos running up and down
his defined arms. He sported his fitted backward, with the ice
around his neck and wearing long denim shorts and white-
on-white Uptowns that looked so clean, you could lick the
sides. His cocoa-brown skin shimmered in the dim light, and
his hazel eyes and trimmed goatee made him out to be a
pretty boy. The ladies loved him, and Ordeal loved them

right back. But he had a reputation as being a real grimy nigga, and if he had love for you, he had love for you. But if he didn't, he could become like the Taliban, really hated and dangerous to your existence. He wasn't scared to buss his gun, and was a stickup kid getting money, until he went off on tour with Ox.

But despite talk of the people he done killed, robbed, or just plain disrespected, whenever Ordeal was around Pound-cake, the two were like in their own world where it was only about them, and nothing else mattered. And he was the last nigga she fucked, and that was almost four months ago.

Pound-cake stared over at Ordeal and couldn't help but smile. Him being so close excited her, and not much excited her. She tried to catch his attention, because she dared not go over to him, but wanted Ordeal to see her and approach her.

Joy stood next to her and ordered her third drink from the bar. "There go Ordeal," Joy mentioned.

"I see him," Pound-cake replied.

"Girl, I know your panties are leaking right now," Joy joked.

"Please, bitch," Pound-cake remarked, turning her attention from Ordeal.

"Don't even fake it, bitch. You know it's been a minute since you had some dick, and there it goes standing right over there for you to snatch up. And you better hurry. You see them groupie bitches all over your man already."

"He ain't my man," Pound-cake said.

"Whatever, Pound-cake. Grow up and go get yours," Joy said, sounding frustrated, and walked off to find her own pleasures.

Pound-cake let her be and decided to order herself a Long Island iced tea from the bar. She glanced over at Sabrina and caught her hugged up on her boo, Shanice, laughing and carrying on.

The bartender soon came over with her drink, placing it in front of Pound-cake. But before he could say the price, Pound-cake heard, "Yo, I got that for her. Don't even sweat it, shortie, I'm gonna take care of you."

She turned and saw Meatball standing near her, pressing for her attention hard. Pound-cake rolled her eyes and sighed. Without even turning to look his way again, she said, "Yo, I'm good, nigga. I don't need shit from you."

"Yo, luv, why you actin' like dat? I'm sayin', I'm trying to be nice and you actin' all stuck-up and shit. Yo, you know who I be?" he barked, anger dripping from his voice.

"Ohmygod, just step, nigga. You ain't my type," she chided.

"What?" Meatball shouted.

"Yo, just let her be, nigga. She waiting on me and my time anyway, ayyite," Meatball and Pound-cake heard someone say from behind them.

Meatball quickly turned, ready to flip on the nigga that was trying to cock-block him and barked, "What, nigga, you need to . . ." he paused, realizing who it was. "Oh shit . . . Ordeal, what's good, my nigga?" Meatball said, his attitude and tone changing abruptly.

"What's good, nigga?" Ordeal returned nonchalantly, giving Meatball dap and a quick embrace.

"I ain't know this was you. My bad, my nigga," Meatball said, stepping back from Pound-cake a bit.

"Yeah, this my nigga, and I don't need your greasy paws all over sumthin' sweet, you feel me?" Ordeal said to him calmly.

"Yeah, I feel you," Meatball replied, knowing Ordeal meant business.

"So step da fuck off, nigga, and bounce," Ordeal growled.

Looking like the meek, Meatball knew not to feel froggy and leap, knowing if he did, he wouldn't survive the night. So he swallowed his pride, and like the wild, he was chased off

and left his catch for the bigger predator in the jungle to enjoy.

Pound-cake smiled and hugged Ordeal with joy and passion. Ordeal gripped her in his arms and enjoyed how soft and warm Pound-cake felt in his arms.

"Ummm, you feel so fuckin' good, Pound-cake." Ordeal picked her up in his arms and pressed his fingers against her ass, while a jealous Meatball looked on.

"Damn, you look good," Ordeal said, eyeing Pound-cake from head to toe and smiling. "You came lookin' like dat for me, right, luv? You knew I was back in town."

"I came to chill," Pound-cake said, smiling.

"Yo, I got that," Ordeal said, passing the bartender a twenty, who was patiently waiting to get paid. "Keep the change." Ordeal stuffed the many hundreds he carried back into his back pocket and focused his attention back on Pound-cake.

"You miss me?" Ordeal asked, throwing his arms around Pound-cake's waist and dying to get into her panties again.

"I thought about you," she returned.

"I know you did."

"Whateva, nigga. You have better been thinking about me," she said seriously.

"You were on my mind every day since I left," he lied.

"You full of shit, Ordeal."

"Nah, you know I would call, but you ain't got a phone like that."

"So, you need to buy me one then, since you ballin' like that," she said.

"I might just do that. I need to keep tabs on you."

"I need to watch you," she said back.

"You here wit' Sabrina and them, right?" he asked.

"Yeah. Why? You think I came wit' some nigga? You jealous?" she playfully said.

"Nah, you ain't that stupid. You know I got that under lock and key," he said, smiling.

Pound-cake playfully pushed him and said, "Don't even gas yourself, Ordeal."

The two hit it off again quickly, like ol' times, and Pound-cake wanted her personal time with him so she could break him off and get her some dick.

Ox finally came over to show her some love, and they hugged, and Ox told her that she looked good.

"Like a family reunion, huh, Pound-cake?" Ox said.

Pound-cake smiled.

"Yo, we onstage in ten minutes," Ox said to Ordeal.

"Ayyite," Ordeal replied.

Ordeal turned his attention back to Pound-cake and asked, "So, what you been up to since I was gone?"

But Pound-cake knew the true meaning behind his words, and she replied, "If you wanna know who I've been fuckin', then nobody."

Ordeal smiled and said, "So, you saving it for me, baby?"

"Don't flatter yourself," she said with a slight smile.

Ordeal eyed Pound-cake down, thinking about that pussy and how tight it must be since she'd been good for four months now. Tonight, Ordeal considered himself a lucky man. But on the road, he fucked countless of women with his boys and didn't once think about Pound-cake, until he ran into her at the Lab. And having her in his sights, he was ready to skip the performance with Ox and go sin for the night.

"Yo, Ordeal, c'mon, we 'bout to get on," Mason shouted.

"Ayyite, nigga, I'm comin'," Ordeal shouted. He pulled Pound-cake close to him and said, "Yo, after I do this show, we fuckin' out."

"It's whateva," Pound-cake replied indifferently.

Ordeal smiled and went off to do what he was paid to do,

be Ox's hype man in front of hundreds, or sometimes thousands, of people.

Pound-cake watched him and took a few sips from her Long Island iced tea.

"You goin' home with him tonight, right?" Sabrina asked, as she walked up to Pound-cake.

"Maybe . . ." Pound-cake replied.

"Please, bitch, I see you throwin' it at dat nigga. Don't get silly. And I know you ain't had none in months," Sabrina said coolly.

"So you think you know my business," Pound-cake said, still kind of upset that she brought Shanice through. "You gonna do you, and I might do me."

Pound-cake then walked off to watch Ox, Ordeal, and a few others perform. The stage was crowded with hood niggas dancing, drinking, and staring down at the crowd of hundreds who waited to see a show.

Pound-cake watched from behind as Ox and Ordeal began to get into their performance, but her eyes were mostly on Ordeal, as she watched him frolic around onstage with the mike in one hand, and a cup filled with some dark liquor in the next.

"Yo, is Brooklyn in da muthafuckin' house tonight?!" Ordeal shouted into the mike.

"Hells yeah . . . Brooklyn!" the crowd shouted.

"Where my muthafuckin' gangsters at?!" Ordeal shouted out.

The crowd of men started screaming, getting rowdy, and throwing their hands in the air, some displaying their gang's signs, some displaying that they were Bloods or Crips.

"Yo, where my ladies at?" Ordeal shouted out next.

The ladies went berserk, screaming and yelling and craving for the attention of the niggas that were onstage doin' their thang.

Ordeal smiled down at a few honeys, wanting to get busy with a few before night's end. "Yo, what bitches in here got love for Ox and me, and the whole muthafuckin' crew that is gettin' money," he shouted.

The ladies screamed and yelled out, "We love you, Ox. We love you, Ordeal."

Soon Ordeal fell back and Ox stepped up, and the crowd got loud and thunderous. Ox stood in front of hundreds with a strong stage presence. He pulled up his jeans barely, with his gleaming long chain dangling from his neck, and looked like a thug straight out of Rikers. He gripped the mike in his hand and yelled out, "Brook-lyn!"

The ladies screamed. Soon the beat to one of his hit singles blared throughout the club, and when the fans heard the beat to "Real Niggaz Do Real Thangs!" the Lab got loud, crazy, and hyped.

Ox started rhyming into the mike, screaming out, "Real niggaz do real thangs, real niggaz get beef, fuck it, we ain't scared to put a nigga to sleep/you step up, come creep through C.I., and end up toe tag, stamped DOA . . . . fuck what you heard, I done made Rikers a second home, had five-oh crashed through my door/pissed on wars/ done flipped so many birds, they call me the wing man/untouchable like the wind/unbreakable like Bruce Willis/we done fucked many bitches, fucked up many nigga/sold crack like I'm the ice-cream man, roll wit' the snub, knowing how to make a nigga bleed and twitch, soon to hear him breathing soft, like a bitch comin' home after curfew, creepin' wit' her sneakers off . . . yo, I know I'm living kind of wild/but who's gonna tell/snitches get stitches/so I do my little dealing/trying to make this million/give my kids a better living/get up out this wicked shit/do my little dirt/so later I can feel like I'm living above the earth/and if you start trippin'/that's when I start flipping/and my forty-five starts hitting/tires start screeching/ Timbs and sneakers start fleeing/'cause they hear shots ring-

ing/ somebody's creeping/this game ain't never easy/every day somebody's bleeding/ just a few niggas getting a little too greedy . . ."

"Yeah, 'cuz real niggaz do real things," Ordeal screamed out, moving and dancing behind Ox, as the crowd got hyped off his lyrics.

Pound-cake nodded to the beat, knowing that Ox and his crew were definitely coming up, because his rhymes were tight and he definitely knew how to move a crowd.

Pound-cake watched as Ordeal looked down at the ladies and even pulled a few onstage to join the show. She wasn't jealous, because she knew once his performance was over, he was coming back home with her to handle his business.

Ox soon went on to perform "Straight Out of Rikers"; it was an East Coast mix from the popular N.W.A. West Coast group's version "Straight Outta Compton" in Ox's own words with the same beat blaring.

The crowd loved it and moved around wildly. The show went on for forty minutes strong, giving the crowd their money's worth.

Pound-cake watched Ordeal become sweaty and hyped as he grinded behind a few bitches, molesting two, and then sending them on their way with their panties moist. He never missed a beat as he rhymed aside with Ox, and was definitely a good hype man.

The ladies screamed out his name, loved his thuggish ways, and Ordeal continued to disrespect them by lobbing his drink down into the crowd, spilling out Hennessy into their hairs, faces, and gear, and laughed about it. Some took it lightly, and a handful of the ladies became tight-faced and trotted off.

Ordeal laughed, grabbed a towel from his man, wiped his sweaty face, and before he walked off the stage, he shouted out, "Coney Island, Brooklyn . . . we don't give a fuck! We about to go fuck!"

His peoples laughed and gave Ordeal dap.

Ordeal then headed back to where Pound-cake was standing. He walked up to her with this confident and wild demeanor and pulled Pound-cake into his arms and said, "Yo, I'm ready to be out. I need some pussy."

Pound-cake was down. It had been months for her, and even though she witnessed Ordeal's vulgar act onstage with the women, she didn't care, because she knew how Ordeal got down.

At times, he could be a bully and a loudmouth, and got carried away with his wild street ways. Like Ox, he was a thug first, a killer next, and being a hype man was least on his list. He partied hard, fucked bitches like a porn star, did drugs, committed murders, robbed dozens of dealers and innocents, and took care of none of his children—some knew that Ordeal was living on borrowed time.

Pound-cake walked over to tell her girls that she was leaving with Ordeal. They all smiled and told her to have fun and enjoy that dick. Her friends were tipsy and were soon ready to commit sinful acts of their own, especially Sabrina and Lady Rah, who had their partners around.

Pound-cake followed Ordeal out of the club, and the two soon caught a cab back to Coney Island. It was after three in the morning when they both trotted into the lobby of Pound-cake's building and rushed into her crib with a hunger burning for each other.

Ordeal cared nothing of how her place looked or smelled, his main focus was pussy. He followed Pound-cake into her bedroom and closed the door behind him. Pound-cake pulled at the thin chain that led up to the single sixty-watt bulb in the ceiling fixture. Her room came to view and it was nothing much to see.

Ordeal quickly pressed himself against Pound-cake, groping her ass and nibbling at her neck. Pound-cake moaned, feeling Ordeal's touch after four months. Her body tingled as she felt his hand tunnel down into her jeans and stroked her smooth-shaven mound.

Pound-cake licked his earlobe tenderly, as Ordeal unfastened her tight-fitted capris, and slowly began pulling them down her thighs. Soon her pink and red panties followed, and Ordeal ogled at her seminude curvy figure in the flesh. Pound-cake stood in front of Ordeal still in her hot pink halter top, but from the bottom down, her nude curves and smooth cocoa-brown skin was making Ordeal extra hard. Pound-cake's legs were defined like a gold medal gymnast and her ass was phat and tight, showing no pimples, stretch marks, or cellulite. Ordeal knew he was the envy of all of C.I., because seeing Pound-cake naked and knowing he was about to fuck was something almost every nigga around the way tried to do. But Pound-cake was a rough catch, and many wondered and fantasized what she looked like without the sweats and T-shirts.

Ordeal began unbuckling his pants, and wanted one thing done at the moment—a blow job. He pulled Pound-cake toward him and asked, "Baby, can you do me that favor?" He asked with Pound-cake, but if it was any other bitch, they were forced to suck his dick whether they wanted to or not. He was a brute and didn't give a fuck about a bitch's feelings.

But Ordeal knew that when dealing with Pound-cake, you had to respect her, or she'll cut a nigga and a bitch.

Pound-cake gently tugged at his size. Ordeal was hanging with the big boys, with his eight-and-a-half-inch dick that he boasted about on tracks and to bitches. Pound-cake got down on her knees, having Ordeal tower over her with a serious hard-on. She then moved his goods to her lips and gently began sucking on the tip of his shaft, her tongue coiling around the head of his dick like a snake.

"Umm," Ordeal moaned, feeling the moisture of her jaws travel down the circumference of his dick. He threw his head back and allowed for Pound-cake to do her business. He had both his hands placed on his hips and watched Pound-cake's head bob back and forth, with his huge size disappearing into her mouth like a long train entering a tunnel.

"Fuck this," Ordeal said. He stood her up and removed her top, revealing her soft tits with her nickel-sized nipples looking like they were dipped in Hershey chocolate.

Pound-cake came up to him and wrapped her arms around Ordeal and began tonguing him down. Ordeal pressed his fingers against her ass and backed her toward the bed. He pushed her down on her back, having Pound-cake spread her long, shapely legs for him, with her pussy looking trimmed, pink and sweet like a bed of roses.

Ordeal removed the remaining clothing he had on and climbed on top of Pound-cake, cupping her juicy tits, and he slowly pushed himself into her, causing Pound-cake to moan and scratch at his back. Inch by inch, he slowly pushed himself into her, opening her up walls gradually. She had no issue fuckin' him raw, because she had love for him like that.

"Mmm, Mmm," Pound-cake moaned, as she felt his thick dick rooted into her like a tree trunk. She straddled him, still on her back and felt his rough thrust as they shook her small mattress.

Ordeal fucked and handled her like the thug he was. He gripped her thighs forcefully, sucked on her Hershey nipples, with his knees sinking into the bed.

Without warning, he pulled out, flipped Pound-cake over into the doggy-style position and began tearing it up from the back, as Pound-cake's hands clasped flat against her bedroom walls. Ordeal pounded into her, smacking her ass red from the back, both of them sweating it out.

Their moans and screams traveled outside the bedroom and carried into Mary's room. But Mary cared nothing about her daughter's rough sexual act. She was in a dope nod, her eyes barely open, with her back against the tattered brown dresser, and the bloody syringe still between her fingertips. And every so often, she would scratch at her neck and look around.

For both mother and daughter, they were in their own heaven for the night.

*   *   *

It was noon when Pound-cake and Ordeal woke up off each other, still naked in the flesh. Last night was crazy for Pound-cake. She knew she dumb out, allowing Ordeal to fuck her raw continuously and when he came, he never pulled out. She wasn't stupid and knew the chances of her getting pregnant by Ordeal were great. He already had four baby mothers, and the nigga's sperm was potent like some high-grade weed. But she didn't stress it. If she was pregnant, then so be it. She had options.

"You good, baby?" Pound-cake asked, staring at Ordeal.

"Yeah . . . shit, what time is it?" he asked, raising up and looking for his watch or cell phone. He rummaged through his clothing and found his Nextel. "Damn, I gotta meet this nigga Ox in da city by one. Fuck!"

He noticed that he had four missed calls, and all of them coming from Ox. He began getting dressed.

Pound-cake followed, throwing her shit together, knowing that she wasn't going to spend the day in the apartment. She wanted to spend some time with Ordeal and hoped that she could come with him to the city.

She rushed into the bathroom, brushed her teeth and washed her ass, and put on some baggy jeans, Timbs, and a T-shirt, her usual.

Ordeal was ready to head out the door when Pound-cake walked out the bathroom.

"I wanna come with you," she said.

"Damn, baby, that ain't happening. I'm gonna be in da city all day taking care of business and I don't need you tagging along. Besides, this is grown folks' business," he proclaimed.

But Ordeal didn't want her to come, because he was meeting some fine groupie bitch in Harlem after the meeting.

"What?" Pound-cake replied, catching a slight attitude.

"I'm saying, don't get mad. I'll be back to scoop you up later tonight, and we can continue to do our thang then. Ayyite, boo?"

"Fuck you, Ordeal!"

Ordeal smiled and said, "C'mon, Pound-cake, don't even be like that wit' me."

Pound-cake knew Ordeal done changed a lot. He'd been an asshole with others in the hood since forever, but when it came to her, he never gave her the runaround. And she knew he was giving her the runaround.

"Yo, let me take you down to the deli and buy you breakfast before I bounce," he suggested.

Pound-cake couldn't refuse the offer. She was hungry and only had five dollars on her. "Fine . . . whatever."

Pound-cake got her shit together and walked out the apartment with Ordeal. She locked her door and turned only to see Sick quickly disappearing into the pissy staircase. She thought nothing of it at first, thinking Sick was high and probably came to the wrong floor looking for Big Jerry for a hit. Like her mother, Sick was a junkie, and was known to be kin to Double-tap, a notorious assassin in the hood, and was one of Brooklyn's deadliest dozen.

Sick was a beanpole-looking figure, with gaunt features and almost no teeth in his mouth. He looked a hot mess with his uncombed hair and clothing sagging off his thin frame. But nobody messed with Sick, because they knew he was kin to Double-tap. And Double-tap had Brooklyn locked down with fear.

Ordeal and Pound-cake walked toward the elevator, both of them quiet. Ordeal wanted to head back to his crib and change clothes for the day, knowing that it wasn't cool to be in the same gear that he performed in and got sweaty in from last night.

When the elevator came to their floor, Pound-cake stepped into the foul-smelling elevator first, then Ordeal. Ordeal pressed for the lobby floor, and when the entrance closed, he handed Pound-cake two C-notes and said, "Take care of yourself today, baby. You know I always got you."

She smiled and nodded, no longer upset with him. Pound-cake stood off to the left, standing a short distance away from the door and peered at Ordeal and all of his finesse, as he slightly leaned against the elevator wall as it descended. He had his hands in his jean pockets, and his posture was somewhat laid-back, but he still had that thuggish demeanor about him. Her pussy made him calm for the moment. He was definite eye candy in Pound-cake's eyes and many other women's.

"So, I'm gonna see you tonight again, Ordeal?" she asked. She definitely wanted some dick again.

"Fo' sure, boo. You know I missed it, and you," he joked.

Both of them weren't aware of the lift coming to a stop at the second floor. The thick door began sliding back into the walls of the second floor, as Ordeal had his eyes on Pound-cake and thought about that pussy. It was too good to him, and if he was to ever become faithful to one bitch, Pound-cake was the number-one contender for his loyalty. She knew how to fuck, her pussy was so good, and she kept it clean and tight for him. And she was a down-ass bitch, fo' sure.

Ordeal displayed a warm smile over to her and Pound-cake smiled back. The elevator now had access to the second floor, and instead of somebody stepping in, Pound-cake's world shook abruptly when a burst of gunfire exploded into the lift, lighting up the small corner, as she witnessed a barrage of gunshots tear into Ordeal viciously.

Boom! Boom! Boom! Boom! Boom! Boom! Boom! Pound-cake continually heard, as the gunfire seemed endless. She witnessed Ordeal collapse, his blood painting the walls. The gunfire was deafening in such close quarters. She couldn't help but to shriek, fearing she was next, with her back pressed against the cold walls of the foul-smelling elevator.

Double-tap walked in, his harrowing figure looming over the body. He was clad in jeans, Timberlands, a wrinkled white T-shirt under a black denim jacket. He gripped the smoking

Desert Eagle tightly. He glared at the shocked Pound-cake, knowing her face.

Pound-cake stared back, not knowing what to do, thinking she was next. She saw Sick not too far behind Double-tap and knew it was a hit.

Double-tap raised his index finger to his lips, indicating for her to be quiet about this. He was dark, with short nappy hair, and was good at what he did—murder.

Pound-cake just stood there and watched Double-tap back out of the lift, the big gun still gripped in his hand and walked away casually, like he didn't leave Ordeal contorted and full with holes on the soiled lift floors.

Pound-cake stared down at Ordeal's lifeless body and staggered toward the doorway. She still had the money he gave her clenched in her fist and felt helpless. She knew she couldn't stick around, knowing that there was nothing she could do for him now. She shook her head and scattered toward the stairway, making her way back into her apartment.

Ordeal had made too many enemies and robbed too many niggas in his twenty-four-year lifespan. He had a contract out on his head that he was unaware of, and word quickly got around that he was back in town to perform with Ox. Ordeal had angered and upset some dangerous, high-profile men in the drug game and made them lose thousands of dollars. They didn't care that he was talented on the mike and was soon to sign a lucrative deal with a record label. They wanted their money back, or his life—and they settled with taking his life.

Pound-cake rushed into her crib and made a beeline for the bathroom, where she dropped down to her knees and began hurling chunks into the toilet. Watching her friend, her lover, get gunned down made her stomach churn, and she couldn't hold it in any longer.

With her head still hovering over the toilet, it actually began to hit her: Ordeal was dead and gone, and last night

was the final night they would ever spend together. She cried and hurled into the toilet again, while her mother was still high and lost in the bedroom.

Joy held Lady Rah's six-month baby boy, Taiwan, comfortably in her arms, nursing him with the warm bottle while hearing the loud pants and moans coming from the bedroom. Her friend, Lady Rah, was turning a trick in the next room, while Joy watched her son on the couch.

Joy didn't mind babysitting in the same apartment that Lady Rah was doing her business. To her it was common, and she was getting fifty bucks for her babysitting services.

Taiwan drank from the bottle and closed his infant eyes, hearing the raving sexual sounds of his mother being fucked like a hog only a few feet away.

Lady Rah was bent over the bed, her panties lying around her ankles, her shirt pulled up to her chest exposing her huge tits, as they jiggled from the force of the thrust her trick inflicted onto her. She cried out, clutching the bedsheets, feeling Jake's hands pressed against her sides as he fucked her and sweated profusely from his brow.

"I'm coming!" he exclaimed. He soon exploded into the condom that was entrenched deeply into her.

He sighed with relief and fell on his back against her bed, looking spent. Lady Rah pulled up her panties, and pulled down her shirt and collected the five twenties Jake had spread out for her.

"Yo, what's up wit' your girl, Joy? She fuckin' or what?" Jake asked, looking up at Lady Rah.

"I got you, Jake. I'm gonna get her to get wit' the program," Lady Rah said, trying to pimp Joy for some extra cash.

Jake had been dying to get at Joy for the longest, admiring her wicked petite figure, and wanted to taste that pussy. Lady Rah had been promising him a threesome with the both of them soon.

Jake collected his clothing and began getting dressed, and was ready to go back home to his wife and kids.

As Lady Rah searched for a pair of jeans to throw on, she heard a burst of police sirens blaring from outside. She looked outside her bedroom window and saw hordes of police cars parked in front of Pound-cake's building.

"Something happened," she said, rushing to get dressed.

Joy heard the sirens too and was peering outside the window, with Taiwan asleep in the bassinet.

Lady Rah came rushing outside her bedroom with Jake right behind her and exclaimed, "Sumthin' went down, Joy."

The two ladies were curious to see what happened so early in the afternoon. Jake wanted to get home to his family, while Lady Rah put on some clothes and was ready to go see what the action was about.

She was near the door, right behind Jake, when Joy shouted out, "What about Taiwan?"

Lady Rah looked over at her sleeping baby boy and said, "He's good. He ain't gonna wake no time soon. Besides, we ain't but gonna be up da street."

"Lady Rah, he's only six months," Joy said.

"And . . . you know he ain't goin' anywhere. The lil' nigga can't even walk yet. And he just ate too. He good, Joy."

Joy looked at her sideways, not agreeing with what she wanted to do. Joy didn't have any kids of her own, and if she did, she damn sure wouldn't be leaving her son home alone. Even though Taiwan wasn't hers, she loved him like he was her own. And she questioned Lady Rah's motherly method sometimes.

"What you lookin' at me like that for? You got a problem wit' what I do wit' my son?" Lady Rah barked.

"Not even," Joy lied.

"So c'mon . . . he's good, Joy. I wanna see what happened."

"Nah, you go ahead. I'll stay and continue to watch Taiwan. It's what you're paying me to do, right," she said, walking back over to the bassinet.

"Fuck it, I'm out," Lady Rah said, running out the door without giving it a second thought.

Joy watched her friend Lady Rah leave and sucked her teeth. Joy was more of a mother to Taiwan than his own mother. Lady Rah turned tricks while her son was in the same room sometimes. She cursed in front of Taiwan, and when someone would correct her on it, her excuse was, "That lil' nigga don't understand what da fuck we sayin' . . . he a fuckin' baby." And she easily smoked weed and cigarettes with her own infant son in the room.

And she left her child with anyone, so she could be able to go out and have a good time—smoking, fucking, fighting, and carrying on like all hell.

Joy looked down at sleeping Taiwan and smiled. "You good, lil' man. Auntie Joy got your back."

She then walked to the window and noticed hordes of people running over to Pound-cake's building to see what the commotion was about. With so much police activity happening, she knew either one or two things: there was a body—or some bodies—or a cop got shot. She glanced over at Taiwan and said, "Welcome to the ghetto."

Lady Rah was mixed in with the large crowd that stood behind the police barricade. Dozens of police and detectives combed the area looking for evidence and witnesses to the murder. Everyone was curious, everyone was nosy, but nobody knew a thing and was helpless to give the police any information about what happened.

"What happened?" Lady Rah kept asking.

"Somebody got bodied just now. I heard they shot him as

he was coming off the elevator," a local bystander informed her.

"Oh word . . . damn," Lady Rah replied.

Everyone wanted to know who it was that got murdered. It was still early afternoon, and even though crime and murders were common in C.I., it was still stimulating news to hear of a murder or murders happening.

"This is body town, fo' sure," a young local thug proudly proclaimed, throwing up his gang signs in front of the police.

Lady Rah waited patiently with the others, waiting to see the body being brought out. She took a few pulls from her cigarette and thought about Pound-cake, knowing that it was her building, and hoped she saw or knew something. She didn't see Pound-cake around and knew she had to be still in her crib fucking Ordeal. *Lucky bitch,* Lady Rah thought, knowing that Ordeal was going to break her off with a few hundreds before he left.

Soon, word was getting around as to who got murdered. A young kid of thirteen got wind of some information he overheard from the detectives and quickly passed it along to others. The detectives tried to keep the identity of the victim quiet, knowing who it was, because he had a long rap sheet with the 60th precinct and was much known throughout the community.

"Yo, is fuckin' Ordeal that got bodied, yo. He lying up on the second floor filled wit' holes and shit," he cried out to his boys.

"Get da fuck outta here, yo. You serious?"

"Nigga, they bodied him and shit. Cops don't wanna say shit, yo," the thirteen-year-old kid said.

Soon it spread from the group of young boys to among the onlookers outside of the barricade and then to Lady Rah.

"What?" she said, sounding shocked.

"It's Ordeal," a young woman repeated to her.

"Get da fuck outta here. You serious?" Lady Rah asked.

The girl nodded. And soon Lady Rah thought about Pound-cake and started to wonder if her homegirl was okay. She quickly removed herself from the crowd and headed back to her crib. She needed to call Sabrina and tell Joy what went down. Ordeal was dead, and God knows what happened to Pound-cake.

Mary finally removed herself from her bedroom with enough cash to get another high for the day. She knew nothing about the tragedy down on the second floor as she moved through the narrow hallway with having a fix on her mind.

Not caring about her daughter in the next room, she made her way out into the hallway and trotted down the stairs to the second floor. She soon came upon two police detectives who were probing the area of the murder. One was tall, like Snoop Dogg, wearing black slacks and a button-down, and his partner was a bit shorter, with a small gut and lighter skin. They both turned to look at her as she emerged from the staircase.

"You live in this building?" the taller detective asked, holding his pen and pad in his hand.

"Third floor," Mary responded, itching for a high and hoping that the police let her be.

"Forget it. She's the walkin' dead," his partner said, noticing the signs that she was a junkie.

They both turned away, but the taller one kept his eye on her somewhat. He watched her walk to a second-floor apartment, an apartment that the two had already knocked at to ask Big Jerry if he witnessed the shooting. But Big Jerry lied and said he was dead to the world when everything went down. Detectives Macomb and Johnson didn't quite believe him, or a few other neighbors they questioned. But they had to let it be. In the hood, no one ever wanted to talk or admit

that they witnessed a crime—no one wanted to be a labeled a snitch.

Mary knocked on Big Jerry's door, the police standing not too far behind her. She scratched at her neck and clutched a twenty-dollar bill in her hand.

Big Jerry heard the knocking and became irate, thinking that it was police again. He walked from the bedroom to the door in his tight wife beater and baggy sweats, saying to one of the dwellers in the apartment, "Muthafuckas are fuckin' up my business. Why dey had to go and murder dat nigga on this floor, and bring police to my fuckin' door? Niggas ain't got no fuckin' respect for business in this gotdamn place."

Big Jerry's apartment looked like something out of *Animal Kingdom* with the funky animal printed furniture, large house plants sprawling out, and having two large boas in two different glass confines.

He went to the door, looked through the small peephole and became more upset when he noticed Mary standing outside his door.

"This fuckin' bitch is gonna get me shut down," he cursed.

The knocking continued and he quickly opened the door and grabbed Mary by her arm, pulling her into the apartment. It would be the first time that she had ever been in his place.

"You gotta be the stupidest bitch on earth!" he screamed. "You don't see police out there, bitch?"

"Big Jerry, I need a fix badly," Mary replied, ignoring his rant.

Slap! Big Jerry swung and struck Mary with his huge open hand and had her crumple to the floor.

"Bitch, you don't come here when police is outside my door. You gonna get a nigga locked up. And I ain't tryin' to see Rikers," he proclaimed, standing over her with a scowl.

Mary coughed and tried to get up, but Big Jerry knocked her back down and said, "You ain't leaving here till ain't no

one in dat fuckin' hallway. Gina, take this bitch to the back bedroom and keep her quiet."

Gina got up off the couch and went over to Mary. She was more considerate than Big Jerry. She hunkered down next to Mary, grabbed her arm gently and said, "C'mon, baby, let's get you in da back before he kills you."

Mary got up and followed Gina into one of the back bedrooms.

Big Jerry went to the door and looked through the peephole again, eyeing the two detectives that were still out in the hallway along with a uniformed cop. He shook his head. "Niggas is always fuckin' up business," he shouted, and then took a long pull from his cancer stick. He turned and looked at Dee, and said, "Yo, when they leave from out dat fuckin' hallway, y'all take dat bitch from out this apartment and let her know, don't fuck up like dat again. I don't care how bad of a fix she needs."

He then walked away from the door, headed toward the master bedroom, scratching at his nuts and continued to watch *Family Guy* and guzzle down a forty-ounce he had on an end table next to his bed.

Sabrina and Lady Rah knocked on Pound-cake's door with a sense of urgency. Sabrina heard what happened to Ordeal and had to check her girl and see if she was okay.

"Pound-cake, open up, girl. Yo, you in there?" Sabrina shouted out, banging on the door like police.

Lady Rah stood behind her with the same worried look on her face.

"Pound-cake, open the fuckin' door!" Sabrina exclaimed.

"I know she in there. She gotta be," Lady Rah said.

Both ladies were relentless to find their friend and see if she was okay. Ordeal's murder spread throughout the hood like wildfire. Rumors started to pour around about who did it and why he was killed, but all were so far from the truth.

Late that afternoon, Ox came speeding up the block in his truck with his crew in tow, and he came running out and shouted, "Yo, what da fuck happened? Where he at? Where my nigga at?"

No one knew how to answer him; they were intimidated by him and the six-man crew he had standing behind him with the same murderous stares.

Two detectives walked over to question Ox and his peoples, but Ox was in no mood to talk to police after hearing about Ordeal being gunned down. He had guns stashed in his truck and was ready to throw away his entire music career for revenge.

But before shit got out of hand on the streets, the detectives promised to find out who was responsible for the killing and asked if Ox could come down to the station to answer some questions. He was hesitant and in a rage, and wanted to see blood spill, but his girl talked him out of it, calming him down some, and soon he and his entourage made their way over to the 60th precinct.

The projects were in an uproar with the police, the onlookers, with the morgue coming through to collect the body, and the gangsters and thugs wondering who took out Ordeal like that.

Sabrina and Lady Rah stayed behind and knocked continuously on Pound-cake's door, not giving up.

"Yo, just kick that shit it," Lady Rah suggested.

But Sabrina didn't want to disrespect Pound-cake's door like that, knowing that she still had to live there. With the both of them out of options, they were willing to camp outside her door until someone showed up, Pound-cake or her junkie mother.

Both ladies sat in front of the door and waited, talking about Ordeal and the shit that was poppin' off.

"Yo, where's Joy?" Sabrina asked.

"She in my crib watching my son," Lady Rah said.

Quickly changing the subject, Sabrina stated, "Yo, I swear, if anything happened to my girl, I'm gonna fuck shit up."

"I'm wit' you, girl," Lady Rah said, extending her hand and giving Sabrina dap, indicating that she definitely had her back.

The girls waited for an hour, talking and watching the neighbors come and go.

Soon Mary finally came looming out from the pissy concrete stairwell looking high and fucked-up. She shot up in Big Jerry's crib, which was a first for any junkie, because no one got high in his place. But Big Jerry needed her to be cool and calm down while the cops were still snooping around on his floor, and for that to happen she needed her fix. So he collected his twenty from her and passed her the product and allowed her to shoot up in the second bedroom.

But when the cops finally became ghost after the investigation, Big Jerry woke Mary up with a vulgar shake, disturbing her high and told her, "Get the fuck out."

Mary slowly came to her feet sluggishly, not wanting to anger Big Jerry any longer and made her way out, with Big Jerry following right behind her. Before she made her exit, he warned her again and then slammed the door behind her.

"Yo, where's your daughter?" Sabrina stood up and asked.

Mary stood in front of the two women, barely able to stand. She wanted to nod off and get ready for another fix. The two girls in front of her did not exist, because at that moment, the world to her was a blur, and if they weren't heroin, then everything was useless.

"Yo, this fuckin' bitch is high," Lady Rah said.

Sabrina sucked her teeth and took it upon herself to search Mary's pocket for any keys to the crib. She found a single key in her dirty sweats and wasted no time putting it in the lock, throwing open the door, and rushing into the place, hoping to find Pound-cake.

Lady Rah was right behind her, and both ladies hurried to

the bedroom and barged in to find Pound-cake lying in her bed, on her side, crying and clutching her pillow tightly.

"Damn, you ain't hear us knocking?" Lady Rah shouted.

"Yo, chill," Sabrina said, noticing Pound-cake's state. She walked over to the bed and sat down at the end, staring at Pound-cake, knowing that she heard the news about Ordeal, but wondered if she actually saw it happen.

"Pound-cake," Sabrina coolly called out.

The room was quiet for a moment, and then Sabrina said, "I know you heard, baby girl."

Pound-cake picked herself up and said, "I'm good."

"What happened?" Lady-Rah asked.

"They fuckin' shot him, and I was right there."

"What? Damn . . ." Lady Rah exclaimed.

"Who shot him?" Sabrina asked.

"Fuck it, yo . . . he's dead. He's dead," Pound-cake stated.

"Who shot him?" Sabrina wanted to know.

But Pound-cake knew the deal—they couldn't do shit if she told them anyway. Double-tap was a nigga they couldn't touch even if they wanted to. He was feared, skillful, and respected. And she knew if Double-tap came at Ordeal, then Ordeal fucked up somewhere and it had to be about money and business.

"You saw who did it?" Lady Rah asked eagerly. She just wanted to know, because it was a juicy secret to know, but she wasn't a snitch.

"Nah, I ain't see no face. They just shot him up from a distance while I was standing in the corner," Pound-cake proclaimed.

"Damn," Sabrina uttered.

"So, you ain't see who did it?" Lady Rah said, sounding frustrated.

Sabrina cut her eyes at her, and Lady Rah just fell back

and sighed. Sabrina held Pound-cake's hand gently and tried to comfort her the best she could.

The three sat in the room and watched TV and let it be. The night continued on, and it was only the second week of the summer, and things were already heating up.

The Holy Cross Cemetery was filled with folks from all over to see Ordeal buried. It looked like everyone from all of Coney Island was present, and Ox and his crew came over four-dozen deep to send Ordeal off the right way. Ordeal's death was all over the Internet and hit the evening news. No one knew who the killer was, but everyone had their speculations.

Pound-cake and her crew stood among the crowd, clad in their dark denim skirts and black T-shirts that displayed Ordeal's image. It was a quick memorial they put together for him. Their eyes were teary, as they stood isolated from the immediate family and looked at the flower-covered casket and heard the preacher say a few words before the body was lowered.

The pastor clutched the Bible in his hands and proclaimed, "But start out bravely with a gallant smile; and for my sake and in my name, live and do all things the same. Feed not your loneliness on empty days. But fill each useful hour in useful ways. Reach out your hand in comfort and in cheer, and I, in turn, will comfort you and in cheer, and I, in turn, will comfort you and hold you near. And never . . . never be afraid to die, for I am waiting for you in the sky.

"May Patrick Ronald Mitchell rest in peace and find comfort in the Lord . . . ashes to ashes and dust to dust, we return this body back into the dust . . . Amen."

After his prayer, Pound-cake turned and saw Double-tap and Sick standing from a distance and observing the cere-

mony. She frowned at their sight, and the display of him brought back the memories of how Ordeal was murdered.

"You okay?" Sabrina asked, standing by her side.

"I'm good," Pound-cake said, remaining strong on the outside.

After the pastor said his words, the casket began to lower, and Sabrina, Pound-cake, Joy, and Lady Rah watched Ordeal's sisters, cousins, and his elderly grandmother cry out loud.

"I'm out. I can't take this shit anymore," Pound-cake said, strutting off from the ceremony.

Sabrina and the rest quickly followed, agreeing with Pound-cake. They caught a cab back to Coney Island, shed their clothing at Sabrina's crib, and lit a blunt to lift their spirits somewhat.

"Yo, anyone see Minnie around lately?" Pound-cake asked with concern.

"Nah, not really," Joy said, taking a pull from the haze.

With the chaos happening, Minnie had been out of the loop a few days, and it hit Pound-cake suddenly and she became worried about her girl.

"Yo, we need to go check on her," Pound-cake suggested.

"It's whateva, yo . . . but right now, I'm chillin'," Lady Rah said, slouching down on the couch and drinking E &J straight from the bottle.

Pound-cake took a few more pulls, closed her eyes and fell asleep on Sabrina's couch. The first thing tomorrow morning, she was going to check Minnie and see if she was okay. She was too high and too emotional to go anywhere for the night, so she ended up spending the night at Sabrina's.

The next morning, Pound-cake was the first to leave. She trotted over to her building to wash her ass and change clothes and then was right back out the door over to Minnie's place.

On the second floor of her building was a small memorial near the elevator decorated with flowers, candles, and pictures of Ordeal. A group of residents tried to keep his memory alive, regardless of his notorious reputation in the community.

Pound-cake hastily walked through Gravesend housing, and crossed the street over to the high-rises. She made it to the ninth floor and knocked on Minnie's door.

"Who?" she heard Minnie call out from inside the apartment.

"Minnie, open the door. It's me, Pound-cake."

Slowly, Minnie opened the door and took a step back and allowed Pound-cake entry to the place. Minnie had her head lowered to the floor, as she meekly stood behind the door and watched her best friend walk in.

Minnie no longer sported her cute long pigtails, but had her hair falling down to her shoulders, and parts of her hair were concealing her bruised and swollen eye. She stood behind Pound-cake looking docile, her lively spirit broken by Winter's uncontrollable abuse and mistreatment of her. She hadn't seen her friends in a week, but that was because Winter tried to have her under lock and key. He fucked her, and then was pimping her for some extra cash that he truly didn't need, since he was working the block for Pain, and had a sizable income coming in daily.

But he pimped Minnie because he could. The other day, he had Duck and June come by to fuck Minnie anyway they wanted for a hundred apiece. And Duck and June didn't hesitate to get at the young, pregnant sixteen-year-old.

Both men had followed behind Winter as he walked into the apartment with a treacherous grin on his face. He had his own keys to Minnie's place, and supplied both her parents with crack and ruled that household like it was his own.

"Minnie, where you at?" Winter had called out.

Hearing his voice, Minnie became petrified, but knew not to keep him waiting and calling out for her too long. She had rushed out her bedroom, draped in a long white T-shirt and some fuzzy slippers. She ran up the short flight of steps and saw Winter waiting for her in a wife beater and baggy Sean John jeans. She then saw Duck and June and knew of their perverted and nasty reputation.

Winter looked at Minnie for a short moment and then said, "Yo, I need for you to handle some business for me."

"What kind of business?" Minnie asked frightfully.

"Yo, don't fuckin' talk back to me, just do what da fuck I say," Winter scolded.

He then turned to Duck and June and said, "Y'all niggas give me my money and don't leave too many marks on my bitch."

Duck and June both passed him a C-note and then smiled at the young Minnie.

Winter looked at Minnie and said, "Yo, you be a good girl and treat my niggas right, you hear?"

Minnie nodded submissively.

But then Winter noticed her unwilling attitude and stepped to her. "Yo, give me a minute," he said to Duck and June. He pulled her into the bathroom and instead of beating on her, surprisingly he said, "You know I love you, right?"

Minnie nodded.

"Yo, I just want you to make some money for the baby, and do what you gotta do, you hear me, baby? Believe me, after the baby is born, it's gonna be good for you and me. I'm gonna take care of you, baby, like I always do. Don't I take care of you?"

Minnie nodded.

"You love me?" Winter asked.

Minnie nodded.

"You trust me, baby?"

Minnie nodded.

"Ayyite." He grabbed Minnie by her chin and held it firmly, staring at her. "So, just fuck these two niggas and call me when they're done. Handle your fuckin' business, Minnie."

He then walked out of the bathroom and told Duck and June that she was ready. Winter shut the apartment door behind him and smiled at his work.

Duck and June wasted no time getting at Minnie. Both their dicks got hard as they gazed at her in her bedtime attire and couldn't wait to strip and feast on Minnie the way they wanted to.

Minnie was extremely nervous. They pushed her on the couch, and Duck began shedding his clothes immediately. June was all over Minnie, licking her from head to toe like a lollipop, his hand squeezing her succulent breast. He stuck his fingers deep into her creamy walls and bit the side of her thigh, causing Minnie to let out a loud cry.

"Chill, bitch, it ain't gonna hurt much," Duck said, jerking his eight-inch erection as he watched his boy molest Minnie on the couch.

Soon, the two were all over Minnie like ants at a picnic. They removed her T-shirt and had her butt naked on the couch. They both were ready to fuck, but that was boring for their taste. They wanted to add some thrill to the threesome.

June had two candles that he bought with him burning on the dilapidated coffee table. When the candles were about to liquefy, he took one of them and held it over Minnie's snatch. Duck held the frightened teen by her arms forcefully and watched as the hot candle began dripping down onto her shaved pussy.

"Aaaaaahh," Minnie cried out, feeling the hot wax splash against her pussy. "Ouch . . . ouch!"

Her panicicked young, sweet voice was turning both men on, and June was hard like steel. He was nine inches in length and gripped his immense dick in one hand, while still

She loved Winter and cried when she thought about the abuse and rape she'd just tolerated. She thought about her baby, and what Duck and June did to her, violating her without a second thought, and at that moment, Minnie thought about giving her own self an abortion with a hanger.

Pound-cake noticed Minnie's place. It was much worse than her apartment, and reeked. "Damn, Minnie, how you living? You okay?" Pound-cake asked, turning to face her.

Minnie still stood by the door, her head lowered to the floor, looking docile like a deer. The past week had been hell to her. Winter couldn't stay off of her, and if they weren't fucking, then he used her as a punching bag. And if he wasn't beating her, then he was pimping her. She couldn't get any peace.

And her parents were no help either. They were constantly high, or yelling at Minnie for dumb shit.

"Minnie, you okay?" Pound-cake asked. She walked up to Minnie and noticed the change. Pound-cake's face suddenly tightened when she noticed the bruised and swollen eye behind the mess of long hair. She grabbed Minnie by her arms and exclaimed, "That nigga Winter beat you like that?"

Minnie was quiet, and frightened to tell her business, even to a close friend.

"Minnie, you better talk to me," Pound-cake said, staring at Minnie with fire in her eyes. "He beat you like this, right? I'm gonna kill him."

"Pound-cake, no!" Minnie cried out.

"Fuck you mean, no!"

"He's gonna know you was here. He's gonna know we talked," Minnie stated frightfully.

"What, he don't want you around us?"

"He says you and Sabrina are a bad influence on me," she said.

"What? Bitch, open your fuckin' eyes. You can't continue to keep living like this. Fuck Winter! I'm gonna beat that

nigga down!" Pound-cake shouted. "What da fuck he did to you?"

Minnie burst into tears and fell into Pound-cake's arms. Pound-cake helped her over to the couch and wanted to know what happened. Minnie was always talkative and lively. But now she looked like the walking dead and had never been so hesitant to talk to her best friend and let her know everything. Winter put the fear of hell in her, and Pound-cake needed to change that.

But, eventually, Minnie opened up to Pound-cake again and explained the hell that she'd been going through the past week. She told Pound-cake about the beatings, the fucking, and the freaky sadistic shit that she endured with Duck and June. She even had the marks and burns to prove it.

Pound-cake was furious, and was boiling over with grief and anger. First she lost Ordeal, but she be damned if she was to lose her friend Minnie to nonsense and by the hands of Winter.

"Get your shit, Minnie. You coming to stay wit' me," Pound-cake stated.

"But, Pound-cake, I can't," Minnie protested.

"Fuck that you-can't shit. He ain't putting his hands on you anymore. Get your shit, Minnie." Pound-cake wasn't taking no for an answer, as she went into Minnie's bedroom and started grabbing things of hers and stuffing them into a black trash bag.

Minnie followed behind Pound-cake, looking reluctant. But she knew when Pound-cake's mind was made up, there was no changing it. She followed behind Pound-cake out of the apartment, watching Pound-cake clutch the weighed-down trash bag filled with clothing, items, shoes, and everything else. Minnie was scared that they may run into Winter, but he was nowhere around.

Soon, Minnie and Pound-cake entered the apartment and Pound-cake let her stay in her bedroom, where she knew Minnie would be safe for the moment.

For once, Minnie's mind felt at ease, as she sat on Pound-cake's bed and stared at the old colored TV propped up on a small old brown dresser.

"I'll be back, Minnie. Just stay tight, ayyite," Pound-cake said.

Minnie nodded.

With that, Pound-cake made her way back out the door and strutted out of the lobby with a burning rage ignited within her. Her eyes were black, and all she could think about was Ordeal's death, and Minnie's uncalled-for abuse at the hands of Winter. She went looking for Winter.

She found Winter a half-hour later chilling with a few of his peoples in front of the high-rises on Neptune Avenue. He was looking smug as he gambled, rolling dice and drinking some Olde E. She was never scared of Winter or his crew, and she was on a mission to do to Winter what many were afraid to even think of.

On her way over to him, with Winter trained in her sights, she picked up an empty beer bottle and clutched it tightly in her fist. Winter and his crew were all enthralled by the dice game to even notice Pound-cake coming their way—they were all gambling so hard, and so much money was up for grabs, that no one wanted to turn from the game. Winter gripped a handful of hundred-dollar bills in his hand and shook the dice feverishly in his fist with the forty-ounce bottle near his feet. He rolled a straight three and cursed himself, picking up the bottle and taking a swig from it.

Pound-cake marched over to the thugs and their game, not even giving her actions a second thought. She was sick of Winter's shit.

With his back turned from her, along with his crew, staring down at the game, Pound-cake leisurely jogged up behind Winter, leaped, and bashed the beer bottle across Winter's head, catching him and everyone by surprise.

"What da fuck!" Winter cursed, dropping money and his beer to the concrete, as he grabbed the back of his head where Pound-cake cut him with the bottle and had him bleeding.

"Fuck you, you bitch-ass nigga!" Pound-cake shrieked, as she continued her onslaught at Winter.

"Yo, yo . . . shortie, chill da fuck out," one of Winter's people shouted, grabbing Pound-cake by the waist and pulling her away from Winter.

The game instantly stopped, of course, and the attention was on Pound-cake. Winter became furious. His hand was coated with blood, and with his eyes beaded at Pound-cake, he wanted to kill that bitch. "Bitch, is you fuckin' crazy? I'll fuckin' murder you, bitch!" he screamed, charging for Pound-cake, reaching for his gun.

But Pound-cake was far from intimidated by him. She tried to free herself from one of Winter's people's grasp and go at him some more. But before Winter and her could go to war with each other, Moe grabbed Winter and said, "Chill, niggah, not here."

"Fuck that bitch!" Winter continued to scream out.

"Stay da fuck away from Minnie, you bitch-ass nigga. Keep your fuckin' hands off her, nigga! I ain't fuckin' scared of your bitch ass. You like to hit women . . . hit me, nigga! I dare you to put your fuckin' hands on me!" Pound-cake yelled out.

"Fuck you, you dyke bitch!" Winter screamed, with Moe still keeping him distant from Pound-cake. "You wanna play bitch, ayyite . . . you ain't got Ordeal to watch your back anymore, bitch! I'm gonna fuck you up, bitch!"

By now, they were causing a scene on the street, and Moe knew not to attract too much attention, because he was dirty along with everyone else. "Yo, Pound-cake, get da fuck outta here!" Moe shouted, pushing Winter back.

"Tell your boy to stay da fuck away from Minnie. I ain't

playing," she warned, glaring Winter down from a short distance.

Some of Winter's men were laughing at the incident, saying to themselves that Pound-cake was definitely a crazy
bitch and had heart to step to Winter like that. They admired
her even more.

Moe dragged the cursing and furious Winter away and
pushed him into the parked truck and was ready to take him
to the hospital to see if he needed any stitches. He drove off
hastily, knowing that the beef between his boy and Pound-
cake was far from over.

Pound-cake glared at the speeding Escalade and wished
she could have done more damage to that nigga Winter.

Vaio and Dejon were the only two of Winter's crew to stay
around. They stared at Pound-cake with much respect and
joked, "Yo, Pound cake, if shit ever pop off, you gotta have
my back."

Pound-cake sighed and walked off, heading back home,
feeling her mission was somewhat accomplished, and knowing that by tomorrow everyone in the projects was going to
hear what just went down.

Sabrina took a long pull from the burning haze and joked
to Lady Rah and Joy about how Pound-cake went upside
Winter's head with a beer bottle. The incident spread through
the hood quick, like food stamps and welfare checks on the
first of the month.

"Damn, I wish I was there to have my girl's back," Sabrina
said, passing the L over to Lady Rah.

"I know, right," Joy replied.

"I heard she gave that nigga Winter like ten stitches in the
back of his head," Joy mentioned.

"Good for that bitch-ass nigga," Sabrina stated.

They were chilling in front of Sabrina's building on
Bayview, mixed among a few other locals, enjoying the sun-

drenched summer day, watching traffic pass and people chilling out across the street in the park. Pound-cake wasn't around, and they hadn't heard from her in a day, but they knew she probably needed some time alone to herself. She went through a lot, with Ordeal's recent murder and then wilding out with Winter on the corner. The three ladies could do without their fourth for a day or two.

Sabrina and the rest lingered and gossiped and talked shit as the day went on.

"Oh, you heard that Carissa is back in C.I. She got out the hospital a week ago," Lady Rah said to Sabrina.

"So, fuck that bitch!" Sabrina cursed.

"Yo, I heard she got the ill buck-fifty across her face," Lady Rah mentioned.

"That bitch ain't pretty anymore," Sabrina replied, smiling.

"I know that's right," Lady Rah said, slapping Sabrina five, approving of the work she put on Carissa.

Sabrina was the one who gave Carissa the scar that lined her right cheek during the fight. A minute before the cops showed up, Sabrina pulled out a small razor that she kept concealed in the straps of her bra and cruelly nicked Carissa with it, drawing blood and slightly disfiguring the beauty queen's flawless features.

Carissa went through minor surgery, but the scar she carried was for life, and would cost extra money for more surgery to her face. She cried all week, and vowed revenge on the bitches that did the unthinkable to her. *Jealous and hateful bitches*, Carissa thought, as she lay in bed with her face bandaged and devouring painkillers.

Carissa's friend Sweety suffered minor cuts and bruises to her face, but came out very lucky from the beat-down she endured by Sabrina and her crew.

Sabrina thought nothing else of Carissa's misery and her trifling ass, as she took a long pull from the second blunt that

was being passed to her. She was enjoying her high, and relished on her fierce reputation in Coney Island.

Her cousin was Corey-D, a notorious hustler that ran with a fierce crew back in '97, '98 and '99, until his untimely death. He was gunned down in front a club on Flatbush by a rival crew one night.

Sabrina's whole family was gangsta, from her father, who was doing life in Attica for double murder of two police, down to her cousins and uncles, who were either locked up for drugs or murder. And she was an apple that didn't fall too far from the tree.

It was reaching late evening, and the girls were making plans as dusk was about to approach. Sabrina wanted to go check her boo Shanice, and get some pussy. Lady Rah had a trick lined up for tonight, she needed some extra cash, and Joy wanted to go see her boo Terry, who lived across town in Flatbush. It would be a personal night for each of them.

Lady Rah took one last pull from her cigarette and dowsed it out on the concrete. The projects seemed quiet all day, and it was getting a bit boring for the group—nothing was popping off. But they all spoke too soon.

Winter's Escalade came to a screeching stop in front of them, and three men quickly got out and came at Sabrina and her clique with a fierce approach. Sabrina's face tightened, seeing Winter and his goons come her way. She quickly stood up, with her two girls glaring and having her back, and was ready to war with Winter and finish what Pound-cake already started.

"Where that fuckin' bitch at!" Winter screamed out, looking heatedly at Sabrina, with his right hand, Moe, next to his side.

"Nigga, you better step da fuck off!" Sabrina retorted.

But Winter had had enough. He was no longer backing down from the bitch. He had a small bandage in the back of

his head, and was embarrassed by the surprise attack from Pound-cake. And then his bitch, Minnie, was missing, and he knew Pound-cake had a hand in that too.

"Sabrina don't fuck wit' me, 'cuz I'm gonna body you and that bitch," Winter warned.

"Fuck you, nigga!" Sabrina shouted, getting up in Winter's face, daring him to do something stupid. "You pussy nigga! I'm glad Pound-cake fucked your head up wit' that bottle."

Winter was fuming, ready to reach for his Glock and shoot Sabrina and her crew down in public. He hated them.

"Bitch, I'm gonna fuck your world up. You just don't know, you stupid bitch. I don't care who your cousin was, or who you fuckin' know . . . don't fuck wit' me, bitch! I ain't the one to fuck wit!" Winter said through clenched teeth.

"Go ahead, touch me and see what happen," Sabrina dared, being up in Winter's face.

But Winter knew that now wasn't the place or time, even though he wanted to kill Sabrina and Pound-cake with a hard-on. If looks could kill, both of them would have dropped dead on sight alone.

A small crowd took notice of the dispute, but nothing major was happening. It was just a few angry and unkind words being exchanged between two individuals that hated each other.

With his scowl still plastered on his face, Winter began moving to the truck and before he got in, he said to Sabrina, "Pain ain't gonna protect you and Pound-cake forever. Soon, you'll be mine to play with." After saying that, he got in on the passenger side and left, leaving Sabrina and everyone else fuming.

Winter left leaving a bad taste in the girls' mouths. The summer was heating up, and everyone knew that it was only going to get hotter.

*   *   *

Pound-cake left Minnie asleep in her bed. Minnie had been at her place for three days straight, and she felt like Minnie's guardian angel. Word on the street was that Winter was looking for the both of them. But she was far from scared. She was on a mission to do justice for her girl and take matters into her own hand.

Pound-cake quickly got dressed in her usual attire, some jeans, a T-shirt, and styled her long hair into a ponytail, and concealed a small blade in her pocket. She then walked out her bedroom and went on her search.

She knew Winter wasn't going to back down, and neither was she and her crew. The streets were filled with too many killers, too many hustlers, and too many crazies, and she wondered where she fit in with the mix.

She walked out into the hallway on the second floor and staked out the small area where she knew she could find her mark at. She watched Big Jerry's door from a small distant corner.

For an hour long, she watched the continuous traffic of junkies knock on his door, pay up, get served, and quickly leave to enjoy their high. She even witnessed her own mother do a rapid transaction. Her mother looked antsy, being dressed down in tattered hand-me-downs, and feeing for a fix. Big Jerry talked down to her like she was less than human, but had no problem taking her money. He had her waiting the longest in the hallway, because he was being spiteful about her stupid mess the other day with the police.

Mary was fidgety as minutes passed, and she knocked on Big Jerry's door waiting for her reward.

"Big Jerry, please hurry, baby . . . I need it bad, baby. I need a fix," she cried out, knocking on his door relentlessly as she clawed at her neck and chest.

Moments later, Big Jerry opened the door again, passing Mary the goodies, and shouted, "Here, take your fuckin' high, you stupid junkie bitch! Go get fucked up, bitch!" He

tossed the small package on the floor and watched Mary dive for the shit like her life depended on it. Big Jerry laughed and slammed the door on her while she was at her knees, and at her low.

Pound-cake witnessed the atrocious act and shed a few tears, watching her mother degrade herself more every day. But she didn't get involved. No matter how much she hated to see the disrespect done to her mother, she let it be, saying to herself, *Mama brought it on herself.*

She remained focused, and continued to watch Big Jerry's door. Soon she saw Sick, the man she was looking for, appear at Big Jerry's door. His clothes hung off him like laundry drying on a clothing line. He was thin like string, with disturbing gaunt features. His skin was filled with acne, and his teeth were rotting out. He was very hard on the eyes.

Sick knocked on Big Jerry's door, but Big Jerry showed this junkie a little respect. He didn't treat Sick like he did everyone else. He knew sick was kin to Double-tap, and everyone knew of Double-tap's deadly and notorious reputation in Brooklyn.

Big Jerry nodded to Sick, saying, "I got you, my nigga, hold on."

He shut the door and quickly emerged again, passing Sick his high and collecting his fee. After that, they both went they separate ways.

Pound-cake watched Sick escape into the staircase and she quickly followed. She knew he had to go somewhere to get his high on and be alone, and there were a few smoke-out spots where a junkie could go to in Brooklyn and smoke their crack or shoot up with dozens of others.

Sick strutted through the projects in a hurry with his drugs clutched tightly in his hand, holding on to it for dear life.

Pound-cake followed him to the corner of West Thirty-seventh Street, where he had entered into a small building complex. It had *drug spot* written all over it, with its shabby

lawn, boarded-up windows, and the constant traffic that was in and out of the place.

Sick moved quickly, feeling desperate for a hit. His eyes were red and huge from not having slept in days, and he reeked so bad that any decent soul would be repulsed by him immediately. But in the spot where he was about to do his drugs, he was like everyone else. They didn't care about image or reputation, the only thing that mattered to them was getting their fix and beaming up like Scotty.

Pound-cake entered the complex and moved through the area carefully and with a sense of urgency. She didn't belong, and some were aware of it, but didn't care because they were too blasted to move.

She spotted Sick in a nearby corner alone, and he was about to prepare his drug that he was about to remove from the small glassine envelope. He looked desperate, moving around fidgety and shit. Pound-cake was about to make her move, and knew what she was about to do was very dangerous, especially when it came to dealing with junkies. She rushed over to Sick and before he could react, she snatched the glassine envelope from his hand and ran off with it.

Sick looked like he got caught in a whirlwind, as he screamed loudly and began to panic. He got up and chased after Pound-cake, ready to kill for what was rightfully his, a decent high he paid for.

No one in the room attempted to help Sick or share their dope with him—everyone was selfish and out for themselves. Sick lost his drugs, then it was his problem. Sick ran out of the drug spot the fastest he could run, and as soon as he met the outside, he was violently met with a baseball bat to his side and back. Sick collapsed to the grass, cringing in pain and crying out. He looked up at his sudden attacker and saw Pound-cake soaring over him, the meanest look plastered across her face.

"You and me need to talk," she stated.

"I'm sick . . . help me," he pleaded, looking pathetic and helpless on his hands and knees.

"You want this back?" Pound-cake asked, taunting him by dangling the dope in front of him.

"Please . . . don't do this to me, I'm beggin' you," he cried out. "Give me my shit."

"First, you need to answer some questions for me," she said.

"Give me my shit," Sick repeated, rising to his feet.

"No, you talk to me first and then you get this."

"Give me my shit!" Sick screamed out, charging for Pound-cake to hurt her and reclaim his high.

But Pound-cake was swift and knew better. He came forward, and she took a step back, and bashed the bat across his knee, dropping him again on his side.

Sick cried out again, clutching his knee and coiling up on the ground.

"You come at me again, and I'll cripple you for good," she warned.

"Help me. I need my fix," he sobbed.

"So, let's talk," Pound-cake repeated more sternly.

Sick knew he couldn't take her. His body was decaying from the many years of drug use, and he couldn't think straight, because he was becoming sick and knew he wouldn't be able to last long without having any dope in his system. His body began to sweat, and he began trembling. He stared up at Pound-cake with pleading eyes.

"Please . . . help me." He coughed and looked like he wanted to die.

"Just tell me where I can find Double-tap, and you can get this back," she said.

"Why?"

"We need to talk."

"My brother don't talk to anyone," Sick stated.

"Oh really," Pound-cake replied. She walked over to the sewer drain and dangled the dope over it.

"No . . . okay . . . okay, he hangs out at this spot on Flatbush called Deuces. He's there mostly on Wednesday nights," Sick informed.

"You sure?"

He nodded. "Please, give me back my shit."

"If you lying to me, I'll find you and finish what I started," she warned.

She trusted his information somewhat and tossed Sick his dope. Sick thrust forward and snatched the glassine envelope from the grassy area and cradled it in his fist. Pound-cake was down the block already.

Sabrina was calm and quiet, enjoying the night and relishing the moment with Shanice, clinched lovingly in her arms, as they both sat in a soothing warm porcelain tub in Shanice's dimly-lit bathroom with scented candles decorating the area. They lay naked; Sabrina's back was against the tub and her tits pressed against Shanice's back, as she slowly moved her hands across Shanice's shoulders, massaging her lover gently, and then moved her hands across her breasts.

It was something Sabrina needed after her run-in with Winter earlier. She was filled with rage beforehand and wanted to blow off her evening with Shanice and handle her business in Coney Island, which meant fighting, beefing, and carrying on. But Shanice wasn't taking no for an answer and was stern when she talked to Sabrina and demanded that they spend some quality time together.

Shanice was scared for her girlfriend's lifestyle. From the stories she'd heard and by her boo's demeanor, she knew Sabrina was a bully to some, and a ride-or-die chick to many. But in her home, Sabrina was her lover, her best friend, and very compassionate. But Shanice loved Sabrina's thuggish ways—it was one of the qualities that attracted her to Sabrina—

but sometimes Shanice felt that Sabrina's ghetto and thuggish ways could be too much and become out of control. She wanted Sabrina not to change, but to tone down her wild ways a bit, especially when it came to the violence she was getting into back in Brooklyn.

Sabrina was a beautiful girl, and Shanice was scared to get that call one day about hearing her lover being in jail or dead. And now with the beef with Winter escalating and knowing how her boo couldn't let shit be, always instigating something, or ready to war with this one or that one, Shanice feared the worst and knew it was going to be a long summer.

But for the night, Shanice's body quivered lightly, feeling her lover's hand exploring her body under the lukewarm water, spreading her lips from below and playing with her kitty cat.

Shanice moaned, forgetting what she wanted to say to Sabrina for the moment. She closed her eyes, rested her head against Sabrina's chest and savored her lover's wicked touch.

"Umm," Shanice fervently cried out, spreading her legs a bit more to give Sabrina better access to her pussy.

Sabrina finger-fucked her and toyed with Shanice's clit rapidly in the tub. Shanice looked like she was short of breath as fingers tunneled in and out of her, and Sabrina kissed and sucked on her neck, almost giving her a hickey. Her tits were squeezed and fondled, and Shanice soon felt she was about to cum in the tub.

"Mmm," Shanice cried out, moving around feverishly and extracting water from out the tub and onto the floor.

"You like that, huh . . . you like it rough," Sabrina said, loving how the pussy felt in her hand.

"Umm, don't stop, I'm gonna cum. Oooh, I'm gonna cum. Oooh, baby . . . Oooh, I'm gonna cum," Shanice chanted, gyrating her hips against Sabrina's touch.

Sabrina loved the way her boo moved under her control.

Shanice's nipples were hard and stiff like quarters, her pussy pulsating and ready to explode underwater, her cries of passion echoing out into the hallway.

Shanice reached around and threw her arm around Sabrina's neck, her other free hand clutching the tub. She was about to explode underwater. Her body trembled being submerged, and soon her juices were mixed in with the bathwater. Shanice looked spent and continued to rest against Sabrina and enjoy her touch.

Several moments passed, and Shanice finally remembered what she wanted to say to Sabrina. She had to take a quick breather from the sexual escapade and get her thoughts together.

"Sabrina . . ." Shanice said, getting her attention.

"What's up, boo?" Sabrina asked, laying down tender kisses against Shanice's shoulders.

"You ever thought about leaving Brooklyn?"

"What?" Sabrina replied, stopping the kisses.

"I mean, why don't you come and stay with me for a while, take a break from Coney Island and do something new with your life," Shanice mentioned.

"You want me to leave my home and come move out here with you, that what you getting at?"

"Is that a bad idea?"

"No offense, but it's too quiet and too uppity out here for me. Staying out here longer than I have to is not my cup of tea. I'm a Brooklyn girl for life," Sabrina stated proudly.

"You don't want to move in with me? I mean, I'm supposed to be your girl, and we're supposed to help and take care of each other. I love you, Sabrina, and I don't want to see anything happen to you."

"Shanice, ain't shit gonna happen to me out in Brooklyn, believe that," she stated surely. "Besides, you want me to flat leave my crew like that and sell out by not being there for

them by moving to Queens. Yo, I can't do that to my peoples. There's too much going on right now."

"You know what, I think you care more about Pound-cake
and your crew than you do about me," Shanice replied angrily, raising up off Sabrina's chest and turning to look at her.
"What about me, Sabrina?" she continued. "I'm here in this
fuckin' apartment alone every night thinking about your ass,
worrying if I'll ever get to see you again, and you got the
nerve to say to me that you can't do that to your peoples.
Think about what the fuck you're doing to me. I'm tired of
your bullshit, Sabrina, the fighting, the beefs, and the attitude. It was cute when we first met, but you need to change
and grow out of that, baby. I wanna be here for you, but I
can't do that if you wanna continue to live like a thug and
spend all of your time in Brooklyn with your fuckin' crew,
and don't want to make a better home for yourself with me."

With that said and done, Shanice stepped out of the tub,
grabbed her bathrobe, and removed herself from the bathroom, leaving Sabrina alone soaking in the tub to reflect
about what she just said.

Sabrina sighed, and hated to see Shanice upset. But she
knew she wasn't changing for anyone, not even her boo. She
reached up and over and grabbed the tightly rolled blunt and
lighter that was on the sink and began taking long pulls, having the piff seep into her system. She leaned back against
the tub, closed her eyes and said to herself, "Fuck her . . . I
should have never got wit' her bougie ass anyway. She don't
understand where I come from."

She did love Shanice, but they both came from two different worlds. And in Sabrina's world, you couldn't look, or be,
weak. Sabrina grew up fighting her whole life. It's what she
did best.

Pound-cake got off the B train and trooped it to Flatbush
Avenue. It was early evening, and the traffic on Flatbush was

like a parking lot. She looked for Deuces and walked ten blocks until she came to Avenue D, and saw a small hole-in-the-wall lounge-bar-restaurant near the corner. So far Sick's information was accurate.

It was a Wednesday evening, and Pound-cake had about thirty dollars to her name, and a hunger to find Double-tap. She walked down the avenue in her short denim skirt, hair flowing down to her shoulders, and a tight halter top that turned heads and made niggas want to come to a complete stop. She needed to look older, so there wouldn't be any questions. And for a first, she applied some makeup to her angelic face, making her look a few years older.

She walked into Deuces and the place was practically empty, except for the bartender and a few employees in the back. No one asked any questions when Pound-cake walked in and took a seat at one of the aging booths. She faced the door to see who was coming and going.

Deuces had an old-time feel to it, with its eighties decor and the still coin-operated Jukebox that was in the back, and the latest track added was Busta Rhymes's "Dangerous." Six retro swivel stools with chrome rings lined the bar, and long-standing pictures of black celebrities of the times and locals heroes of Brooklyn lined the walls of the restaurant.

Pound-cake sat, observing the place and thought it needed a serious makeover. *It's a miracle they're still in business*, she said to herself.

Soon a young waitress who looked to be in her mid-twenties, with her hair styled into a bun, walked over to Pound-cake with a pad and pencil in hand and said, "Welcome to Deuces. My name is Maria, and can I get you something to drink?"

"Water would be fine for now," Pound-cake said.

"No problem," the waitress said and walked off.

Pound-cake sighed and hoped Double-tap showed up soon, or at all. She sipped on the glass of water the waitress brought and waited for the small sandwich she ordered.

An hour passed and a few people came, ate, and quickly went on their way. Pound-cake continued to sit, and ordered a soda the next time around. She yawned, getting tired on waiting for Double-tap to show up. She started to second-guess herself, thinking Sick lied to her, knowing Double-tap probably wouldn't even show up.

Two hours passed, and the waitress started to question Pound-cake's lingering around. She finished her small sandwich long ago and was ordering petty shit like glasses of water and sodas.

Just when Pound-cake was about to give up hope and leave, Double-tap finally showed up. He walked into the place coolly, clad in a dark denim jacket with a wrinkled white T underneath, and some tarnished beige Timberlands. He made his way over to a nearby booth and faced the door, like a killer should always do. By the look on everyone's face, he was a regular.

Pound-cake got her nerves together and knew it was now or never. She was about to face the man that gunned down her lover right in front of her. She didn't know how to approach him, nor did she know what his reaction would be when he saw her again. But she was willing to take that chance.

Pound-cake stood up and quickly made her way over to where Double-tap sat. In one quick motion, she slid into the booth opposite of him, eyed him, and boldly said, "I wanna talk to you."

Double-tap already had his 9 mm out, cocked, and it rested in the seat next to him, not too far from his reach. He stared at Pound-cake with a deadpan expression, and knew by the look in her eyes she didn't come to bring him no harm. He couldn't place her face right away, but he knew it was familiar in his eyes.

Double-tap's rough features could be intimidating for many, with his short nappy dark hair, unkempt beard, with

many murders in his eyes and his strapping, chiseled six-foot-two frame that he attained doing seven years upstate for various crimes.

"I know you," he said incredulously, with his raspy voice.

"Nigga, you owe me," Pound-cake replied.

Double-tap let out a chuckle. "Let me guess, I killed someone close to you?"

Pound-cake nodded.

"Well, don't expect me to apologize," he said.

"I don't want your fuckin' apology," Pound-cake barked.

"What do you want?"

"A favor."

Double-tap chuckled and then said, "Get the fuck outta here, little girl. I don't do favors for anyone."

"You murdered Ordeal right in front of me two weeks back. I was that bitch in the elevator you warned to keep quiet," she informed him.

The information recharged his memory, and he suddenly remembered the hit. "By keeping you alive, I already did you a favor," he said coldly.

"I'm no snitch," she said.

"You know better," he returned. "But what's done is done. You're a cute girl; you can find many niggas to fuck you. Ordeal was a piece of shit," he added.

"I'm past that, nigga," she said.

"Good, then fuckin' leave me," he sternly said, hating to repeat himself.

"I want someone dead," she stated.

Double-tap let out that infamous snub chuckle of his, and said, "I don't have time for games, little girl, and you can't afford my time."

"I can come up with the fee you charge," she said.

"How? And do you know how much?"

"I'm very resourceful. I found you, didn't I?" she proclaimed.

Double-tap smiled somewhat, knowing it was true. But he knew who told her his whereabouts, and he would deal with his younger brother in time.

"Sick could become very violent when you mess with his drugs," he said.

"I had to do what I had to do."

"Is he okay?"

"He was never okay," she replied with a little sarcasm.

"Well, it won't happen again," he assured.

"Look, I'm not here for games wit' you. I'm here for business. And I'm not a little girl; I know how to handle mines, so take me serious, nigga. I've done played wit' the big boys before and held it down plenty of times. Now, I can get you your money, or I can pay you in pussy . . . however you want it. I just want the job done," she made known.

Double-tap just sat there and eyed her, admiring her wits and heart. "Keep your panties to yourself. I'm no cradle robber," he stated. "You serious about this, huh?"

"Nigga, I never been more serious in my life," she replied.

"You got heart, shortie, I'll give you that. But this line you're about to cross, it's more than just beating bitches down in the projects, talking shit, and carrying on like a thug. There ain't no turning back from murder. Once it's done, it's done, and you gotta live with it till the day you die."

"I've been living wit' a lot of things that's heavy on my heart. It'll be just more fuel to the fire in my fucked-up life," she uttered out.

"Well, my fee is fifteen large for a body. You come up wit' that, and we can do business. If not, you can get you a gun for cheap and become an entrepreneur on the streets, if you think it's that easy," he said.

Fifteen large was a bit over Pound-cake's head. Even if she went out and started turning a few tricks, it would take months to come up with that amount and she didn't have months to wait.

"Look, you do a favor for me, and I'll do a favor for you," she bargained.

"I don't do favors; I do cash money, half before, and half after. Don't waste my time with anything else."

"I know you need sumthin' done, and I'm that bitch that can pull it off. I don't have fifteen grand on me and for me to get that money, it'll take months, and I don't have months. I'm being real wit' you. I need it done ASAP," she said.

"Like I said, you can cross that line yourself with a cheap gun."

Pound-cake was becoming fed up with his arrogance and high pricing. But she knew not to disrespect him. She thought about killing Winter herself, but knew of the repercussions to come. He worked for Pain, and Pain controlled C.I. and parts of B.K. Her and Winter had continuous beef, and if she did murder him, it wouldn't take the cops long to trace the dots back to her, and she wasn't trying to go to jail for that asshole. Her options were limited.

Pound-cake stared at Double-tap and thought she wasted her time by coming to see him, thinking he would be reasonable since he did murder Ordeal, leaving her to witness.

"You know what, I'm out. I'll find another way to get it done." She removed herself from the booth, but before she left, she said, "And I'm nineteen, nigga, and far from the little girl you think I am."

Pound-cake went over to the waitress, paid her bill, and left out the place feeling upset, but not knowing that she left quite an impression on Double-tap, who thought about her awhile after she left.

Pound-cake made it back to Coney Island around nine that night, and saw that something major had popped off on the corner of Neptune Avenue and Thirty-third Street—police was everywhere, lighting up the streets with their blaring red and blue lights, and yellow caution tape restricting the locals from moving any nearer the crime scene. A few detectives moved

through the onlookers asking the locals questions, and the old heads shook their heads in disgust at the violence that took place tonight.

Pound-cake walked toward the crowd and looked for her crew. She spotted Sabrina not too far away and greeted her, and asked what happened.

Sabrina sighed and informed, "Yo, they just shot Bones."

"What?" Pound-cake replied in shock. "He's dead?"

Sabrina nodded.

"Why?" Pound-cake asked.

"They think he had sumthin' to do wit' Ordeal's murder. I heard a car just pulled up and gunned him down like that. They just took the body away," Sabrina said.

"Damn," Pound-cake muttered.

"You know him and Ordeal never did like each other," Sabrina said.

She felt for Bones and his family, but she didn't know the nigga like that—he was cool peoples. And she definitely knew that Bones had nothing to do with Ordeal's death. She knew that Ox's people were looking to retaliate, and anyone that looked like they had something to do with Ordeal getting murdered, they were going after. It was about street rep, and not looking soft in the ghetto. Pound-cake knew that Ox wasn't involved in the shooting directly, but he definitely gave the word to his underlings to handle things.

Sabrina suddenly noticed Pound-cake in her short denim skirt and halter top, and was taken aback. "Bitch, where you coming from looking like some hip-hop princess?"

"I had to take care of sumthin'," she mentioned.

"What, you got you some dick?"

"Nah, business," Pound-cake said, being short with her.

"Business?"

"Yeah, I'll tell you about it later," Pound-cake said. "I'm out."

"Ayyite, we'll talk," Sabrina said, watching her friend walk away, with her skirt riding up her backside and her legs looking smooth and perfect.

Sabrina noticed other niggas watching, like a hawk, Pound-cake walk away, and even heard one dude standing next to her say, "Damn . . . Oooh, I wanna fuck that bitch."

Sabrina chuckled and said, "You wish, nigga."

Pound-cake walked into her dark apartment, leaving the chaos on the streets where it belonged, and went straight for her bedroom. She wanted to see if Minnie was okay, but when she opened the bedroom door, Minnie was gone. She checked the bathroom, and even her mother's room, but there was no sign of Minnie. Pound-cake then noticed that the trash bag filled with Minnie's clothes was also missing.

"Minnie, no!" Pound-cake exclaimed, knowing she probably went back to her apartment, or went looking for Winter.

"Fuck," she cursed, rushing back out the door and headed over to Minnie's apartment.

She hurriedly moved down the pissy stairway and exited out the lobby. She got to Minnie's apartment in no time and knocked on the door like she was police.

"Minnie, open up . . . you here?" she called out.

A short moment later, Minnie's mother, Aria, opened the door abruptly and cursed, "Bitch, what da fuck you bangin' on my gotdamn door like you da fuckin' police." She stood in front of Pound-cake with a dirty housecoat opened and hanging off her shoulders, panties and bra showing, and a cigarette dangling from her lips.

Pound-cake glared at her, obviously disgusted by her lack of parental guidance to her daughter and the fact she loved her crack addiction more than her own family.

"Minnie here?" Pound-cake asked in an indignant tone.

"I haven't seen dat bitch in a fuckin' week. I don't know where she be. But if you see dat little bitch, tell her Winter's

been lookin' for her ass too. I'm tired of that nigga being up in my ass about my gotdamn daughter. She ain't a fuckin' baby anymore," she mentioned.

The look Pound-cake gave Aria said it all, and she picked up on it.

"Bitch, you think you're better than me? Huh? You ain't better than me, bitch . . . you tryin' to be a mother to my fuckin' daughter?"

"Obviously you ain't," Pound-cake commented back.

"Fuck you, Pound-cake! Your family is just as fucked-up as this one, so don't come to my fuckin' home and judge me, bitch. I ain't da one to fuck wit!"

Pound-cake just gave her a smirk and knew she could wipe the floor with Aria any day. *But why bother,* she thought. The bitch was high or dying slow every day and it would be a waste of her time. Her main concern was finding Minnie and seeing if she was okay.

"Minnie never had a fuckin' chance living here," Pound-cake said. "No wonder she looks for love in the wrong places."

Pound-cake had said enough and walked off, leaving Aria fuming.

"Bitch, what you tryin' to say, huh? Fuck you, Pound-cake. Don't come to my home anymore, you dyke bitch!" Aria screamed out into the corridor.

Pound-cake walked out of the building, trying to maintain her temper and hold her anger. Too much was going on for her. She went back to her place and stayed in all night, tired of dealing with the bullshit.

Minnie cried out agonizingly as Winter beat her viciously with his belt in a room with six niggas watching. They all stood around, encircling Minnie and did nothing to help the frightened young teenager. Winter had stripped Minnie butt-ass-naked, with her raw business exposed to his peoples, and he took the pleasure of abusing her for everyone to watch.

He gripped his long leather belt in his hand and came down hard on Minnie's skin like a whip, striking her in the face, her bare back, the back of her thighs, and arms, as she raised them up trying to defend herself.

"Ouch . . . aaaaaahh, Winter, I'm sorry, noooo . . . please stop . . . I'm sorry, baby," she cried out, being glued to the floor and feeling like she was about to lose consciousness.

Her skin was black and blue, her lip trickled blood, her eye swollen and bruised again. She had left Pound-cake's place and went looking for Winter, tugging the black bag in hand, and wanted to say she was sorry for leaving. She was scared, not having many options for herself, and even though Pound-cake was her friend, how was she going to take care of her? Minnie asked herself. So she decided to take her chances with Winter and apologize for her absence.

But Winter was far from considerate or understanding, when he saw Minnie walking down the street, tugging her bag of clothes behind her and sweating. He was furious. He waited till she was standing right in front of him and shouted, "Bitch, where you been at?"

"I'm sorry, Winter," was all Minnie could say.

Winter grabbed Minnie aggressively and pushed her against his truck. He swung open the back door and pushed her inside forcefully, and said, "I'm gonna fuckin' teach you not to defy me."

"Winter, I'm sorry," Minnie said, but she got the door slammed in her face. He wasn't trying to hear her pleas.

Winter then grabbed up the black trash bag she was tugging and dumped all her clothing and belongings out on the streets. He scattered around everything, while Minnie watched in shock, seeing everything she owned lay out on the streets for the locals to rummage through and easily take from her. She cried, because now she definitely had nothing. Everything she owned was out on the streets—all she had was the clothes on her back.

At an unknown place, Winter beat Minnie until she could no longer get up. Her naked battered flesh lay against the cold tiled floor, leaving her breathing soft, her bones aching, and her spirit broken for good. She worried about her baby, but it was apparent that Winter cared nothing about her pregnancy—or that it was his child she was carrying.

Minnie was still alive, even though she no longer wanted to be. She was sobbing as she lay in the fetal position, unable to move, and felt the eyes of many staring down at her, looking uncaring of her abuse and her pregnancy. Winter surrounded himself with monsters, because only a monster could watch what just went on and not intervene and remain unemotional about her attack.

Winter took a few pulls from his cancer stick, and glared down at Minnie. She looked a hot mess.

"Bitch, you okay . . . get da fuck up!" Winter said.

Minnie remained frozen to the floor, still crying.

"Bitch, you hear me talking to you!" he shouted.

"I can't," Minnie murmured.

"What?"

"I can't . . ."

Winter got angry and kicked her in the stomach, shouting, "Don't get me upset again, Minnie!"

Minnie winced in severe pain, letting out a loud shriek as she clutched her stomach. She panicked about her baby. Her body felt like it was about to shut down.

"I need a hospital," she cried out.

"Yo, lift this bitch on her feet and take her to the back bedroom," Winter instructed a few of his goons.

They walked over to the crying Minnie and picked her up with no remorse about her situation. They were like robots, dragging Minnie to the back bedroom so she could shut up. They dropped Minnie on the bed, and left her lying there in the dark, crying, in critical pain, shutting the door with their exit and muting her out from the rest of the place.

All night Minnie had no help, support, or no medical attention. She cried and cried until she finally passed out. She had blood spots coming from her wound and severe abdominal pain.

The next day, Winter had a personal doctor he knew come through to check on her. He couldn't take Minnie to a hospital, 'cause he knew they would question her about the bruises, and there would be cops around, and he didn't want to deal with the risk. So he had a friend—a personal MD he paid handsomely—come through whenever medical attention was needed on one of his bitches or if a crew member got injured, and they didn't need doctors and police in their business.

The MD informed Winter that Minnie definitely had a miscarriage, and she needed medical attention ASAP. Winter doubled his pay if he could do what he had to do and be discreet about it. The MD took the money and went to work.

Minnie blacked out when she heard the news. Her baby was gone—*her baby was gone.* The one person who she knew would truly love her as she would have loved him or her was dead.

She felt so empty, and not loved by her boyfriend, her parents, and now her baby left her.

When the doctor left, Winter looked more compassionate. He closed the bedroom door and sat down on the bed next to Minnie. He held her hand gently and said, "You okay, baby? I know it's hard, but we gonna try again and get my son, right? I was trippin' last night, but you know how I get. I just missed you and you had me so worried about you. But it's gonna be all good. I got you, boo. I'm gonna take care of you. Don't worry about losing the baby; we'll just make another one, ayyite."

Minnie still had her head turned from Winter's attention, and continued to stare in blankness. He might as well have been speaking in Spanish, because she wasn't hearing him.

She just lay still and thought about her fucked-up life and her baby being dead.

It had been a week since Minnie left Pound-cake's crib, and Pound-cake couldn't help but to worry about Minnie. But she had to go on with her life. Pound-cake started spending time with her crew again and doing what they did best: smoke weed, fight bitches, and steal from the bodegas and shoplift anything from clothes to bullshit from the main department stores.

The crew saw less of Winter the past few days, and it kind of worried Pound-cake, because she didn't know what he did with Minnie. Every day she thought about getting herself a gun and taking out Winter. But it was just a thought.

She and Sabrina were by each other's side every day, and that was making Shanice jealous. After their little dispute, Sabrina decided to take a small break from Shanice, and Shanice was upset. She called Sabrina on the Nokia she bought her, and they were arguing with each other like some old married couple.

"I guess being wit' pussy ain't that much different from being wit' dick," Joy joked.

Sabrina heard Joy's little smart comment and flipped her the bird while she was still on the phone with Shanice. Pound-cake and Lady Rah laughed as they smoked the haze they rolled up.

Once again, Coney Island was somewhat peaceful and quiet for the day. Everyone was laughing, smiling, getting high, joking around, and it looked like the drama and chaos took a day's vacation. And even though Pound-cake was laughing and enjoying a peaceful summer day with her friends and neighbors, a small part of her was still worried about Minnie. Sabrina had asked about her, but no one knew where she was.

Even Pain and Coupe came through for a minute to see what was up with Sabrina and her peoples. He was cool like that, a hustler and gangsta for sure, but still made time out from his money-getting agenda to check on his homegirls.

Pain asked Sabrina how things were going, especially between her and Winter, but Sabrina had no kind words at all to say about Winter. Her and Pound-cake had hate for Winter till they die.

Pain wanted to see whatever peace there was between them for the moment to remain. His block was quiet and getting plenty of money for once. And he didn't want anyone fuckin' it up for him and his paper.

He talked to Sabrina for a short while, and before he left, he blessed Sabrina with two hundred dollars easy. Sabrina took the cash, smiled, gave Pain a hug and then watched him drive off in his sixty-thousand-dollar truck. She quickly pocketed the cash, not informing anyone of her girls about the money.

Pound-cake took her umpteenth pull from the haze and guzzled down almost half a bottle of Olde E, and afterward, she had to go take a piss.

"Yo, I gotta go pee, I'll be back," she said, walking off to her building.

She rushed up the stairway, and when she got to her door, a neighbor greeted her and said, "Pound-cake, you just missed some girl that was looking for you. She looked upset and slid a note under your door."

"Word?" Pound-cake replied.

"Yeah, she looked young, about sixteen or seventeen, and her face looked like someone took some boxing training on it. She was lookin' fucked-up," she revealed.

"Minnie," Pound-cake said out loud. "Thanks, Jackie."

Pound-cake quickly opened her door and saw a small note. She quickly picked it up and began reading:

*   *   *

*Hey, Pound-cake, I know you missed me for a mo-
ment, but shit is fucked-up. I'm sorry I left your crib
without telling you, but I can't have you worrying
about me and taking care of me like that, you got
your own life to live, but thanks for looking out. You
my girl for life. I lost the baby, Winter beat da shit
outta me, and now he wants me to make another
one with him. He must be fuckin' crazy. I thought he
loved me. But I couldn't even find love with my parents, so why did I expect Winter to love me anymore
than my own flesh and blood didn't. You like a sista
to me Pound-cake, and I will never forget you, Sabrina and everyone else that tried looking out for me.
I'm gonna finally leave Winter for good. I have the
courage now, Pound-cake. I ain't got my baby anymore, so I don't give a fuck what happens to me. You
remember the night Winter took my virginity on the
rooftop of my building, I was like thirteen and his
grown self talked my ass into giving him some
pussy. And it hurt like hell my first night. Who knew
that hurt was gonna continue more in my heart and
body. I can't do shit right, Pound-cake. And guess
what I just found out, I got the monster, Pound-cake.
Doctor told me that I'm HIV positive, of course, only
me right. But it's good for Winter's ass; I hope he dies
a slow and painful death. 'Cuz me, I ain't going out
like that, no more pain and hurt for me Pound-cake. I
can't live like this anymore. So I finally got the
courage to leave Winter from where it all started. I
love you always; Pound-cake, you and Sabrina are
the only family I ever had, so Peace from your girl,
Minnie.*

*   *   *

Pound-cake was in shock, she knew it was a suicide note, and she feared she was too late. She rushed out her apartment, raced down the stairs, and headed for where she knew Minnie would be—her building rooftop. She sprinted through the building projects like a fast discharge from a loaded gun, with the letter gripped tightly in her hand. She darted across thirty-third Street without looking for oncoming traffic and continued running at high speed toward Minnie's building. It looked like she was being chased.

Once she got to the lobby of Minnie's building, she went straight for the stairs and hurried upward, leaping up the steps two or three stairs at a time. She went up eleven floors, reaching the rooftop, and pushed open the rooftop door, and yelled out, "Minnie! Minnie!"

She saw Minnie standing by the edge of the roof, and Pound-cake looked at her in shock. Minnie had her back turned from her friend and peered down at the ground, ignoring Pound-cake's calls. She was naked. Her clothes were spread out a few feet from her, and she looked like a statue standing still in one location.

Pound-cake approached closer, and noticed the marks and bruises that covered her back. "Ohmygod," she said. "Minnie, please . . . don't do this."

Minnie stood still, her eyes fixated on the cold hard concrete below. The courtyard was practically empty, so she knew it would be an easy fall.

"Minnie, look at me!" Pound-cake yelled out.

Minnie took a deep breath, and then slowly turned to face her friend. She stared at Pound-cake and said, "You know Winter fucked me and took my virginity right there." She pointed to a spot not too far from where she was standing.

"Like I said in my letter, it hurt the first time, but I let him continue because I loved him," she continued. "Why you here, Pound-cake?"

"Why you think? 'Cuz I love you, Minnie. You're my sister, and I can't let you do this. Don't kill yourself, especially over Winter," Pound-cake pleaded.

Minnie began crying. "I'm sick, Pound-cake. You know that . . . that bastard made me sick. I lost everything, my baby, my health, shit; I don't give a fuck anymore."

"Minnie, you still got us. You got Sabrina. You know you our girl, you know we gonna always look out for you. You know I always had your back, Minnie. You were never alone," Pound-cake proclaimed.

"I need to be alone. I need to go away. I'm not strong like you and Sabrina. I can't do it," Minnie said.

"C'mon, Minnie, you is family. Please, don't do this. Yo, we gonna get through this. I promise you, Minnie. I'm gonna help you get through this. Don't let that nigga win by taking your own life," Pound-cake pleaded. She had tears streaming down her cheeks as she looked at Minnie naked and standing just inches from the edge.

Minnie cried and exclaimed, "It hurts, Pound-cake. It fuckin' hurts."

"I know, baby girl. But we gonna make it better," Pound-cake said, approaching Minnie slowly.

Pound-cake extended her hand and wanted Minnie to take hold of it. "C'mon, Minnie, I promise that nigga will never touch you again. We got your back."

Minnie looked at Pound-cake and knew she could always be trusted. Tears flowed from her eyes and she wanted to grab onto Pound-cake's hand and be safe and taken care of. But the fear of Winter and living with HIV made her think otherwise. Minnie dried her tears with the back of her hand and smiled over at Pound-cake.

Pound-cake returned the smile and asked, "You trust me, Minnie?"

"I always did, Pound-cake. You were always my best friend."

"So trust me now."

Minnie nodded. Pound-cake came closer and reached for Minnie with a smile. Minnie continued to smile and said, "You gotta trust me, Pound-cake. I love you."

Minnie then took a few steps back and dropped abruptly, disappearing from Pound-cake's view, and letting gravity do what it did best. Pound-cake rushed forward, screaming, "Minnie, *Nooooooooooo!*"

She stood near the edge hollering and screaming. She was scared to look over and see Minnie's body. Pound-cake dropped to her knees crying like a baby, with Minnie's letter clutched tightly in her hand. It was the second time this summer that Pound-cake had lost someone close to her.

Sabrina, Lady Rah, Joy, and Bubbles were still camped outside Sabrina's building and enjoying the day. Sabrina noticed Pound-cake had been gone for a long while and joked, "That bitch probably had to take a shit, or sumthin'."

Everyone laughed.

Sabrina took a small sip from the E&J she had in her hand, and sat on the steps looking over at the park. She loved Brooklyn. She loved Coney Island. She loved her crew. And the summer for her had been crazy. Sabrina thought about Shanice and wanted their relationship to work, because Shanice had some good pussy and she was good company too. But they came from two different backgrounds.

Lady Rah smoked on a Newport and wanted to get ready for two of her tricks tonight. She was making plenty of money selling pussy and even had Joy get into the business with her. Both girls started stripping at nights at this spot on Atlantic Avenue, and were making some nice paper. Lady Rah had plans on pimping bitches, and wanted Joy underneath her. She would be her first ho.

Joy was reluctant at first getting into the business with her friend Lady Rah, but when she saw the money Lady Rah was

making, she was tempted to get in. But unbeknownst to her friends, Joy was six weeks pregnant by Terry. And she needed the money, because even though she loved Terry, he was a broke-ass nigga still struggling on his rap career.

Little by little each of the girls were moving on to something new for the summer, they still had each other's back, but they were growing older and getting into different things.

As the girls lingered around, with the day about to turn into dusk, they heard a siren blaring from a distance. Soon, they heard another siren, and saw a few marked police cars speeding down Neptune Avenue, headed toward the high-rises on Thirty-seventh Street. Soon they saw a few individuals running over to the incident.

Sabrina looked and wanted to see what had happened. A neighbor came trotting, and Sabrina called out to her and asked, "Michelle, what happened?"

"I heard someone just jumped off the building and killed themselves," she informed, running to see who it was.

"Get da fuck outta here," Sabrina exclaimed.

All four girls went running over to where the suicide happened. They wanted to see who the victim was; unaware that it was one of their own, Minnie.

The ladies made it over to the courtyard where the body of a woman lay dead. Police were already on the scene, taking notes and investigating the area.

Minnie was sprawled out like a twisted doll, her young naked body contorted and mangled against the cold concrete. It looked like she had fallen apart, leaving a crimson stain underneath her. It was a gruesome sight, and had the locals in awe and some had to turn their heads from the appalling death. Police didn't get the chance to cover the body yet; they had no identification of the woman so far.

Sabrina looked and she knew something wasn't right. She couldn't see the face because of the way the body was positioned. But her heart said it was someone she knew. She

looked around and tried to collect information from those that stood around her. No one knew of the victim yet, because her face was badly mangled.

The girls shook their head in sadness and just watched the police do their job from a short distance. Everyone was talking; some said a prayer for the victim, and some just didn't care who it was.

A short moment had passed, and Sabrina noticed Pound-cake being escorted away by a few detectives. She looked distraught as two detectives guided her to the nearest squad car. They knew she had witnessed the suicide and needed to talk to her. They took the note Minnie had wrote as evidence of her suicide.

"Yo, Pound-cake . . . Pound-cake," Sabrina called out, rushing over to her, with Lady Rah and the rest following.

Pound-cake looked up, her eyes stained with tears, and her mind traumatized by seeing the death of her young friend. But she held strong and moved along with the detectives, with one agenda on her mind, and that was to kill Winter.

Pound-cake looked at Sabrina and heard her say, "Girl, where you been? And who's the jumper?"

Pound-cake didn't have to say a word; the look she gave Sabrina said it all. It suddenly registered in Sabrina's head—it was Minnie's building, the jumper was young from what she was hearing, and there was no sign of Minnie anywhere.

"No! That's not Minnie," Sabrina cried out. "No, she wouldn't do no stupid shit like that."

Joy and the rest caught on and they looked at the body closely from afar. And they knew it was Minnie. Knowing that it was a close friend of theirs made it much harder for them to look at the contorted body. They remembered her as a young hip girl and loved her like a sister. Everyone was in tears, wondering what pushed Minnie to throw her own self off a roof.

Soon the body was finally covered, and word quickly got around that it was Minnie, and the crowd mourned and became saddened by her violent demise. People loved and adored Minnie and knowing that she was pregnant made it much harder to endure her death. Pound-cake was the only one who knew that she lost her baby before she jumped.

As the evening continued, the neighborhood was gray with grief and those that heard later on were shocked and devastated. When the news finally reached Minnie's parents, Aria was so high that she couldn't even comprehend her daughter's death. They found her in a local crack house, and wearing only a long, soiled T-shirt. She was taken to the 60th precinct, and detained.

Minnie's father was in the apartment, and when cops came with the neighbors to inform him about his daughter's suicide, he thought the cops were there to take him to jail, so he lunged at them with a large knife. Shots were quickly fired and Joseph was shot twice in the shoulder and stomach. He would live, but was arrested and taken to jail.

The neighbors were disgusted with both of Minnie's parents, and knew she needed a proper burial. So a few of the residents put together a collection for the funeral, and by week's end, they collected over three thousand dollars.

Toward the end of Minnie's funeral, Pound-cake, Sabrina, Lady Rah, Joy, and the rest wanted to get high and get their drink on. Pound-cake needed to get high especially, because she was going through it—two funerals in the past three weeks. Everyone knew that she witnessed Minnie jump and they knew she tried her hardest to stop her. But Pound-cake felt that she could have done more to prevent it from happening. She hated feeling helpless.

At the funeral, Pound-cake noticed Double-tap in attendance from a far distance, like he was at Ordeal's funeral. She thought nothing of it, or said nothing to anyone. She said

her good-byes to Minnie, tossed a single white rose onto her casket, and knew her death wouldn't be in vain.

Winter was nowhere at the funeral. He'd been ghost the past week or two, and everyone thought that he was in hiding. Sabrina and Pound-cake knew that when they saw him, on sight alone, they were fucking him up and probably would kill him.

Pain came through to the funeral too to give his condolences. He brought a bouquet of flowers with him and would have given money to the family, but Minnie had no other family. The only true family she left behind was Sabrina, Pound-cake, Lady Rah, and Joy.

Pound-cake agreed to meet with everyone else in an hour at the Astroland amusement park. She needed to change clothes after the funeral. Pound-cake strutted up the stairs and exited out on the third floor, only to see Sick standing in front of her door.

She became cautious and asked, "What the fuck you doin' in front of my door, Sick?"

"Double-tap wants to see you," he informed.

"For what? I ain't got no business wit' him."

"He wants to talk," Sick said, ready to leave and get his high on. Double-tap paid him forty dollars to relay quick information to Pound-cake.

"He's on the roof waiting for you right now," Sick mentioned. He then took off into the stairway, feeling he accomplished what he had to do.

Pound-cake stood in front of her door, contemplating if she should meet with Double-tap. She had nothing to lose, and thought that maybe he'd changed his mind about the hit. She walked up the stairway and slowly made her way onto the rooftop. She spotted Double-tap standing alone with his back turned and peering out into the hood.

Eric Gray

He was in a black T-shirt and jeans and smoked on a New-port. Pound-cake approached him warily. She wasn't scared of the man, but suspicious about meeting him.

"I'm sorry about your friend," Double-tap spoke, in his raspy voice. He didn't bother to turn around to face Pound-cake. He simply stood erect like a soldier and peered over Coney Island and admired how beautiful the Verrazano Bridge looked from a distance.

"What you want wit' me?" Pound-cake asked, being abrupt.

"You left quite an impression on me the other day," he started. He took a pull from his cigarette and glanced at her.

"And?" Pound-cake uttered. She stood near him, staring him down and admired his physique. His forearms and arms were well defined, and even though his appearance was rough and he kept his hair nappy, there was something that she liked about him.

"I thought about your proposal, and it got me thinking," he started. He took one last pull from the cigarette and tossed it off the roof. "You can't afford to pay me, so I came up with another option," he stated.

"You wanna fuck me?"

"Don't flatter yourself, little girl. I don't collect in pussy," he said.

"You gonna stop calling me a little girl," she barked.

Double-tap let out a faint smile, eyed Pound-cake, and said, "You don't fear me like everyone else."

"I fear no nigga," she quickly proclaimed.

Double-tap nodded, admiring her fearless demeanor. "I like that in you."

"And?"

"Listen, I need someone on my team, someone I can trust, someone who I know is bold when it comes to this game. I need someone who is subtle and can get at certain individuals in a heartbeat," Double-tap proclaimed.

"You need an apprentice," she said, staring strongly at him.

"I need a ride-or-die bitch to have my back and that ain't scared to use pussy to get at certain marks in a heartbeat. You can do that, you have the looks and attitude, and anyone that's fearless of me, I know can definitely hold their own."

"What about Sick?" she asked.

"Sick is my younger brother, and I got love for him. But he's weak, and he's a junkie. He gave me up for his drugs, and I can't afford to have that happening. I have enemies," he said.

"So what makes you think you can trust me? You don't fuckin' know me."

"I can't, but I'm willing to see how it plays out with you," he said.

"And if I let you take me under your wing, what do I get outta this?" Pound-cake asked.

Double-tap stared at Pound-cake, examining her and feeling her out. He reached into his pocket and pulled out a small piece of paper with some writing on it. "I'll give you Winter," he said.

"So, you'll do the hit for me?"

"I'll let you carry it out yourself, just say yes, and I'll pass you everything you need to know about Winter, his kids, where he likes to hang out, who he's fucking . . . I have it all written down on this piece of paper," he said.

"I'm not like you. I'm not a professional killer," she said.

"You could be."

"And risk going to jail for killing that asshole?" she said.

"But you want him dead. And I can guarantee that you won't see a day in jail. I know you, you got heart for this . . . just let yourself go, and do what comes natural. You need to

rise beyond this ghetto beef and fighting, and get paid for being ruthless. There's a lot of money in this business, and I see it in your eyes, you can do this," Double-tap proclaimed.

"I'll think about it," she told him.

"It doesn't work like that. It's either yes or no right now," he said steadfastly.

Pound-cake and Double-tap locked eyes and stared at each other. Pound-cake thought about her options. She thought about everything that went on this summer and knew things needed changing.

"So, what's it gonna be? I need an answer," Double-tap said coolly, staring at Pound-cake and waiting for her to say it.

Winter sat at a small round table at one of his underground spots and tossed down a bottle of Grey Goose, with Minnie on his mind. He didn't care for the funeral, and cursed Minnie for doing something stupid.

"Stupid bitch had to go and kill her fuckin' self . . . what kind of dumb shit is that, Moe? What kind of dumb bitch throws herself off the fuckin' building? I knew that bitch wasn't wrapped too tight," he ranted.

Moe shrugged and looked at his boy. "Yo, it is what it is. Ain't no bringing the bitch back, so fuck it, nigga . . . you got other bitches to look out for."

"Bitch had some good pussy, though, and she was making me some money, but she was a dumb young bitch, Moe. I swear, yo, I don't know why I got that bitch pregnant. She couldn't even keep the fuckin' baby," Winter said, taking another swig from the bottle.

Winter was slouched down in a chair, drinking his worries away. The table in front of him was cluttered with booze, weed, money, and his .380. Winter and Moe were the only occupants of the spot, and wanted to lay low from C.I. for a

week. Since Minnie's suicide and Bone's murder, the block was hot like grease on the stove.

Moe kept his boy company and listened to him rant about Minnie's stupidity. He drank his cognac and was mostly quiet, throwing in his two cents here and there.

"I'm gonna still get money, my nigga," Winter uttered.

"That's what's up, my nigga," Moe replied. "But yo, I gotta take a piss, you gonna be ayyite?"

"Yeah, my nigga. I'm good," Winter replied, taking a long mouthful of the Grey Goose.

Moe stared at the .380 on the table near Winter's reach. "Yo, I'm gonna take this wit' me, you fucked-up right now, and I don't need you doin' some stupid shit."

"Nigga, I ain't gonna kill myself like that bitch, Minnie. I got better sense than that," Winter said.

"Ayyite, I believe you, my nigga . . . but to be on the safe side, this shit is comin' wit' me," Moe said, picking up the gun and leaving out the room.

"Nigga's tryin' to babysit me now," Winter complained, taking another swig from the bottle.

The room was quiet, and Winter mumbled a few things to himself, as the bottle touched his lips every minute or so. He thought about getting some pussy for the night or just wilding out with his crew. He sat with his back facing the exit and clutched the half-empty bottle.

Like ninjas in the night, Pound-cake, Sabrina, Lady Rah, and Joy silently walked into the room, glaring at Winter. Sabrina displayed a tiny smile and cracked her knuckles, waiting what felt like forever for this moment. Winter was right in front of her and vulnerable like prey to a pack of hungry-ass lions—and they were hungry to fuck Winter up for all the pain and heartache he caused Minnie, and for disrespecting them.

Winter heard some movement behind him and said, "Moe, that's you. Yo, I'm ready to be out this bitch."

He turned around, only to catch havoc. He jumped back, seeing Pound-cake come at him swinging a one-liter bottle at his head—but he was too late. The Absolut peach smashed over his face and he cried out, "Aaaaaahh . . . fuckin' bitch!"

Winter stumbled and then fell over the chair, and landed on his side.

"Yeah, muthafucka, what now!" Sabrina shouted. She raised her size six sneaker and came down on Winter's face vigorously.

Joy and Lady Rah promptly joined in on the assault, beating him with fists, chairs, and smashing bottles over his head. Winter tried to fight back, but the ladies were aggressive, and when he tried getting up, another bottle was smashed over his head. They were brutal; they tore into Winter with so much hate and anger that he began crying like a bitch.

"This is for Minnie, nigga!" Sabrina yelled, kicking Winter in the back of his head.

He balled up into the fetal position, but it didn't help much. Pound-cake picked up another wooden chair and shattered it across his back. Winter cringed in pain, opening himself up for attack to his chest, and Joy put her boot so deep into his chest that she felt the nigga's heartbeat.

Winter coughed up blood and tried scrambling for cover, but they were on his ass like flies to shit. The punches and kicks rained down on him like a perfect storm, and Pound-cake was brutal when she took her Timberlands boot and crashed them down onto his genitals not once, but three times. Winter was in tears, his face coated with blood, his clothes torn, and his arm broken.

He could no longer move. He just laid there looking helpless—crippled almost. He looked up at all four ladies with his one good eye, and said, "I ain't kill her. Y'all know I ain't touch that bitch. She did it to herself."

"You did it to her, nigga. You pushed her, wit' your bitch ass. It ain't so fun when a bitch hits back, right. Yeah, nigga,

what you gotta say now, wit' your bitch ass?" Sabrina said, breathing hard from the fight.

Winter remain sprawled out on the floor, wishing he had his .380 on him and thought, *Where the fuck is Moe?* He coughed up more blood and knew these four bitches were serious.

"Get up, muthafucka, so we can beat your bitch ass back down again," Pound-cake said, towering over Winter's battered body.

"Fuck y'all bitches . . . fo' real," Winter cried out, preparing himself for the worst.

"What, nigga . . . fuck you, nigga . . . fuck you!" Pound-cake shrieked, kicking Winter in his grill and had him spit out three teeth.

It was a wrap, he was a done deal.

"C'mon, Pound-cake, let's be out. He ain't gettin' back up no time soon," Sabrina said.

Lady Rah and Joy were backing out the room ready to exit, and Sabrina was ready to follow. But Pound-cake lingered behind.

"Y'all go, I'll be wit' y'all in a minute," Pound-cake said to them.

"Hurry up, girl," Sabrina said, leaving the room.

Pound-cake turned and stared furiously at the crippled Winter. He was definitely fucked-up. He couldn't move, and could barely speak with all the blood coated in his mouth. Pound-cake watched him for a short moment, and thought about all the pain he done put Minnie through.

She then pulled out the .380 Moe had gave her before his exit out the building and pointed it down at Winter.

"That's my gun, bitch!" he uttered out.

"So you know what time it is," she said.

It didn't take a genius to know that Moe had set him up for the assault.

"Your boy gave you up, stupid. He's done wit' you. Moe got paid lovely, though," she informed him.

"Shady-ass muthafucka!" Winter cursed.

Pound-cake continued to stare down at him. She needed to ask.

"Why Minnie, nigga? She was only sixteen. She was young, and she loved your dumb ass so much. But you didn't give a fuck about her, all you did was beat her and pimped her," Pound-cake proclaimed.

Winter looked up at Pound-cake and said with a smirk, "Why not, bitch? It was that easy to get into that bitch's head. You lucky I ain't get into your fuckin' head too, and pimp that dyke ass of yours. But I guess Ordeal beat me to it."

"You a piece of shit, Winter. I hope you burn in fuckin' hell," Pound-cake exclaimed.

"I'll see you there, bitch," he countered.

Feeling all the rage and hate she felt for him, and knowing he was the one responsible for Minnie's suicide. Pound-cake trained the .380 at Winter, locking eyes with the man, and then squeezed off—*Bam! Bam! Bam! Bam! Bam! Bam! Bam!*

Winter lay dead in her eyes—being sprawled out in a bloody mess on the cemented floor, with holes in his head, chest, stomach, and dick. Her first kill—her fist hit, and she didn't regret doing it. It needed to be done. Pound-cake sealed her fate when she squeezed off that first round into Winter. Now she was under Double-tap's supervision and he would mold her into the perfect assassin.

She didn't tell Sabrina and the others of her true intentions. She wanted to, but Double-tap warned to always keep your mouth shut about a kill. But they would know that Pound-cake killed Winter, because they left her alone with him. But they would never snitch on their girl.

Pound-cake dried her tears, thought about Minnie for a short moment, and then walked out of the building, concealing the gun on her person.

"You good, Pound-cake?" Joy asked.

"Yeah, I'm good, let's be out. Now Minnie can rest in peace knowing that nigga got his," Pound-cake said.

Fall 2007

The summer finally came to an end, and the girls were moving on with their lives. Everyone still thought of Minnie, and they had a small memorial displayed up where she fell. Flowers, pictures, poems, teddy bears, and burning candles were her memorial, and many paid tribute to it everyday.

The drama in the fall still went on with the fighting, the beefs, the drugs, and the murders, but it declined somewhat.

But the same shit went on with Big Jerry pushing drugs out of his apartment, Duck and June fucking bitches in a perverted manner, Pain still running things with his right-hand man, Coupe, and Sabrina and her crew still holding down the block with their reckless ways, fighting and carrying on, and still stealing out of bodegas.

Pound-cake was still hanging with them, but not as often since she got down with Double-tap. He was training her to be his right-hand, and teaching her the use of different guns, and how to kill a man perfectly. She took a liking to Double-tap and felt an attraction to him. He was a cold-blooded killer, but was an intelligent male, who knew history, current events, and just about everything else. He was subtle with things, and pretty much kept to himself. In Pound-cake's eyes, Double-tap was more than meets the eye. He kept his past a mystery, and didn't talk about himself much. His main thing was business and surviving in the streets of Brooklyn.

Winter was Pound-cake's first kill, but she knew that there would be more.

With November reaching and the days getting colder, so was Pound-cake's life. Her mother Mary died of an overdose in September, and the body stayed rotting in the apartment

for a week. Pound-cake had moved out in August, getting her own place on Mermaid Avenue, and never went back to check on her moms. She had love for her mother, but knew she would end up killing herself off the drugs she used daily.

Life in Coney Island was no fairytale for so many folks.

Epilogue

Big Jerry was sweating profusely as he thrust his fat six-inch dick into Lady Rah. He gripped the wrinkled bedsheets, grunting and fucking, being in the missionary position with Lady Rah's thick, defined legs wrapped around him.

Lady Rah clawed at his back, thinking she had bigger and better dick, but a trick was a trick, and the two hundred dollars Big Jerry was paying her was worth the sweat, fat, and his little thick dick that she had to endure.

His huge gut rested on Lady Rah's stomach as he fucked her rapidly like a fast bullet.

"Slow down, baby, the pussy ain't goin' anywhere," Lady Rah said, holding onto Big Jerry so she wouldn't fall off the bed.

"Ooh, your pussy is so good, shortie. Oh, shit," Big Jerry cried out. He then started sucking on her nipples.

"You gotta cum, nigga. I ain't got all day," Lady Rah said, glancing at the time.

He'd been in the pussy for thirty minutes, and she wished he was a minute man. But Big Jerry was far from being a minute man, taking Viagra daily and beating his dick twice a day.

"I'll give you an extra hundred for your time," Big Jerry stated, trying not to lose his rhythm in the pussy.

"That'll work," Lady Rah mentioned gladly

They continued to fuck when they heard an unexpected loud knock at the door. The apartment was empty and the knock echoed back into the bedroom where they both were.

"What da fuck," Big Jerry exclaimed. He paused the fucking and listened. "Fuck it, they'll go away."

He continued to thrust into Lady Rah, but the knocking at the door continued and became louder. Big Jerry became annoyed, and pulled out the juicy pussy and threw on his boxers. He thought it was some local junkie coming to see him for a fix. He was going to show them.

"I'll be back, shortie . . . let me take care of this fuckin' fool real quick," he said, storming out of the bedroom.

The knocking was relentless. Big Jerry removed his metal baseball bat from behind the door, looked through the peephole and saw what seemed to be a junkie clad in a gray hoodie and some old jeans.

He swung open the door with force, with the bat clutched tightly in his hand and shouted, "Yo, don't fuckin' come to this door when I'm doin' my fuckin' business."

But the person in the hoodie looked unyielding, as they stood in front of Big Jerry unemotional and fearless, with their hands in their hoodie pocket and eyes lowered to the floor a bit.

"Yo, you hear me fuckin' talkin' to you?" Big Jerry shouted.

"Yeah, I hear you, you fat, greasy bitch-ass nigga," they said.

The hoodie soon came off, and Big Jerry had a look of shock displayed across his face. He didn't understand the reason for Pound-cake being at his door. She wasn't a user, but then he thought, he did have Lady Rah in his back bed-

room twisting that pussy out, and the thought of a threesome got him extra hard.

"Pound-cake, you came to join the party with your friend?" Big Jerry asked.

Pound-cake looked angrily at him, and then she pulled out a silver 9 mm from her front hoodie pocket.

Big Jerry's eyes widened. He took two steps back before Pound-cake put three holes into his fat stomach and chest. Big Jerry dropped suddenly and was dead to the world.

The gunfire was loud, echoing throughout the hallway and apartment, causing Lady Rah to jump up with panic when she heard the shots. Before she could run to the door to see what had happened, Pound-cake was striding down the stairway with her hoodie back over her head, with the gun concealed in her pocket, and rushed out the building to meet up with Double-tap who was waiting nearby in a parked Expedition.

Big Jerry was fucking up, that's why he was dead. He was late with money always, or short with thousands, and Pain sent word out that he was done doing business with Big Jerry. And when Pain was done doing business with you, you didn't get fired or laid off—you got exterminated.

Lady Rah saw Big Jerry laid out dead in a pool of his own blood and panicked. She ran back to the bedroom, quickly got dressed, grabbed up her things and rushed out the apartment trying not to be a witness to anything.

It would be the second time within four months that police would come to investigate a murder on the second floor of the building.

Sabrina sat in the passenger seat of Shanice's plush burgundy BMW. It had been three months since they decided to go their separate ways and end their one-year relationship. It was getting cold outside, and the two were talking, being friends.

"I see some nigga gave you the big belly," Sabrina said.

Shanice was three months pregnant, but not in love with the baby daddy. He was just a sperm donor so she could have a baby.

"I felt empty, Sabrina. I wanted this child. I wanted us to have a baby. I want a family. I want to be happy," Shanice proclaimed tenderly.

"Well, I'm happy for you," Sabrina said.

"Thank you. You ever thought about having kids, Sabrina?"

"Me, nah . . . I ain't trying to have any little brats running around. I ain't into the family thing . . . that's your dream, Shanice, not mines. Like I told you, I'm a Brooklyn girl. I come from the streets, and I'm gonna love it out here till the day I die," Sabrina said.

Shanice felt kind of saddened that Sabrina felt that way. She was still in love with Sabrina. But she could never change her mind about them moving in together and either adopting or getting pregnant by a sperm donor, and starting a family together. Sabrina and she definitely came from two different backgrounds, and having two very different motives in life.

"So, what you gonna name your baby if it's a boy?" Sabrina asked.

"I like Michael or Jeffery," Shanice said.

"Michael is cool, but I don't know about any Jeffery, you tryin' to get your son fucked-up before he's even born," Sabrina joked.

"You silly," Shanice said, chuckling.

"And if it's a girl?"

"I like Tanya and I like Octavia."

"That's cool. I hope you have a girl, because you come up wit' better names for them," Sabrina stated.

"I know, right."

The two talked for an hour, being parked in front of Sabrina's building.

"You do look good, though, Shanice."

"Thank you, and you look fine yourself. Are you staying out of trouble?" Shanice asked.

"I don't look for trouble, it be finding me, and when it do, I send it running back," Sabrina said with assurance.

"You were always a wild girl," Shanice stated.

"Yeah, but it's in my blood. I do me."

Shanice smiled.

"Sabrina, you ever think about us, about what we could have become if we stayed together?" Shanice asked.

"Sometimes, but it's best this way. You do your thang, and I'll do mines. I mean, you're happy, right?"

"Yeah, but—"

"No buts," Sabrina interrupted. "Just think about your baby, and don't dwell on the past. I never do," Sabrina said.

"You're right," Shanice said, smiling at Sabrina.

"We'll see what happens in the future, right?" Sabrina said.

"We'll see." Shanice smiled.

"I gotta go, but you better call me when your baby is born. I gotta see how cute my godchild is going to turn out," Sabrina said.

"You know I will. You be safe out here, Sabrina."

"And you too . . . take care, baby girl. Get home safe and don't be a stranger."

"I won't."

The two hugged each other tightly and then went on their way. Sabrina stepped out of the BMW and watched Shanice drive off until she turned the corner. She would always have love for Shanice.

Unaware that she was being watched by an unpleasant individual for the past hour, Sabrina began walking toward the building lobby. It was getting nippy outside, and Sabrina

wanted to get out of the cold and get ready for the date she had planned for the night.

Sabrina was a few steps from the lobby entrance when she noticed a vague figure quickly looming her way. But before she could react, a .357 was raised to her head, and the last thing Sabrina heard was, "You remember me, bitch?"

Carissa quickly put a bullet through Sabrina's head, dropping her dead where she stood. It was her revenge best served cold.

So Seductive

By Mark Anthony

January 2007

Rock Bottom

I had to hustle and do what I had to do to get my money up. I was never the type to depend on a nigga for shit. But on the flip side I was never the type to depend on a legitimate nine-to-five either. With a six-year-old daughter though, I had to get that bread and provide for her the best way that I knew how, so I resorted to shaking my ass all over New York City and New Jersey to pay the bills.

My daughter Tarsha was what and who I lived for. Unfortunately, I had her when I was fifteen years old, and due to my immaturity I often made big-time mistakes, and like most young people from the streets I had huge lapses in judgment.

Clearly my biggest lapse in judgment came on a cold winter night about a year ago. My babysitter had called and canceled on me at the last minute, and being that it was already close to 11:00, there was no one that I could call to come over to my apartment and watch Tarsha while I went out and made that money.

"Fuck!" I screamed into the phone.

"Cinnamon, I'm sorry but there's just no way I can make it tonight. I—"

"You know what, kill it. Just stop! Denise, you are fucking me up big-time. You don't even understand," I said to my babysitter, cutting her off in the middle of her explanation.

"Cinnamon, I know and I promise you it won't happen again. Like I said, it's just that I been in this emergency room with my moms since like four this afternoon and I thought we would have been outta here by now."

I blew some air into the phone before speaking. "Look, what if I pay for your cab from the hospital to my apartment, and for tonight I'll even double what I normally pay you?"

"Cinnamon, it's not even about the money. You don't understand. I just can't leave my mother up in the emergency room without even knowing what's wrong with her or how she's gonna get back home. You feel me?"

In the background I could hear what sounded like someone speaking through a PA system, so I figured that Denise wasn't bullshitting me and I had no choice but to give her a pass. Really, what else could I do? It wasn't like I could just reach through the phone and snatch her up. So I was stuck.

So there I was without a babysitter for the night. But it wasn't just any night—it just happened to be the night of legendary New York DJ Kay Slay's birthday party at the Players Club in the Bronx. I couldn't miss a night like that, because it was sure to be one of those jam-packed nights where I could make mad money. At the Players Club I always had one good night where I made enough dough to make up for any slow or missed nights.

I knew that my rent was due in two days. So I had no choice. I set the alarm to the apartment and left Tarsha asleep in her bed. I didn't feel good at all about doing that,

but the apartment was located in a quiet section of Rockaway, so I figured she would be safe for the night.

Cinnamon, what the fuck are you doing? I remember
the little voice inside of my head asking me when I bent over
to kiss my daughter on her forehead while she slept so
peacefully in her bed.

Those same words replayed through my mind as I started
the engine to my black Denali and pulled off, making my
way toward the highway.

She'll be a'ight, don't worry.

That's what I convinced myself as I sparked some weed
and turned my music up full blast in order to drown out any
other uncomfortable thoughts that were trying to pop into
my head.

Before long the weed had kicked in and my head was feeling really good. As I approached the club I could picture my
daughter's face as clear as day. I remember getting this awkward feeling that instantly made me hold my stomach like I
was about to throw up or something.

I shook the feeling off and continued to head into the jam-
packed club, and as I made my way to the dressing room I
wondered just how much money I had already missed out on
since I was arriving pretty late.

As it turned out, I made off pretty good. I made off with
about fifteen hundred dollars, and I knew for a fact that I
would have made more had my mind been at ease and not
on my daughter. It's always been hard as hell for my body to
get into something that my mind was not into. And that night
my mind was definitely not into lap dances and flirtatious
talk. It was strictly on my daughter.

I normally would bounce from the club at 4:00 AM when it
closed. But on this particular night I decided to leave at a little past 2:30. When I got to my truck I knew that I should
have probably hung around the club for about an hour or

some longer and drank a bunch of water in order to take away some of the effects that all of the alcohol that I had been drinking had produced in me.

But I didn't go back into the club. Instead I just started up my truck and made my way to the Throgs Neck Bridge, high as a kite and drunk as a motherfucker. The thirty-minute drive home went pretty quick, and I couldn't wait to hit my bed and sleep my ass off. I could just tell that I was definitely in store for a hangover.

I made it to Rockaway and stopped at the McDonald's drive-through before heading in to my apartment. And after I left the McDonald's I proceeded toward Shore Front Parkway, and as soon as I turned onto Beach Eightieth Street where I lived, immediately my heart fell to my feet.

"Oh shit! What the fuck happened?" I said to myself, thinking out loud.

I quickly turned off the radio and rolled down my window, which ushered in the cold-ass winter air that smacked me in the face like a ton of bricks.

The cold air was the last thing that I was concerned about. All I could see were a shitload of bright-red fire trucks and blue-and-white police cars everywhere, and they were accompanied by two ambulances. All of the emergency vehicles had their flashing siren lights on, which reflected off of the front of my high-rise apartment building.

"Oh my God! My baby! Tarsha! Tarsha!" I screamed as I jumped from my truck and left it running right there in the middle of the street.

With stilettos and all, I raced toward the front of my building, which was roped off with yellow and black emergency crime-scene tape. It seemed as if every resident in the building was standing behind the yellow tape, huddled together to keep warm. Some were in just their pajamas and slippers, while others were in their coats and shoes.

"Miss, you can't go into the building!" one of the cops said to me as he had to practically bear-hug me in an attempt to restrain me.

"I know I know I know. Listen," I said frantically while breathing so heavy and being so nervous that I began hyperventilating. "My daughter—is in there and—I gotta get to her!"

"Miss, we have all of the emergency responders doing an apartment by apartment search and we just can't let anyone in the building right now," the cop continued to explain.

"Uggh! Mister, please, you just don't understand. My daughter is really young and she was home alone with her elderly grandmother and I just want to make sure everything is okay," I lied and said.

"Ma'am, I understand your concern. Believe me, I do. Everyone out here has been out here for a couple of hours now and everyone wants to get back into their apartments and assess things. We understand that. Believe me, we do. But there is an investigation going on, and for the time being we can't let anyone into the building."

I placed my face in my hands and I decided to just fall back for a few moments and just not get completely freaked out. But I knew that I had to get into that building to check on Tarsha and I also knew that I couldn't let them get into my apartment and realize that Tarsha had been home alone.

Think, think, think! I urged myself as I slowly paced next to the other neighbors and onlookers.

"Excuse me, I just came in from work, and I was trying to figure out exactly what happened . . . like I can smell the smoke so I know there was some kind of fire, but was it in an apartment, in the laundry room? What's going on?" I asked one of my white neighbors.

Fact was the majority of my neighbors were white, and that was exactly who I had purposely chosen to live amongst. Living in the white part of town provided me with a certain level

of anonymity, which was just how I liked to roll, considering that I was a dancer, and especially since I was always scheming to get money in some kind of way that wasn't always legit.

"Yeah, well, from what I'm hearing there was a fire that started in one of the apartments on the sixth floor—" my shivering neighbor said to me before I cut her off.

"The sixth floor! Did you say the sixth floor? Oh my God! I live on the sixth floor!" I screamed.

I ran back over to the officer and I explained to him that I lived on the same floor that the fire had started on and that I really needed him to try and help me find out if my daughter was okay.

The officer looked at me and seemed kind of annoyed that I had resurfaced. But I didn't give a fuck how annoying I was being. I needed to get some information and I needed to get it pretty quickly before I had a nervous breakdown or some other psychotic episode.

"Show me some ID and I'll see what I can do for you," the cop said to me.

"ID? Okay, wait a minute. I just gotta run to my truck and get it and I'll be right back."

I walked as briskly as I could to my truck, which was still running idle in the middle of the street. I retrieved my Prada bag and turned off the ignition and I quickly made my way back to the officer.

"Here you go, sir. I'm Charlene Anderson. I live in apartment Six D," I said, attempting to confirm the exact same thing that my driver's license said.

The cop shined his flashlight on my driver's license and then he got on his walkie-talkie and asked for someone to come and assist him.

Before long a black female officer came over to where we were standing and she asked me if I was Ms. Anderson.

"Yes, that's me," I said, sounding kind of nervous.

"Can you walk with me, Ms. Anderson?"

"Yes, but is everything okay?" I asked jittery and anxious as shit.

When we were out of earshot of the other tenants the black female officer held me by the hand and she explained to me, "Ms. Anderson, it appears as if the fire started in your apartment and spread to two other apartments—"

"Nooo, don't tell me that!" I said, cutting off the police officer. "Please don't tell me that!" I burst out into tears and I felt like I was going to pass out.

The officer slowly shook her head and she compassionately said, "I'm sorry and I wish I could tell you that, but I can't. Fortunately though, Ms. Anderson, the fire department was able to contain the fire and get it under control rather quickly. But *unfortunately* I have to tell you that they did find a little girl in your apartment who was unconscious and they had to rush her to the hospital."

When I heard those words all I could remember was my legs getting weak and me falling to the ground and someone repeatedly tapping me on my face, asking me if I was okay.

As it turned out, I was okay, and more importantly, my daughter Tarsha was okay. She had been overcome by smoke inhalation and she had been rushed to Jamaica Hospital. From what I had been told, the firemen got to her just in time. They had found her in her bedroom huddled underneath her bed clutching a teddy bear. The flames had spread from the kitchen and made it to just outside of Tarsha's room.

I wasn't able to speak to Tarsha until the following day and when I did speak to her, she and I both burst out into tears and we hugged each other so tightly when we saw each other.

"I'm sorry, Mommy, I'm sorry!" Tarsha said to me in a pleading tone. "Please don't be mad, Mommy."

My daughter went on to explain to me in heartbreaking fashion that she had woke up in the middle of the night and went into my bedroom and when she didn't see me or the babysitter that she got scared. So she went to call me on my cell phone and when I didn't pick up she started crying and she went to the kitchen and tried to make hot chocolate for herself on the stove.

Hot chocolate with marshmallows was something that she always drank before she went to sleep and it was sort of like a comforting thing for her.

She went on to explain to me that she would have been scared to go to sleep if she didn't drink any hot chocolate and that was why she tried to make it on her own.

"Are you mad at me, Mommy?" she asked.

"Nooo. Oh, no way, sweetie. I'm not mad at you. Mommy is so mad at herself. I should have never left you alone. Oh God," I said as I exhaled and I hugged my daughter even tighter. "I'm just so glad that you're all right."

My daughter was okay in the physical sense, and for that reason I could exhale and be happy. But emotionally I knew that she would be touched and bothered by my stupid lapse in judgment, and our lives would be altered due to my stupidity.

And, boy, was I right. I ended up getting arrested before I left the hospital and charged with one count of endangering the welfare of a child, which was a misdemeanor, and one count of reckless endangerment, a felony. I got shipped off to Rikers Island jail and I lost custody of my daughter, who was placed into the foster care system.

While I was in jail waiting for my case to go to trial, it felt like I had hit rock bottom or something. I knew two things—I had to figure out a way to get the hell up outta that jail and I had to figure out a way to get my daughter back.

I was on a mission and I was willing to do whatever. As far as I was concerned, it was on!

February 14, 2007

Scam Queen

At about 6:30 in the evening on Valentine's Day I found myself in the living room of this hustler from Queens who went by the name of Midas. And, to be specific, I was butt-ass naked on my knees, sucking Midas's dick like a pro.

"Yeah, just like that, baby. Suck that shit! Deep-throat that motherfucker!" Midas commanded me while simultaneously gripping the back of my head and forcing my face to move further down the shaft of his dick.

I relaxed my throat, and somehow I managed to get all of Midas's fat-ass dick into my mouth without gagging and throwing up.

"That's what the fuck I'm talking about!" Midas yelled out.

I then began stroking his dick, hoping like all hell that he would hurry up and cum.

Thankfully, after about two more minutes of sucking and stroking his dick Midas finally came all on my face.

"Wow! Your head game is sick!" he shouted. Then he instructed me to put some of his cum on my finger and to lick it and swallow it.

Although I didn't want to, I complied with his wishes.

After Midas had bailed me out of Rikers Island I felt like that was the least that I could do. Plus, he was putting me up in his crib with him, since my apartment was a wrap, due to the fire. So I would have been a fool to not comply with what he liked.

I swallowed some of his cum and then I stood up and smiled. "Tastes just like Cask and Cream."

Midas began laughing, and I knew that his ego was boosted. And I proceeded to ask him where his bathroom was so that I could jump in the shower and freshen up and feel like a human being.

He pointed me in the direction of the bathroom and I sashayed my full-figured light-skin ass toward it.

"Damn, you fine as fuck! Look at all that?" Midas said to me as he got dressed.

He wasn't lying because, truth be told, I looked a lot like Halle Berry, only I was much thicker in all the right places and I was way more ghetto than Halle. And I had the tattoos and the attitude to match.

After I had taken my shower Midas, who was from Queens but lived out on Long Island, drove me to the mall and got me about two thousand dollars worth of clothes. And then we headed to Red Lobster to get something to eat.

"Midas, you just don't know how thankful I am that you looked out for me on this bond thing," I said as we waited inside the jam-packed Red Lobster restaurant.

"It's all good, ma. But don't get shit twisted. Those clothes that I got you and this dinner and all that, it ain't about nothing other than me looking out for you so you can get me this money. You feel me?"

"Yeah, no doubt. I gotchu," I explained to Midas.

When Midas came to visit me in jail, he had agreed to put up the money for my bail and let me rest at his crib, so long as I was willing to get that money for him once I hit the bricks. Truth be told, I had no idea just exactly what I would be doing for Midas, but I assumed that he was planning on putting my ass out on the track so I could suck dick and sell my pussy for him.

Really though, I was just so fucking desperate to get out of Rikers. I wanted to start the process of regaining custody of my daughter and just finding out where the fuck she was. I was so desperate that I was willing to cross that line into *whoredom* and sell my ass, if it meant reconnecting with my daughter.

But as it turned out, Midas had a completely different plan in mind for me.

When we finally sat down to eat our fried shrimp and lobster tails, Midas began breaking things down to me.

"Okay, see, I got this white chick, bad as hell right"—Midas paused and literally began licking his fingers and slurping on them and shit.

"Okay," I said with a smirk of embarrassment.

"She's down for me when I need her to be. I turned the bitch out and got her open off of black niggas and black culture." Midas stopped to drink some of his Hennessy and Coke. He burped and then continued on.

"The bitch is from Stony Brook, like way out there on Long Island and shit, and she ain't never really been nowhere before. So you know how I do, had her in the six hundred, taking her ass to different industry parties, popping bottles and all that, right. And she meeting Diddy, Hov, T.I., and she's buggin', just all on my dick, right. But at the end of the day she ain't nothing more to me than a straggler bitch and some white pussy, but what was wild was, wherever we went it was all eyes on me and her, like in a major way and shit. So I was saying to my man that if I wasn't around she would have all kinda niggas flocking to her ass. And so on two occasions I fell back and played the background just to see what would happen, and just like I thought, motherfuckers were all over her ass."

Midas paused and focused on trying to get the lobster meat from its shell, and after dipping it into some butter he put it into his mouth while I chewed on my fried shrimp.

"Where I was getting with everything is this: I know for a fact if you and this white chick name Simone were to hook up and was out in the city, partying and up in these clubs, that hands down y'all would shut down every spot that y'all walk into, without question! You already know the kind of attention that you attract on your own. Now just imagine you with a bad-ass white bitch. It would be fucking bananas!"

I sipped on my drink and I smiled because I just loved Midas's swagger.

"So, okay, I'm with the white chick and we partying and hitting the clubs and all that, but then what?" I asked.

"A'ight, y'all will have niggas asking to buy y'all drinks and all that, right? The niggas with the jewelry and the three-hundred-dollar jeans and shit."

"Yeah, yeah, the doe boys. I can spot them a mile away. I'm following you," I said.

"Okay, cool. Now you'll be able to spot them out easier than Simone will be able to 'cause that bitch can't distinguish between frontin' motherfuckers and the niggas that's really getting it. So this is the thing, flirt hard with them mother-fuckers and get them open to the point where they think they can fuck for the night. But the thing is, have them thinking that they about to have the fantasy of their life come true, a random threesome with a bad-ass white chick and a bad-ass black chick. You feel me?"

"I feel you. That ain't shit," I said in a confident manner. "I do that shit every night up in the strip clubs."

"Exactly!" Midas stressed. "But the thing is, in the strip clubs you ain't leaving the club with the niggas, you just gassin' them to get that gwop."

Midas and I both laughed and he continued on.

"Now all I want y'all to do is leave the club with the niggas and get them to the truck that I'll let y'all hold. Get the mother-fuckers in the backseat of the whip and get their pants down to their ankles and start giving them a blow job. I mean, I re-ally want them niggas thinking that they died and woke up in a porno movie or some shit. And then me and my man will run up on the truck and put gats to them niggas' heads and bounce with they shit." Midas paused and looked at me, wait-ing for a response.

"Motherfucka, that's all I gotta do?" I asked with a huge smile on my face.

Midas smiled and replied, "Yeah, I mean I'll break the shit down some more so that the shit will go off without no slipups, but that's it. It ain't nothing, right?"

"Nigga, I'm the fucking scam queen out this bitch! Hell no, that ain't shit. I gotchu. I'm wit' it. Ready when you say go."

Midas nodded his head and reached out his fist for a pound.

"That's what I'm talking about," he said as my fist touched his. "You always been a down-ass chick."

"And ain't a damn thing change!" I added as we got up from the table and prepared to make our way out of the restaurant.

Midas counted out seventy dollars and dropped it on the table, and as we exited the restaurant, my thoughts went to that of my daughter. And I wondered to myself just where in the world she was at and if she missed me? And more importantly, I wondered when I would be able to see her again.

February 15, 2007

It's On . . . Let's Do This

I was happy as hell to finally be waking up in a normal bed. Although it was Midas's bed and not my own, at least it wasn't a bed that was attached to a jail cell.

The fact was that I really didn't have a place of my own. My apartment had been damaged extensively because of the fire and needed major remodeling. But with me being shipped off to jail, the owners of the apartment building moved quick as hell to get me evicted from that apartment. And since I had in essence committed a crime by leaving my daughter unattended in the apartment, the judge had no problem in okaying my eviction.

I had friends and family that I could have called on for fi-

nancial help, but the thing was, I didn't want them all up in my business, especially not my family. None of my family members knew what I did for a living, and I was planning on keeping it that way. The toughest part about my not being open and up front with my family was that I couldn't even reach out to them, in terms of asking them to help me out with my daughter Tarsha by taking custody of her. But it didn't matter, because I was a fighter, and for all of my life I had been used to doing shit for myself and by myself, and the current plight that I was facing was gonna be no different.

By the time Midas and I got outta the bed it was a little past 1:00 in the afternoon. I decided to make breakfast for the two of us, and as we ate the grits and bacon that I had cooked, Midas got Simone on the phone and told her that he needed to get up with her later on that afternoon.

"So we doing this tonight?" I asked with a strip of bacon in my mouth.

"Fo' sho. Tonight it's on!" Midas said with a huge grin on his face. He stretched a little, showing that he was obviously still tired from the two hours of fucking that he and I had managed to get in after we had left Red Lobster the night before.

"This bitch better not fuck this shit up," Midas said, in reference to Simone.

"Midas, she won't fuck it up. I got this. This is what I do," I assured him.

After breakfast I was able to reach out to the city's department for children services, and they constantly kept giving me the runaround in terms of my daughter. The social worker who had been assigned to me when I was on Rikers Island had all but vanished, as did the bullshit public defender that had been assigned to me. I was getting tired of the bullshit, and somebody had to tell me something!

"Miss, listen to me. I know that you're just doing your job.

I understand that completely. But what you're telling me is that you don't know where my daughter is at? And you expect me to be okay with that and all calm and collected? What the fuck is that?" I vented into the phone. I couldn't believe that the bitch was actually telling me that they wasn't one hundred percent sure where my daughter was at.

"Ms. Anderson, if you're going to use that kind of language then I am going to have to end this phone call."

I blew some air into the phone to vent my frustration. But I knew that I had no choice but to humble myself. So I kept quiet and tried my best to be patient.

After a noticeable pause the white social worker continued on. "Now—what we're saying is that we know that your daughter was placed with a foster care family, but for some reason our system isn't giving me the information that I need in order to know exactly where she is and—"

After I heard that, my short-lived humbleness and patience had worn thin and my short fuse was blown. I cut the lady off in the middle of what she was saying and proceeded to curse her ass out.

"Stop! Just stop and hear what the fuck I'm saying. I can already tell where this is going, and I see that you're trying to get slick. I don't play that disrespectful shit. That's number one. Number two, we are talking about my daughter! She is a fucking living, breathing, human fucking being! She's not a got-damn file that was accidentally misplaced! What the hell is wrong with you? You're the social worker handling my daughter's case. That's what I was told. Now what the fuck I'm telling you is this, if you don't call me back within the next motherfucker hour and tell me where the hell my daughter is I will personally come down to that office and whip your white ass! You hear me?" I screamed into the phone.

The social worker didn't bother to even respond to me and immediately hung up the phone.

"Ugggh!" I grunted in frustration. "Midas, I swear to God

I'm gonna kill one of those social worker bitches down at that office."

I explained to him what had happened and he tried to sympathize with my situation, but at the end of the day I could tell that he didn't really give a fuck and was more worried about me helping him pull off his scam. He was also more preoccupied with introducing me to Simone, who had arrived at his crib while I was on the phone with the social worker.

"Babe, don't worry about that. You know how dealing with the city is," Midas explained.

And just as I was about to continue rambling on and expressing my dissatisfaction, Midas introduced me to Simone.

"Simone, this is Cinnamon. Cinnamon, this is Simone."

I shook my head and twisted my lips and just walked over to the couch and sat down.

"Hey, Simone. Don't mind me, just these motherfuckers is fucking with me and my daughter and just pissing me off."

Simone, who looked like the splitting image of a thicker version of the actress Jessica Alba, looked visibly uncomfortable with my loud mouth, so I decided to calm down and try to relax and take things down a notch.

I went and got a drink, and Midas fixed Simone a drink, and the three of us sat around in the living room and got more acquainted with each other. As we talked I could tell that Simone was cool, but she was definitely a little rough around the edges, and she appeared to be one of those white people who was trying way too hard to fit in and be black.

But at the end of the day she was 'bout it and she was a down-ass chick. As soon as Midas was finished going through the details of the scam, I could see Simone's green eyes light up like a Christmas tree.

Most chicks woulda been hemming and hawing and asking a million and one questions if they were asked to be down with a scam like the one Midas was proposing. But with

Simone, right from the gate she was with it and she made me laugh because she sounded like me using one of my sayings.

"*It's on*," she said. "Let's do this." She stuck out her hand and gave me a pound. "I'm good to go just like this?" she asked, referring to her outfit, which consisted of these hot-ass Jimmy Choo stilettos and skin-tight Citizens of Humanity jeans and a top that showed off the cleavage of her double-D titties.

I smirked and I laughed and told her that she was good and that her outfit was fire.

"Well, it's on then, let's do this."

Later that Night

Mike's Cabaret

At about 10:00, me, Simone, Midas, and his boy LQ arrived at this white strip club spot in midtown Manhattan called Mike's Cabaret. LQ had suggested we work that club because he had been there before and it was always packed with executives, CEO's, and the Wall Street–type dudes who had real long money. He figured that they would be easier marks than the usually frontin'-ass street niggas that be up in the black spots.

So with the change to the white venue, we figured that Simone would sort of take the lead and help break the ice at the bar and I would tail her and help draw the white dudes to us, especially the white dudes who would give anything for some black pussy.

I had never worked in any of the white strip clubs, but I had been to them before on a few occasions. They were cool, but at the end of the day the white clubs just weren't real to me. It wasn't raw enough, but that didn't matter because they

made a hell of a lot more money than the black clubs, and that's what it's all about.

Well, anyway, after getting frisked, LQ and Midas made their way into the club and nonchalantly walked off ahead of us so that they wouldn't give anyone the appearance that they were with us.

"This what the fuck I'm talking about! Simone's in the motherfucking house! Heeyyy!" Simone screamed out loud, trying to draw attention to herself.

"Simone, would you shut the fuck up?" I barked into her ear.

She sounded as brand-new as you could sound and stupid as hell. She had been drinking the whole way there and was twisted.

"Simone, you gotta chill and maintain before you fuck everything up!" I added.

"No, no, no, I'm cool. We'll be fine," Simone added with this huge smile on her face.

We made it to the bar and it was packed with no place for us to sit, so I kinda had to bogart my way through the throngs of people until I was able to get the bartender's attention.

"Yeah, let me get a bottle of Rémy Martin!" I yelled to the bartender as I pulled out a huge knot of Midas's money. The money was like a prop in our little acting skit.

The bartender walked off and came right back with the bottle.

"And let me get two glasses," I said while I counted off a bunch of twenty-dollar bills and handed it to the sexy white blond-haired, blue-eyed bartender.

As soon as I handed Simone one of the glasses, this cute white dude with black hair stood up from his seat at the bar and asked me if I wanted to sit down.

"Oh, thank you. That was so sweet," I said to the white dude, a cheery smile on my face.

He smiled back and then he tapped one of his friends on the shoulder and got his attention and pointed toward Simone. His boy got the picture and stood up right away and gave Simone his seat.

"You must be Greek, right?" I said to the guy who had given me his seat.

"Oh shit, how did you know?" he said with an accent, while grinning from ear to ear.

Oh, we got these niggas, I thought to myself.

I was trying to do all of the talking and break the ice just so that Simone and her drunk ass didn't fuck shit up before we had a chance to really get things popping.

"Because of your black curly hair and your accent," I said, popping open the bottle that I had.

The two guys introduced themselves as Rick and Tony, and as they began making small talk, I started to scan the strip club, trying to locate Midas and LQ, just to make sure that their eyes were on us. Midas and LQ were sitting in the VIP area, and when my eyes made contact with his, Midas held up his drink in the air to let me know that he saw me.

Rick and Tony were unaware that I acknowledged Midas by nodding my head to him, and then I resumed the small talk with Rick, Tony, and Simone.

"So, Tony, are you Greek too?" Simone asked.

I was thankful that she seemed to be maintaining.

"No, actually I'm Italian," he replied. "So what are you ladies doing in here?"

"Just chillin', having some drinks, and looking at the ladies," I replied.

"Oh, so you like to look at the ladies too?" Rick asked, a curious grin on his face.

I sipped on my drink and then explained to Rick and Tony that in my opinion all women are at least slightly attracted to other women.

"You think so?" Tony asked.

"Hell yeah," Simone chimed in. Then she reached over and pinched both of my boobies with her right hand.

I was wearing a push-up bra with a real tight cleavage-revealing top, and my nipples were standing at attention and trying to bust out and break free.

"How could someone not love a woman's body when it's so soft, and the curves and all of that? Like, look at Cinnamon's boobs—don't they look good to you?"

Rick and Tony both nodded their heads, and Simone commented that my boobs also looked good to her.

"What is that? VSOP? No, you can't drink that. That's garbage!" Tony blurted out over the loud music.

"Let me get a bottle of Louis the thirteenth," he shouted over to the bartender.

Jack-motherfucking-pot! I thought to myself. From my experience in the strip clubs I knew that only true ballers for real could afford Louis XIII, considering that in the clubs they charged upward of two grand for a bottle.

Tony reached into the pocket of his tight butt-hugging jeans and pulled out a huge bankroll of nothing but hundreds and handed the bartender a fistful of cash.

Before the bottle could even be set before us, Simone had taken hold of it and popped it and poured herself a drink. She was drinking it straight with no chaser.

"Never tasted nothing like it, right?" Tony asked.

"Oh shit, this is off the damn chain!" Simone replied.

I, on the other hand, was trying to play things cool and not look so brand-new, and while Tony poured me a drink, I reached out and grabbed Rick's hand and pulled him closer to me and guided him so that he could lean down toward my titties.

"Is it true what they say about Greek guys?" I whispered into his ear.

Rick looked at me and smiled and then he asked me to stand up.

I stood up, and he pulled me close to his body and guided my hand so that I could feel the rock-hard bulge in his pants.

"Yes, it's true, but most of the ladies that I'm with can't handle it," he explained.

From the feel of things, Rick was definitely working with something, so he probably wasn't bullshitting. Although I loved anal sex I doubt that I would have wanted his big dick sliding into my asshole either. But since this was strictly about gaming him, I had to roll with things.

"You ever been with a black girl?" I asked him, still rubbing on his dick.

He shook his head no.

"You been missing out then," I said to him. Then I reached up and kissed his earlobe and whispered into his ear and told him that I could *handle it* however he wanted to give it to me.

"Tony, I love these two," Rick shouted to his friend, referring to me and Simone.

Tony had Simone all giggly and jittery, and with the way the liquor was being passed among us, I was sure that we were gonna get at Rick and Tony and turn them into vics.

Before long, the whole bottle of Louis XIII was gone, and my head was buzzing like a motherfucker. I was drunk, but I was trying to maintain control of myself and the task at hand. I grabbed Simone by the hand and then guided us toward the bathroom.

"We'll be right back," I said to Rick and Tony as we walked off.

"I gotta piss like a fucking racehorse!" I said to Simone.

"Yeah, me too!"

"Simone, we got these two motherfuckers."

"Tell me about it. I got Tony's head so far up my ass, it's crazy. He was talking so much shit. But I know the dude got money. He told me he owns four BMW dealerships," Simone informed me.

"Say word?" I shouted.

"I'm serious."

We both made our way into our separate stalls and handled our business and came out and freshened up before we headed back to Rick and Tony.

"Everything good?" LQ asked us as soon as we stepped outta the bathroom.

"Yeah, we 'bout to make this happen. We're getting ready to get up outta here with those two dudes we were wit'," I quickly explained to LQ, and then we kept it moving so we wouldn't look like we were scripting anything.

"You don't want anything else to drink?" Rick asked me as we made it back to where they were standing.

"No, I'm good. You already got me too drunk as it is." I chuckled.

After I said that, I turned and looked and saw Simone and Tony lip-locked and shoving their tongue down each other's throats.

"She's a freak just like me," I whispered to Rick. "Why don't you come with me to my truck?" I said to him.

"To your truck?"

"Yeah," I said as I reached down and gently massaged Rick's crotch.

Rick paused and thought for a minute and then he asked, "You're not a cop or anything like that, are you?"

To totally remove any inhibitions that Rick might have had and to assure him, I unbuttoned the tight black satin pants that I was wearing and positioned myself next to him in a way where no one could see what we were doing, and then I guided his hand into my pants and let him massage my shaven and pantyless pussy.

"Frisk me and you tell me if you think I'm a cop," I said to him.

Rick's middle finger was soon inside my wet pussy, and I

know that he was turned on to no end and any reservations that he might have had about me all went out the window.

He walked over to Tony and spoke into his ear, and before I knew it, Tony, Rick, me, and Simone were heading out of the club and across the street to this parking lot where LQ's truck was parked.

I had the keys to the truck and disabled the alarm, and the four of us got in the backseat. The truck had a remote ignition, so the engine came on and began running idle.

Simone and I had already rehashed with each other exactly how this scenario would play itself out so that we were sure to be in control of any situation that was to pop off.

So immediately we instructed Tony and Rick to pull their pants down, and Simone and I both began giving them blow jobs. What we wanted to do was make sure that their pants were pulled down to at least the calf area of their legs. This way, when LQ and Midas showed up, the dudes wouldn't be able to easily bounce and run.

Rick had the biggest dick that I had ever seen on either a black dude or a white dude, and I had to really work to get that shit in my mouth. Simone was doing the damn thing to Tony, and I could tell that Tony and Rick were both enjoying the unexpected blow jobs that they were receiving.

But I didn't know where the hell LQ and Midas were at, and part of me began panicking because I didn't want Rick or Tony to bust their loads before Midas and LQ got there. And, sure enough, just what I feared would happen, happened. Before long, Rick and Tony were both asking me and Simone to get naked so that they could fuck us.

It wasn't like me and Simone could front and say no at that point, because it would have ruined everything and made us look like frauds. But I played it off good.

"Well, that's round two. This is only round one," I looked up at Rick and said, my heart beating a little bit faster.

Rick wasn't going for that, though, and he reached and grabbed at my pants and started tugging on them until they ripped.

"Damn, baby, I gotchu," I said. "Let me do it. I'll take them off."

As soon as I said that, both of the side passenger doors were violently ripped open, LQ on my side of the truck, Midas on Simone's side of the truck.

"Y'all know what time it is! Run your fucking shit!" Midas shouted at the two dudes.

"Motherfucker!" Tony yelled.

LQ told me and Simone to step outta the truck and he asked us if we were okay.

"Yeah, we good," I said as I got outta the truck and stood off to the side.

"Hurry up and run your shit! I want everything! Hurry the fuck up!" Midas continued to bark orders.

I looked over LQ's shoulder and I could see Tony and Rick both reaching in their jacket pockets, and they handed over their possessions. Simone stood off a few feet and acted as a lookout.

"There's fucking more! Hurry up!" LQ barked.

Rick and Tony then began rummaging through their pants pockets and just as Tony was preparing to hand over a bankroll of cash, Rick popped his hand up from around his ankles and fired a shot at LQ.

Bang!

That was the sound that I heard, and being that it was dark outside I could actually see the bright red muzzle flash. "Oh shit!" I screamed.

And in less than a split second I heard another loud gunshot that Rick had fired in Midas's direction.

I looked and saw LQ fall to the ground, writhing in pain, his gun laying on the ground beside him.

"NYPD, freeze!" Rick yelled out as he held out his badge

and quickly exited from the truck and began chasing Midas, who had apparently not been shot.

Bang! Bang! Bang!

I heard three more shots, and then Simone and I ran halfway down the block and took cover behind a parked car.

Then next thing I knew was that within like sixty seconds I heard sirens coming from every direction and there were plainclothes cops running up the block on foot and marked police cars quickly making their way to the scene.

"Simone, come, we gotta get the fuck up outta here!" I shouted to her.

The two of us quickly began walking as fast as we could down the block heading toward Sixth Avenue.

"We gotta hurry up. Oh shit, I can't believe this shit."

"What happened?" Simone asked.

"That motherfucker was strapped, and he was a fucking cop! Gotdamn! I hope my prints wasn't in that motherfucker car. Oh shit! Motherfucker! Aint this a bitch?" I agonized as Simone and I had finally made it to Sixth Avenue.

By this time the cops were literally everywhere, and just as Simone and I managed to slip into the subway station on Thirty-fourth Street and Sixth Avenue, the cops began roping off blocks and blocks of city streets so that they could mark off the area as a crime scene and preserve any evidence that they could use in order to lock our asses up at a later date if they caught us.

I just hoped LQ and Midas were all right, but the bottom line was that I knew that I had to look out for myself and worry about getting my daughter back.

Penn Station

By the time me and Simone made it to the platform of the Penn Station subway, we were way outta breath and huffing

and puffing like we had just run a marathon. It wasn't that we were that much outta shape, which was part of the reason we were breathing so hard, but it also had to do with the fact that we were both nervous as hell.

"Simone, I can't believe that motherfucker was a cop!" I whispered to her in distress.

Simone just shook her head and looked at me. She looked like she was scared as shit, and I can't say that I blame her. We decided that we would jump on the Long Island Railroad and head out to Simone's house and sort things out once we got there.

"Where the fuck is this train at?" I said, sounding anxious like a motherfucker.

I peered into the dark subway tunnel, hoping that I would see the headlights of a train, but I didn't see nothing.

Fifteen more minutes had passed by and still there was no sign of the train that we were supposed to get on.

"That train shoulda been here by now!" Simone said in frustration.

The platform quickly started to fill up with passengers, and instead of it looking like the late-night hour that it was, the subway platform started to look more like the height of rush hour. All of the passengers began murmuring and getting visibly restless and agitated.

Then we heard an announcement coming over the PA system that said that due to police activity all of the train service coming in and out of Penn Station had been halted due to the investigation.

"Ain't this about a bitch!" I screamed out. "Come on, Simone, we gotta bounce."

Simone wanted to chill and just wait it out, but I knew from my experience dealing with street niggas that we couldn't chill, and that it was more than time to bounce up outta that subway or else we would be on our fucking way to jail.

"Simone, don't fight me! Trust me. In five minutes cops is

gonna flood this station with bloodhounds and the whole nine yards. We gotta bounce! Now let me get your driver's license."

"For what?"

"Simone, give me the fucking license, shit!" I barked on her ass.

Simone quickly reached for her driver's license and handed it to me.

"Is this the address where you live at?"

Simone nodded her head.

"A'ight, here, take this," I said, handing Simone a hundred-dollar bill. I explained to her that we had to split up and go back outside and hail down separate cabs. "We'll meet up at your house. I got your driver's license and I'll keep this with me so I won't lose your address. Let me get your cell phone number, and when I get out there I'll call you from a pay phone just to double-check on shit and make sure everything is all good."

Simone said okay, and then she started to ask a bunch of questions.

"We gotta bounce right now. We'll talk later," I said to her, sensing that things were about to get hectic. And, man, was I right. As soon as Simone and I headed toward the subway exit we were greeted by an army of cops on foot. They were in full riot gear and accompanied by bloodhounds.

"Fuck! Simone, come on," I screamed to her as we quickly turned in the other direction and tried to blend in with the other passengers.

Thankfully, Penn Station was a huge train station with a bunch of exits and a ton of shops and all kinds of square footage to get lost in.

"Just go that way and try to get to a free exit, and I'm gonna go this way," I said, as me and Simone split up, and I briskly walked away praying that I would see an exit. My

heart was thumping and I wanted to run, but I didn't want to bring any attention to myself.

I finally saw some steps leading to an exit and headed straight for it.

Hurry hurry hurry! I urged myself.

Just as I got to the top of the steps, I saw another army of cops with shotguns and bulletproof vests, but thank God they didn't have any bloodhounds. I had no choice but to go past those cops if I wanted to get outside, and I knew that I had to go for it because if I went back down the steps into the subway then I would have definitely gotten bagged by the bloodhounds.

Maybe it was just in my head, but I was sure that one of the cops seemed to have his eyes locked on me. There were other passengers around me, but it wasn't nearly the throng of people who had been gathering on the platform. So I felt kind of like a fish outta water.

As I approached the army of cops, this one cop seemed like he was just locked in on me and I knew that it was time to go into full-fledged acting mode in order to save my ass.

I tried my best not to break my stride as I walked and I began coughing a fake cough and covered my mouth while I coughed. And when I was about ten yards away from the officers I began coughing really hard and bent over, to hide my face. But what I was really doing was sticking a finger down my throat, and I didn't want the cops to see me when I did that.

My finger touched the back of my throat, and I pressed down as hard as I could. And as I stood up I began puking my brains out. I knew that I had to be extra dramatic with it, so I let the vomit run all down my top and some of it got on my pants and shoes. I brought my hands to my mouth and wiped some of the excess vomit away, but I whisked my hand across the front of my face in a way that caused me to fling some vomit chunks into the air.

"Uurrrghhh! Urrggghhh!" I violently coughed as hard as I could, and by this time, with me looking like a straight vomiting mess, I approached the same cop who appeared to be looking at me when I was first coming up the steps.

"Excuse me, I know there's some kind of police emergency, but I'm pregnant and I'm throwing up and I just feel horrible. Are there cabs running? I really need to get home," I said to the cop with my heart in my stomach. I was playing it up good but was trying to not overdo it.

"Uhh, yeah. Well, no, actually this whole zone is a frozen zone. We have to lock everything down until we are done with our investigation," the cop said as he looked as if he was thinking of what to do.

"Just walk outside. Let one of the officers outside know that you're pregnant and they'll help you out."

"Okay, thank you," I said as I walked out of Penn Station. I knew that I had to get the hell outta that area as quickly as I could. And I also knew that if it was a frozen zone I wouldn't be able to catch any cabs in that vicinity, and even if I did, I was sure that the cops would be checking each and every car that came in and out of that frozen zone. Plus, I had to hurry up and get the hell outta dodge, just in case there was an APB out on me and that cop that I had spoken to wised-up and realized who I was and that I had been bullshitting him.

Thankfully, I was able to walk about twenty blocks to Fifty-third Street, and in that area there was no frozen zone, so I was able to hail a cab with no problem. I got in the cab and told the Arab driver where I was going. As the driver pulled off and headed toward the Fifty-ninth Street Bridge I was able to exhale and relax just a little bit.

I knew that I wouldn't be able to relax fully for some time to come and I knew that shit was gonna get real hectic for me. I hoped like all hell that the cops wouldn't be able to lift my fingerprints off of anything inside of LQ's truck or off of

anything inside the strip club. I would just have to wait and see how things played out. But for starters my wait-and-see game was gonna start with me waiting to see if Simone was able to successfully make it.

Time would soon tell.

Headline News

As it turned out, while I was in the cab driving out to Long Island, something told me that it probably wouldn't be the smartest thing to head straight to Simone's crib. Because, after all was said and done, I was operating in the blind so to speak. I mean, I had no idea if the cops had dusted the car for prints, and if so, what if they found Simone's prints and her prints just happen to be inside of some kind of database? If that was the case, then it would just be a matter of hours— if not minutes—before the cops would be arriving at Simone's crib.

I also was operating blindly in the fact that I didn't know what was up with Midas and LQ. Like, I didn't know if they had got arrested and were being questioned, and if so, what if they bitched up and started snitching and ratting me and Simone out?

Wheewwww. That was the sound that I made as I slumped in my seat in the back of the cab.

"This shit is crazy," I mumbled under my breath.

"Excuse me, driver, excuse me. Listen, I changed my mind about my destination. I need to go to Queens instead."

The Arab driver, who was musty as hell, slid the partition to the side that separated the front of the cab from the back of the cab. He seemed to be annoyed and was yapping about something, but I couldn't understand a word he was saying. But, from the sound of it, it sounded like he was pissed off that I had changed my plans.

"What the fuck difference does it make? I'm still gonna pay you! Shit!" I barked at the cabdriver.

He mumbled something back to me, but I ignored him.

"Hollis. Hollis, Queens. I want to go to H-O-L-L-I-S. Do you understand the words that are coming out of my mouth?" I screamed.

The cabdriver really seemed like he was pissed off. He quickly exited the Expressway and prepared to head back in the opposite direction. And as soon as he made it back on to the highway he hit the gas pedal as hard as he could and was soon doing like ninety miles an hour. He was weaving in and out of traffic and driving like a gotdamn fool.

"Hey! Hellloooo!" I screamed as I banged on the clear fiberglass partition. "You fucking towel-head dot-head motherfucker. Slow the fuck down! What the hell is wrong with you?"

The driver totally ignored me and continued to speed, and in about fifteen minutes we were exiting the Parkway and weaving our way to Hollis.

"Let me out at Two hundred and first Street and Hollis Ave."

The driver still paid me no mind but made his way to the location. And as soon as we reached the location, he made sure that he locked the doors until I paid him.

"Ain't nobody not trying to pay you? What the fuck you locking the doors for?" I said as I looked at the meter and I could see that the fare was gonna cost me sixty dollars. I took out my money and counted off sixty dollars exactly and handed it through the partition.

"You ain't getting shit else. Now let me the fuck out."

He unlocked the doors, and I exited from the cab. When the cabdriver pulled off, I walked a half a block up 201st Street until I made it to my on-again, off-again homegirl's house. Her name was Denise, and she was a corrections officer. But the thing about her was that she was cool and was the type

that you would never expect to be in law enforcement because she was so ghetto.

The only thing about Denise was that she really had these jealousy issues that would make her just stop speaking to her friends over nothing. Like, let her see me in a new car, and she would cop an attitude about something and stop speaking to me. But without a doubt her biggest jealousy issue was when it came to dudes. She had this thing about her where she felt like every dude had to like her and give her the time of day. And if a dude didn't, then it was no problem, unless it was a situation where a dude showed me or one of my girls some love or tried to kick it to us but didn't show Denise any love or didn't try to kick it to Denise. God forbid that happened because she would lose it! And then the next thing you know is that she would be talking behind our backs and dissing us for absolutely no reason.

Well, anyway, I reached Denise's side door and, mind you, it was now well past twelve midnight. I didn't care, though, and I started ringing her doorbell. After about five minutes or so, she came to the door and she asked who it was while simultaneously opening the door.

"Cinnamon?"

"Yeah, it's me."

"What's up? What's going on?"

"Fucking drama like crazy!" I replied as Denise let me in.

I was reluctant to tell her everything that had gone down, but I desperately needed to stay there with her that night, so I knew that I had to come clean.

"Okay, Denise, I'll be straight up with you, but please don't trip the fuck out."

"Yeah, yeah, come on, you know me. What's up? What happened?"

I started breaking down what had happened, in terms of the robbery going bad with Midas and LQ. But I kept it generic in the sense that I only told her that we were leaving

the strip club and that shit just jumped off. I didn't tell her that we had planned on setting the dudes up and that our plans went bad.

"No fucking way," Denise said. "I was just watching that shit on CNN. That shit is like breaking headline news on every station," she explained, and then she ushered me into her living room.

I gazed at her flat-screen television as Denise flipped the channels until she found a news station that was talking about the shooting. And as I listened in, right off the bat I knew that shit was fucked-up and that I was neck-deep in some serious shit. It turned out that both Rick and Tony were undercover vice cops who had been investigating suspected prostitution and drug sales at Mike's Cabaret.

I shook my head as I thought about how fucked-up and how corrupt those cops must have been. Because not only did they have shitloads of money that the NYPD does not pay them or would even let them borrow for the investigation, but they were both literally getting blow jobs from me and Simone and was ready to fuck us. So, from that alone, I knew that they were dirty cops, but it didn't matter. The only thing that mattered was that they were indeed cops and they were on duty when we struck.

According to the news, LQ had been shot and killed. He died on the scene. Both cops had been shot and were expected to make it. One cop was in critical condition, and the other was in stable condition. As for Midas, he hadn't been shot, but he was apprehended about ten blocks away from the crime scene.

But the words that I definitely didn't want to hear was that the cops were looking for two female suspects who were believed to be with Midas and LQ at the time of the shooting.

"Cinnamon, you? They talking about you?"

All I could do was nod my head.

"But you was just locked up on the Island? What hap-

pened? I mean, it seemed like when my last shift ended I was saying bye to your ass and a few days later this shit?"

"Denise, I know. I fucked up."

Then, sure enough and true to her nature, Denise started questioning me about Midas.

"So you was fucking Midas?"

I kept quiet because I didn't even want to go there, and I was trying to see if I should just lie and tell her what was up.

"You know he used to try to kick it to me, right? I mean, that nigga always wanted to fuck me, but I ain't never give up the drawers to that nigga. He the type that keeps money, but he be frontin' too. I mean, he don't have real long money. I was like, I didn't think it would be worth the hassle."

I kept my mouth shut because there was absolutely no reason for Denise to even be telling me all that she was telling me.

Then she stood up from the couch and smiled this sinister smile and said, "Let me find out you was trying to get at my leftovers."

"Your leftovers?" I replied.

"See, I knew it. So you was fucking that nigga," Denise replied as if she had really caught feelings.

"Okay, Denise, honest to God, I had only fucked the nigga one time. That's it. It wasn't nothing there. I mean, I reached out to the nigga and told him what was up with me and how I needed to get out of Rikers so I could see what was up with my daughter. And I asked him if he could help me out. He looked out for me and got my bail money up, so the least I could do was give the nigga some pussy."

Denise kind of twisted her lips and smacked this smirk on her face that I just wanted to slap right the fuck off.

"Yeah, I mean, whatever. You just doing you, right?"

"That's it."

Denise was quiet for a minute, and I could tell that she was kinda tight over me fucking Midas.

"So, you know you can't stay here, right?"

"Denise, I know, and all I'm asking is to just let me spend the night and I'm out in the morning."

Denise shook her head and blew some air outta her lungs. "A'ight, I'm just saying, I gotta protect my job. They find out you was staying up in here and I'll be assed out and fired."

"I completely understand. I promise you I'll be out in the morning."

Denise finally got off of the jealous shit and offered me something to eat and drink and asked me if I wanted to take a shower. She even offered to give me a few of her old outfits and shoes and sneakers so I could have some changes of clothes during the upcoming days.

That was definitely much appreciated, and I took her up on all that she offered. And that was the thing with her. She was fucking Dr. Jekyll and Mr. Hyde. But that's just how she was, and there was nothing that I could do about it.

So after I took a shower, changed my clothes, and ate some food I told Denise to turn the television off because I was tired of hearing the news talk about the whole cop-shooting thing. I decided to switch topics and talk about my daughter and I began to explain to Denise how I couldn't believe that the system had fucked up and literally had lost my daughter.

To my complete surprise and shock Denise said that she wasn't surprised because she had seen it happen firsthand on different occasions while she worked at Rikers.

"Yeah, all the time single moms are getting locked up and even single dads get locked up, and it's like the kids just get swooped up and go into some kind of black hole or some shit," Denise explained.

She did offer me a bit of hope and said that she was almost sure that she would be able to get assistance from someone in the department of corrections and help me track down my daughter. She asked me if there was a way that she could reach me tomorrow.

I ended up giving her Simone's number and told her that if no one picked up, to just leave a voice mail with any information that she could muster up.

Only thing was that now I was just hoping that Simone was all right on her end and that I would be able to hook up with her or at least make contact with her.

I was living a crazy life, but it was real!

Two's a Crowd

When I woke up a few hours later I was tired as hell, but I wanted to respect Denise's wishes and her crib. She had given me a small suitcase, the size that you would use to carry on an airplane. So I packed the few outfits that she had given me and I called a cab.

While I was waiting, Denise woke up to get ready for work.

"You up already?" she asked.

"Yeah, I'm-a bounce. I know you gotta go to work, and I wantchu to have that peace of mind when you're at work, knowing that I left," I said as I zipped up the suitcase.

Denise asked me if I needed anything.

"Yeah, if you could just call me today about Tarsha and look into all of that today, then that would be all that I would really need."

"Yeah, I gotchu on that. I'll hit you up on that number before this afternoon."

With that I hugged Denise and thanked her for looking out for me. She gave me a phony halfhearted hug and told me to be safe and to be careful.

My cab pulled up to her house and blew the horn, and I stepped outside and asked the cabdriver to drive me to this diner in Rosedale called USA Diner.

With only forty dollars to my name I sat down and ordered

breakfast. I asked the waitress if she could get me five dollars worth of quarters, which she gladly did.

While my food got prepared I walked over to the pay phone and dialed Simone on her cell phone.

"Shit," I said to myself as the phone rang out to voice mail. I didn't leave a message and I thought about what I should do. *Just call back and keep calling till you get her.* That's what I said to myself and I repeatedly called Simone's phone. And thankfully, after having wasted almost two dollars in quarters, Simone picked up the phone, sounding tired and groggy as hell.

"Simone?"

"Yeah, hello? Who's this?"

"Simone, it's me, Cinnamon. You 'sleep? Get up!"

"What time is it?" Simone asked.

"Simone! Listen to me—wake the fuck up."

"Okay, all right, I'm up. I'm up. What's up? I thought you were gonna meet me at my house."

"Listen, Simone, I gotta talk real quick, but just listen to me. Have you ever been fingerprinted before in your life?"

Simone explained that she had been because she was a former nursery school teacher.

"Okay, you gots to get the fuck up and bounce from your crib right now. They bagged Midas and LQ got killed."

"No! Don't tell me that."

"Yeah, he's outta here. I didn't know if the cops had bagged you or what, so I couldn't take a chance on heading out there. But here's the thing, you can't stay there because if your prints is anywhere up in that truck or in that club and the police happen to lift the prints and run a check on them then you'll be bagged. If Midas drops dime on you, then you're bagged."

"But, Cinnamon, I was thinking about this, and at the end of the day me and you didn't do anything."

"Simone, are you mad? All anyone else has to do is con-nect Midas with us and we'll be up under the jail."

I explained to Simone that she had to trust me and that she had to get dressed and get her ass out to Queens and hook up with me at the USA Diner.

Simone agreed to meet me. But, truth be told, as far as I was concerned, Simone was really a liability to me, more like carrying around deadweight. Plain and simple, being that I was on the run I knew that two was a crowd, but at the same time I knew that Denise would be calling Simone's cell phone as soon as she found out any info on my daugh-ter. Plus, I also knew that Simone had access to a car and access to some much-needed cash.

I asked Simone if she had access to any car that wasn't registered in her name, and thankfully she said that she had access to her brother's Nissan Altima, being that he was away at college.

"Good, so drive that instead of your car, and if you got any dough, try to roll with like five hundred dollars."

Simone kinda understood where I was coming from with my line of reasoning and my rationale but still was on, she's innocent and didn't really have to worry. But I knew that that was just because she didn't understand the laws and the sys-tem and how shit worked like I did.

There are two fucking cops that are shot, and we basically was in on the scheme to rob them. So any sensible street-smart person would have known that that was an open-and-shut conspiracy charge. But I didn't have time to grapple with her about those issues over the phone. I simply had to, and was able to, get her to trust me, and I convinced her to get her ass out to Queens.

Two hours later once Simone arrived I explained to her that we would wait to hear from Denise, and as soon as we did, that would determine our next moves and all she had to

do was follow my lead. In the interim I had to make some moves and reach out to certain connections that I had so that I could get my hands on some heat. I wanted to try to scoop up some phone numbers of certain people that I definitely wanted to reach out to that I felt would be able to help me figure out shit.

Anyway, Simone finally got it. But I knew that I would still have to make an investment of faith in her ass. I was going on faith that having her around during this crazy hectic time would be better for me than not having her around.

I definitely hoped that I was right and that my *investment* paid off.

Only time would tell.

Pistol Pete

Simone proved to be a good straggler investment for me. Although she was essentially a white trick, she knew a little bit about computers and the Internet. And it was her idea that we go to a local library and check out the information that Denise had provided for us.

It turned out that Denise was able to run a nationwide check on Tarsha, and she found out that she was registered in the New Jersey public school system by a legal guardian whose last name was Anderson. Now, how the fuck she ended up in New Jersey? I have no idea.

Denise literally could only talk to me for like thirty seconds, and she couldn't provide no specific details. She had to cut shit short with me because I knew that she was worried about tapped phones and all kinds of shit pertaining to my ass. But I appreciated any little thing that she could do for me. All she said was, "Cee, I can't explain how or why, but Tarsha is in New Jersey, and she's in the New Jersey public school system. Check into that and you'll be good. I gotta bounce."

That was all Denise said to me, but I ran with it, and it gave me all kinds of hope.

"Cinnamon, I think I got something that we can go off of," Simone said while I nervously scoped out the library to make sure I wasn't being watched too closely by anybody.

"Whatchu talkin' about?" I asked.

"Look. See all of this on the screen? Well, I did a people search on Yahoo for all of the people with the last name *Anderson* that live in Camden, New Jersey and this is what came back."

"All of those fuckin' names!" I stated with disbelief and some disappointment. "How the hell are we gonna know which is the correct Anderson?"

"Well, look at this." Simone pointed at the computer monitor.

"We can kind of narrow it down by the ages. We should just start with all of the Andersons that are thirty and older. It's more likely that your daughter would be with a family in that age range, like I couldn't see the system putting her with some old-ass family or someone that was too young," Simone reasoned.

"A'ight, that makes some sense, but now what?" I asked.

"Well, now, we need to pay for this info to get the full addresses and all of that," Simone stated.

"Credit card? Bitch, are you fuckin' stupid or what? I ain't got no got damn credit cards! This is how you're supposed to be helping a bitch? Typing in shit like you a fuckin' Bill Gates computer whiz and shit! Simone, you ain't helping me, and I need to find my daughter!" I said in a real vexed tone, while not trying to attract too much attention.

"Look, you got three hundred dollars cash on you, right?" Simone asked.

"Yeah."

"Give it to me and I'll get the info. Just watch me work."

I really had no choice but to trust that Simone knew what the hell she was doing. I gave her the three hundred dollars, and within a matter of minutes she had spotted a mark in the library. She found a middle-aged white man and she explained him her plight and he agreed to let her use his credit card in exchange for the hundred-dollar fee that Simone proposed.

"See, it is a safe Web site," Simone explained. "It is nine-ninety-nine for every name that we search and I wanna search twenty names so they'll charge your credit card two hundred dollars and I'm giving you three hundred dollars so you are making a hundred dollars right off the top."

The white man thought about it for a moment and then he complied. "It seems legitimate to me," he stated and took out his credit card while proceeding to type in his credit card number. "You know with so many identity theft things happening you have to be careful," he stated.

Although the man had helped us out, I could sense that the real reason that he had helped was because he probably thought he could kick it to Simone in his own little white way.

So to make sure that everything went over real smooth I tapped Simone and silently mouthed the words, *"Kick it to him."*

Simone smiled and then she reached for a piece of paper and a pen and wrote down her number. "Here, I want you to have this," Simone said as she handed the white man her phone number.

"What's this?" he asked.

"I wantchu to have that, and call me during the week and I'll make sure that I *really* thank you for this," Simone said in her whorish-sounding tone.

The white man looked like a nerd, but he caught on really quick as he began to turn bloodshot red from embarrassment.

Simone then walked off with him and left me at the computer. As I sat there, I remember feeling nervous with anticipation because I could sense that I just might possibly be reunited with my daughter. And the simple thought of just possibly seeing her was way too much for a bitch's blood pressure to handle.

Simone made her way back to the computer, a wide smile on her face.

"What the fuck is so funny?" I asked.

"Nothing. It's just that I could have got that dude for like two hundred and fifty dollars for a blow job. I know I could have!" Simone confidently stated.

"Yo, you got more game than a little bit. Fo' real, fo' real!"

"Yeah, but we gotta get this info. I'm gonna print it out, and then we should be good. We just gotta hope that Tarsha is at one of these addresses," Simone explained.

When we were done printing the info, I was more than ready to get the hell up outta that library. Being in certain spots just made me feel way too uncomfortable, and whenever I got that uncomfortable feeling I knew that it was time to bounce.

We made our way to the Nissan, and I let Simone do the driving. Even though she wasn't from New Jersey she navigated her way to the New Jersey Turnpike.

"Yo, you think Denise was bullshitting with this information?" I asked Simone.

Before she could answer the question I shot back with another question. "Simone, you think we should park up the Nissan and just go rent something? You think we pressing our luck in this ride right here?"

Simone was ready to answer me, but again I cut her off. "Word to everything! If that bitch Denise is sending me on a wild-goose chase, I'll go back to New York and fuck that bitch up! Word is bond!"

I finally paused from my nervous barrage of questions and comments.

"Well, you know her better than I do, so I really don't know what to say. I mean, I don't see why she would send you on some wild-goose chase," Simone reasoned.

I guess she was right, and the fact was, I really didn't have much to lose.

Underground Ho Spot

1:30 AM, Philadelphia, Pennsylvania

"You sure this the spot?" Simone asked.

"Yeah, this is it. I know this area. He told me Old York Road, not too far from Temple University."

"What address did he give you?"

"He didn't, he just told me on Old York Road," I replied.

As Simone navigated the car down Old York Road, I was in search of this dude named Tito, a hustler from Mount Vernon, New York who had relocated to Philadelphia. Tito told me to meet him at an underground ho spot. Tito was my nigga that had let me rest at his spot in Philly with my daughter a few years back after I had shot up this hatin'-ass chick's crib and needed to lay low for a while. He was also my "Clyde" and I was his "Bonnie," back in the days and even somewhat recently. Our hustle was to go from borough to borough robbing motherfuckers.

I had contacted him while me and Simone were on the New Jersey Turnpike because I figured he would know a little bit about Camden, and the last thing I wanted to do was go up in Camden blind not knowing what was what, and fuck around and get bagged by the cops on a humble. So Tito had told me to meet him at the ho spot on Old York Road and we would build from there.

"This gotta be the spot," I said to Simone as I had her park the car. There was a slow stream of traffic coming from an apartment, which was situated above a storefront. And I just knew that that had to be the spot.

"A'ight, we gonna park here, and you just follow my lead. I'm gonna play it off like you tricking tonight. A'ight?"

"Okay, cool. I gotchu," Simone said, sounding like she was a black girl from Bed-Stuy and not some white ho from the suburbs in Long Island.

As we approached what we hoped was the ho spot, Simone spoke up.

"Yo, I gotchu, Cinnamon. But on the real, I hate spots like this 'cause you gotta be careful as hell because spots like this are always getting raided," Simone said. "That's why I never really went up in spots like this. The clubs was always my thing. I'll walk the streets and hit up these clubs any day instead of being caged up in a spot like this waiting for undercovers to come raid it."

"Yo, shut the fuck up and move yo' ass!" I yelled at Simone. She didn't know what the fuck she was talking about. I didn't need her talking about all of that getting-raided-by-the-cops bullshit, but I moreso yelled at her for the madam-ho effect.

As we had made our way up to the metal security door, a bodyguard-looking cat stepped out from inside the door.

"What's good?" I asked the bodyguard-looking dude.

He didn't respond to me, and I didn't want to just straight-out ask for Tito because I didn't know what was what at that point.

"Yo, what's the tip in, and what's the tip out?" I asked.

After saying that the bodyguard looked at Simone and sort of relaxed his position.

"Who you wit'?" he asked.

"I'm wit' Tito."

The bodyguard nodded and then asked, "How many girls you got? Just her?"

"Yeah, just her."

"A'ight I'm-a frisk y'all, and then y'all just see my man right behind the security booth and make your way upstairs."

With that we were in. I went to the security booth and asked about the tip in and tip out.

"It's just her with you?"

"Yeah, just her."

"A'ight, let her go straight upstairs."

Although Simone claimed that she knew how to operate in spots like this, while we were in the car riding to the spot I schooled her on how she should move once we got inside. She was a quick study and definitely came across like she knew the ropes. She quickly went upstairs and did as she had been instructed.

As Simone opened the heavy steel door that led to upstairs, the loud sound of thumping music rushed out at me.

I get money money I got . . .

Those were the words of the 50 Cent track that blasted in the background.

"Yo, a'ight with the tip in—" the guy behind the security booth said before he was interrupted.

"Ohhh shit, muthafucking sexy-ass Cinnamon! What's really good, my lady?" Tito yelled as he came up to me and gave me a bear hug and a kiss on the cheek.

"My nigga!" I said. I was happier than a bitch to see Tito.

"Tip in? You brought some hoes witchu, Cinnamon?" Tito asked as I smiled.

"Yo, Cinnamon you is one hustlin'-ass bitch! I thought you was coming to see about your daughter and here you are bringing hoes to the fucking spot!"

As a ho came downstairs dressed in high heels and fishnet stockings, you could here the music still thumping in the background, only now the record had switched up to a Rick Ross song.

Every day I'm hustlin' hustlin' hustlin' . . .

Right on cue with the music I said to Tito, "Yo, Tito, Every day I'm hustlin' hustlin' hustlin' . . ."

The two of us laughed, and then Tito took me to a back room that looked like it doubled as a recording studio during the day. There were three hoes in the room, and each of them was giving someone a blow job.

"That's you if you wanna hit," Tito said.

At first I thought he was talking about one of the hoes, but then I realized that he was referring to the lines of coke that was laid out on the table.

Normally just chronic and Hennessy was what I fucked wit', but as stressed and anxious as I had been over my daughter, I was ready to get high off of whateva.

I sat down at the table, and before I knew what was what, I had snorted two lines of coke. And after snorting it I reclined back in my chair, closed my eyes and waited for the drug to do its thing.

Tito rolled a blunt and after sparking it said, "So, yo, where you resting at?"

Over the loud music I replied, "I'll probably just stay at a hotel near the airport tonight."

"A'ight so, yo, I'm bouncing up outta here at about five in the morning. Just holla at me at like twelve in the afternoon and I'll scoop you up and we'll take it from there," Tito stated.

"A hundred!" I replied as I gave Tito a pound and took like five pulls from the blunt.

I was definitely feeling high like a muthafucka as Tito

poured us both some Hennessy and we made our way upstairs.

When we got upstairs I saw a stream of hoes, most of
them choice dime pieces. There were also a bunch of dudes
standing around getting wall dances and making proposi-
tions to the hoes.

"Yo, look at this thick white bitch up in here butt-ass
naked!" Tito shouted in my ear.

"Yo, that's me!" I shouted back at Tito.

"Say word?"

"Word is bond."

Tito started laughing as he said, "Yo, Cinnamon, you are
about the grimiest bitch that I know!"

He continued to laugh as he said, "Cinnamon, you could
have at least bought the bitch a pair of stillettos or some
stockings or something! Oh shit, that is hilarious god! The
bitch is walking around butt-naked with a pocketbook! What
the fuck? I ain't never seen no shit like that before."

I had to admit that Simone did in fact look funny. Not that
she didn't look sexy or appealing, it was just that all of the
other chicks were walking around in thongs, or something
provocative and sexy-looking, with makeup on and all of
that. And Simone was white as a mouse walking around with
no clothes on, and it just looked wild.

The thing was, I had never planned on *pimpin'* Simone. It
was just something that just happened. But with the coke,
weed, and liquor flowing through my body I was open as hell,
and the thought of Simone getting me some money was
sounding like music to my ears.

A Jay-Z track was booming in the room as Simone spotted me and Tito and walked over to us. "What's up?" Simone
asked.

"What's up?" I replied with a disgusted look on my face.
"Get this money, that's what's up!" I totally caught Simone

off guard with my demeanor and she looked at me kind of confused.

"Don't stand around looking at me, bitch! Get this money!" I shouted over the music.

Simone looked at me and walked off and sort of began to follow the lead of the other hoes. And before long she was walking off with a nigga ready to service him.

By the time we left the spot it was just about 5:00 in the morning, and Simone had done good. In the span of about four hours, she had made about four hundred and fifty dollars, which she had no problem handing over to me.

"Cinnamon, at least you could have told me that you wanted me to trick for you. You did it on some ol' chump-ass bitch shit," Simone said as we piled into the Nissan.

I was feeling like I was hungover even though I hadn't drank that much. So I wasn't really in the mood for much of Simone's bullshit. I was gonna flip on her, but at the same time I was sensible enough to realize that I needed her to help me get my daughter, besides the fact that we both were on the run and needed each other.

"Yo, pull out and make a left at the corner and then make another left at the first light." I was feeling like I was ready to throw up. "We gotta make our way to the Hilton over near the airport."

Simone remained calm and quiet as we navigated through the dark Philadelphia streets.

"On the real I wasn't planning on you getting us no money tonight. It just happened. Yo, make a left right there and get on the Interstate and you'll see the signs for the airport. Follow those signs and you'll see a bunch of hotels. Just exit near the hotels and navigate your way to the Hilton. My ass is feeling sick, and I gotta go to sleep," I stated as I reclined back in my chair and went to sleep.

Camden, New Jersey—USA Homicide Capital

Tito had met us at the Hilton and suggested that we call the phone numbers that we had, to narrow down the search for Tarsha even more.

It was an excellent idea, and that was when Simone's white accent came in good for us. She dialed number after number and asked if she could speak to Tarsha.

And with each call my hope began to fade as caller after caller claimed that no one by the name of Tarsha lived at the residence.

Not until the sixteenth or so call that we made did we feel like we were on to something.

Simone had the phone on speakerphone as she asked, "Hello, may I speak with Tarsha?"

"Tarsha?" the person on the other end asked, sounding somewhat curious. "May I ask who is calling, and what this is in reference to?"

"Oh, I'm sorry," Simone replied. "This is Nikki. I'm a friend of Tarsha's. We were in the same dorm at college last year, and I no longer go to that college anymore, so I was just calling to say hello, actually to surprise Tarsha and to talk about old times."

I immediately knew where she was going with her line of talk.

"Oh," the party on the other line stated. "I think you have the wrong number."

"Well, doesn't Tarsha live at this address?" Simone asked as I was prepared for yet another letdown.

"Yes, Tarsha lives here, but she is way too young for college, so I think you may have dialed the wrong number," the person said.

"Oh, I'm so sorry. I got this number from off the Internet."

"It's not a problem," the lady replied before hanging up.

My heart was racing a mile a minute as I said, "That's it. I know she's there."

Tito asked to see the address and then quickly stated that he was almost sure he knew where the address was located. "Yo, if that is where I think it is, on the real, it don't get more ghetto than that area! Word. Camden is as wild as it is. It's the murder capital in the country, but that particular part of Camden is the fuckin' slums!" Tito informed us.

I thought for a minute in silence.

And after breaking my silence I said, "This is what we gotta do. I don't wanna take a chance driving the Nissan, so we'll go to the airport, rent a car and head over to Camden and scope everything out before we make any moves."

"Baby, we can't rent no car without a credit card," Simone replied.

"She's right, Cinnamon," Tito added. "But we'll be a'ight. Let's just roll in my ride."

We all piled in Tito's all-black quarter-to-eight BMW, a car that he informed me he was able to get, thanks to this robbery that we had committed at this spot called Brooklyn Café.

"Cinnamon, that's why you'll always be my nigga fo' life. You attract money like a magnet," he stated.

In a matter of minutes we were in Camden, and it didn't take long to see what Tito had been talking about. Being from New York, I had seen my share of ghettos. But southside Jamaica, Queens; Brownsville, Brooklyn; or the south Bronx all couldn't touch Camden, New Jersey in terms of ghettoness. The shit looked worse than the slums of Baltimore, Maryland.

"Yo, I can't believe the system got my daughter growing up in this shit! They would have never did that to no white kid!" I yelled, as I could care less that Simone was white.

"This is the block," Tito said as he pulled in front of a local

store. There were a number of people out on the block who looked as if they were just going about their business.

"The house is probably about midway down the block," Tito stated.

"Okay, cool," I said. "But what we gotta do is circle the block one time and look for anything that looks suspicious. And then we wait about a half hour and do the exact same thing before we make any kind of moves. The last thing that I want is for the cops to get lucky and roll up on us. I can't be this close to Tarsha and get knocked!"

Tito complied with my instructions and started up the car, and we cruised down the block in what was a normal driving pace for a residential block.

"Y'all see anything?" Tito asked.

"Nah, everything looks cool," I replied.

"That's the house right there, the brick one on the left," Simone informed us.

My palms were sweaty from my nerves. With all that I knew about stickups and running up in niggas' cribs and doing robberies, I was more than ready to walk up to the door with my .45 and do my thing and come out with my daughter.

"You think she's home?" Tito asked.

"Yeah," I quickly replied as thoughts of Tarsha's dad popped into my head.

"So how we gonna do this?" Tito asked.

Simone stated that she could walk up to the door and act like she was at the wrong address just to get a feel for what the house looked like on the inside and to see who was home. But we thought that that would raise too many red flags since we had already called and asked for a Tarsha. That would have made things look way too suspicious.

"We gonna have to come back tonight when it gets dark and run up in that bitch," I said, knowing that it was always very risky to run up in someone's house without knowing what or who was inside.

As Tito turned and was headed back toward the direction of the store that we had been parked in front of, he stated, "Yo, did y'all see that Escalade that was parked all the way at the end of the block? It was just before we made the turn. That was the only thing that looked outta place to me. That whip don't belong here," Tito stated.

"Nah, I didn't see it, but why you say that?" I asked. "You be around here like that to know what niggas is driving? Maybe some nigga is just hustling and got dough and his girl lives on the block or something," I reasoned.

Tito didn't say anything, and neither did Simone.

"Yo, let's go get something from McDonald's, and then we can circle back, but let's just come up the block from the opposite direction," I stated.

As we made it to the McDonald's drive-through Tito said, "Them *federalees* be driving them high-end whips and be trippin' up motherfuckas, so that's why my radar went up."

Tito was street, so if that's what he was suspecting, then I trusted and respected his gangsta, and I knew that we had to proceed with caution.

My nerves were so on edge that I couldn't even bring myself to eat. As I sat and waited for Simone and Tito to finish their food, I wondered if Tarsha still liked McDonald's. I wondered when was the last time that she had been to McDonald's. And buying Tarsha a McDonald's Happy Meal quickly became another motivator for me. *Tonight*, I told myself, *the first thing that I am gonna do is buy Tarsha a happy meal. Word.*

Tito and Simone were finally finished eating, and Tito started up the car and made his way back to what we hoped was Tarsha's block.

When we were about two blocks away, Tito turned down the music and said, "Yo, the Escalade is gonna be on the passenger side if it's still there. We'll just roll through at a nor-

mal speed, and we can look as hard as we want to at them 'cause they can't see through the tints on this ride."

As we came up on the Escalade the first thing that Simone noticed was that it had Pennsylvania plates. And that made me think even more so that it was probably not the feds because the feds would have likely had New Jersey plates.

"So what?" Tito questioned. "Who cares about the plates? I wanna know who is in the muthafucka."

We passed the Escalade and chills ran down my body, and so did rage and anger.

"Son of a bitch!" I screamed.

"What's up? What?" Simone and Tito asked as he continued to drive.

"That fucking bitch Denise played my ass!" I yelled.

"What happened?" Tito asked.

"That dude in the Escalade is Pistol Pete the OG from New York!"

Simone and Tito pressed me for more of an explanation.

"Chill! Just give me a fucking minute to think!" I yelled.

All sorts of thoughts ran through my head. I wanted to know what exactly was Pete doing on the same block that I thought Tarsha lived on? Maybe someone in my family got into the foster care system and located Tarsha so that she would be in good hands? Maybe Tarsha didn't even live on this block at all and I was in fact on a wild-goose chase? I was really starting to trip out.

I finally began to explain to Tito and Simone exactly who Pistol Pete was. He was a first-cousin to Midas, and the thing was, he was a straight-up hitman for hire. And I knew that with him being out there he had to be planning to make a hit on my ass to take me out, to prevent me from dropping dime on Midas over the whole shooting shit that went down with Rick, the cop and LQ. I knew that since LQ had gotten killed during the robbery, and me and Simone got away and were

on the run, that Midas would be trying to pin everything on LQ, me, and Simone. The best way to prevent us from coming up with a different story if we were to get arrested or if we just out-and-out snitched on his ass was to make sure that we were dead so that we couldn't talk even if we wanted to.

"So where is the connection to Denise and Pistol Pete?" Tito asked.

"I don't know," I lied, not wanting to tell them my hunch was that Pete was there to carry out a hit on me. "But this ain't no coincidence!" I added.

Simone butted in. "This don't seem right because Denise never straight-up gave you Tarsha's address. We found that shit by narrowing it down from a bunch of possible names. So I don't see how it's connecting."

She had a good point. And she continued on.

"Tarsha has to be at this address because what are the chances that Pete would be here on this block, especially if Denise never gave you the exact address? The only way that you and Pete could have ended up on this same block is if there is a common thing on this block and that common thing is Tarsha your daughter."

Simone was right, but I didn't need this complication. I was nervous as hell and didn't know what to do, but I couldn't leave Camden without at least knocking on that door and checking for my daughter. But if I moved too quickly I knew that I could be walking into a booby trap.

Why the fuck is Pete in an Escalade with Pennsylvania plates? I asked myself. I also didn't know who that other dude was that Pete was with.

"Yo, this is the deal. We saw them and I know they don't know my whip or who is in this car, so we got the upper hand right now. We need to move on them niggas. I say we drive by they shit and spray the bitch up with slugs. Shoot first and ask questions later," Tito reasoned.

Pete ain't working with no feds, I said to myself. *Ain't no way, unless it's some kind of deal where if he can give information on me it would help to spring his ass from some kind of jam that he might of got himself into with the feds.*

I had to stop thinking like that and use common fucking sense. So right there I convinced myself that any thoughts of the feds being involved was stemming from pure paranoia on my part. But it was hard to not be paranoid. I mean, I didn't want to believe that Denise would do me dirty, but at the same time I had to remember that this was the streets and anything goes. And I also had to remember how Denise had acted real shady over some jealous-bitch shit one night when I showed up to party at Brooklyn Café decked out in a fifteen-hundred-dollar outfit and all laced out in diamonds. And she was always just one of those phony-ass bitches that would hate from the sidelines and be in your face like she was cool witchu, but really she was just trying to keep her enemies close to her.

"Fuck this shit! Tito, pull over," I ordered.

Tito pulled to the side of the road, and I climbed in the backseat with Simone and instructed her to climb in the front seat. We had switched positions in the car without exiting simply because I didn't want any attention being drawn to ourselves.

"Yo, this is the plan, and I need y'all niggas to just ride wit' me and follow what the fuck I say," I commanded, but not in an arrogant way.

"No doubt," Tito stated.

"Tito, we gonna drive down the block so that the driver's side of our car is on their passenger side of the car. Simone, while we're driving I want you to start sucking Tito's dick. Suck that shit like you trying to win an award! And, Tito, while she's sucking your dick, I want you to have your gun in

your left and have it sandwiched in between the driver's door and the driver's seat so that nobody can see it and you have your right hand on the steering wheel. And, Simone, here, take this," I said while handing her a loaded .45. "This gun is gonna be under Tito's lap and won't be visible to nobody, and you just keep sucking his dick and don't stop. I'm gonna be lying down in the back on the floor with my .45 in my hand and what we gonna do is roll up next to the Escalade and, Tito, you do the talking. Roll down your window and have Simone still sucking your dick and start telling Pete and whoever else is in that ride that your ho is scared to walk the block because she thinks that they're cops. Then at that point you just flow with the conversation from there. And when you say, 'See, Simone, they ain't cops,' that is when I'm gonna pop up and jump out the backseat and run up on Pete and his people before they can know what's what. And I want you to immediately draw your gun on them and, Simone, I want you to grab the forty-five from under Tito's lap and aim that shit at the Escalade like you ready to lay a nigga out! Y'all got it?" I asked after having given the long-winded instructions.

Everybody said that they got it and that they was wit' it.

"Yo, Tito, on the real, this is a real live-ass nigga. As live as they come, so if you see anything not looking right don't hesitate to buss a nigga. If y'all see anybody running, then buss a cap in they ass. Simone, when me and Tito draw our guns and you get the gun from under Tito's lap, I want you to immediately look around to make sure that there ain't nobody across the street in another car or walking down the block that might be with Pete. If you see anything like that, just start shooting first and asking questions later. A'ight?"

"A'ight," Simone said as I could see that she was nervous about what was about to go down.

Even Tito looked a little uneasy, but I think that was because he wasn't sure if Pete was in the truck with a cop or if

there were other cops right on that same block waiting to swarm in on us or what.

With the dark tints that were on the car I was confident that Pete wouldn't see me.

"Y'all good up there?" I asked as I finally had fidgeted into a comfortable position and at that point wasn't moving.

"Yeah, I'm good," Tito stated. Then he started to chuckle. "I've been in some shit and I've seen some shit go down but I ain't never run up on nobody while getting a blow job! Word up, son!"

All of us started laughing as I heard Tito unzip his pants.

"I gotta pull my pants down a little bit so that it'll be no question that I'm getting a blow job. And, plus, it'll help hide the gun that's under my lap," Tito stated.

"Simone, you a'ight?" I asked.

"Yeah, I'm okay," she said. Then to lighten the mood she added, "Tito, you better not be no minute man because I puts it down with my head game!"

Everyone in the car laughed at Simone's comment, and I felt good that the tension had been broken.

Before I knew what was what I could hear Simone in the front seat slobbing and slurping on Tito's joint.

"Tito, now do I take care of you or what? You got twenty-something gees with me last time on that Brooklyn Café robbery and now you getting some good head in the whip."

"Oh shit! On the real, Simone, your head game is sick. You gonna make it hard for a nigga to focus."

Simone sounded as if she came up for some air as she laughed and then she went back to sucking off Tito.

"A'ight, we rolling," Tito said as he put the car in drive and headed toward the Escalade.

"Cool. Tito, just make sure all of the doors is unlocked," I stated as now my heart rate was beginning to pick up.

I could hear the window being rolled down, and I felt the air

that quickly filled up the car and I knew that we had to be just about right up on the Escalade.

The car stopped. I could hear Simone still slobbing and slurping away.

"Yo, my man! My man! Can you roll down the window for a second?" Tito shouted out of his window.

There was an awkward silence, and I wondered what the hell was going on.

"What's up, fella?" Tito asked Pete while continuing to get his joint sucked.

"Everything is everything, patna," Pete responded with an OG accent.

Tito was quiet, and I was hoping that he didn't front on me.

"Oh shit. Ahhh. Hol' up a minute, baby," Tito stated.

Simone seemed to have come up for some more air. And in my mind I was screaming because they were already not following the plan.

"Yo, no disrespect, but it would help a nigga out if the two of y'all wasn't posted up on the block just chillin' like fucking po-po. You kna mean?" Tito stated.

A'ight, cool, I said to myself. I was liking Tito's flow. Then right on cue I could sense that Simone had went back to sucking his dick and her timing was perfect.

Pete had made no reply to Tito, and neither did anyone else inside the Escalade.

Tito went on, "I got my girls scared to come and walk on the block 'cause they don't know who y'all are."

"It's cool," Pete responded.

Tito seemed like his flow had left him. And Simone must have sensed it too as she stopped sucking on Tito's dick and spoke up and asked Pete if she could go for a ride in his truck.

"Nah, sweetheart, we good. You seem like you got your hands full already," Pete replied.

"What about your man? He don't wanna go for a ride with me around the block?" Simone asked.

Pete didn't respond, and Simone went back to sucking on Tito's dick.

"Get ya money patna. We from outta town and we ain't trying to knock nobody's hustle. We just waiting on our man," Pete explained.

"No doubt," Tito replied. "Just making sure y'all ain't fucking feds."

There was no reply from anyone in the Escalade.

"See, Simone, they ain't cops," Tito remarked.

I knew that was my cue.

Without hesitation I sat up as quick as I could and burst out of the BMW and quicker than an alley cat I was up on the Escalade with my .45 pointed at Pete's head.

Tito was also scrambling to get out of the car. He had his gun in one hand pointed at the Escalade. And with his other hand he was trying to pull up his pants and cover his exposed erection.

"What the fuck is the deal, Pete!" I shouted as Pete held his hands up in surrender.

"Nigga, if you even flinch I'll murder yo' ass!" I screamed at Pete's boy, who was in the driver's seat.

At that point there were some people on the block and they saw the guns that we had drawn, and while some people quickly got outta dodge, there were other hood rats that had to come rushing toward the excitement.

Simone got outta the BMW and held her gun on the hood rats that were rushing to see what was going on.

"This ain't a party, people! Get the fuck outta here!" she barked at the onlookers while she kept them at bay.

At that point Tito had pulled his pants up and had made it to the driver's side of the Escalade.

"Both of y'all, get the fuck out!" I ordered.

"Pete, this is a young man's game, baby! Midas shoulda told you that you too old to play ball now, my nigga!" I boasted as I had Pete right where I wanted him and he knew it.

"Look, youngblood, you and your partner need to calm the fuck down!" Pete yelled, as he and his partner reluctantly got out of the Cadillac.

"Shut the fuck up!" Tito barked.

"Get in the backseat!" I ordered. "Simone, you drive the BMW and follow us. Tito, you drive the Escalade, and I'll keep my heat on these old bitch-ass niggas."

Before complying with my wishes Tito showed his street smarts by telling me to hold up. He quickly frisked both Pete and his boy and then he looked under the seats and other obvious and visible areas in the Escalade to make sure that there was no guns or weapons or cell phones.

"Gimme this fuckin' shit!" Tito barked as he snatched a loaded gun that Pete had tucked away in an ankle holster.

"We good now!"

And with that we ordered Pete and his man to get inside the truck and we were out, with Simone following right behind.

I shook my head because I knew that Tito had just confiscated the gun that was more than likely gonna be used to murder my ass.

"Cinnamon, that is your fucking problem! You're a gotdamn hothead skanky fucking ho!" Pete scowled as he looked at me with disgust. He knew we had his ass and was probably just trying to go out with a bang. He had to know what time it was.

"Nigga, fuck you!" I replied. "What the hell are you doing out here?"

"What am I doing out here? I'm visiting your daughter! I'm the one who's been putting food in her mouth ever since your ass was locked the fuck up for that dumb shit! Yeah,

Midas ain't tell you that shit, did he? And I bet you he ain't tell your ass that I was the one who put up that bail money for you. That's what the fuck I'm doing out here! This is some gotdamn bullshit," Pete replied with convincing disgust, but at the same time I could tell that he didn't have his usually confident OG street swagger in his voice.

"That's bullshit!" I shouted as I continued to hold my gun on Pete and his man. "This motherfucker is lying. Ain't nobody even know where my daughter was! So how the fuck was you putting food in her mouth?"

I knew exactly how to call his bluff. "Denise put Midas on to me and my daughter, and Midas reached out to yo' ass and now you out here gunning for me for that, nigga!"

Pete's silence had sealed his fate. In my heart I knew I had guessed right. And even if I was wrong the fact remained that Pete was a big threat to my existence and you don't pull a gun on a man like Pete and not use it.

"Listen, Cinnamon—"

Pete's man began to talk, and I immediately cut him off. "Nigga, did I tell you to open your mouth? You don't even know me, dude!" I yelled.

"Johnny, it's okay," Pete said in an attempt to ease the tension.

For Denise's sake I hated to do what I was about to do to Pete because I knew that she was gonna now be roped up in some bullshit that her ass wasn't built for. But I was too close to being reunited with my daughter and I couldn't let Pete be a threat to that hope I had. My daughter was the only hope I had and the only thing worth living for. I was feeling desperate like a caged animal.

Bladow! Bladow! Was the deafening sound that came from the .45 that I was holding? I had pumped two shots into Pete's head, and his body immediately lay limp and lifeless.

Bladow! The third shot from my gun managed to hit Johnny right in the throat, and he immediately grabbed and

clutched his throat. He had one of the wildest, most panicked looks on his face. It's a look that I know will haunt me in the future. It's a look that you can't describe. It's a look that only a human that knows that they are about to die can muster up.

As blood flowed and squirted out of Johnny's neck, Tito managed to maneuver our way back to Philly. And before long, Johnny had stopped clutching his throat. His body lay limp as an eighty-year-old dick, while his eyes rolled to the back of his head.

I rolled down the window and instructed Simone to go to the gas station and to purchase some gasoline and to put some inside of whatever type of container that she could find.

"Put it in a soda can if you have to," I yelled. "I don't care what you put it in, and then follow us.

"Yo, Tito, I just killed one of the wildest OG muthafuckas from Harlem!" I said as the reality of what I'd done began to set in.

"You did what you had to do. If you didn't pop that nigga he would have made it his life mission to come after me and you until he murdered us," Tito accurately stated.

"Word is bond! But you know what? Pete was too old for this shit! I mean, I hate to see the nigga shot up like that 'cause I got respect for the game and I had nothing but love for his cousin, but at the same time, it's like only the strong survive, and I ain't no weak muthafucka," I stated with heavy street confidence, all the while on the inside I was shitting bricks.

"You did what you had to do, baby girl."

Simone purchased the gas and quickly followed me and Tito as he maneuvered the Escalade to a desolate area.

The two of us quickly got out and retrieved the gasoline from Simone, which she had placed inside of a gallon-sized milk container.

Tito doused the inside of the Escalade with gasoline and he also poured gasoline on the roof and on the hood of the Escalade before tossing a match inside the truck and setting it ablaze.

The three of us jumped inside the BMW and waited until the fire was fully engulfing the Escalade and then we sped off.

There were hardly any words spoken by the three of us. And it was for obvious reasons. I mean, all of that gung-ho gun-toting shoot-'em-up shit that you see in the Mafia movies where cats kill somebody and then go and chill with their family like everything is all good. Well that ain't how it really goes down.

It goes down like it was going down inside of that BMW. You feel like shit, like the scum of the earth after taking another human being's life.

I broke the silence by telling Tito that I was sorry for having roped him into that whole murder shit. I had definitely not planned for things to go that way but that was just how things played themselves out.

"Tito, on the real, as soon as I get my hands on some real cake I'm-a come see a nigga and hit you wit' like ten gees for this shit. Word!" I emphatically proclaimed, and I meant every word of it.

Tito downplayed everything, but that was the type of cat he was. Real street, and real thorough, but at the same time he was real humble.

"So what's the deal with your daughter?" Tito asked.

I shook my head and then blew some air out of my lungs. "Tonight I gotta make my move and get her. I'm just running up in the crib, and the only way I ain't coming out with her is if they take me out of that crib in a body bag," I said and then I paused.

"But, Tito, we got it from here. Just take us back to the

hotel and let us pick up the whip, and me and Simone will head back to Camden on our own. You already did more than enough. We got this shot from here."

"Cinnamon, I got your back. Just say the word. It ain't nothing," Tito replied.

I knew that he would have my back, but on the real, all I needed at that point was for Simone to ride shotgun in the Nissan and I was gonna get my daughter. There was no need for help at that point.

"You sure you gonna be a'ight?" Tito asked again as we pulled up to the Nissan.

"No doubt, I got this," I replied as the BMW sat idling next to our car.

"I gotta move tonight and get Tarsha as soon as it gets dark. This whole shit with Pete, it kinda spooked my ass, and I just wanna get the hell up outta here and start over."

After I said that there was nothing but silence in the car. Then Tito turned on the radio to break the awkward silence.

"Yo, turn the music down for a second," I requested.

"Tito, on the real, this is what I need you to do for me . . ." I said as I took a long pause. "If I get killed tonight or if I get bagged by the cops—"

Tito cut me off. "Cinnamon, come on with that nonsense."

"Nah, god, this is real talk. Word! If I get killed or bagged, just give me your word on this one thing. Wait for shit to die down and when it does, I need you to tell my daughter that I love her and that I miss her and that I don't want her to ever be afraid or scared of anything!" As I said that I had to watch myself because I was beginning to get real emotional.

"Cinnamon, you got my word on that," Tito said. "No doubt."

There was another pause as I reached into my pocket. "Here. Make sure that she also gets this." I handed Tito a passport photo of myself that I had taken at a Walgreens drugstore in Brooklyn.

"Okay, definitely," Tito replied. "I'll look out for her like she was one of mines. But you know what? Everything is gonna be a'ight, kid."

Camden, New Jersey—11:00 PM

I was beyond tired by the time 11:00 PM came. And I was tired for good reason. The night before I was in a whorehouse drinking and smoking until like 5:00 in the morning and then on only a few hours of sleep. I was drained from the day's activities, which included killing two gangsters in cold blood.

But now wasn't the time for no tiredness. I had one objective to complete, and then I could move on with my life. That objective was to get my daughter.

I had Simone park right in front of the house that Tarsha was staying in. There was gonna be no casing the house and trying to figure shit out. My mind was already made up to just march right into the joint and get my daughter, even if it meant someone had to get killed in the process.

"Simone, keep the car running and keep it in drive with your foot on the gas pedal. And when I come out and hop in, you don't ask no questions and you don't hesitate. You just floor this bitch and get the fuck up outta dodge as quick as you can. Okay?"

Simone nodded her head.

"I said *okay?*" I reiterated because I wanted Simone to formally acknowledge my words with more than just a head nod.

"Yeah, okay," Simone verbally responded.

With that I tucked my .45 into my waistband and exited from the car. I blew a whole lot of anxious air from my lungs and walked toward the yard, to where Tarsha was staying.

The yard looked a mess and there were two sickly-looking stray dogs that were in the front yard. I noticed that all of the

lights seemed to be on inside the house. Which was a good thing, I guess.

I didn't know what I was gonna say once I knocked on the door. I didn't know if I was gonna play it off like I was lost and needed directions or if I was gonna say that my car had broke down and that I needed to use their phone. I wasn't sure. I had even contemplated just walking up to the door and asking for Tarsha.

Just be natural, I said to myself as I knocked three times on the door.

"Auntie Sandra somebody's at the door," a little voice yelled.

I was certain that that was my little girl. My heart was racing, and I couldn't wait to see if that in fact was her.

Becoming more and more impatient, I knocked three more times on the door.

"Just a minute, I'm coming," the lady inside the house yelled.

There was no screen door, so when the lady came to the door and opened it, she and I were face to face.

My eyes immediately got wide. And I was sure that she could see my chest rise from inhaling and then deflate from exhaling.

"Yes, can I help you?" the lady asked as she sort of positioned her body behind the door and let only her head be visible.

I thought about pushing in the door but quickly decided against that.

"Yeah, I am so sorry to bother you, miss, but my car broke down and I was just wondering if I could use your phone to call triple A," I said, hoping that I was being convincing enough.

The lady looked at me with much suspicion and hesitated before saying anything.

"I mean, you don't have to let me inside. If you have a

cordless phone or a cell phone you could bring it to me," I added for good measure.

The lady still looked unconvinced. And just as I was about to reach into my waistband and pull out my gun and rush the door, a little hand appeared near the doorknob as it gripped the door and attempted to pull it open.

"Tarsha, go upstairs to your room!" the lady barked.

My eyes got wide like a drug addict and I instinctively reached for the door and slightly pushed it but not in a threatening way. That was my daughter and I needed to see her at that moment.

"I wanna see," Tarsha said as she ignored the lady's orders and pulled at the door, attempting to open it.

It was almost like she knew it was me at the door or something.

Cinnamon, push open the fucking door and grab Tarsha and be out, bitch! I yelled to myself.

Finally Tarsha was able to make some headway and she snaked her head around the door and her beautiful face was now in my full view. She just looked so beautiful and she looked as if she'd gotten so big. I wanted to melt right there on the spot.

"Mommy!" Tarsha yelled.

A Kool-Aid smile splashed across my face as I was happy as hell that Tarsha remembered me. Then she began to struggle with all of her might to get from behind the door.

"Mommy?" the lady questioned.

At that point I knew that I had to make my move and grab Tarsha and be out.

"Baby, who is that at the fucking door this time of night?" a deep-sounding male voice shouted from inside the house.

"Mommy! Mommy!" Tarsha yelled again with more excitement in her voice.

Fuck this! I said to myself as I pushed the door in, while simultaneously reaching for my .45.

"Come on, Tarsha! Mommy's here!" I stated as I drew my gun and was ready to blast anybody that tried to stop me from leaving with my daughter.

Reunited

When Tarsha reached out her arms to me, I quickly bent over and scooped her up. Holding her in my left arm and gripping my gun in my right hand, I backed away from the front door and then I spun and ran toward Simone's car. I ripped open the rear passenger door and I shoved Tarsha in the backseat and hopped in the car.

Simone knew what time it was and before I could even close the door she had hit the gas pedal and we were out.

"Where are we going?" she shouted to me.

"I don't know. Just drive!" I shouted back.

Tarsha's little body was getting whipped around from the sharp turns that Simone was making, and she reached out to me and grabbed hold of my leg.

"Mommy, I'm scared."

"Oh, baby. It's okay, you're with Mommy now. Don't be scared. You don't have to worry about nothing."

"You think I should go back to the hotel?" Simone asked.

"Yeah, go back there, and we'll sort everything out when we get there."

Simone wasn't sure which way to go, because obviously we weren't from around those parts, so she just continued to drive and tried to feel her way.

After we had drove for a safe distance from the house that Tarsha had been staying at, Simone slowed down just so we could catch our breath for a moment.

"Oh, she is such a cutie!" Simone said.

"I know. I just wanna eat her up," I replied and I grabbed Tarsha and started hugging her as tight as I could.

Tarsha laughed and she told me that she couldn't breathe because I was squeezing her too hard.

"Mommy, I missed you. Why did you take so long to come get me?" Tarsha asked with so much innocence. She was obviously clueless as to what had been going on and what she and I both had been through.

"Baby, Mommy is so sorry. But I promise you that I won't leave you anymore."

Simone then suggested that we stop at a McDonald's that we were driving past. So we pulled into the McDonald's and we went through the drive-through and we ordered up a storm. I ordered Tarsha anything and everything that she wanted and then some. All she wanted was a chicken mc-Nuggets happy meal, but I also ordered her a vanilla shake, cookies, a hamburger, an apple pie, and apple dippers.

I knew that she couldn't eat all of that, but it was like I just so desperately wanted to make up for what I had put her through all because of my stupid decisions.

We sat in the parking lot stuffing our faces and talking and listening to the radio. I asked Tarsha a million and one questions because I definitely wanted to know how she had been treated during my absence. Thankfully, based on what she had divulged to me, she had not been mistreated or beat or abused in any way. But I still just felt so guilty

So as we sat and ate, all of a sudden we heard and saw a massive amount of police cars driving by with their sirens blaring.

"Simone, let's get the fuck up outta here and go back to the hotel," I said.

Simone immediately started up the car and she began maneuvering her way towards the highway, and about fifteen minutes later we were approaching the parking lot of the

hotel that we were staying in and when we turned on to the block that led into the parking lot we saw an army of cops.

"Oh shit, Simone, back the fuck up! Hurry up," I screamed.

Simone put the car in reverse and tried to hustle us out of harm's way without drawing any attention to ourselves. Unfortunately, luck wasn't on our side and cops quickly pounced on us.

"Just drive, Simone! Drive! Run them motherfuckers over if you have to!" I screamed.

"Your daughter's in here—we can't do that, Cinnamon!"

"Fuck! Shit! No!" I screamed as cops ran up on the car with their guns pointed at us and barking orders.

"Keep the doors locked!" I screamed.

I grabbed hold of Tarsha and I explained to her that no matter what happened that I wanted her to know that Mommy loved her and that Mommy would always love her.

"Mommy, you're gonna leave me again? Please don't, Mommy. I'll be good. I promise," Tarsha said in heartbreaking fashion.

I just put my head down and clenched my teeth as I remembered that I had fucking used my ATM card to book the hotel room.

"Oh fuck!" I screamed out and banged the dashboard. "Fuck! Fuck! Fuck!"

I shook my head in defeat because I knew that I had gotten careless and forgot that I shouldn't use any ATM cards or credit cards or no traceable shit like that.

"Baby, you are the best child in the world. You are good. And Mommy loves you so much," I said to my daughter.

Just as I said that the cops broke the car windows and reached in and unlocked the doors and yanked me and Simone out of the car and threw us to the ground and cuffed us.

"My daughter's in there. She's just a baby. She's a kid. Don't hurt her!" I screamed and begged.

"Mommy!" Tarsha yelled as a cop took hold of her and whisked her away.

"It's okay, baby, don't be scared," I screamed out to her.

With my face smashed up against the concrete I knew that I had just lied to my daughter. Because the fact was, things weren't gonna be okay, and the truth of the matter was that because of dumb decisions that I had allowed myself to make all of my life, my daughter was now gonna have to grow up without her mom.

So, yeah, more than likely, she was gonna be scared. What kid wouldn't be scared growing up without their parents?

The seductive fast life that I had lived had finally caught up to me. Yeah, that life was *so seductive,* but when it causes you to lose everything that you love, it makes it so not worth it.